# Horrible Women, Wonderful Girls

A Jaycee Grayson Novel

DARTMOUTH PARK

Horrible Women, Wonderful Girls: A Jaycee Grayson Novel
Copyright © 2025 by Julie Ann Sipos

DARTMOUTH PARK

Published by Dartmouth Park, LLC
PO Box 547446
Orlando, FL 32804

Copy Editor: Beth Attwood
Cover Art and Design: Damon Freeman/Damonza
Interior Design: Robynne Alexander/Damonza
Author Photo: Thelma Vickroy

First Dartmouth Park hardcover edition 2025 Library of Congress Control Number: 2024924598

ISBN:
979-8-9919-9940-3 (hardcover)
979-8-9919994-9-6 (paperback)
979-8-9919-9941-0 (ebook)

This book is a work of fiction. Any references to historical events, real people, or real places are used fictitiously. Other names, characters, places, and events are products of the author's imagination, and any resemblance to actual events or places or persons, living or dead, is entirely coincidental.

Copyright © 2025 by Julie Ann Sipos. All rights reserved. This book or any portion thereof may not be reproduced or used in any manner whatsoever without the express written permission of the publisher except for the use of brief quotations in a book review.

*For Mary Beth*

*We did it, my sister*

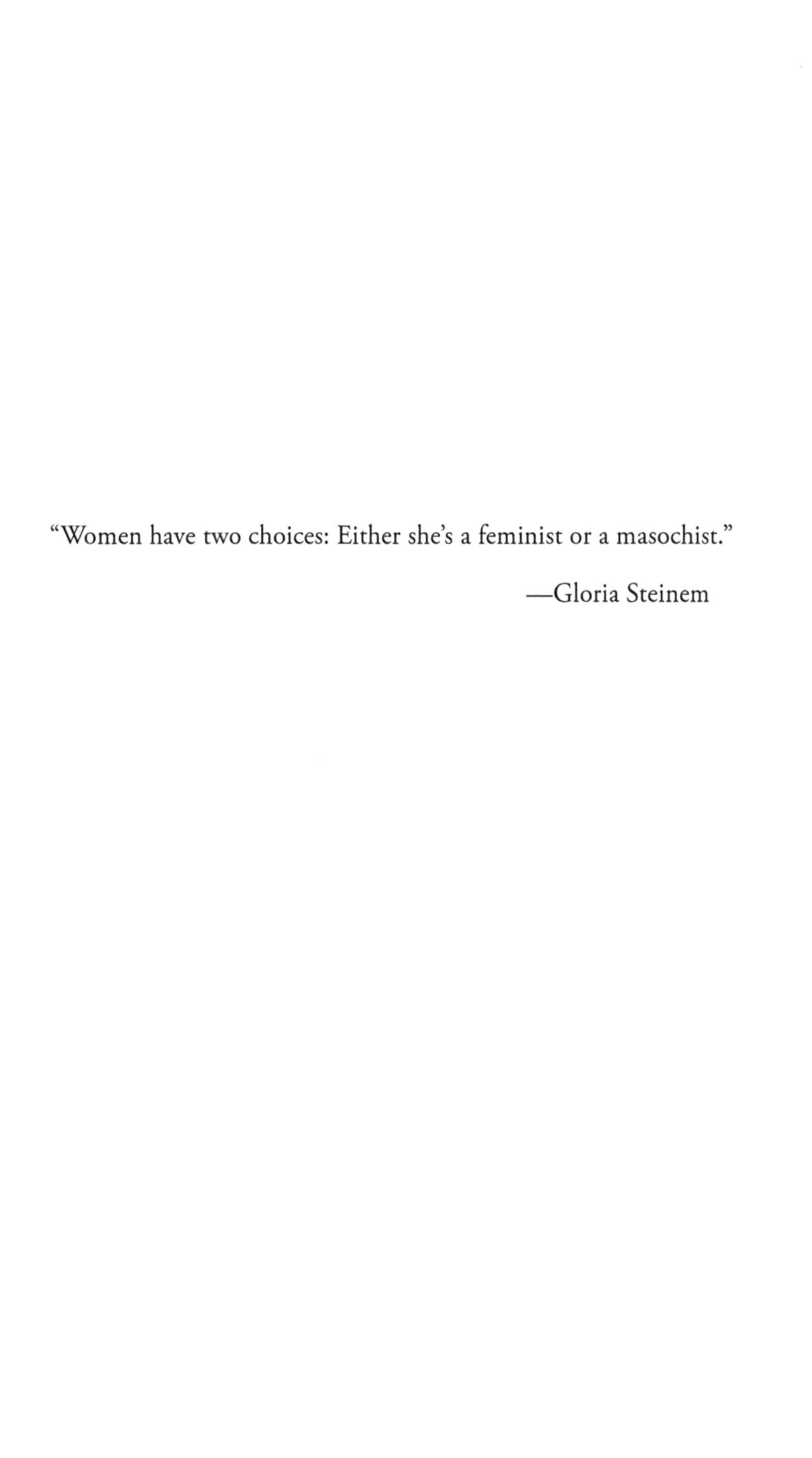

"Women have two choices: Either she's a feminist or a masochist."

—Gloria Steinem

ALSO BY THE AUTHOR

**Naomi's Recipe Box:**
A Jaycee Grayson Novel Companion

**Postcards from Littleburgh WI:**
A Jaycee Grayson Novel Companion

**Love from Morning to Night:**
Poems & Songs for Mommy and Baby

## ACKNOWLEDGMENTS

To Hal Ackerman, Richard Walter, and all my formidable mentors in the MFA screenwriting program at UCLA, I thank you for teaching me what a story is, and for living inside my head virtually every time I sit down to write one. Thank you to my friend and mentor, Thelma Vickroy, for being here in the real world to coax Jaycee to life through the nonjudgmental gaze of a documentarian. My humble thanks to lifelong friends Jen McComb and Elizabeth Heilman for volunteering your voracious fandom in the genre to help me sharpen multiple drafts of the adventure. Rebecca Harris, you lived that adventure with unflagging spirit while turning my words into songs that sing themselves on the page. To Beth Rahko and Janet Cabot, along with so many other dear friends at Madison Symphony Orchestra, my heartfelt gratitude for rooting my Wisconsin journey in purpose, belonging, and all that glorious music. For the beautifully rendered graphics, inside and out, much gratitude to the very patient Claire Walker and to the entire Damonza design team in New Zealand. To say it takes a village is an understatement, with Beth Attwood in Canada and Lucy Littlejohns in the UK earning transatlantic shoutouts for eagle-eyed editorial work. To my students, you are fearsome talents who teach me more than you know, especially when questioning what I am teaching you. Drs. David Lee and Perri Johnson, your countless hours of silent empathy from either point on the map gave name to my "Why," literally. I thank Karen Currie and the ladies of Albright House at Smith College for embracing our sisterhood in the shared loss of a sister with characteristic grace. All due credit goes to my long-time entertainment agent, Judi Farkas, who casually tossed out the brilliant title for my literary debut one afternoon over lunch. Finally, my persnickety mom, Marianne Sipos, has my undying gratitude for instilling the basics early on, and for declaring everything I've written since an instant bestseller, if only in the furthest recesses of a retired eighth-grade English teacher's mind.

# Horrible Women, Wonderful Girls

A Jaycee Grayson Novel

CHAPTER ONE

# Jaycee Grayson, the Most Wonderful Girl at the Betty Ford Center

MY SISTER, MEREDITH, SHEPHERDED MY treacherous path through the Hollywood trenches as unswervingly as if it were her own. Just out of a graduate program certain to improve my fortunes, I buckled under the weight of protracted failure, false starts, empty promises, and compounding student loan interest. She forged ahead, splaying herself out beneath me like a human safety net, and refused to stop smiling when I dared to glance down from my sagging tightrope.

"Krispy Kremes!" Meredith announced at my screen door with a box of assorted doughnuts and an accompanying bag of holes. Elbowing her way in, she bestowed me with a doll from one of those ridiculous Hallmark kinds of shops for people with sizable balances available on their credit cards—a "You Can Do It Wish Doll," wearing a "Hang in There!" dog tag and a bracelet with "Go Girl" and star-shaped charms dangling from it. "Her name is Aurelia," she said. "That's how she grabbed me, anyway. Don't you like her?"

"I wonder how much I can get for her at the Fairfax Flea Market on Sunday," I said. "I rented a booth."

Meredith had caught me in my pajamas, dragging my things from drawers and closets and sorting them into bags and boxes, with every brand of knickknack and whatnot stacked up around the house. I had received an eviction notice on my last safe haven, a one-bedroom Craftsman tucked inside a bungalow village rendered in ice cream colors, originally built by the studios in the 1920s.

"Totally unlawful," Meredith pronounced the whole ploy, even if the landlord did plan to move in his son. "I'll be keeping an eye on that; any idiot knows that's how you break rent control."

"Who cares? I'll be living in some low-rent efficiency in the Valley."

She lived in the Valley, where we'd both grown up. Her lovely canyon ranch home came with a well-padded husband who had a pretend job in high finance while she quietly bankrolled their tony lifestyle at a top Beverly Hills law firm. "I brought you some more coffee, but I forgot to steal another ream of paper." She plopped some stale foil packets on the counter, pulling handfuls of sugar substitute and shelf-stabilized creamer from her pockets. "Will you be okay for a while?"

"Do I look okay for a while?" I was living off dollar-store eggs at the time, making myself sixteen-cent omelets with parmesan cheese packets from a pizza she'd brought by on her way home from the office, or a squeeze of salsa from a late-night taco run.

In her mind, my plan to raise some cash for myself provided irrefutable evidence I intended to throw in the towel and become a bag lady at the bottom of an undesirable exit off the 101 Freeway.

"You can't sell your plates, Jaycee, how will you eat?"

She had bought me the plates and the matching plate rack, involving a lot of hand-painted daisies. She came across another rejected gift, a set of buffalo-check MacKenzie-Childs porcelain candlesticks that Dr. Seuss might have imagined. "Do you know how much these cost me?"

"I couldn't make them work." Hurting her feelings was nearly impossible, given her capacity for self-delusion.

"Just give them back to me." She picked up an oversize shoulder bag from IKEA and started stuffing things in as though the Swedes had announced a Blue Light Special on everything America never wanted. "I'll take it all. How much?"

"For my life? You want to buy my life?"

"How much? I'll write you a check."

I kicked open the screen door and she trailed me onto the porch, where you could almost see the Hollywood sign when the fog lifted if you craned your neck hard enough to risk injury. Well after nine o'clock, Meredith still wore her no-name internet catalogue suit for the busy plus-size professional. Her feet looked swollen in the sensible heels she'd overpaid for and clung to well beyond their prime. "Why don't you go somewhere and focus on yourself?" I politely inquired. "You're overdue for highlights and your brows belong on a yeti."

"Fine. I'm taking the doughnuts."

"Fine. Leave the holes."


THE MOVIES UP AND DISAPPEARED over the next ten years, giving way to infinite cinematic story worlds worth billions of dollars to those who liked that sort of thing. I learned to display an inoffensive artfulness in latching on to some nerd boy's overamped comic book spectacular with my concept for a cute DVD extra or fun digital game that only became more popular with the next new technology to play it on, with, or against.

I cashed in my dream of becoming a filmmaker for a thin thread of credits unspooling like silent screams at the tail end of all the most meaningless summer blockbusters. Some days I hardly hated myself at all.

Even stupid success came with a reliable pay package and assigned parking on an only vaguely insulting corner of the backlot, alive at dawn with the click of bargain stilettos purveyed on the sly from some distant Loehmann's or lesser Nordstrom Rack.

Putting all that out of my head on my walk to the center of the universe, I painted on a smile with the new lip-colored lipstick suddenly so popular among women determined to feel better about our mouths. Showing up in the right dress for the right table read, I said the right things about the right guy's new feature deal. Known for my knack at sniffing out only the best material, in truth, I could spin the worst of it into gold without vomiting all over myself at the right crafts table.

Oh, I'd earned my rumored promotion to Vice President of Extended Story Play at the world's largest entertainment company, a title so sexy I made it up myself. Who could have foreseen my fortunes turning with such immediacy that even Meredith would find herself at a loss for words, possibly for the first time in her life?

"You're bringing in a mint for those people!" she sputtered on the phone. "What possible grounds could they have for denying your promotion?"

"Grounds? We don't need grounds in this town. We're masters of illusion and mistresses of suspended disbelief."

I tried to explain the HR person's version of events, however false and one-sided, but I was half in the bag outside some overcrowded NoHo hipster bar on the slim hope a taxi might come along and take me to another one. The sun felt like a spotlight, harsh and unforgiving in the dreaded San Fernando Valley.

"Was your supervisor in the room?" Meredith demanded. "Was she taking contemporaneous notes?"

"Why would she stick her nose in this and go down with the girl ship? She's only, like, twenty-six. They skip college now, it's a *stragety*," I slurred.

"Stra-te-gy," she correctly pronounced. "Are you drunk on the job?"

"Everyone drank. They bought the drinks."

It didn't matter who bought the drinks. A woman saying yes to the right guy, or no to the wrong one, in the right or wrong place at a good or bad time, could indeed get her hired or fired on the spot.

"We had a glow-in-the-dark bowling party to celebrate a record quarter. A couple of clowns from Corporate Synergy viewed this as an ideal opportunity to break in the new crop of high school interns."

"That is absolutely vile," Meredith said.

"Then they came for me. Apparently, my sweater was too loose for their tastes in the dim light of the glow-and-bowl."

"Too loose? I'm sorry, how are you the one in the hot seat right now?" asked Meredith, incredulous.

"Because I'm a grown woman with the nerve to divert attention from twelfth graders in shorter skirts. Also, because I stole a pair of giant thumbless balls."

"I don't know what those are, but I'm getting a very unfortunate visual."

"I must have become disoriented in the dark and reached into the shared ball return," I said. "Maybe I did lob a big neon pair in the general direction of some highly offensive catcalling, is that so wrong?"

"You bowled your bosses?"

"While somehow scoring a spare for the team," I said, claiming momentary bragging rights. "That should only prove it was all a freak accident, though, since I'm not that great of a bowler with the lights on."

Meredith needed a moment to let this compute, drumming her fingers on the desk. "You rarely see age discrimination *and* juvenile sex crimes in the same legal action," she said. "I've never even heard of a toxic workplace environment at employee fun time. Give me that HR genius's name, and I'll name her personally in the wrongful termination suit."

"Are you insane? I can't sue a hundred-and-fifty-billion-dollar global corporation."

"I can."

"You have laws in your business. Not to mention ethics, manners, and ordinary decency."

"That's stretching it," she said with a dismissive snort.

"Has a colleague ever interrupted a meeting to go take a poop with the door wide open, while reminding you to send another case of Kit Kats to his boat, and also complaining about some stripper's insufficient bikini wax?"

"That's random."

"Not necessarily."

"Jesus Christ, Jaycee. Give me that guy's name, too."

"That *guy*? I could go on for days before I get to the concerning part. Even if I win, I lose, don't you get it? Dumb is okay. Slutty is awesome, as long as she keeps her mouth shut—but nobody likes a spoilsport. I'm done, Meredith. Over and out."

Something in her knew I was right. "Hollywood isn't the end of the world."

"It literally is," I flatly reminded her. "The whole town is about to fall off the edge, that's a scientific fact. You would know this had you ever given my unproduced earthquake comedy the respect it deserved."

"You need to get sober, Jaycee. Own your part in this, get some help."

"Please stop being right all the time. It's boring."

I stopped short of reminding her she was fat, since she probably knew that already. What made her job so awesome, hurling invectives at trembling Chinese drywall contractors hiding construction defects under their tiny power suits all day?

Her firm recently paid for her troubles with a mandatory weekend conference on female anger in Sacramento—no, not Las Vegas or even Reno.

How did her big blowhard husband end up with the bigger closet, the better car, and the zero-dollar paycheck? I could have asked her to take a good, hard look in the mirror for once.

I didn't want her to stand there and cry for a thousand years; what would be the point of that? The two of us had made some unspoken agreement shortly after birth that no matter how things went, she would be available to save me, and I would be free to fall apart. I just wished I could stop taking her up on it.

"Okay, I'll get help," I said. "Now what?"

SHE PLANNED TO TREAD LIGHTLY in negotiating my banishment, while also trying to engineer a short-term opportunity of some kind. People love to talk, but they also have limited memory spans.

Meredith knew much more than she should have about how the industry worked, having spent years reading the trades, plotting my next move as I stood paralyzed on a chessboard awaiting rescue from the queen. I would be back soon, she felt confident, and no one would remember to talk about me with any reliable detail.

In the meantime, lying low in Palm Desert might not make a half-bad getaway. Unfortunately, I had mistakenly envisioned the Betty Ford Center as more upscale spa and wellness resort, less poorly staffed cuckoo's nest.

I was still stuck in the women's detox unit when I encountered a faceless, hulking guard known only by the thunder of his steel-toed boots skulking through the ward with a flashlight shined in our faces as the new meat slept in our lacey underthings on tearstained pillows, taking his sweet time scribbling random observations across a clipboard. *"Night sweats. Mouth breather. Fetal position, partial wedgie."*

Naturally, he startled me when I caught him lurking over my bed, so naturally, I sat up and beat him about the head and face. A gentleman in his golden years, as things would turn out, he suffered job-related eye strain and macular degeneration. I'd broken his thick old-man glasses and bloodied his spider-veined senior nose.

I felt terrible, of course, and asked a passing orderly if he knew where I could find the poor fellow to apologize. "We had a little run-in last night, nobody's fault. Frankly, I can't imagine why they'd have somebody skulking in and out of here at all hours."

"Let's have a sit-down, you and me, give that a think." He pushed past me like he owned the place and helped himself to a seat on the bedside chair where I'd hung my only decent blouse—one hundred percent Mulberry silk, both practical and stylish—in case I needed to leave in a hurry. "The name's Mr. Y."

"Why what?"

"Y period. I'm your sober counselor."

"Shouldn't you be a woman?"

"Not last time I checked."

Had the world's leading authority on healing and hope seriously assigned this walking wall of graffiti as my confessor?

"Are you the one who releases me to the women's residence hall?" I asked. "There's no vending machine in this unit and I'm getting ready for my monthly infusion of chocolate. You understand."

"I'll file the usual report. Let's get back to the assault."

"Assault? I just told you it was an accident!"

"You've had a few of those lately." He leafed through my chart while scratching his back against my blouse in a blatant display of disrespect for better fabrics.

"I also need an iron, preferably with a cooling and steaming function, can you report that? And I couldn't find a clothesline in the bathroom to rinse out some personal items. Right now I'm supposed to be here for four weeks, but I will have to rethink that if I'm already running out of basics."

"Anything else bothering you?"

"Again, there's the chocolate situation."

He got up and headed for the door. "Next time you want my help, you'll have to ask."

"I asked this time," I politely reminded him, following him out to peel my blouse off his back. I hadn't even paid for it yet and didn't know when or how I was going to, it occurred to me. "I guess we can forget that iron."

"Ever heard the expression it's hard to pet an angry dog?" he asked.

*Did someone ask this thug to pet me?*

"Somebody needs to check on that gal who sits out by the pool all day dangling her ankle monitor over the edge and crying nonstop," I told him. "I'm worried she might electrocute herself."

"That gal is a flight attendant with the skills to shoot up her old man at thirty thousand feet," he said. "She could have Narcaned the dude, but she got herself too geared to notice he keeled until the feds boarded and popped her for Man One."

How had this individual ever passed muster with whoever did the hiring around here in the name of Mrs. Gerald R. Ford? He wore a backwoods preacher's sweat-dampened shirt sleeves, with a snake tattoo peeping over his collar and a pair of see-through earlobe stretchers providing a painfully clear view of the rear wall through either side of his head. A reformed Hells Angel, I figured, he'd become disenchanted with group bar fights and riding his hog down the freeway in formation; another disaffected youth scared straight by an overdose of quality public television.

"There's no candy machine in detox so we can track what you've ingested when somebody goes south," he said. "Clotheslines ended badly for a couple of previous guests. Nobody goes tits up on my watch."

He continued down the hall, but I raced in front of him and stopped him flat.

"You don't know anything about me, Mr. Why Period. I'm only here to take a little break on some things that don't feel like much fun anymore. I won't be going 'tits up' or tits anywhere else, for that matter. I have never given up on anything in my entire life. I wouldn't know how."

"You're a real smart lady."

"Thank you," I said, truly humbled.

"Too smart," he added. "You need to dismount that high horse of yours and focus on going all the way down. Rock bottom, rolling around in the mud. Then dig yourself an even deeper ditch and lie there for a good long while sucking in the taste of your own dumb."

I FELT I HAD SUCKED in about enough of my own dumb by the time Meredith visited nearly three weeks later. She had gotten stressed out at work, which was never a long ride, and our scant calls over the residence landline had become shorter and more strained. As my hall mates shuffled out with their heads down to greet perpetually disappointed loved ones, I spent the previous Family Days in the rec room watching the *Forensic Files.*

Nobody asked Mr. Y. to join me on the overstuffed couch, but he had all kinds of helpful observations about recent advancements in FBI blood spatter analysis leading to the capture of various serial killers.

He also seemed to think I'd need support at home in order to ensure my long-term sobriety. To my mind, though, their fake family dinner party served only as a message that things would go better for us on the inside once a concerned loved one ponied up another hefty co-payment and skedaddled.

"This looks nice," Meredith observed weakly after I ushered her in from a long queue outside the dining hall.

She and I bore a family resemblance, despite our differences in shape. Though she was nearly five years my senior, I stood five inches taller by the age of eight, with a slim-hipped body type to her slightly squat endomorph. We both had enviable eyelashes without the aid of mascara and thick chestnut hair requiring little daily maintenance. We'd worn the same blunt shoulder-length bob for so long she barely noticed that time I went rogue and got bangs.

"Ignore all this, they've put on a ruse," I whispered. Flickering LED candles and real linens masked Formica tables typically littered with clogged saltshakers and crusty ketchup bottles. "Normally we get Turkey Meatloaf and Pine Sol. I hoard applesauce cups in my bathroom cabinet, but somebody stole my stash."

"I brought a picnic," she volunteered brightly.

The guards had rifled through her favorite Congolese market basket purchased in the free trade aisle at Whole Foods Market, along with the well-worn full-grain leather barrister briefcase our dad had presented her the proud day she graduated law school from their alma mater at Cornell University. She gripped them at either side like a pair of shields marking her superior life rank should she need to deflect a junkie uprising at the Shawshank Café.

"Can we sit down, please? Inside or out, you pick."

Me? That was a first.

Leading my own charge anywhere seemed flat-out cheeky with the general in the house. I slid open a glass door onto the picnic area, breathing in the arid high desert air, and showed her to the welcome shade of an umbrella table.

I snatched the basket pawed by the gate louts and inventoried her manhandled Mediterranean-themed menu. A wayward marinated Kalamata olive freed from an herbaceous heirloom tomato salad seemed like fair game, but she caught me in the act and slapped it out of my hand.

"Can you wait? Let's get the paperwork out of the way first."

"What paperwork?"

She wore a look of quiet detachment I'd never seen and couldn't quite read. Negotiating her usual iron grip like a pair of safety wheels with a screw gone missing, I pedaled only tentatively during our brief time apart. She would swoop in to stand me up, dust off my bottom, and then whisk me off to somewhere better even as I lamented her interruption of another glory freedom ride. That's how we'd always done it; I didn't make up the rules.

Something told me that this paperwork of hers would draw a line in the sand between us forever changing the game.

"Meredith," I began ominously. "What have you done?"

"Exactly what I said I would do, relax."

She handed me a fancy lawyer pen that turned out to be a cheap knock-off emblazoned with the name of her firm and slid over a legal document. "This is a basic nondisclosure agreement. You can't ever tell your side of the bowling story because there is no bowling story."

"I think in stories, though, it's how my brain works," I said through a stolen mouthful of scratch-made pita chips and a swipe of baba ghanoush she'd stayed up the night before to hand-flame with a kitchen torch. "Maybe the whole debacle becomes my next screenplay, the one that finally gets made. Oh, the delicious irony."

"Sign here, initial there." She laid down another two documents, and two more after that, with the casual affect of a blackjack dealer doling out the last of a hopeless deck.

"What if one of my film school friends wanted to feature me in a documentary about inequities for women in entertainment, or—"

"And then you'll countersign here, here, and here. They've agreed to a mutual release of claims for any multimillion-dollar damages they may feel due them for alleged injuries, real or imagined."

"Damages due *them*? You were so set on *us* getting the big payday."

"That was before you came down here and beat up an old man."

11

"We made up. I gave him a bunch of free theme park passes I found in my overnight bag and now I get extra dryer sheets."

She remembered another document, tapping a finger on its signature line. "Neither they nor any of their agents may harm your reputation in any way, while you resign to pursue other interests with a small merit bonus and ninety days of health care that will more than cover your delightful stay here. You're welcome."

Once Meredith said that there was only one acceptable response. "Thank you, my sister. I don't know what I would do without you."

"It wasn't very complicated. Don't make it that way in your head."

I felt a renewed kinship with an Orange County housewife in group therapy who loved droning on about her ugly high-stakes divorce. Abandoning the whole of her self-worth on a sheet of Xerox paper, she sighed her last sigh across a cavernous conference room while staring blankly into the void. Come Monday morning, the same county clerk cloaked in the dream of a department store celebrity fragrance would stamp and certify the death of ours even as we forgot each other's first names and last initials on adjacent Betty Ford stair climbers.

"Everything's going to be okay," Meredith said. "I promise." She reached across the table to give my hand an upbeat double tap—just as a Canada goose flapped nearby, startling us both.

An aggressive flock of the dirtiest creatures ever to drop out of the sky marked the outlying trails with excrement, picking it up in stinky mounds with their shifty black bills to feather nests along the breezeways.

"They refused to migrate through last winter," I said. "They've stayed put and taken over for some reason, but it turns out they have federal protection. Nobody wants to risk arrest and court-martial cleaning up after them, unless they're looking to collect the big Family Day bonus, and then they get out the firehose and make them really mad."

"I get it already: Family Day is a grift and you haven't gotten a thing out of the program."

"I've learned how to shake my margarita in a baby bottle *while* I'm feeding the baby lunch so my wealthy older husband is none the wiser."

"That reminds me," Meredith said, leafing through her files. "I received an intriguing job inquiry on your behalf, although I'm not sure it's quite up your alley."

Recoiling my hand from a Canada goose thrusting its hissing beak within an inch of the last falafel ball, I turned to Meredith, stating the obvious. "Try me."

"Have you heard of Wonderful Girls? They make those amazing lifelike dolls."

"What's lifelike about them? They're not actually alive."

"Don't be ridiculous," she said. "They have dozens of unique characters, each with her own set of quirks and challenges. Children see them as best friends and role models."

"That's interesting," I replied, although it seemed ordinary in terms of the exciting things going on out there. Artificial intelligence and robotics. Virtual and augmented reality.

"They've expressed interest in your running their new entertainment studios. You'd be working for and with other women," she added, dangling the bait. "Pretty much exclusively."

"What? Get out."

"You don't see *any* men in their stores," she insisted. "They don't even have a men's room. They have two ladies' rooms, one for mommies, one for girls and dolls."

"Where would I fit into that mix?"

"The female empowerment," she insisted. "I went to their flagship store in La Jolla to pick up something for my assistant's twins and dropped a load on Wonderful everything. They put on the fiercest all-girl show to get that Amex Black fist pumping high and proud."

Company founder Happy Lindstrom had been a small-town librarian whose family traveled around the Midwest in a converted mobile home. Re-creating female achievements in history through theatrical skits performed at state fairs and flea markets, Happy sold an array of costumed dolls, clothing, and toys and grew a thriving catalogue business, recently acquired in a billion-dollar deal with ZZZZZoom!, the Japanese gaming giant headquartered in San Francisco. The company preserved its own brand purity, Meredith said, from home offices in Littleburgh, Wisconsin.

"Wait, where?"

"It's not far from Madison," she said.

"Which is where?"

"Near Chicago."

"How near is near?" I asked.

"Couple hours. It's really in the middle of everything, depending on your perspective."

"I have a different perspective, Meredith. We talked about New York. Atlanta, Toronto, maybe London. Didn't we make a list?"

"It was just an idea. You go ahead and put the whole thing right out of your head," she said, inhaling the unmistakable perfume of New Poop by Canada Goose. "Stay here indefinitely if you like, while I keep looking around for something, somewhere. Your call."

"Just take me home."

"Now? How would that work? Nothing to do with yourself all day but wander around the Farmers Market in dark sunglasses hoping you'll make it through happy hour without a slip?"

"Maybe I could come stay with you for a while. Would that be okay with your husband?"

"You are always welcome in our home, don't be ridiculous," Meredith said.

They had a yard three times the size of the house itself, with an outdoor kitchen and a pool and Jacuzzi with a waterfall overlooking the canyon. The lawns were expansive enough for a putting green, bocci ball, horseshoe, and badminton courts.

Patches of lavender, thyme, and mint became most fragrant in the noonday sun, and trees dropped citrus, figs, and stone fruit for snacking.

A self-service lunch would be displayed in portion plates behind the glass door of a Sub-Zero fridge, and on weekends she'd cook dinner in a wood-burning brick pizza oven in the soft light of hanging lanterns bobbing from overhead olive branches. It was everything Betty Ford should have been and more!

"I guess I wouldn't mind getting around to some of my own projects," I said, savoring the thought.

She walked it way back. "Obviously, I'll have to clear the details with Butch—the whats and wheres, the how longs. You know how he is about having a lot of people around eating his groceries and sitting on his furniture. There was that time you did something crazy with his remote?"

"They're called channel presets. God, forget it. How much are the doll people offering?"

"I really think that's the best choice."

"How much?"

"I can promise you they will come in with a generous compensation package. You don't have to commit right away. You'll go up there and have a look around, meet the team."

"Don't look behind you," I said under my breath. Raising a chorus of honks and hisses, the full flank of Canada geese was closing ranks around a baking dish of homemade pistachio baklava.

"Leave it. Pick up the briefcase," I added calmly.

She put her hands in the air and backed away.

"Now run!"

We jumped through a small gap in their tightening encirclement, giving way to the proverbial wild goose chase as we made our escape from Betty Ford.

Later discharged in absentia AMA, against medical advice, I did not stop to pick up my baggage.

On, Wisconsin.

CHAPTER TWO

# Casey Klinkhoffer, the Most Wonderful Girl with a Death Wish and a Key to the Warehouse Store

GROUCHO MARX BETRAYED HIS FAMOUS advice about never joining a club that would have you with an all-knowing flick of the limp cigar that actually got him in the door. Coupled with that weird eyebrow thing, it might as well have been a secret handshake to a closed club that wanted him just fine.

Pulled by this strange and wonderful concept of female unity, I stepped off the plane in Madison expecting some milky-skinned ambassador smelling of good sense and native optimism to show me the way to our secret retreat. Quite an ambitious title, the Great American Heartland. If nothing else, these doll ladies had moxie.

Marked by the absence of a jetway enveloping passengers in climate-controlled bliss, unfortunately, Dane County Regional deposited its scant midsummer arrivals down a clunky stairway onto the melting black tarmac against a wave of humidity I could practically stand up and surf.

The senior leadership team at Wonderful Girls hoped to have me onboarded by late August, when they would ramp up for the holiday season. We barely had time to teleconference and hammer out the particulars before they arranged my house-hunting trip on this sweltering Fourth of July weekend.

"I'll admit the view is spectacular," I told my sister over the phone. "I'm not so sure about the commute from here."

Flopped across my king-size bed at the Edgewater Hotel, I surveyed the panoramic Wisconsin State Capitol building looming over a wide expanse of Lake Mendota in the heart of downtown Madison. "Don't they have something out near their little village factory I could walk to in a blizzard?"

"I don't think you want to walk anywhere in a blizzard. They obviously want to razzle-dazzle you, show you the whole area."

"They didn't send a car, though. I don't even see the customary fruit basket." I ripped open a nine-dollar bag of Fritos from the mini-bar with my teeth. "What's up with Wonderful Human Resources?"

"I'm sorry, have you already forgotten that Human Resources is never your friend?" she said with a chuckle.

"Human Resources." I echoed her familiar refrain. "Neither human nor resourceful."

"The woman in charge has been on maternity leave. If something slipped off somebody's radar on a holiday weekend, that's a good thing. Why don't you go out and enjoy yourself while you get your bearings on their nickel?"

A FARM-TO-TABLE GASTROPUB, GRAZE HAD a menu of spicy, exotic comfort food reflecting the conflicted imagination of a James Beard–winning "Sconnie" with Korean roots.

Situated directly in front of the majestic capitol building, it teemed with young legislative aides and assistant state attorneys, a blue-hued sea of tie-loosened power suits recessing for the long holiday weekend.

I asked the bartender for the Gochutgaru Virgin Bloody with Hand-Crushed Summer Tomatoes.

Seated at a community table running the length of a modern glass atrium, I leafed through some real estate pamphlets I'd picked up in the hotel.

A fresh-faced young lady tapped my shoulder and asked me to pass the pig. "The bacon basket," she prompted. "I can't reach it."

"They give you free bacon at the table instead of bread!" I told my sister on the phone, speaking over the festive din. "I mean, you can have bread, but why would you want it?"

"It sounds like a bar. You went straight to a bar?"

"Didn't I just say it's a gastropub? You said I should enjoy myself."

"I said you should get your bearings."

"I am. Here, talk to the girl next to me. I think she works for the governor," I added conspiratorially.

"Find a place to live!" Meredith barked and hung up the phone.

I paid the tab and walked back to the hotel, watching families assemble along the shoreline. They jockeyed for prime lounge chair positions to enjoy "Shake the Lake," the weekend-long musical fireworks spectacular.

The University of Wisconsin–Madison waterski team stacked up on one another's shoulders in breathtaking formation, veering around foamy wakes of every size, shape, and variety trailing a network of private, party, and excursion boats powering past. Maybe I would take up trick skiing; it had to be good exercise and I couldn't rely on finding any respectable kundalini yoga in the area.

I went upstairs to call my sister back and add this to my general concerns, but my hotel room phone rang before I could dial out, and a woman started talking.

"Hello, dear, this is Gloria Bohring, the Realtor. Are you ready to take a ride with me around town?" she asked in a strong, nasal voice with openly rounded consonants and long, dragged-out vowels against a rapid-fire cadence.

I interrupted to ask where she was from, and it took her a good long time to say Manitowoc by way of Menomonee Falls. "But I went to college in Wauwatosa and met Mr. Bohring way up in Ashwaubenon, so you're probably hearing all of that."

"I was interested in how you found me," I said flatly.

"Oooooh," she said, as if wrapping her entire face around a light bulb. "Your sister, Meredith, thought you could use a hand."

I ran back downstairs and strapped myself into the cramped passenger seat of a red Mini Cooper, driven by a middle-aged blond who wore chunky gold highlights to match the key-shaped badge on her lapel. She exited the porte-cochere of the striking Art Moderne tower opening onto the city's ornate Mansion Hill District, dappled with sunshine.

"This looks beautiful now, don't get me wrong. Navigating winter is my chief concern." I shivered at the thought of it.

She dismissed me with one hand while the other applied frosted raspberry lipstick the exact shade of her nail polish and coordinating cotton twill pantsuit. I wondered which she'd purchased first, or maybe this was her daily uniform, a branding statement about the ease and comfort of becoming one with your ice cream cone. "Winter is just a story."

"I'm pretty sure it's a true story. I've seen it on TV."

"That's all fake news."

"Oh, is the weather girl in on that?" I hadn't considered how the culture wars might controvert the gender wars at bay inside my cozy dollhouse just down the street, but I figured I'd steer the topic toward one that existed. "Are there any good condos in Littleburgh?"

"You're funny. As I was saying, we might get a powdery snowfall by Thanksgiving or Christmas. Nothing sticks until January, and it's all pretty much over by mid-March."

Where had Meredith dug up this climate denier, and how slaphappy did she think we were on the coast?

She hit the gas hard to fly by the ornate residences flanking Capitol Square. Pristine studies in Queen Anne Revival and Italianate style, they featured low-pitched roofs, broad eaves, and decorative framing around the doors and windows.

"They used to call this Millionaire's Row, before partitioning it off as rentals," she said, scrunching her nose as though she'd inhaled something so rank, she needed to stop it halfway up. "You wouldn't want anything like *that*."

"A rental? I don't know. They want me to start in a few weeks and I'm open to anything doable in that window, I suppose." I didn't mention I'd signed a two-year contract with a healthy bonus if I chose to extend, given the unlikelihood of that ever happening.

"Let's start at the top and work our way down," she said. We couldn't have driven five blocks before another large lake appeared. "This is the Lake Monona side. We are talking lakefront?" she asked.

"I hadn't really considered the idea of a dock for my fleet of restored wooden boats."

"Where do you plan to keep them?"

"I don't actually have any boats," I said.

"Well, you'll have to get some."

Situated on its titular Isthmus, the Madison area is shaped something like the female reproductive anatomy, a skinny spindle of prime real estate pointing upward with fertile feeder lakes fanning out on either side like a pair of swollen ovaries.

We traced the north shore of Lake Mendota, where she planned to show me the tony neighborhoods along the shorter route to Littleburgh.

"Shorewood Hills is the old money. Spring Hills is the doctor money. Bishop's Bay is the country club, do you golf? You'll want to get on the waiting list right away or they'll kill you with greens fees."

"Yeah, we may not be aligning here on my price range," I said.

"Did I mention Meredith and I worked together on the buyback offer for your LA house? Quite the hardliner, your sister." A company program arranged for the purchase of homes for relocating executives as part of the compensation package, and Meredith had insisted I grab at the opportunity to let them do the legwork on the front end. "You'll find quite a market differential between here and LA."

"Oh? I've been wondering how much I'd get here in exchange for my two-one in the Burbank Equestrian District." A converted stable, its second bedroom formerly doubled as a hayloft and still smelled vaguely horsey when it rained. I hadn't gotten any further in the Southern California real estate market over the years, and even that rare find stretched my midlevel executive pocketbook to its limits.

We pulled up to a hillside, four-bedroom, three-bath midcentury modern split-level set on a private hill point with panoramic views of Lake Mendota. "Are you familiar with the Prairie School of Design?" she asked. "Look at how the flat lines and horizontal bands integrate with the landscape. Compare that with what you saw downtown."

Vaulted ceilings, a wood-burning stone fireplace, and a wall of massive windows graced the open-concept interior great room, while a four-season sunroom accessed a wraparound terraced lookout, a backyard paver patio, and a screened gazebo lined with a curtain of hundred-year-old maple trees facing the outlying marshland. "It needs some work here and there, but that's the fun part," she said. "You'll take a drive over to Viroqua and grab a couple of the Driftless Amish. They make wonderful carpenters, and they practically give away the furniture."

"I don't know. It probably costs a mint just to heat."

"You can close off the whole downstairs. You'll also catch a nice breeze off the lake in summer, so you'll save on cooling. Exactly how Frank Lloyd Wright designed it."

"Frank Lloyd Wright? Come on."

"We've never clearly authenticated his involvement, but he would have had his reasons for thwarting that," she said. "He lived just up the road. They say he built this place for his mistress after people started talking."

"About what?"

She looked at me knowingly. "Drive out there, take the tour. They'll tell you *everything*."

"Okay, but can I seriously afford to buy something like this?"

"It includes a ten-acre parcel of marshland, so you'll want to build a boardwalk for picnicking, birdwatching, that sort of thing. And you're not in the village proper, so you'd have to hire a private plow to clear the service road when we get a storm coming off the lake."

"And how much would that cost?"

"Fifty bucks a pop."

"I need to call my sister. She'll probably want to get that down to forty."

MY VERY LOW OFFER ON a rumored architectural masterpiece with a supposedly checkered past meant I could return to LA to pick up my things immune to bad jokes about calling Littleburgh, Wisconsin, my home for the duration.

Any Golden State resident with an unkind word about my running from the mob or offsetting premenopausal hot flashes in wintry bliss would receive a copy of my property tax statement and a pound of free bacon compliments of the governor. Oh yes, he and I chatted casually once or twice over the next days while passing the pig—about clean air, cheap gas, and a new generation of aggressively available artisanal cheese men.

I did want to try out my commute the afternoon I flew out, so I squeezed in a last-minute visit to the office. Avoiding the downtown congestion exiting the hotel, I bypassed the Isthmus and drove all the way around Lake Mendota, tracing its northern shore and intersecting wide, marshy expanses and protected natural conservancies, flanked by the hilly family dairy farms concentrating around the Village of Littleburgh.

I drove my rental car to a back gate of the twenty-five-million-dollar Wonderful Girls campus. Three warehouse outbuildings and a soaring glass-topped conservatory housed an office space, flanking a desolate backdrop of seven hundred acres of preserved wooded prairieland donated in trust by company founder Happy Lindstrom, a noted environmental enthusiast, Gloria Bohring had heard somewhere.

The gate arm sat upright, with some nine hundred surface-level parking spots deserted. I hesitated to enter without a nod from a security guard I expected to appear, listening to the hum of the tallgrass, alive with the sounds of whistling bird life and chuckling prairie dogs. I'd been drinking this in for only a moment when a navy blue minivan with New York plates pulled up beside me and a young woman got out.

"Excuse me, is there a reason you're just sitting here?" In her early thirties, she wore a stylish boho kimono over a tank top and denim shorts with a pair of classic Ray-Ban Clubmasters. "Security took off today, everybody's off." She lifted her glasses onto her head to get a better look at me. "Are you Jaycee Grayson by any chance?"

"Was it something I said?" *I hadn't said a word.*

"Oh, hi! I heard you might be in town, which didn't make much sense. Everybody takes off for their cabins up north this week. The lucky ones stay for two or more, or even the rest of the summer."

I made a mental note to purchase a summer cabin up north. How much could that set me back?

She extended a French-manicured hand clanging with Moroccan bangle bracelets. "Casey Klinkhoffer. I'm the new Photo Studio Manager."

As a series of plaintive wails emitted from the minivan, Casey's voice lowered several startling octaves. "Marshall, Pendleton, give Mommy a minute." She turned back to me and shrugged. "Boys."

"Right. Well, I guess I chose pretty much the worst week of the year to make the trip out," I said. "It's like trying to get a meeting in LA during Sundance."

Her face lit up as though welcoming an old friend. "I'm just in from the opposite coast!"

Born and raised in Madison, she eagerly shared, Casey Klinkhoffer had spent the last ten years working her way up on the morning talk show circuit in New York. Hailing from a long line of Wisconsin royalty, her mother was heiress to the MooMoo Spreadable Party Cheese fortune; her father had been lieutenant governor for most of the nineties and later became a cable news political pundit. Though Casey held rightful darling status among a wide swath of the donor class in media and entertainment, she kicked in her own doors in an overcrowded field.

"I can't wait to work on the new ecommerce site from the ZZZZ-Zoom! people but shooting a mail-order catalogue feels like a step down," she said. "They had this job available, and with the boys in school it felt like the right time to come home. We just have the two, six and seven. Marshall and Pendleton," she added after an awkward pause.

I had often watched less qualified moms, and altogether unqualified dads, jump over me again and again across the corporate checkerboard. An expanding family photo set appeared on a rising executive's desk from time to time, perhaps just as it had come packaged in its shiny new frame—proving a superior mastery of illusion at the very least.

"Nothing ranks above family, Casey, not a single thing in this life." I smiled. She smiled. We both smiled. It would take me a while to trust anyone with too much information in this mysterious world built by and for the fairer sex.

Casey jogged back to the minivan to tend to another round of impatient whines. "Hey, did you want to buy some dolls and toys to take home?" she asked me over a shoulder. "Employees have a lot more to choose from since the ZZZZZoom! acquisition." She pointed conspiratorially to an unmarked warehouse across the lot. "I still have a key to the warehouse store. Used to work there in high school."

THE FIVE OF US PROWLED the windowless aisles without turning on the lights. Casey found a shopping cart and raced her boys up and down the aisles, all three screaming in wicked delight. "I'll write up everything and charge it to my employee badge," she said, sailing past out of breath. "You can Venmo me or whatever."

Cranking up the music on the store system with Marshall and Pendleton bouncing along to the beat, she struck me as a fun mom pulled from the pages of the company catalogue.

Rounding a corner, I joined a wall-to-ceiling showing of the nation's Wonderful Girls, standing up to salute me in their clear jewel boxes, presenting a riot of accomplishment in costumes and regalia accented with remarkable detail. They represented virtually every corner of the country, moment in history, hobby, craft, sport, skillset, passion, and pursuit.

Fran MacNeill, the Most Wonderful Girl on the College Football Field, caught my eye. Originally hailing from the traditionally African American suburb of Avondale in Cincinnati, Ohio, she overcame gender bias, generational poverty, and a pediatric bone disorder to become an eight-year-old placekicking prodigy. She stood at a feisty two-foot-nothing beside a certified National Collegiate Athletic Association goal post designed to scale. Holding a tiny genuine cowhide leather Wilson football, she wore regulation padding beneath a nonbranded uniform. When I picked her up, a motion sensor cued a marching band crackling from an embedded packaging speaker.

My adult perception that this all felt a bit hokey vanished in favor of its certain meaning to girls.

Casey climbed a sixteen-foot-high wheeled industrial ladder to reach a top warehouse shelf. She stood on one leg on her tiptoes, removing her hand from the guardrail to feel around for a display box, raining dozens of packs of a popular ZZZZZoom! trading card game into the outstretched hands of the squealing boys below.

In that moment, I saw a slightly younger soul sister mirroring my steep upward climb. A fine, strong woman of the plain, she came from good pioneer stock who bore many generations of Klinkhoffers without benefit of the modern epidural. No hooky-playing bourgeoisie would stand between this woman's boys and their toys!

"Let me run something by you," I said, once she had both feet safely on the floor. "The ladies upstairs see us handing off feature production to outside partners. To my mind, that runs the risk of losing control of the brand message."

"Trust me," she said with a chuckle. "They'll want to control everything."

"What if we converted our existing photo studios into a working soundstage? San Francisco is taking their time building our play portal. Why not start feeding that beast with some games and videos? We could shoot simple stop motions with all this product on hand, and line up a couple of college interns to do the post."

"I don't know where we'd put them, though. We're pretty tight for space already." She paused and thought a moment before telling me about a warehouse abandoned when manufacturing moved offshore years earlier, used ever since as a "doll hospital" where girls sent defective merchandise for repair.

"That could work," I said.

"Are you hearing a barking dog?" she asked.

I could hardly hear anything with the Muzak cranked up. "It's probably one of the new combat toys." I gestured to the playtime military training her boys had undertaken at the far end of the aisle. "They're going big with cavity-embedded sound effects."

I told her I'd need to work up a proposal for my soundstage idea to get the brass on board. "You haven't spoken to them about this?" she asked.

"Not yet. I haven't even met the whole team."

She hesitated, sucking in a breath. "Most of us are from here, born and bred. The ones Happy put in charge never left. If you run at them too hard, they'll dig in their heels and gun it in reverse."

"They brought me here to plow forward, though."

"Oh, they need ideas, don't get me wrong," she said. "The big fear is the new guys move in and shut us down, ship the whole operation to San Francisco."

"That's a tech town," I told her. "They don't have the creative talent to make that work any more than we do."

"What do I know?"

"Listen, I appreciate both the honesty and the intel," I said. "I've worked with a lot of guys over the years who weren't always so collaborative."

"To excel is to reach your own highest dream. We must also help others, where and when we can, to reach theirs," she said. "Barbara taught me that."

*Barbara who? Boxer? Bush? Streisand?* Such casual disinterest in executing a proper name drop filled me with promise for our fertile workplace alliance. I let it all spill out. "I don't have a family. Single, forty, no kids. It's just me, and honestly, I feel really energized talking to you."

We collected the boys and rolled our cart full of booty outside into the blinding sun of the plain, where you could smell centuries of promise in the air—and stared down the barrel of a police-issue semi-automatic M4 carbine.

"Hands up," a deep voice ordered through a bullhorn over a ferociously barking dog.

A cop crouching behind the door of an official Tahoe squad sitting on elevated monster tires stood up, covering himself with the long gun.

Just then, a sixty-pound Belgian Malinois police canine broke loose from its lead and bounced over to Casey, licking her face.

"Pavlov, look how big you are!" she cried, plowing forward to love him up alongside the equally delighted boys.

With that, the cop lowered the gun, signaling a radio clipped to his shoulder.

"Two-Oh-One, false alarm on that ten-sixty-two. Two-Oh-One, ten-seven-B out."

He looked at Casey, mystified, wiping the sweat from his brow with an honest-to-God linen hankie pulled from his shirt pocket. "Didn't you hear me ordering you to come out with your hands up?"

"I'm sorry, Chief. We had the music cranked up and those warehouse walls are super thick."

"Jeezaloo, kid, you scared the living bedoodle out of me, tripping all kind of alarms."

He leaned against a police SUV, catching his breath. "Your security team went fishing who knows where for Lord knows how long. I can't be catching these breaking-and-enterings out here alone. I'm an old man."

Not an old man at all, he struck me as kind of sexy for a guy who said "jeezaloo" and "bedoodle" when he got agitated. I couldn't help but empathize with men in uniform, having brought so many to life in the world of digital shooter games. The player generally takes on the role of the cop, rendered as both a badass and a good guy fighting assorted evildoers to win back control of his soul while securing the public's safety.

The small-town archetype battled an army of cornfield demons quietly waiting to pounce, often the most vicious and slippery demons of all.

"Meet my bestie's dad," Casey said.

*How old was her bestie, twelve?*

This guy seemed grizzled beyond his forty-odd years, wearing a gray-flecked beard with a much younger set of hazel eyes that turned to fix on me, even as he continued speaking to Casey. Cops do that kind of thing to catch a subject off guard. "Who's your accomplice, kid?"

"Jaycee Grayson," I interjected. "Executive Producer and Vice President of Global Entertainment."

We had wrangled over my title in contract negotiations, and I had some trouble spitting it out, since I'd never said it before, and I felt a little giddy, what with the foiled heist and potential of high-powered gunplay.

"Abel Dreaux, Village Police Chief." I extended my hand, but he had already turned around to fumble with the blue light still swirling on the dash of the squad.

"I didn't realize you had a village department," I said. "I haven't detected a lot of humans out this way."

"You won't see small-town policing around much longer; it'll all roll up to the counties. Course, I'll be dead and buried by then."

Some imagined creaky old age might be a ploy to draw my attention to the fit and muscular form he cut in his crisp khaki uniform as he leaned into the trunk of the squad to stow his weapon.

"Did you need to bring us in or anything?" I asked. "We can get all of this straightened out, whatever you need."

"No, you're good," he said, mildly amused by the suggestion.

"Thank you, sir. I need to catch a flight and what with all the excitement I'm a bit pressed for time."

"Golly, I guess I'm the one who got you all excited there."

"Pardon me?"

"Or maybe it was Pavlov here. We're still working on settling this one down."

I laughed, somewhat tentatively. Maybe there'd come a day when I wasn't braced to fend off a tasteless remark from the most unassuming place.

"I could give you a lift over to the airport," he volunteered. "Send someone out to pick up your rental car."

"That is thoughtful, but completely unnecessary." I opened the trunk of the car to find a place in my luggage for two-foot-tall Fran MacNeill and her clunky box.

"Alrighty then. Did you need a hand with your dolly?"

I really didn't but stepped aside anyway to allow him to make room for the box without crushing it. He wasn't shy about manhandling my intimates to create some padding, taking full command of my delicate mesh train case to do away with the extraneous personal items inside of it. Feminine powder. Bath salts. Body butter.

"Put these in your purse," he directed me.

I could easily imagine him ordering around his share of girl perps spot lit through the fog of flashing headlamps alongside deserted country roads.

"A police escort," I mused after he zipped up and shut my trunk with a great display of confidence in his handiwork. "What a cool way to wrap up my visit. Are you sure you have the time?"

"He has the time," Casey interjected. It's important to have a support team that knows how to take the temperature in the room even when out of doors. I was going to like that girl.

"Did you want lights and sirens, ma'am?" asked Village of Littleburgh Police Chief Abel Dreaux, who must have felt unusually youthful in that moment to even suggest such a scandalous breach of protocol.

"Jaycee," I said. "Can I turn them on myself?"

CHAPTER THREE

# Trudi Oldham, the Most Wonderful Girl with Your Preferred Cookie, Giant Pie, and Desk Candy of Choice

I FLEW HOME WITH A smile on my face and a mad crush on Wisconsin, seized by the strange and wonderful thought that all of this was meant to be. Could my life in hiding become more than a passing fancy? Why had I bucked and kicked against the idea of reaching for something entirely new and running with that, wherever it might take me? Having neglected to pursue anything else of significance while doubling down to reach for an elusive dream, my Hollywood life had become predictable shortly after I began living inside of it. Maybe an even unlikelier dream, with vast, uncertain edges, awaited in the middle—alive with the grand mystery of whether my second chapter would reveal something unattended at my core in the first.

On my last day in LA, the movers picked up my prized Porsche Cayenne and loaded it up for its two-week hopscotch to a place I still couldn't pick off a map.

For an Angeleno, handing over the car keys to anyone but a uniformed valet outside Mr. Chow represented the ultimate leap of faith.

I Ubered over to my sister's, where I planned to sleep over to give the movers some room the next day while they packed up everything else I owned. Surprisingly, I found the lights dim at Meredith's sprawling ranch home. Letting myself in, I called out, "Meredith? Anybody home?"

I found her in the backyard looking out over the starlit canyon with a hot cup of tea, her feet up on an oversize rattan ottoman. I could count on one hand the number of times I'd seen her doing any one of those things. "What's up?" I asked.

Startled from a far-off revery, she sat up and sprung to her feet. "Jaycee! I was about to corn the beef for the movers."

"Can't we just give them a tip? Really, it's a bit much to be corning their beef."

She slid open a wall of French doors crisscrossed with fragrant night-blooming jasmine. "Never mind. They tend to treat your things better when you make it personal."

I followed her into the dimly lit kitchen, where she pressed a packet of spices into the fatty flesh of a five-pound brisket and set it to simmer on a bronze-trimmed La Cornue stove. She flitted about turning on some lights. Something seemed off in the O'Cochlain house.

"Where's Butch?" I asked.

"Working." Okay, now I was really concerned. Butch was working while she lolled around the pool gazing at the moon. "He's giving a seminar on estate planning," she added.

"What does he know about estates or planning? Or seminars?"

"He took a class, will you stop? It's a fabulous opportunity with a generous commission. He's really been buckling down lately."

If he was out convincing old ladies to hand over a piece of what their husbands had left them instead of hitting up my sister for lunch money, frankly I was good with that. "Why has he been buckling down, though? Did you have a fight or something?"

"You know we don't fight."

What I knew was she devoted a *lot* of energy to keeping him on a relatively even emotional keel.

Recovering from a childhood bicycle accident and multiple subsequent brain surgeries, he'd been coddled by women his whole life—his mother, his sisters, doting nurses, pretty nuns. It probably wasn't all that hard for him to fall in love with himself. By the time she hooked up with him, he was Dr. Jekyll and Baby Huey. One minute he'd be belting out Broadway show tunes entering a clubby old-school eatery like Dan Tana's, and the next he discovered his favorite table was unavailable. He'd need to go outside alone and stand still with his teeth and fists tightly clenched until it passed. Either that or his head would explode all over Santa Monica Boulevard and Meredith would have to clean it up. Her choice. He'd always made that very clear, to be fair.

"I want to talk about you," Meredith said. "Do you have any idea how jealous I am? Here you are going off without a care to pursue another dangerous undertaking."

"I wouldn't exactly call it dangerous. The deal's been sealed, what could go wrong now?"

All kinds of things were going wrong at that precise moment, I would later decipher, such as serious talk among the nice Wisconsin doll ladies of how to demote me while keeping my sister's rock-solid contract in relative tact. Against a wall of picture windows opening onto the lush Littleburgh marshlands, my friendly workplace intimate Casey Klinkhoffer may well have spent that very morning selling me down the river among her reunited gang of gal pals.

"We need a mom, a millennial mom with my life experience, to deliver brand authenticity on the production side," Casey would tell the senior team, pitching as her own *my* idea to build out an entertainment studio on-site. "Let the new guys bring the tech. We can start feeding the beast with the product we have and get in some college interns to do the post."

Oh yes, Casey Klinkhoffer would prove herself more stealthy and cunning a soul than even I could have imagined with all my executive storyteller skills and training. A cold, unblinking frontierswoman, she advanced across contentious ground inside my brain—and she was willing to scalp me for it.

Blissfully unaware as I prepared to leave LA in the rearview mirror, I intercepted my sister's foaming cauldron of corned beef boiling over her upmarket French stove. The water must have evaporated altogether from a pot of boiled potatoes while she had been outside earlier, reducing them to an inedible mass.

"Did you get fired today or something?" I asked.

"Ha! I wish. My partners don't fire rainmakers who successfully arbitrate fifty-million-dollar cases by group text."

She put the burnt pot in the sink and filled another one with reverse osmosis water from a tap. She threw in a fistful of coarse Kosher salt and opened a fresh bag of Russian Banana fingerling potatoes.

"I met a high-ranking police officer on my trip," I said. "The chief, actually."

"Oh? And how did that one escape you until now?"

"You've been kind of tough to nail down these last few weeks. I call you with a problem with my house closing or a question about the mortgage insurance and your assistant calls me back."

She fiddled with a predictive wireless meat thermometer on the blink. "I do have that other job to get after from time to time between servicing your assorted issues."

"Do you want to hear about the cop I met or not?"

Though it had been only a passing encounter, something struck me as different about Abel Dreaux, barely sixteen when he married Sally Baker, pregnant by another boy who'd rejected her.

"Abel didn't blink, gave up his whole future," I told Meredith. "He raised the baby as his own and they had three more girls before things fell apart. Now everybody's all grown up and married, and Sally lives in a tiny house on the edge of Abel's property so they can all be a family when they want."

"That sounds complicated. I have questions." Meredith was having trouble with her twenty-two-thousand-dollar pilot light, a potentially explosive situation as she stuck her head inside the oven to light it manually.

I felt it a risky time to pull focus, so I left out the part where Abel and I had a few extra minutes at the airport. He and I drove up to the top floor of the airport parking garage and shared a cup of coffee listening to the two-way radio in his squad. Just as I demonstrated my fluency in police code, a holdover from my gaming days, it started raining and Pavlov had to pee, so we didn't get to exchange numbers as I hopped out at the curb. *Cops can get numbers on their own*, I told myself.

"Who knows, maybe you'll get a chance to interrogate him personally if you make it for Thanksgiving," I prodded Meredith. "We're still planning that, right?"

"Uh-huh. I guess."

Now she had the hot corned beef in the tenuous grip of a pair of stainless-steel clamps, raising it from the pot over a waiting roasting pan. The dripping haunch dropped from her grasp and slid off the counter onto the floor. Without missing a beat, she reached down and grabbed it with her bare hands, chucking it into the pan and picking it up. "Get the oven door!"

I tried to—but lost my footing on corned beef grease, tumbling backward onto my elbows. She gave me a hand, but also slipped to the floor, letting loose of the pan on her way down, again sending the meat flying.

She crawled after it on hand and knee, picked it up, and lodged it into the oven pan-free, slamming the door shut behind her with a foot. "There we are."

We sat up against the cabinets, dissolving into hysterical laughter.

"I'm going to miss you, my sister," I finally managed to get out through a series of snorts.

"Me, too, my Jaycee." With that, she stopped laughing and fought back tears, her lower lip quivering.

"What? What?"

"I'm pregnant," she blurted out.

MY NEW BOSS, TRUDI OLDHAM, seemed unusually sympathetic when I asked for a week off to go home for Thanksgiving on my first day at work.

"Take two weeks if you want. Take as much time as you need."

She sat dwarfed behind a disproportionately large glass desk improbably devoid of dust and smudges. I figured she'd occupied the same spot for much of her twenty-year tenure with the company and a succession of larger and more streak-free office furniture probably came with her annual bonus package.

"I can't even imagine such a distance from my sisters during one of their pregnancies, especially a risky one," Trudi said. "They like to have their babies at home, with everybody right there."

"We'll have to consider something like that," I totally lied, since Meredith and I both felt strongly about modern gynecology.

Positioned on the top floor of the executive suite, Trudi's office had floor-to-ceiling windows overlooking a five-acre glass-domed garden and conservatory called the Happy Wonderful Place, where employees could gather for on-site festivities even in the harsh winter months. Beyond that, Lake Mendota stretched itself like a lazy yawn across a measureless expanse of prime Midwest horizon.

Trudi had ethereal blue eyes a bit too large for her face, effecting a cartoonish expression of genuine surprise she could wield as a superpower should she possess the native canniness to consider this a useful option. Locally raised among a prominent family of eight, she enjoyed limitless bulk frozen food from the supermarket her father managed. Her fashionable high-collar doctor jacket, positioned over white stretch denim jeans, hid a belly and backside amply fed off the fat of the land. In terms of life's little trade-offs, I thought, put me down for extra butter and moving up a dress size or two.

"May I tell you your skin is flawless?" I couldn't help but share.

"It's soap and water, no big secret," she said, somewhat uncomfortably. "Of course, we don't get much sun up this way."

"Soap, water, not much sun up this way." I jotted it all down. "Now that we have the priority items out of the way, were you able to get to my proposal for expanding the Photo Studios into a working soundstage?"

"And we love it!" she announced. "I do think we should let Casey Klinkhoffer's team run point on that, along with the Facilities people. You don't want to get your hands dirty with dump trucks and electricians."

"Well, there's quite a lot more to getting a studio up and running than the physical plant," I said. "Casey's terrific, but she might need some guidance setting up the—"

"And all that rolls up under Marketing, anyway. Catalogue. Ecommerce. We're looking at you as a pipeline to the entertainment industry," Trudi said. "Think about mining your existing contacts. Traveling, conferences, that kind of thing."

*Fabulous. In hiding for twenty minutes, and I'd received orders to return to the front and face the kill squad.*

"Maybe I'll take a trip to Miami for Kidgitalscreenfest. Nothing actually happens at that kind of thing, but everybody needs to get in there and conference about it." *Hopefully I wouldn't be expected at the executive bowling bash.*

I could see Casey down in the glass dome over Trudi's shoulder setting up for my Happy Wonderful welcome. She looked up at me with her huge, cornfed smile and gave me two thumbs up.

"We hope you'll join us in the conservatory for the big pie," Trudi said. "That was boysenberry, right? You may also expect a snickerdoodle and strawberry ice cream party on your birthday, and we'll send you home the day we wrap up the Christmas rush with a family-sized box of dark chocolate peppermint patties."

"You gals are good," I said, duly impressed.

"If we expect to raise joyful, thoughtful girls, we need to be joyful, thoughtful women." She referred to the company motto scrawled across the wall of the outlying hallway in Happy Lindstrom's own handwriting.

Getting up to close the blinds, she shut out the growing buzz of the party ramping up below. "We need you to stay focused on the big picture, forging valuable partnerships across the industry to keep us from leaning on San Francisco."

"Those guys have a strong tech team, but they don't bring anything to entertainment. That's why, and this goes back to the on-site studios, I recommend—"

"And you'll be hitting the ground running on finding us a big LA partner for our feature deal."

Why did she keep starting her sentences with "and"? There's no conjunction necessary when you're interrupting someone. Either she addressed the universe with one loosely connected thought, or she took partial ownership of everything she ever heard in her entire life.

"I'll get going on lining up some directors we could shop something around with," I said. "This will of course depend on which characters we feel are right to develop for the screen."

"And you'll have to crunch the numbers on that. Some will cost more than others to produce, so you'll want to call a meeting first and get a lot of opinions from across the teams."

"Oh good. I love a lot of opinions."

Had she bothered herself with a small chuckle this would have come off as a joke rather than lying there between us as a boldfaced lie.

"And let me show you your office," she said.

I didn't know what to do in my office, other than crunch numbers and set up meetings to collect a lot of opinions, but it was just across the hall from hers, where it looked like it had been vacated in a hurry.

"I thought all this had been cleaned out for you." She told me that the previous occupant had resigned on short notice. "I believe her mother became ill. Or was it her father?"

"How awful. Where was she from?"

"You know, I didn't get to know her all that well; she wasn't here long, unfortunately."

*They had to have known her pie flavor and cookie profile, even without the forwarding address to send her large box of preferred Christmas candy.*

"Keep whatever you want," she urged me. "Some of this takes a while to requisition."

A hastily discarded desk set was branded in the familiar trademarked Pantone shade of Wonderful Lavender, as were the scissors, light switch plate, and circular trash can. "Happy was a stickler about displaying Wonderful everything," she said.

When I asked if Happy ever came around nowadays, Trudi pointed to a magnificent office suite at the end of the hall. Its wide double doors opened onto a dreamlike study in shades of light purple set against the hazy blue sky and verdant green meadows I pictured blanketed in white during the winter months. "She's been living her own life for some time now, the grandchildren, the various charities. I understand they have a spectacular second home in Arizona."

I vaguely recalled reading in my onboarding literature that Happy Lindstrom had never felt comfortable in the spotlight after she and her family retired from the road. She rescued recent UW–Stevens Point graduate Trudi Oldham from a grim future in genetically modified soy or some such when the Lindstrom offspring showed no interest in growing Happy's home business into today's megabrand.

A personally handwritten résumé and cover letter from the well-mannered double major in food engineering and agricultural marketing apparently so impressed Happy that she set aside obvious concerns and asked Trudi to help create a brand ambassador the two of them came to call the Wonderful Mrs. Happy.

Mrs. Happy would be depicted not only by Happy Lindstrom herself on occasion, but also by any number of young moms in the pages of the catalogue, and by multiple actresses on stage in retail stores around the country.

Trudi shortly became company spokeswoman and was promoted to Executive Vice President and General Manager, the senior-ranking official on-site, in the acquisition deal that made Happy Lindstrom one of only four self-made female billionaires in the Midwest.

"She's getting on in years," Trudi told me. "And Hank isn't well. He drinks a little."

*He drinks a little! How hideous!*

An assistant leaned in to tell Trudi she had an urgent call, and she picked up the phone on my desk. "I think a nice balloon bouquet," she said. "Yes, lots and lots of them, something cheerful, fill the whole funeral home."

She hung up and told me that the natural father of her adopted toddler had died suddenly. "It's that opiate epidemic," she said. "Twenty-three years old. I'm flabbergasted."

She did look utterly shocked, but again, wearing a look of earnest, bug-eyed surprise could well be Trudi Oldham's secret power. "This boy was no good to anyone, certainly not to my son," she said on her way out.

*It was his son*, I wanted to call after her. Recovery is real, drinking a little doesn't make a person "unwell," and lots and lots of balloons might not be the best way to mark the devastating loss of an addict. I began to wonder if Trudi Oldham was my kind of joyful, thoughtful woman—although the jury would be out on that for a while.

Then again, why not leave my own addiction story in the past, along with skincare products and low-fat dairy? If that's what it took to earn my place under Trudi's Wonderful wing, I would coax my long-awaited movie to life and plant it in the ground like a victory flag for girls who rarely saw themselves at the center of anything, let alone standing ten feet tall at the local multiplex.

I pulled my Fran MacNeill from her Wonderful Lavender shopping bag and stood her upright on my desk, football in hand, eye on the goalpost. She and I had survived some things, and in that moment, she was my one true friend.

CHAPTER FOUR

# Meredith Grayson-O'Cochlain, the Most Wonderful Girl with Pastry Skills and a Following in France

MARKED BY A WIDE, EXPANSIVE skyline over endless summer grasslands, Wisconsin scored so highly on presentation and artistry I hardly noticed the tiny fault lines detracting from its structural integrity lingering just beneath the surface.

As for me, neither a feminist nor altruist by nature, both of which would imply a strong outward focus, I had far less interest in changing the world than in upgrading my kitchen and master bath.

"I bought three Shaker-style four-poster beds, two dressers, an armoire, six nightstands, a dining room table and chairs with a matching china hutch, and a spalted maple pub table." I made a giddy accounting of my afternoon shopping haul over the phone to Meredith. "Don't ask me what that last thing is, but it's fabulous, and everything cost in total what you paid that guy in Calabasas to make your shoe cubbies in the laundry room."

"I think I'm in the wrong life again," she said.

I envisioned Meredith at home in Laurel Canyon, working on a legal brief the size of a phone book with her feet up on one of three nesting pedestal coffee tables from Restoration Hardware. Factory-made somewhere in Appalachia, supposedly, it had been marked up beyond all reason by the snippy Brentwood designer of a partner's stay-at-home wife. "I don't know how this keeps happening to me. I could have been a French pastry chef. In France, where my handiwork is appreciated, and the people understand me."

"Why don't you pack a bag and walk away?" I prodded. "Leave everything, you don't need it."

"You're hilarious."

"I'm not kidding, Meredith. I'm going to have plenty of room here once I get things all fixed up. Me. Imagine that."

I was driving back toward Littleburgh from Viroqua in the epicenter of the Wisconsin Driftless Region, where Amish settlers pumped out generous examples of old-world skills from roadside farms near antiques shops bursting with rusty barn finds. "Maybe you and I could put down some real roots here after the baby comes."

"What about Butch?"

"Butch? Who invited him?"

"Oh, stop."

I veered around a slow-moving horse-drawn buggy with my top down as the end of the humid summer gave way to fall. Farm families worked the fields dressed just as they had in the sixteenth century, with women and girls in opaque white bonnets and matching aprons over plain cotton dresses and layered petticoats. Men and boys wore gray shirts and trousers, with matching suspenders to hold them up and black felt hats to shield their eyes from the crisp autumn sun.

"He's working very hard these days," Meredith said firmly. "He goes off to work in his suit and tie, and most nights he comes home right afterward. He hardly ever golfs a full eighteen holes on the weekend, either, and he's really excited about becoming a dad."

I watched a man raking hay into rows of hand-tied feed blocks lining the horizon as far as the eye could see to keep the family animals alive through the long winter months. "It's hard to picture Butch being that kind of dad," I said.

"Why would he need to be? I don't get where you're going."

"It just feels different here, how people depend on each other to get by." A gaggle of farm boys lined up along a hand-hewn fence to watch my silver Porsche Cayenne zoom over a hilly crest.

Piles of hand-thatched baskets, a patchwork of quilts, and neatly stitched feather down pillows obscured my passenger windows, with a hundred-year-old wagon wheel wedged into the hatchback. "That's going to be your headboard in the room next to mine," I told Meredith.

"This is all so exciting," she said. "Maybe I will try to make it for Thanksgiving."

"What are you talking about? It can't be safe for you to get on a plane by that point."

"The whole total bedrest thing turns out to be controversial," she said. "They're not supposed to treat you like your hair is on fire because you have risk factors."

I wondered how much weight she had gained but didn't want to ask, in part because I had no idea how much weight she was supposed to gain (or lose) and asking would only mean a fight about who was doing a worse job putting her overall health front and center in this new chapter.

"Isn't forty the cutoff age for the more serious geriatric pregnancy issues?" I slipped in.

"'Geriatric' is an outmoded term," she said. "'Advanced age pregnancy' is more successful than ever before in human history." She'd been referred to a maternal-fetal medicine specialist for advanced genetic testing. "Hopefully all that's looking good, and I don't end up with gestational diabetes or preeclampsia as things progress, which is a whole other ball of wax. Do we have to keep touring the inside of my uterus or are you good?"

That was so like her, dodging reasonable questions while simultaneously informing the medical profession at large how all this was going to go.

She would run me off to a world-class hand surgeon if I got so much as a hangnail, but she'd never been interested in scheduling her own well-woman exams and was intensely tight-lipped about the outcome when she did. I once invested months researching medical horror stories to get her to a dermatologist for treatment of a suspicious growth above her right eye.

"You'll have to wear a patch if you have some kind of ocular cancer," I chided her as the thing grew, magnified beneath an oversize lens of her Warby Parker eyeglasses. "That look only works for older gentlemen in the foreign intelligence community."

It turned out to be a benign skin tag, she reluctantly revealed, which she had to self-pay to remove after her insurance company deemed it a minor cosmetic option. "You always end up costing me money," she said. "In the future, please mind your own bodily issues and stay out of my face."

I pulled over along an ancient ridge to check out Vernon Vineyards, one of the few places in the state of Wisconsin with sufficient elevation to produce estate-grown vintages. Meredith must have heard the cheer from a raucous wedding reception underway in a high-ceilinged party barn where three hundred or so Madison Cheeseheads got smashed on the famous cranberry wine sourced from adjacent bogs before the first freeze.

"Where are you?" she asked with some suspicion in her voice. "Not some backroads bar, I hope. Nothing good happens in those places."

"It's an Amish candy store," I lied. "They make everything from scratch and tourists get excited when they take out the big fudge." I had no idea what that even meant.

"Big fudge? How big is it?"

"I didn't see it, okay?"

Once I'd moseyed my way down the road a bit, I mentioned I was going to start attending the local twelve-step meetings. "Littleburgh is so small I don't want to risk running into people from work," I said. "I'm checking into something a town or two over, did I mention that?"

"No, but I'm glad to hear it," she replied.

"Please promise me you'll take good care of yourself."

"Promise me you will," she said.

"Yes, fine. I promise," I lied again.

THE TRUTH IS MOST DAYS I focused singularly on a high-stakes battle so insidious I rarely saw it coming—informally at my desk, in passing over a copy machine, across the hot soup station in the company cafeteria. I never knew where I would encounter a formidable workplace warrior I came to call the Prairie Karen.

Overtly, she seemed a cheerful sort, the friend and helpmate I'd come a great distance to join in the warm spirit of our uniquely feminine collaboration. Beneath that lay the black heart of a viper, who'd cut you in an instant with the dull edge of a table knife concealed under the almond crumb coat of her grandmother's famous Danish Kringle.

"Did you want a slice of the Pineapple Upside Down Jellykugen?" asked Belinda Rockland. Though in her early forties, she appeared to have stopped growing around the seventh grade.

Belinda styled herself as though headed to the mall to hang out with her daughter's girlfriends, wearing an outdated bowl haircut and a denim jumper that fit awkwardly on top, further flattening a deficient bust. She had no intention of serving me, for heaven's sake, but she did make a big show of sliding over the blue and white Delft plate she'd brought from home.

Belinda viewed the company's foray into theatrical features as gilding the lily, given the quality thirty-second holiday commercials she had produced as head of Marketing over the years.

"We've picked up so many awards I've stopped counting. I can't imagine you showing any hint of originality this morning, what with the breakthroughs we've made with the moving image," she said, smiling brightly. "Big day for you. I'm excited to hear your ideas."

Unsure how to respond, I picked up a wedge of the jellied pineapple thing and shoved it in my mouth.

"Did you need a plate?" she asked. I didn't need anything from Belinda Rockland.

The executive conference room overlooked a wall of windows onto the warehouse distribution center, a bustling network of ramps, catwalks, and towering industrial shelving tended by forklifts jerking about. Merchandise manufactured offshore arrived here for sorting on conveyor belts and shipping around the world to fulfill a purchase made either online or through a busy on-site phone bank.

As the team settled in, I closed the blinds to eliminate all distraction and dabbed my mouth with a Wonderful Lavender paper napkin. Bolstering myself with a swig of coffee, I fired up my laptop, synching a PowerPoint presentation to the whiteboard behind me.

"Today's girls want familiar stories consumed in a bold new way," I began, cuing up stills of the brand's three original characters, Clara, Tara, and Sara. "Let's take it all the way back to the Great American frontier."

"I hate to interrupt, but haven't we done that to death?" asked Prudence Atwood, showing no outward appearance of hating to interrupt anything. A pert brunette with impeccable taste, as she was quick to share in our initial meetings, Prudence graduated top of her class in English Lit from UW–Eau Claire. Besting a pool of top candidates, or so she claimed, Prudence joined her mother, Louise Atwood, in the highly challenging editorial management of the three-inch illustrated storybooks that came inside the doll boxes.

"*Clara, Tara, and Sara* was Happy's first stage play," Prudence made clear, in case this bit of company history had slipped anyone's attention.

The lucrative brand was built on the backs of Clara, the Most Wonderful Girl on the Frontier; Tara, the Most Wonderful Girl on the Reservation; and Sara, the Most Wonderful Girl on the Underground Railroad. Leveraging a successful crochet business, the plucky fourth graders opened a home for orphaned war babies, remaining loyal to one another even after their parents killed each other by accident in a series of culturally insensitive mishaps.

"Thank you for that refresher, Prudence," I said. "Since the original trio consistently ranks among our top sellers, let's rejoin them on a cinematic thrill ride—into adulthood!"

"What's fun about adulthood?" asked Rebecca Lavery, who oversaw Brand Management.

The youngest among the senior team, Rebecca wore a uniformly calm expression, I would come to observe, even after delivering a chaotic brood to school each morning. Once the temperature dropped to thirty below, her mass of strawberry blond curls still wet from the shower occasionally broke in half at her shoulders, and she sat in meetings fiddling with a fresh bob tucked behind her ears.

"Exactly how does a doll grow up, anyway?" she inquired.

*Did they not have movies in this one-horse town?* "We would cast actresses to play them at different ages, into their teen years, and explore marriage and motherhood in later screen stories."

"Marriage! Motherhood!" cried Summer Jessup, as if she been stabbed twice through the heart in rapid succession.

Histrionics aside, men probably found Summer very attractive. Men don't even know when women overtone a comely feathered blond mane they should have lopped off years earlier to celebrate the end of a bad starter marriage, or so went the office scuttlebutt. Responsible for Research and Design since the tenth grade, Summer Jessup had answered a help-wanted ad in the local Penny Saver and marched into Happy Lindstrom's garage toting an impressive collection of *Teen Vogue*, along with a portable Sears Kenmore at the ready on her desk to this day.

"Our girls are nine and little," she said. "They play dolls with a friend who's nine and little. The grown-ups are down the hall."

Dispensing with reflections on parental neglect from the high school dropout, I had little choice but to invoke the great Laura Ingalls Wilder. "She *grows up* and becomes a teacher. Mary runs a home for the blind, and—"

"They're real people. Our girls like made-up stories," Louise Atwood said firmly. She had edited all fifty words of each made-up story, and while I had serious trouble making sense of this woman's salary and benefits package, I moved on to *Anne of Green Gables*. "She's a *grown-up* twenty-two. All the *Little Women* grow up—even Beth powered through, and she had scarlet fever. There's Wendy Darling—"

"Wendy Darling growing up is perhaps the most heartbreaking irony in all of children's literature," said Prudence Atwood, who felt this another good time to remind us she knew everything about everything.

"She's a doctor's daughter," Louise piped in.

"She's a doctor's wife," added Prudence.

The two of them would interject this incongruous inside joke into most any conversation impossible to correlate to either medical science or familial relations.

"The point being that today's girls don't want us holding back the realities around what happens to them next," I said.

"She's not wrong," said Rebecca Lavery.

With a stunned jolt to attention, the others looked at her as though she'd just sprouted a second freshly shampooed head.

A merchandising wunderkind, Rebecca had shadowed Happy for a college project and landed a job running Insights and Analysis by the end of her sophomore year. While numbers rarely lie, Rebecca had killer instincts and steely confidence, relying on both to prioritize a flawless record of wildly successful initiatives.

"Girls age out of doll play younger and younger every year," she said. "Defying social predictors is how we disappear altogether, regardless of who shows up here waving around another big wad of cash."

Emboldened by my tentative friendship with the smart one, I clicked on the poster art imagining seventeen-year-old Clara, Tara, and Sara at the center of the Klondike Gold Rush. "They'll conquer the Yukon, win a dance hall smackdown, and establish a sanctuary for abused palominos across the Old West."

Oh, I knew they liked it. How could they not like a teenage dance romance delivering a message on horseback?

"So, we'll dress up our dolls in the hot little numbers these booby actresses are running around in." Summer thought this through, toying with a tomato-shaped pincushion she wore on her wrist in case you forgot she could hurt you in a random office sew-off. "You bet girls will want in on that, provided Mom has completely lost her mind."

"A teenage doll could be issued in limited release as an ancillary item to market the film," I insisted. "Imagine the crossover brand appeal for a 'Happy Meal' type of toy."

"Marketing would need to lead that conversation," Belinda said. She hadn't been paying much attention since the jellied pineapple exchange. I pictured her dressing in doll clothes to amuse her husband and hated myself for this, of course, but she'd been the one to challenge the full breadth of my imagination with the moving image.

"Entertainment doesn't market the product," I said. "It *is* the product."

My next slide illustrated that story reduced to numbers even the Atwood gals could compute. "This one narrative—spun out across games, social, interactive—has more profit potential over the next fiscal year than the rest of the line combined."

"And this is fantastic," my boss, Trudi Oldham, announced, wearing her signature look of surprise and delight. She hadn't spoken a peep, as was her way, reserving her own opinions based on the aggregate of all others in a savvy chess move that would maintain her absolute power while eliminating all creative risk. "I love an ensemble, I love a wider audience, I love an adventure right-sized for girls," she said. "Let us reconvene when we've gotten a tad closer on a brand-friendly concept."

While I had no idea what, if anything, Trudi just said, rendering it impossible for me to execute upon it in any small way, she seemed delighted with her success in providing me no clear path forward. She gave me an encouraging pat on the shoulder and rose from the table, signaling an equally enthusiastic show of uninvested schadenfreude on the group's exodus.

I sighed, bowing my head as I followed the catwalk to the adjacent warehouse and slinked into a remote ladies' room. I sat down on a toilet in a distant row of stalls and discovered I'd gotten my period a few days earlier than expected. Fishing around for a wayward tampon in my purse leftover from last month, I heard the bathroom door open and two women whispering.

"Either she has no idea what she's doing here, or she has no idea what we're doing here," said one voice. I'm pretty sure this was the mother, Louise Atwood, though I couldn't say for sure. "Really, we can't blame her for either thing," she added. "Trudi will have to deal with them more effectively when they come."

I wondered who "they" were and decided I would have to invite Louise Atwood to lunch sometime and test her unique level of function in plain and direct speech, like a battery separated from its pack in the kitchen drawer.

"She's so Hollywood," said a voice I believed to be the self-important daughter, Prudence. "Do you see how she holds her car keys when she walks into a room? It really says something about who she is on the inside."

I would have to take a good, hard look at how I held my car keys and what that said about who I am on the inside, but for now I was stuck bleeding into a toilet and had a couple of bigger fish to fry. "Does anybody have a tampon?" I pleaded from the far stall.

Apparently, nobody did. What kind of self-respecting doctor was keeping these two around the house? "I'd take a pad in a pinch—mini, maxi, I'm not picky. I don't want to ruin these nice panties I bought at Frederick's of *Hollywood*."

I heard some muttering about a machine by the cafeteria bathrooms downstairs and the shuffling of shamed doctor brethren feet shuffling out the door.

Not even a full month in and I could Prairie Karen with the best of them.


"DIDN'T I WARN YOU TO take it slowly with them?" Casey Klinkhoffer whispered in the cafeteria. By early September, she had entered advance production on the holiday catalogue and picked artificial snow from her hair while keeping an eye out for a diverse lineup of nine-year-old-girl models running around on a quick break.

"Ashta! Ling-Ling! No junk, no spills, and do not snag another pair of velveteen tights for me to have to Photoshop," she barked.

We huddled in a corner behind a central fireplace dividing a large airy dining area that had yet to be fired up for the season. Most employees sat outside, beyond a soaring wall of windows around picnic tables overlooking the sunny preservation area.

"Now I'm pretty much back to square one. Even if we do agree on an action-adventure piece, I'll never find someone qualified to deliver it."

"How do you mean?"

"They'll want experience, of course, but nobody hires women for action-adventure. How's that for a *catch-22*?"

The girl models were overfilling their cups with forbidden treats from a self-service dessert bar. "Savannah Svensson!" Casey shouted, clapping her hands. "If you get that fro-yo on your dirndl skirt, I will fire you on the spot because we don't have another one that fits. Go get your mommy!"

The girls disbursed in abject terror as Casey glanced at her Apple Watch. "I've got to go back in. We're short on producers for a shoot this size."

"I know you're overwhelmed with getting the new studios up and running," I said. "I still can't figure out how that landed in your lap, but I wanted to pick your brain about another idea."

"Please, not again." She pushed a hanging wardrobe heavy with every size and color of girl- and doll-sized holiday outfit and accoutrement.

"Here, let me help." Trailing alongside her down the hall, I volunteered my thoughts on a virtual film festival, inviting every age group to enter projects themed around our characters. "Whatever their interest—art, design, computer graphics—they could share an original video on the website and upvote their favorites."

"What makes you think they'd come up with anything near our standards?" she asked.

"They're out there with their iPhones by age nine making stop motions with our dolls and getting fifteen million YouTube hits."

"I heard the ZZZZZoom! legal team is putting all that out of business," she said.

"What? The whole point is to build engagement, not break it down. In fact, I'd invite our film fest finalists to a summer lab in the new studios."

I followed her inside the Photo Studios, where a magical winter wonderland erected for the holiday catalogue shoot rivaled any I'd seen on a Hollywood backlot. "Wow," I said. "This is spectacular, girl."

She flagged down a young woman wearing bright red lipstick, elf ears, funky eyeglasses, and Converse high-tops. "Meet my set designer, Selena Leon," Casey said. "She's a freelancer in from Chicago."

"Jaycee Grayson, head of entertainment." I handed her my business card. "You're very talented, let's stay in touch."

She couldn't hide her smile as she bopped off to exalt with her elfin clan.

"Hands off, she's mine," Casey said, wagging a finger.

"I just want to pick her brain about a diversity initiative I'm thinking about. We've got all kinds of representation in the brand, but that great wall of white upstairs is alarming."

I tried to help sort the hanging costumes onto an empty rack but only messed things up more. "Just let me do it," Casey said.

"Sorry. Maybe I am overreaching, but I really want to show the world what can happen when women and girls work together to raise a voice."

"What a lovely notion," said the Wonderful Mrs. Happy, who happened to pass by with a cart of holiday storybooks. She looked a bit like your typical Mrs. Claus in her wire-rimmed granny glasses, though she was fit and slender, costumed in a red velour catsuit with her hair knotted into an elegant silver-gray chignon.

"Mrs. Happy likes my idea," I said to Casey.

"That's not Mrs. Happy. That's an eighty-year-old fashion model.

Mostly she does brochures for old people's cruises. I've got two more of them on tap in the green room in case she needs a nap."

In a far corner of the studio, the diminutive Belinda Rockland assisted a videographer staging a holiday promo for the website. She directed an ever-rowdier assortment of tiny tots costumed as Santa's helpers, each carrying identical baby dolls. Mounting a faux-snow crest, Belinda raised an oversize bullhorn. "Quiet on the set!"

The pixies only grew louder, squealing after pastel-colored snowballs dangling overhead from fish wire. "Do not eat the faux-balls, they will ugly your teeth and nasty your tummies." Another staccato series of whistles, followed by a change in tone and the sharp slate of a clapperboard. "Back to one, you little brats!"

"How complicated does this need to be?" I asked Casey, bewildered. "Why not turn the camera on what's happening in the studio instead of staging some other thing? Today's girls want an authentic experience—and we could put out ten times the content for a fraction of the cost."

"Nobody's going to take your side against Belinda Rockland no matter how much sense it makes." Casey looked around, lowering her voice. "You do know they all went to high school together?"

"Who?"

"The Big Five. Trudi, Louise, Belinda. Summer dropped out early, some family issue, and Rebecca was more my age, but she ran around town with their crowd, and they ruled the halls of Littleburgh High for years. Student council, yearbook, homecoming."

"How unusual they'd all end up back here together."

"Or maybe it was part of their grand master plan to never grow up and rule the world forever."

It all came into place when I saw Wonderful Girls not as a small town but rather a big high school, where everyone behaved, dressed, and talked the same—and here came the new kid. There would be no spare tampons for me, and I would never hold my keys in a way the in crowd deemed acceptable. I was lucky I'd escaped being pantsed in the lobby on day one!

Perhaps I had been guilty of wearing a kind of West Coast elitism in the confident swing of my hard-won Fendi bag, or a casual overhead flip of a pair of newly affordable Gucci sunglasses to show off a professionally glossed head of hair I had to do myself all those years over the bathroom sink.

If I had to trade in my Jimmy Choos for a drab wardrobe of Ugg boots waterproofed just as instructed with an inexpensive rubber spray from Amazon, so be it. I had come to play, and I was not about to lose to the popular group because I enjoyed a nice edamame salad on my lunch tray over a pile of ground beef and tater tots swimming in cream of celery soup. I could learn to love my Minnesota Hot Dish Casserole with a side of corn and green beans for extra fiber nobody had to know about.

My head swam with thoughts of proving to these ladies they had nothing to fear from me as Casey and I finished stringing the lights. "When do you leave again?" she asked.

"Not for a few weeks. I've got a million things to do beforehand."

Little did I know Casey also had a million things to do beyond grabbing advance credit for my ideas and putting them on ice for the winter. I'd created a whole new set of challenges in our latest exchange, and claiming my job during my brief absence wouldn't be nearly enough. She'd have to buckle down and figure out how to do it.

CHAPTER FIVE

# Marion Mahoney Griffin, the Most Wonderful Girl under Frank Lloyd Wright's Cold, Dead Blowhard Skin

ON A BRIGHT SATURDAY MORNING, I woke up early to take a country drive to the local twelve-step meeting I'd promised my sister I would check out.

Outside my front door, an early fog had dissipated into a blinding wall of sun. At the bottom of the steps, I nearly tripped over a bouquet of colossal mixed-color dahlias. A brown cardboard carton of eggs in shades of pale green accompanied a loose bunch of heirloom carrots pulled from the earth with their floppy green tops attached.

I couldn't find a note, and though I might have considered this a lovely welcome surprise from a friendly neighbor, I didn't have any within a good half mile on either side.

My storied house, set on a desirable point of verdant marshland jutting into the lake, had seemed so charming up until that moment—when something about it suddenly felt isolated, maybe even a little creepy.

Only a listing Realtor had showed up at the closing, harried and somewhat confused. A Mrs. Kristela Heywood from Kenosha Falls Realty allegedly made the four- or five-hour drive in "bumper-to-bumper" traffic, a literal impossibility on all fronts, unless she diverted to Chicago and took in a Cubs game that went into extra innings.

Providing scant details, she claimed to represent the estate of an elderly couple who passed away some time ago and left the property to distant relatives living abroad. They'd only recently gotten around to selling—and located her, she said, through a small Myspace ad placed by an "internet-crazy" daughter-in-law.

Maybe she was the Betty Davis of Racine County. Maybe she deserved her own reality show. Maybe she and Gloria Bohring were a pair of flimflam artists working with the snow plow guy to control the foul weather services market, but what did I care? I'd gotten quite the bang for my buck, Frank Lloyd right or wrong.

Or so I thought.

By the time I returned from California to meet the moving van in the sweltering August wetlands, the driveway lined with towering pines had become so overgrown I could no longer imagine beautifully manicured gardens in its mass of twisted vines.

The house itself needed more work than I'd originally anticipated, with leaky plumbing and shaky electricity. I could easily overtax a fuse when I plugged in a hair dryer after an evening bath or set a kettle on the aging stove to make a cup of tea before bed. I'd have to run outside barefoot with a flashlight, shivering against the damp chill of the lake in my thin silk nightgown, and fiddle around with the box to get things back up and running. I did not look forward to the first frost.

That morning, the outlying forestation remained thick with overbrush on the cusp of fall. Standing there on my front steps with my anonymous gift, I had a fleeting thought that if someone had been watching me in the month or so since I'd arrived alone to take up residence on my sprawling property, I wouldn't have known it.

"Beautiful day, ma'am. Let me squeeze right past ya there."

I wheeled around to discover the mailman putting a stack of bills in the box at the foot of my steps. "Oh my God! You scared me, creeping up like that."

A postal service Jeep had been parked on the service road at the foot of my drive. "Aw geez. Why ya so jumpy there?"

I showed him the mysterious offerings left on the steps. "Somebody left this for me," I said. "Either last night or earlier today, but I was here, and nobody knocked."

"Hmong," he tossed off without a second look. "They live off the grid. Nice folks, not gonna hurtcha. Probably looking for work, but too shy to come up and give ya a quick shout."

Laotian guerilla fighters recruited by US forces in Vietnam, the Hmong resettled here in the years after the war with the help of religious charities.

"Haven't had an easy go of things, the Hmong," he said. "Good farmers, very hard workers. The whole family shows up at the village market on Sundays, then off they go to who knows where."

"I do need some help, that's for sure. I only just hired someone to get started inside," I said. "An Amish guy from Viroqua."

In his early twenties, Elijah Petersheim, who wore a mass of dirty blond curls and stood a good seven feet tall, was a tad peculiar, come to think of it. Exhibiting stunning hardwood cabinetry and intricately interlaid butcher-block countertops, he worked intently by an old barn way off the main road I stumbled upon when I got myself turned around hunting for quality Driftless furniture on the cheap.

He didn't speak much in response to my offer of work on badly needed improvements to my kitchen and ensuite master bath. Looking back on it, I proposed the hourly rate and work schedule, while the only word he uttered over the course of our conversation was "Jah."

"You keep an eye on all that then," the mailman warned me, wagging a finger. "Hmong and Amish, they don't tend to mix. And whatever you do, steer clear of those Mennonites."

*Was there a way to tell the difference?*

"The Mennonites drive the cars, and you've got your Amish riding around in the buggies there," he said. "Things get bloody from time to time. I read the papers."

"Thank you for the heads-up," I said. "I wouldn't want to start a land war on my front porch."

"You betcha." He dipped the official letter carrier bucket hat with snap-up sides secured with a string at his chin and jogged back to the Jeep.

I didn't want to be alone just then.

Hurrying to my car, I followed him to the end of the service road and turned in the opposite direction to meet a windy two-lane highway leading to the neighboring Village of Spring Green.

There I would happen upon a famous residence, which, just as my Realtor foretold, bore a distinct resemblance in architectural design to my hilltop home overlooking that lonely corner of Lake Mendota.

In this sprawling masterpiece drawn into the landscape like a watercolor and preserved over time, years earlier the domestic help brutally massacred seven women, children, and houseguests.

My day was about to get weird.

A BESPECTACLED UW–MADISON FOREIGN EXCHANGE student with mangy blond hair streaked Kool-Aid blue introduced herself to my tour group, referencing the name badge she wore around her neck.

"*Astrilde*, after the Norse goddess of love. *Larsdatter*, daughter of Lars. The goddess and my father were not a couple, or my mother would have killed him."

I'd wager she made that well-worn stab at forbidden love affair humor in response to numerous guest comment cards noting her lacking people skills. A modern architecture major with a minor in gender studies, Astrilde spent a lot of time on the walking tour of the eight-hundred-acre Taliesin Preservation ignoring my raised hand.

Reading from a stack of bulleted index cards, she offered up key details on the short life and tragic death of one Mamah Cheney.

"In the early part of the twentieth century, the Ohio housewife

57

abandoned her husband and children to enter into an outrageous romance with the greatest American architect."

"What was so outrageous about her?" I asked, waving my raised hand. "Didn't he have like twelve kids by three wives and countless mistresses?"

I had spent some time in the gift shop reading up on old Frank, who felt that his only real transgression had been failing to inform the newspapers he'd eloped with another man's wife. She held up a finger in my direction as if to stave off another salacious detail I would surely request if given the briefest opening.

"A serial nonmonogamist, he left behind his family to travel Europe with Mamah in one of the great scandals of the Victorian era," Astrilde continued. "They returned together to Wright's family homeland, Taliesin, from the Welsh 'shining brow.'"

She would stick to the script if it meant switching back and forth among nine Germanic, Uralic, and Caucasian languages in which no American dared question her proficiency, least of all me.

Along with the original home Wright built for his publicly pinched paramour, a windmill, school, barn, and extended family housing perched on the edge of a luscious forty-thousand-acre valley. Each breakthrough design represented nearly every subsequent decade of the master's career, continuing through his death in 1959.

"While he tried to shield Mamah from relentless scrutiny, villagers traced the lovers here, to their stolen hideaway," she said. "The press crudely dubbed the maestro's most timeless design the 'Bungalow of Love.'"

"Can we get back to the mass murder?" I asked.

We had reached the grounds of the personal residence, still under construction when Wright was away in Chicago one random summer midday.

A handyman poured gasoline on the dining room floor during lunch and lit a match, butchering seven people with a hatchet as they attempted to escape the smoke and flames. The dead included Wright's carpenters and draftsman, along with Mamah and two of her children.

"I've already told you that couldn't have had anything whatsoever to do with your little house on the Burgh," Astrilde said firmly.

"My house in Littleburgh," I corrected her.

I asked her to take one more look at an architectural rendering in the Taliesin brochure against the little fixer-upper I'd photographed extensively with my cell phone.

"Look at the striking similarity in 'the harmony between structure and environment.'"

"Yes, I can read the promotional copy," she said. "It's called biomimicry, but I don't see it standing out in your example."

"Really? My house has the same open floor plan, though. It's all designed to flatter the broad Midwest horizon. 'Not on the hill, but of the hill, belonging to it.'"

"Yes, well, Wright's Prairie style has influenced more than a century of international design," she said. "No need to put his stamp on another rural claptrap down the road."

An audible gasp emitted from the group. They hadn't seemed interested in our previous exchanges, but now that it was getting ugly between me and this Scandinavian snit they looked over my shoulder to take up sides.

"And furthermore, why would he build this nothing little house down the road for Mamah, as this Realtor of yours implied, when he'd already given her all this?" She had the nerve to tap her Birkenstocked foot and wait for a reply.

I knew when I was licked.

"Was the handyman Amish, by any chance?" I hoped *she* wasn't Amish, judging from her expression.

"The handyman came from Barbados, madam," she sniffed with all the finality she could muster. "Does anyone else have a question?"

Nobody knew why the handyman snapped, although some say he suspected he would soon be fired and hadn't received proper notice. I figured I better not fire my handyman, Elijah Petersheim, without proper notice, especially if it turned out he drives cars, which seemed to be a matter of great suspicion for my mailman.

Elijah appeared on my property randomly with a thermos of hot coffee whose aroma I smelled as the only indicator he was standing behind me. While I hadn't specifically seen a hatchet in his toolbox, I would certainly treat him with kid gloves going forward.

Astrilde walked the group around the courtyard where some of the workers had escaped the final death blows with their clothes aflame, summersaulting down the hill to safety. They had handcrafted these hipped roofs and overhanging eaves, laying bricks for the broad chimneys, and forming the wood-banded casement windows distinguishing a loggia running the span of Wright's living room.

I peered inside the celebrated drafting studio, where the Organic Architecture movement came alive. "Excuse me, are we allowed to use Frank Lloyd Wright's bathroom?" I asked Astrilde, the nominal Norse love goddess. "I really have to go."

"Certainly not. In fact, the residence has closed to tours today for a private function this afternoon."

A sizeable gathering of well-heeled ladies who lunch exiting the shuttle from the Visitor Center gathered on the terrace for a fancy reception of some kind. "You'll have to take the shuttle back and use the facilities at the main entrance." She invited me to rejoin the walk through the gardens that would conclude with a spectacular view of Wright's ancestral valley, but she probably only wanted to make sure I ponied up for her tip.

I LEFT THE GROUP FOR the supposed shortcut to the outer terrace—but got myself turned around and couldn't find the shuttle stop.

I checked the map both right side up and upside down and really had to pee by the time I gave up and began the trek on foot—or maybe not.

I ended up at a service door on a lower level behind the residence, where I happened upon an older woman pulling some flats of cups and saucers from the back of a van.

Although she had the kind of pep in her step one hopes for at eighty-five, hauling around forty-eight cups and saucers at a clip had turned out to be a bit risky. "Can I help you with that?"

"Oh, would you be a dear? I'm under the gun to finish setting up down here."

I took one of the flats from her and made sure she had a good grip on the other one as we walked inside the staff kitchens together.

Wearing a smart black silk blouse and matching tulip skirt, she had a cute silvery pixie haircut, a strand of pearls with matching earrings, and a pair of white slip-on Keds.

"May I use the ladies' room? I can't make it to the Visitor Center."

"Just to your right through the swinging doors, dear. Leave the teacups on the side table." I rushed through the doors, pausing quickly to drop the cups, and ducked into a bathroom door propped open with a rubber wedge.

Frank Lloyd Wright's forbidden water closet turned out to be a ho-hum utility restroom added in the 1970s to accommodate event guests and kitchen staff. While I'd been expecting the fruit of an intriguing system of waterfalls and hydraulics designed by the father of modern plumbing, I couldn't afford to be picky. After I washed my hands and left, I forgot to prop the door back open, and it slammed shut behind me.

I returned to take in the spectacular interior dining area stretched out beneath the sweeping, slightly elevated loggia. The woman hurried about, putting the final touches on a fancy dessert table stretching the entire length of the great room, flanked by signature Prairie School high-backed slatted formal side chairs. "I think I locked us out of the bathroom," I said. "I'm sorry."

"That's the second time today. You'd think someone hid money in the ballcock the way they lock down that toilet."

"I got the same impression," I said, chuckling. "Then it turned out to be nothing to write home about."

She gestured to the hubbub beyond the glass on the upper loggia. "We're having a progressive fundraiser; maybe we can work on improving the facilities. The big wallets come in from town and go from room to room for each course."

While she was fighting the clock, she struck me as too proud to ask for help. "I'm not in any rush," I volunteered. "Do you need a hand?"

"Aw, would you be a dear? The caterers should have been back with the beverage service a half hour ago." She asked me to finish arranging the desserts on porcelain towers set intermittently along the table for the ladies to help themselves. "I'm always rushing," she said. "I don't know why I do it to myself."

After what I'd been through earlier, I had an agenda of my own to address and let her know right off how disappointed I felt with the snippy guide. "Instead of a juicy story about my own little Bungalow of Love, I found out some gossipy Realtor figured a California airhead made a good mark."

"I'm not so sure about that," she said, cocking her head to digest the details. "My name is Helen, by the way."

"I'm Jaycee. Do you have something I could cut the strings with?"

She handed me a plastic table knife to help slit open stacks of craft paper boxes tied with narrow grosgrain yellow ribbon, certified with hand-embossed black-and-gold labels from Madison Chocolate Company.

"Don't you believe anything you heard from that two-bit docent. Frank had plenty of talented women through here in his time; did Miss Norway tell you that?"

I shook my head no, piling tiered serving plates with an assortment of delicate pastries—hazelnut madeleines and buttery palmiers, flaky date-crusted parmesan galettes, and a rainbow of marshmallow macarons stuffed with caramel nut fillings.

"Come to think of it, Marion Mahony Griffin might be your girl. A Frank Lloyd Wright colleague and close, personal confidante, Marion had been instrumental in helping cement his vision by using her skills as a draftsman to bring his structures to life on paper in Japanese-style watercolor drawings."

"I thought those were *his* drawings," I said. "They're all over the gift shop."

"He stole them from her without any attribution," she said. "Even after she made him famous, he took sole credit for the Prairie style. Then she bruised his ego by marrying another architect he saw as a much more serious rival."

"Isn't that just like a man," I said. "If a woman did have a hand in designing my house, though, maybe it was her only way of escaping from under the great master's thumb."

"Bingo. And that's a much better story, my dear."

I finished stacking syrupy canelés alongside finger-shaped vanilla bean custard eclairs, and bittersweet chocolate truffles dusted with gold and dipped in flaked coconut. Bite-size coconut mousse cups dotted with whipped cream and crowned with a single black, purple, or yellow Porter's Patch Raspberry made the top tier.

When she leaned down to hide the last of the empty china palettes behind the swinging kitchen door, I heard the sound of a beach ball inflating, followed by a loud pop. She glanced down at her belly.

"Oh no!" she exclaimed.

"What happened?"

"My shit bag's blown up!"

"What?"

"My ostomy bag. Oh, will you look at this mess."

She lifted her blouse and ripped open a Velcro belt, soiling her hands with the contents oozing from a ruptured bag hanging from her torso. "I'm still getting used to the damn thing. You eat too fast, you get gassy and boom."

Just then, the catering truck pulled up outside the back door to deliver a team of cater waiters dressed in crisp white shirts and pressed black pants hauling the coffee service to the back door.

This arrival timed itself precisely with the shuffling of feet from the outer loggia, where the ladies signaled their progression downstairs, trapping us in the middle.

The master's open-concept design started to feel something less than brilliant when integrating oneself with time and place meant nowhere to duck for cover with a ruptured colostomy bag. Obviously, this lady and I would not be making a run for the loggia to roll down the lawns like those who'd survived the fire. A hundred years later and that lame brain Frank Lloyd Wright had neither bothered himself to design a decent service bathroom nor create a reasonable escape route for future victims of their ire.

"What a disgusting world we live in," Helen said, sinking into the famed origami-inspired armchair constructed from a single piece of folded plywood, resigned to displaying herself artfully to the inevitable onslaught. "Why come for the cookies when you've got a good scandal to dish? My husband drinks a little. It's been the talk of the town for years."

"Listen to me, Helen. Do you have another bag on you?"

"In my purse. It's in the kitchen."

I ran to the door and locked it, leaving the confused cater waiters standing outside with their simmering urns. Then I raced up to the door leading to the loggia and locked out the yammering socialites.

I jogged back to the kitchen to soap up a dish cloth by the sink, gave it to Helen to wipe the mess from her skin, and dipped into her purse to rip the paper from a fresh kit. "I guess this is pretty self-explanatory," I said, peeling off a detachable flange. We heard the impatient hum of the gathering guests and a few knocks outside the door leading down from the loggia.

"Yoo-hoo, Helen, is it time for the sweets?" asked an elderly lady's voice.

"Just a minute, ladies," Helen called out in a panic.

Outside the kitchen door, someone seemed to be fiddling with an oversize janitor's ring of keys.

"Last week at work I got stuck on the john without a tampon," I said, tearing open a foil packet of gauze and dampening it with alcohol before popping on the fresh bag. "It wasn't fun. Not like this. This is big fun."

We both burst into laughter. I stood her up and secured everything with a Velcro waist belt, wiped my hands on the dish towel, and tucked the used bag inside the disposable paper one. "I'll take this. Go get your friends."

She showed me her freshly cleaned hands and grabbed both of mine in hers. "You, my dear, are a thoughtful, joyful girl."

CHAPTER SIX

# Linda Lovejoy, the Most Wonderful Girl Who Answers Late-Night Raccoon Sex Nine-One-One

"Yup, I'm pretty sure I met the real Happy Lindstrom yesterday," I said to my sister on the phone the next night while getting ready for bed. "The tagline, the bravado, the twinkle in her eye."

"If that was the real Happy, why would she introduce herself as the real Helen?"

"Happy can't be a Christian name. Maybe it's a nickname the other kids gave her when a tornado took out the barn that last time and she refused to let it get her down."

"Are you hitting the sauce?" Meredith asked.

"No! Why would you ask me something like that?"

"Because this has got to be the most bizarre chain of events I've ever heard."

"It gets weirder, though." I lay on my bed and flipped open my MacBook. "I tried to find a picture of Happy Lindstrom on the internet to either confirm or deny my suspicions and there aren't any. Zip. Nada."

"What? How is that even possible?"

"All kinds of Wonderful Mrs. Happys pop up. I don't know how many models and actresses have played the role over the years. On official announcements, press releases and such, you'll get a picture of my boss, Trudi Oldham. That makes sense; she's been the company spokesperson since the beginning."

"Well, Happy wouldn't be the first entrepreneur to become a bit of a recluse once things got big. Why do so many billionaires end up surprised and embarrassed by it all?"

Meredith was curious, though. I could hear her clicking around on her own keyboard over the phone line. "What about in the old days, when the family hit the road?"

"They have some pictures in our front lobby in a glass case," I said. "They look a little grainy, though, and they all wore these cute masks to intermix the different characters with the dolls on stage. We sell them. We sell everything."

"Have you asked around at work? People must have snapped a picture with her at a holiday party or the company picnic."

"Yes, but even that gets confusing, with all the Wonderful Mrs. Happys working in the studio and interacting with children of employees. How would anybody recognize the real one?"

"Right. Could have been your friend from today. Who knows?" Meredith never minded putting on her lawyer hat to talk through one of my theories, but we would come to a point where her practical side needed to move on.

I could hear her multitasking—organizing file folders with a metal clamp, clicking a ballpoint pen to scribble out checks for this month's utility bills. I nudged her a step further. "Meredith, listen to me. Do you think it's possible Happy Lindstrom never existed?"

"No. I do not think that is possible for a single minute."

"Wait. Hear me out," I said. "The five women who run the company all grew up together. What if these college friends came up with an idea for a premier doll company and conjured up Happy Lindstrom to put out front? She represented everything they didn't. Warmth. Confidence. Kindness. They made her an icon of feminine principles who influenced moms all over the country with certain concerns about their daughters' playtime with that sexed-up Malibu crowd in the beach house."

"Why hide it?" Meredith asked. "Inventing a brand ambassador wouldn't raise any red flags. Mrs. Butterworth isn't real. There's no Uncle Ben or Captain Crunch."

"Maybe they got into something they couldn't get out of. Who cashed the billion-dollar check in the massive buyout?"

"That's a whole other can of worms," she said. "Unless they disclosed all of this prior to the acquisition, we'd be looking at a federal crime."

"Like a prison time kind of federal crime?"

"Absolutely. You'd have overvaluation of assets, because Happy Lindstrom *is* the company. SEC violations, defrauding the stockholders, and a whole bunch of fiduciary issues, but as for the good news…" She shouted into the phone so loudly I had to take it away from my ear. "NONE OF THIS HAS A THING TO DO WITH YOU!"

"I work there, Meredith. I'm in it already."

"You're not in anything that did or didn't go down twenty years ago inside your brain! Should any of this ever turn out to have a shred of truth to it, you walk away with a fat check to compensate for the nullification of your fraudulent contract and a good story to tell."

"Why are you so mad? Sheesh."

I'd been tossing all this out there as an intriguing idea. Now she'd left me with no choice but to conduct a more detailed investigation at the earliest opportunity.

"You promised to attend a sober meeting today!" she said. "But no, you were too busy novelizing Laotian guerrillas working as sharecroppers at night in your garden."

"My mailman said that, not me."

I looked out the window to see if by chance my Hmong had arrived to set up shop, but I didn't see any farmer's market families tending to neat rows of heritage vegetables by moonlight.

"I didn't make up anything about the Mennonites, either," I politely reminded her. "I just said they're locked in a brutal religious war with the Amish and my handyman is kind of scary."

I was still creeped out by all that. Who wouldn't be? I was already downstairs double-checking the locks on the wall of glass doors looking down on the lake.

"I know what you're doing," Meredith said as though she'd embedded a spy camera in the center of my forehead. "The real world is so disappointing you have no choice but to retreat into an endless internal dialogue of suspicious characters, and strange goings-on, and people out to get you—such as Norwegian tour guides who need to be investigated by the University of Wisconsin for academic incompetence. It must feel so exhausting living inside your head."

"Sometimes. Other times I find it highly productive." I headed back upstairs to wash my face and brush my teeth. "In my business, you have to let your mind wander and see where it takes you."

"They call that playing make-believe, which is fine until you turn five. Then you grow up and accept the fact that most people are doing the best they can today to remember to thaw the hamburger. I understand the value of an overactive imagination given the nature of your work, but you can't be making up stories all day every day about how your colleagues aren't the right kind of nice."

"They're Midwest Nice. It's a thing, look it up."

She breathed in deeply and exhaled a long, cleansing sigh. "Please don't run around exposing your crazy to a region of the country that thrives on its own normalcy or people will believe you. Trust me on this."

"They have some exciting work for me here, Meredith, but I don't feel any urgency to it, and with what they're paying, that just seems odd."

I opened my bedroom closet to pull down from a top shelf the luggage I'd only recently unpacked on arrival. "Meanwhile, everything's pretty much on hold while I head off to this conference at the end of the week, and I don't exactly know what they want me to do down there."

"You're supposed to meet people," she said flatly. I'd obviously visited this tirade with her before.

"I already know everybody," I said. "I want to create avenues for women overdue for a break, but these are mostly men who already had theirs and didn't deserve it the first time."

"I agree it won't be easy facing the whole Hollywood power crowd again so soon," she said. "You'll just have to suck it up. It's five days, for God's sake."

At that point, Meredith probably felt around the floor for the shoes she'd slipped off somewhere earlier and could never find when it came time to put them back on. Perhaps she would happen upon a different pair—comfortably worn penny loafers—and walking around on top of their collapsed heels would work fine wherever she needed to go next.

"I've got to finish up here. Are we done?" She signaled our nightly wrap-up when I would have a split second to jump in and inquire about her issues.

"Wait, how are you feeling? Did you take all those tests?"

"I'm fine. I'm still at the office."

"The office? It's nine o'clock on a Sunday night. You said you'd work from home now. You should be powering down prenatal vitamins and drinking whole milk."

"I had to come in for a partner thing; we had clients in," she snapped back. "And it happens I'm eating yogurt."

She wasn't eating yogurt. She wouldn't eat yogurt if the Yoplait people paid her in nonqualified stock options.

She had probably been picking from some foil platter overheating on gel burners delivered from a low-rent Chinese catering menu—like shrimp in boiled-down lobster sauce, or a solid mound of Buddha's Delight, whatever its earlier form had taken.

Some harried paralegal likely assembled this weak expression of dinnertime resentment after Meredith couldn't jump off an earlier conference call to offer up some Thai-Jamaican fusion discovery tucked in a nearby alley and dictate multiple courses culled from top reviews. Everyone would have loved her for this and lingered over the meal together to decompress.

Her punishment for having failed them involved force-feeding herself greasy mouthfuls of whatever landed between two splintered chopsticks.

Meredith loved everything about food, stealing every possible opportunity in her scant free time to research, plan, shop, cook, and share it with others, but I'm not convinced she ever connected her own shape to what she did or didn't eat.

She had always been round. In pictures I drew of us together when we were kids, she came out as all smiley round circles. I looked like a collection of short skinny lines. I first began to sense what would become her mute geometric battle with herself when I found some diet pills she'd started taking in the seventh grade.

"Give them back and shut up," she warned, slamming the bathroom door.

I would never tell a soul.

I had joined the Brownies earlier that year and could only conclude revealing this terrible discovery to anyone would mean revocation of my long-awaited invitation to join her at Girl Scout camp that summer. If we wouldn't be eating the roasted marshmallows, what was the point of going?

My fears were met with the happy news that I would be eating her marshmallows along with my own, and also that she had achieved the rank of Woodland Forest Queen, or some such. Every evening at sundown, she would clean the willows from a twig with a pocketknife and start a bonfire by scraping a piece of steel against a flint rock she wore as a necklace.

As if that weren't enough black magic, she'd melt a square of chocolate with a perfectly burnt marshmallow and sandwich all that between two graham crackers, passing around this life-altering confection known as the "s'more" while teaching the brown-beanied uninitiated a chorus of complex stomp-and-clap songs.

I never quite got any of this down, despite my sorority with scouting royalty, and would often simper off to my bunk in frustration, leaving her green majesty to deal with the mess I left behind in flagrant defiance of the Brownie way.

When all was said and done at summer's end, Meredith still looked round, though briefly smaller around the edges. I became a taller stick. She didn't want to talk about it.

She did want to talk about getting up to blow the reveille together. "Jaycee got to raise the flag," she bragged. "I oversaw the arts and crafts, and Jaycee made the best lanyard ever. They also made me teacher of the Sunfish class, and don't you know Jaycee was first to sail across the pond."

Not a single word of this was true, at least not on my account.

I never woke up in the dark to march off and blow some dumb bugle; I barely got up off my stinky cot after she blew it herself, while managing to raise the flag one-handed under full, white-gloved Girl Scout salute.

Meredith finished my dodgy red, white, and blue lanyard when I got frustrated with its mass of ugly knots and foisted it off on her to fix.

She had to jump in and walk my stranded Sunfish across the shallow pond after the sail deflated and fell over. I'd started to cry over a scraped knee I got earlier by falling out of my potato sack and losing the race to a nasty chorus of Brownie taunts and jeers.

I never knew how I got to be the hero of my sister's story, but long after we grew up it was always a good time to talk about me.

"Did I tell you they call the mosquito the state bird of Wisconsin?" I asked her that night on the phone, pondering a smattering of swollen red lumps on my ankles from my earlier walk in Spring Green.

"Oh no. I hope you have Benadryl on hand," she said. "I'm pretty sure you're allergic; I've been telling you that for years."

"I'll definitely get some before my trip to Miami." I clicked the button on my cell and asked Siri to remind me, submitting to the ranks of most people, as Meredith suggested earlier, just trying to remember to defrost the hamburger.

With that, my day soared from the heights of greatness forever memorialized in the Wisconsin landscape, to the depths of excrement in a basement toilet near an unremarkable service kitchen.

My sister remained incapable of self-reflection, paralyzed by the possibilities of late-life motherhood, while a former debutante I met in passing immersed herself in philanthropy to forget a humiliating shutdown of aging bodily systems.

The handiwork of anonymous mistresses and their children, along with faceless artists and craftsmen, all murdered one random day in the last century over an unremarkable lunch, showed me what precious little time any of us has to leave something of note behind, and I couldn't invest mine dwelling on the perplexities of "Midwest Nice."

People are indeed capable of crazy things, but I would take Meredith's advice and keep my crazy to myself. I would become of the pond rather than stand back and look over a pond awash with ordinary ripples while my sister towed my boat.

"How is the baby?" I asked as I climbed into my hand-hammered, Shaker-style either Amish or Mennonite bed, blanketing myself in the warmth of a million single stitches connecting its hand-dyed flannel patches.

"We're all okay," Meredith promised. "She's a girl, by the way."

"She is? Oh wow. I can't wait to go shopping for little girl everything."

Meredith would often toss in the kind of gigantic news at the end of a conversation that other people rent planes to write across the sky for the whole wide world to applaud. "I'm going to be class valedictorian," "I got accepted at Smith," or the boldest one of all, up until now, "I'm planning to stay in Paris after my junior year abroad." She didn't end up doing it, but the announcement she'd embraced such an extraordinary life plan should have been a much bigger deal.

"The gender test is only about seventy percent accurate because it's so early," Meredith said. "They do an anatomy scan in week eighteen. Butch really wants a girl so fingers crossed."

"Yeah. The last thing we need is an extra dick around the house."

"Go to sleep, nutbag."


HAD A MAN NOT WALKED across my roof at four o'clock that morning, Meredith's good news might have been the thing I remembered best about the events of that weekend.

I bolted upright in bed and heard another man's footsteps, and then the sound of both men stomping around directly overhead.

They started running back and forth, over and over, racing across the flat-pitched layers of tar and gravel upon which one of Frank Lloyd Wright's long string of denigrated girlfriends may have crowned the midcentury modern gem Marion hid from his jealous clutches.

There was a short cry, met with mournful weeping, before everything went silent beneath the whoosh of the wind over the marsh.

I picked up my cell and frantically hammered on it. "Nine-one-one, Village of Littleburgh, Mrs. Linda Lovejoy speaking. What's your emergency there, real quick?" responded a close relation of my mailman, judging from her energetic elocution.

"A man was walking on my roof with another guy, but one of them fell off and died and the other one got away," I whispered. "That's my best guess."

"The chief's gone off duty for the night, hon. Did you want me to get him up? Or maybe we'll wait until after he's come back in and had his breakfast."

"Isn't there anyone else?"

"I could get you over to the fire station at Yahara, but that'll be a couple of hours. How about you go out and look around quick while I sit on the line. It's probably nothing. We had a hailstorm earlier up in Pheasant Branch."

"Get me a cop out here with a gun right now!"

"You betcha."

## CHAPTER SEVEN

# Sally Baker-Dreaux, the Most Wonderful Girl Twice Pregnant at Anowaka High

I PACED MY SQUEAKY oakwood flooring at a safe distance from the pulldown ladder Police Chief Abel Dreaux mounted in a hidden corner of the hall outside my bedroom, poking the upper half of his body around my attic with a flashlight.

"Do you see anything?" I asked.

"Nope, but I bet they're looking at me, the crafty little buggers," he said with a muffled voice.

"Oh my God, they're watching us? Well, I'll have to move if they've taken over the place."

He chuckled.

"You didn't hear what I heard earlier," I said primly. "At one point it was obvious that one of them had choked an owl to death up there."

"Golly, that's odd this time of year," his voice said, wholly perplexed. "They'll usually take a break through fall and hunker down somewhere for the snows before they start going at it again."

"Going at it? What I heard was…raccoon sex?"

"Yep. You woke me up in the middle of the night for raccoon sex."

As disgusting as that image was, I found Abel Dreaux very attractive from the waist down and didn't want him to leave after he climbed down my ladder to meet my gaze.

He rolled it up with great efficiency and reached up to slam shut the attic door, slapping his hands together as if to dismiss the whole nasty mess.

"Wait, what are you doing?" I asked, fully panicked. "You're not going to just leave them there."

"That's where they live," he said, heading down the hall. "There isn't much to be done about it at this hour."

I trailed him downstairs, wearing a London Fog I'd set out for my trip and thrown hastily over my long silk nightgown before opening the back door to him earlier. "Maybe you can help me address the issues attracting them inside the house."

"I'm more worried about the littler guys you'll see bedding down for winter—the woodchucks, the squirrels, and field mice. You'll want to evict the bats hanging from those rafters—that's the top of your food chain."

*Bats? There were bats?* I thought seriously about ducking to the floor and continuing the conversation on my hands and knees.

"You're doing a pretty fine job raising nature's wonderland out here," he said. "I might have to call you Snow White."

"That would work," I said with a shy smile, feeling better about things already. What woman would turn down a princess nickname from an attractive officer, even if it did mean reawakening the bubonic plague in her attic?

"You're surrounded by a federally protected area, though. You'll have to take it up with the alders if you want to cut back that overgrowth by the marsh."

He trotted toward my mudroom exit and stopped to wash his hands at a utility sink. "May I?"

"Oh. Of course."

I gave him a squirt of pumpkin spice hand soap and a hand towel monogrammed with my initials. I'd bought them as decorations but much preferred watching him put them to use wiping his hands and gray-flecked beard, along with the back of his neck.

"Course, that won't reverse the damage I'm seeing to your soffit and fascia. I'm going to guess you've been having some electrical problems. Fuses popping. Lights flickering."

"Have you been watching me?" I asked, perhaps a bit too hopefully.

"Educated guess," he said with an embarrassed laugh. "They like to chew on the wiring."

"Drats," I said, snapping my fingers.

I wondered if he would flirt back, standing there hugging my flimsy trench coat against a cold gust of wind coming off the lake.

I wore the bouncing lambie slippers Meredith gave me as a parting gift, hoping I didn't look too dumb lingering on the back steps near where he'd parked earlier to have a look around.

"I suppose I could watch you if I wanted," he said. "I'm just across the lake on the bluff."

Sure enough, a clear shot about a mile off held no obstruction between us across the blades of rippling black water. A flashing light over a small lock connecting the lake to an adjacent river system persisted through the fog. "You live in a lighthouse?"

"Not on the regular. I do go up there from time to time to put the village to bed. Gives me a sense of calm, especially in winter."

He looked around like he could see it coming, barreling through the forest like an ogre he knew how to tame with some advance work among the villagers.

"Yep, you're going to need to reinsulate the attic; they've got your slag wool all chewed up. You might want to rethink your lookout access so they can't climb up and take over at thirty below. Course, all that'll be tough to permit after the first frost."

"And when is that scheduled?"

"Next week. We've got a big weather system coming through."

"It's barely November!"

He seemed bemused by my terror level. "We probably won't get anything sticking for a while, but you'll get a good pounding."

Even standing there shivering in the moonlight talking about the good pounding I would get, I honestly had no way of knowing if Abel Dreaux was flirting with me. Maybe he just talked that way.

"If you wanted my cell, you could call me directly next time. Course, I don't always pick up when I'm dead to the world," he said. He pulled the crackling two-way radio, a cop's lifeline, from his hip. "How about you take this, and I give you a private frequency?"

"I can't take that from you," I said.

"I've got a spare in my squad, and the one by my bed never powers off. You know how to work it?"

"Roger that, Two-Oh-One. Two-Two-Two, over."

I was telling him my call sign. I already knew his, imprinted both on his badge and on the side of his squad.

"I got your six, Two-Two-Two," he said. "Radio anytime. I never met a civilian before who speaks police code. Did you say you used to produce some big video games?"

"The dream was to produce some big movies, but it all started to blend," I said with a sigh. "Let's say I know very well how to call in Seal Team 6, but when I get really scared I summon all my little elves and fairies to keep me company under the bed."

"You don't have to be scared of anything here. I'm just across the way."

Though this could have been an awkward moment, I stumbled upon a well-timed gift. At the foot of the steps, my Laotian friends had left more eggs, a bunch of mustard-colored mums, and some finger-shaped radishes, along with the last of the season's tomatoes arranged in a raccoon-proof crate.

"Got to love the Hmong," said the chief. "Sleep well, Snow White."

"Don't go, Two-Oh-One. I'll make you some breakfast."

RAISED IN MINNESOTA BY A single mother, Cherie, along with two older brothers, Abel Dreaux had French Canadian blood mixed with First Nation.

He described "Slim," the last of a string of "stepfathers," as the only man he ever hated, joining the family to wander south from Duluth when Abel was a kid. The family tried unsuccessfully to connect with a distant relative believed to have struck it rich in underground gaming years before Minnesota negotiated tribal-state casino compacts with eleven Native American tribes.

A compulsive gambler, Slim supported Cherie and the kids off his winnings while Cherie worked part-time as a cocktail waitress, moving out of cheap motels and onto the road when Slim's luck ran out. Sometimes he did well enough for long enough to provide an apartment with dishes, furniture, friends, and even school—but abandoned all that in the middle of the night if he suffered another losing streak by the time the rent came due.

"He'd come out of a gas station with a pack of Twinkies and make my brothers and me wrestle over who got breakfast."

Half the size of either brother, Abel had suffered a bout of spinal meningitis as a baby, from which he narrowly recovered.

"My mother always thought I should have been taller," Abel said. "The Cheyenne and Sioux on her side of the family were giants."

He looked perfectly tall to me, though he would not win any wrestling matches with two beefy siblings and didn't want breakfast, anyway. Slim had either stolen it or gambled for it and neither met with the strong religious principles instilled by Abel's preacher father, whom Cherie had walked out on to seek her elusive share of the extended family's ill-gotten gains.

"My mom left when I was five," I volunteered, something I rarely do, sitting in front of my fireplace with Abel as dawn broke in a riot of color over the lake. "My sister jumped in to fill in the blanks."

"Did you get regular meals?"

"I got whatever she wanted me to want, whenever she wanted me to want it," I said. "If I missed something, I wouldn't have any way of knowing it."

"It didn't go like that for me," Abel said. "I had a lot of shame."

He knew early on he did not belong with this bunch, and the road to redemption shined like a beacon one day on the way to Anowaka High School.

Sally Baker, a pregnant tenth grader who desperately needed to be rescued, met a boy who desperately needed to do some rescuing. Sally spent the next twenty-five years hating Abel Dreaux for that.

MY SISTER DIDN'T NECESSARILY BUY Abel's version of events when I spoke to her on the phone later in the week from the office.

"What do you mean?" I asked, incredulous. "Here this great guy wanted to marry her, and again the baby belonged to another boy. Her parents made Abel jump through all these hoops to prove himself good enough for her."

"Such as?"

"He wanted to join the military, but they made him go work for her father making sheet metal desks."

"Sheet metal? That's not cool. He should have at least held out for engineered wood."

"Why are you being like this? I feel like we have a real connection. He spent half the morning hammering my fascia."

"Hello," she said lewdly.

"Don't be gross. He only spoke about this in vague terms, but by my guess, the guy hasn't had sex in maybe ten years. She started early, she finished early."

"Do you really not know the ex-wife is always crazy?" Meredith said. "There might only be one ex-wife who runs around maxing out all the credit cards and drooling into her soup."

"This is my interpretation, not his," I replied. "Abel speaks highly of her because she's the victim and everything was his fault. They couldn't even get married until Sally got herself knocked up a second time—

that's twice now, by two different boys—before she finished high school. He had to become a Catholic so she could still be a saint."

"That does sound a tad hypocritical," Meredith said. "Can you imagine Dad's reaction if we showed up in that situation?"

"No, because we would both be dead. Meanwhile, after their girls grew up and left the house, Sally cheated on him with one of the county sheriffs."

"How could she? That is a much larger and more important agency!"

"She could have gotten him killed. Those guys cover for each other when they go out on the big drug busts."

"How many of those do they actually have up that way?" she asked, nonplussed.

"All kinds of them, according to Harlan Meidlemeister."

"Who?"

"My mailman. Please try to keep up. When Abel found out about the affair, Sally left *him*, selling *her* transgression as a badly needed taste of the freedom Abel had robbed her of all those years. She didn't even make it on her own in Minneapolis for a year before she hightailed it back here and planted herself in a chicken coop on his property."

"I thought they'd made their peace," Meredith said. "Why would he plant her in a chicken coop?"

"Abel converted it into one of those fashionable tiny houses that he built with his own hands. Sally wants Abel to believe they've made up, but Harlan Meidlemeister thinks she has something up her sleeve and so do I."

"I see a few red flags."

"You always see a few red flags."

"As your sister, that's my job."

"I'm not dating her, why do I care where she lives?" I asked. "Anyway, if we do pursue something, I won't be hanging out over there as a matter of respect for the mother of his children."

"How about some respect for the woman he's dating?"

"The only man I need in my life at the moment is Elijah Petersheim, an Old Order Mennonite."

"The FedEx driver?"

"The handyman! Don't you ever listen?"

I CONFIRMED ELIJAH PETERSHEIM'S RELIGIOUS affiliation when he arrived at my house behind the wheel of a black late-model Buick alongside his equally taciturn wife, Naomi, and another young couple in their late teens whose names I didn't catch. In keeping with the *Ordnung*, a book of rules set forth to guide behavior in alignment with the spiritual world, the car radio had been removed, leaving a mass of twisted wires where it should have been.

"Is there something weird about those folks?" I asked Abel.

He'd stopped by later in the week before work to direct them in tackling the amorous raccoons. They would have to be trapped and removed before the openings in the roof they'd chewed into could be permanently sealed, and this would require some vigilance while I was away. "I've never had a family of Mennonites house-sit for me and the mailman has concerns."

"Harlan Meidlemeister? He likes to talk, what else does he have to do running door to door but deliver a lot of chin-wagging?" Abel said.

"Really? I hadn't noticed that about him."

"These groups outwardly reject violence of any kind, but you do hear about sexual abuse, inbreeding, runaways. I wouldn't buy into any of that bunk about witches and warlocks."

"Witches and warlocks?" *Thankfully, Harlan Meidlemeister had left out that bunk.*

"Good and bad folks exist everywhere," Abel said. "I don't think you have anything to worry about with the Plain People."

While toweling off after my shower, I glanced out my bathroom window, watching Abel with a foot against his squad as Naomi passed around a thatched pail of home-baked pastries wrapped in waxed paper.

The men wiped their brows and put down their tools, helping themselves to a pitcher of that fresh-roasted hot coffee whose fragrance heralded Elijah's quiet arrivals.

In the distance, I got a glimpse of the secluded Hmong, a multigenerational family of a dozen or so living in a camper near the preserve.

Watching life play out like a silent movie on the perimeter of my world, I remembered the untethered noise of my own childhood as I sat on the kitchen counter watching *Sesame Street* on a small kitchen TV set, and Meredith barked the morning orders to get me off to school.

"Do not forget your lunch," she chided. "I stayed up late baking homemade bread because Dad loves it and so do you."

"It's okay. I like how Wonder Bread squishes up into a ball."

"That's disgusting. You're getting peanut butter and jelly, because that's also your favorite. Do not trade it for salami and cheese. You'll only get diarrhea again and the nurse will have to come bug me in class, like what comes out of your butt is my problem. Put back that apple; you're getting a tangerine."

She ran a tight ship, my sister, as the nice ladies who came around from time to time expecting to find two little girls in need of a mommy would quickly discover. They mostly worked at my dad's firm, from what we could tell, and wore wide-shouldered blazers with flouncy skirts to match their confident smiles, as though they had big lives elsewhere and only came by to check us out as an option.

Always polite, Meredith set out an extra plate and cloth napkin and made sure I finished my homework early, so I'd be available for leisurely after-dinner conversation.

"What am I supposed to say?" I asked.

"Talk about hair, ladies like that."

"Hair? Hair's dumb," I said.

"They spend a lot of time on their hair. Putting it up, letting it down."

"I could talk about hamsters," I suggested. "They take up a ton of time. You have to get in there every morning and change out the wood chips, depending on how much pee and poop you find."

"Ick, no. Do not talk about hamsters," she said. "Just follow my lead."

Meredith was nine, what did she know?

She couldn't even tell me why our mom had left, the few times I tried to ask. To my mind, it happened slowly over time. Mommy would be in her room a lot, and then her room would be empty, and she would be off visiting friends somewhere, Meredith said, or staying overnight in a place where she had liked being alone before she married our dad.

One day she didn't come back for a long time, and I asked Meredith when she would.

"Probably never," she said off-handedly, looking up from her book under the weeping willow tree in the backyard. "She wanted to be happy, and I guess she is."

I don't know if Meredith ever believed that herself or if she tried to protect me from a harsher reality.

Regardless, my sister had dinner on the table every night at six thirty, and if Dad didn't make it home in time, he got a covered plate on top of the microwave with a foil tin of homemade biscuit dough she directed him to pop in the toaster oven separately so it would develop a proper crust.

I had to be in the tub by eight and in bed by nine, and Meredith was high-minded about my TV time—a half hour on weeknights, and only if I finished whatever book she'd liked best herself at my age and lined up neatly on a shelf by my bed.

My rebellion against her started in the eighth grade, when I came down with mono and got to stay home from school for an entire month watching *I Love Lucy* reruns. Meredith would bring me my homework and stand at the door with her arms crossed as Ricky spanked Lucy over his lap for selling off their crappy furniture while he was out auditioning chorus girls for his famous nightclub act. The live studio audience really ate it up when Lucy started crying, but at that age I had serious trouble extracting the big yuks from domestic violence.

Meredith had no patience whatsoever for this kind of thing. "Did you lie around watching this junk all day?"

I studied the macabre choreography of a merry-go-round chase sequence that ended with a hilarious marital beating. "It isn't junk. It's been on for like a hundred years for a reason."

"Oh? And what reason is that?"

"I'm trying to figure that out. Please shut the door behind you."

Meredith went off to college the next year and TV replaced her as a governess with some real intrigue. While cartoons filled my Saturday mornings with a riot of color and clatter, after school I got hooked on a twisted net of adult soap operas whose storylines I could probably loosely follow to this day. I developed a widely contradictory taste in sitcoms, both current and classic, whether I found them the least bit funny.

My need for a more complex pixelated fix often drew me to a Ventura Boulevard bus stop on Saturday mornings. Welcoming the echoing chill of the cavernous Sherman Oaks mall, I bought one ticket for the G-rated matinee at the Cineplex and sat alone in the dark, sneaking in as many others as I could before some smart-ass usher with a screaming case of acne brought around a manager.

Meredith would call home from a faraway Massachusetts time zone, shut safely away in her big deal dorm at Smith. Some fawning house mother probably touched her up with a feather duster as Fancy Pants politely inquired how I expected to get into a decent college myself someday if I refused to study.

"I am studying, you dodo," I'd tell her, lying on the couch to dissect the onslaught of reality television, serialized teen drama, prime-time game shows, and most exciting of all, Super Nintendo, Sega Saturn, and PlayStation. These ranked among the hottest topics across the expansive geek network I courted online.

I became a multiplayer legend among legends while rarely leaving the living room. My sister would call from her college dorm or, after that, her apartment at law school in Boston. "Did Dad make it home for dinner?"

"Nope. Steaks at Morton's with a client."

"Don't sit around eating SnackWell's. Broil a nice piece of chicken or something, you like chicken."

What I liked was picking my own Lean Cuisine from a stack in the freezer, two of them if the mood struck, alternating between them both with the same fork while standing at the kitchen counter.

ALL THOSE YEARS LATER, THAT'S exactly the ritual Casey Klinkhoffer caught me reenacting when she passed by the office kitchen.

"Hey, I thought you already took off for Miami," she said. "What is that, Swedish Meatballs?"

"With Thai Sesame Noodles," I said, spearing either one to make the perfect bite. "Call me a culinary adventuress."

"You're an unusual girl."

"And you're just noticing this now?"

She seemed harried, juggling a stack of file folders, grabbing a minute to pause between meetings in the executive suite.

"I'm about to get an Uber for the airport," I told her. "The chief was going to drive me, but he got a call."

"Yeah, I saw him dropping you off earlier. That looks like it's progressing nicely," she said, fishing around for some dirt. "What call did he get?"

"I don't know. Some police call, I guess. Listen, I wanted to ask you something."

"Robyn isn't still in the picture, is she?"

*Robyn? Who was Robyn?* "I haven't met Robyn," I said. "I haven't even met Sally."

"Robyn Apuna, his ex-girlfriend. She's like twenty," Casey offered up. "Can you see your dad dating a twenty-year-old?"

"My dad is dead, so definitely not."

There went my theory of Abel's ten-year dry streak.

Where would he even meet a twenty-year-old interested in a man twenty-five years her senior who peppered his speech with "*by gollys*" and "*loads of malarkey*"?

He had mentioned sexual abuse and runaways at one point; I hoped Robyn hadn't been a victim he'd met in his line of work and swore an oath to protect and serve. If she were some adventurous young sheriff's cadette, on the other hand, I suppose it would have made sense at the time to give old Sally a little tit for tat, so to speak.

"None of his daughters would even talk to him while he lived with her," Casey said.

*He lived with her?*

This had to have gone down during Sally's great Minneapolis exodus and quick turnaround to guard the foot of his drive like a gargoyle. Either way, it all seemed to me to be lacking in good taste. His daughters were grown with children of their own, he'd shared with me earlier in the week after getting in the habit of popping by both before and after work. We took a walk down to the lake at sunset to pick some crabapples Naomi had asked him for permission to add to a batch of maple jelly.

"Is it weird she asked you and not me?" I asked Abel.

"She probably sees you as an outsider."

"She's making jelly in my kitchen."

"She may not even have electricity at home. You're probably the wealthiest, most powerful woman she's ever interacted with up close and personal."

"I used to take the plastic jelly tubs from restaurants so I could live on toast for a week and not feel resentful," I said. "It wasn't all that long ago."

"Wow. Did you ever feel like giving up?"

"Every day. You get good at retreating inside your own head."

He reached up for a greenish-red fruit the size of a plum, placing it firmly in my hand.

"There you go, Snow White."

I thought better of biting my tiny apple pending further investigation into either the huntsman or the prince.

"You never got married or had any kids?" he asked.

I did not want to tell this man that I forgot to have children because I was busy watching TV, or that playing video games made a better measure of my teenage years than those he'd devoted to raising them.

I flashed back on sitting at my dad's favorite car wash with my first crush, the guy who owned the place, sharing an early video game I'd sketched out. I depicted him as a giant silverback ape, with me at the wheel of a convertible cuing his simian lust in a shower of hot wax to escape our both getting sudsed to death.

The Car Wash King of Canoga Park shot my dad an uncomfortable grin. "You'll have to watch out for this one when her boobs come in."

I slipped on a slimy flat rock by the shoreline, and Abel reached for my hand—the first time he ever touched me—as a stiff gust whipped up over the lake.

"You'll want to think about some heavier things you can slip on and off through the worst of it," he said.

He, too, had once been a newcomer to the Village of Littleburgh. After he graduated the police academy, Sally developed panic attacks that made life in the Twin Cities so overwhelming he accepted the chief job over a much more exciting offer with the Minnesota Bureau of Criminal Apprehension.

The eldest daughter, Eugenie, had done more than her share of the heavy lifting, and Abel adored her, he said, for being the first of the four to make him a man.

"I think you and Eugenie could get along," Casey said, trailing me from the kitchen to my office to watch me pack some things for the conference: Wonderful brochures and leaflets, Wonderful mini doll souvenir keychains. "Just don't pick up a shotgun every other week and try to kill yourself, and you'll be a big improvement over Robyn."

*Multiple suicide attempts. Could this plot get any thicker?*

I glanced toward Trudi Oldham's door across the hall, relieved that she was not at her desk. I had run into her earlier at the employee warehouse store, where she selected art materials for her son's preschool class.

I'd stopped in to pick up some things for my reclusive Hmong family. I filled a half dozen Wonderful Lavender backpacks with toys, dolls, and school supplies to leave by the back porch, along with some coats in various sizes I'd picked up on sale online at Macy's. It appeared they had been clearing and planting my land for a good long while, and I wanted to honor our unspoken contract in some small way.

"My husband does the yard work," Trudi said. "I guess I got one of the good ones."

She probably wanted me to say my husband either was or was not one of the good ones. "I also have some Mennonites working for me,"

I volunteered. "The wife gets up before dawn to roast coffee beans and grind them by hand. I bet right along now she's putting a crabapple sauce cake in my oven."

This portrait of domestic relations seemed a bit exotic for Trudi Oldham's taste, as though we were all living under the cover of night on some clothing-optional hippie commune and couldn't manage regular groceries in the perfectly well-lit aisles of her father's supermarket.

"So, what did you want to ask me?" Casey said, checking her watch at my office doorway. "I've got a bunch of meetings up here today; I need to get moving."

"Oh, right. I wondered if you have any contacts with the village alders. I need a permit for some work on my house and it might be tricky."

"Freddie Weissfluggen," she said. "They just elected him council president. He's got his eye on an open congressional seat, and he's kind of a straight arrow, anyway, so I wouldn't count on any special favors. Abel knows him," she added. "Freddie's his new boss."

It occurred to me that part of Casey might have enjoyed delivering the more unsavory details of Abel's past she so casually tossed off while purporting to be busy with these mysterious upstairs meetings.

She had happened upon a casual meeting between me and her freelance set designer, Selena, earlier that week about a new DEI program I wanted to put in place. "Don't talk to my people, ever, about anything," she said, her eyes flashing as though she might self-combust and burst through the atrium of the Happy Wonderful Place.

I looked at the crackling two-way radio Abel had given me, propped up on my desk.

This would represent our only way to communicate when I got in from the airport later that week to face, literally, the eye of the coming storm. Did Robyn have her own private frequency? Did Sally?

I sighed, powering it off, and left it right where it sat.

CHAPTER EIGHT

# Belinda Rockland, the Most Wonderful Girl Drunk Out of Her Big-Girl Panties at the Kidgitalscreenfest Awards

SEATED BESIDE BELINDA ROCKLAND ON the plane to Miami munching on warm mixed nuts from a ramekin, I dared not close my eyes against her covetous gaze.

"Are you going to eat those?" she asked.

"I am eating them."

"You're picking out the almonds."

"I eat the almonds first," I said. "Then I cruise through the cashews and move on to the pistachios. I can take or leave the pecans, depending on if I'm still hungry and what, if anything, they're serving for dinner. It's a system."

"I don't really care," she said.

Is it possible for a traveling partnership to break up prior to leaving the ground?

I still had time to make one of those scenes with the flight attendant that ends up on social media and gets you removed from the flight, but given my personal history with provoking fellow executives, any number of whom I was likely to run into over the next few days, I felt it best to maintain some element of surprise.

"I'm after your collectible nut ramekin," Belinda said. "I've assembled quite the trove of airline logo items over the years. Matchbooks. Facial tissues. Playing cards. We like to fly around the country and pick up our awards in person."

"Do you have to add a new shelf from time to time?" I asked. "Or do the awards get their own private shelves you erect in an annual awards ceremony for the awards?"

Wonderful Girls had been honored by every creative, media, product, design, publishing, and parenting group with an honor to foist upon us. We needn't do much more than fill out the entry form, and our submission would be passed up and on through the next round until it received another Grand Gold Jury Prize of the Year for Excellence in Everything.

When the flight attendant asked if Belinda wanted a drink, she claimed to be moderating and waved him on. She tugged his sleeve to call him back. "Although would you be a dear and bring two or three of those cute vodka bottles for my home collection?"

He hesitated a moment, perhaps considering her pocket-sized stature relative to the legal drinking age, but quickly made the easier choice and handed her three one-ounce bottles of Smirnoff.

"And did you have two or three of the teensy vermouths to make these a matched set?" she asked with another quick tug.

Her moderation plans altered significantly nearer our destination, when the pilot's voice on the speaker warned of severe turbulence over the Florida Panhandle.

When she began pouring rum and Cokes from an impressive stash in her flight bag, I recognized all the signs. While Belinda Rockland possessed the cool demeanor of an amateur sky thief, she could comfortably call herself a business-class drunk.

By the time we approached Miami, where we would join eighteen hundred colleagues to share insights and analyses, Belinda let loose a few of her own.

"Do you really think we're going to let you put our name on a forty-million-dollar theatrical release?"

"Why else would you have hired me?"

"We were acquired over a year ago," she theorized. "We've done quite well for ourselves before you people appeared to help us little yokels reinvent the wheel."

"I have no interest in disturbing the Wonderful brand halo," I said. "However, you might be surprised by the level of talent I'm able to connect you with down there."

"Ha! I wasn't all that enthralled when we found *you* down there."

Indeed, I had spoken in a small breakout session the previous year, on the "Convergence of Entertainment and Technology." "I don't recall meeting anybody from a doll company," I said, a bit confused. Of course, the whole event had been a bit of a blur as I neared the end of my own drinking career.

"Oh, I wouldn't attend something like that," she sniffed, checking a compact mirror to rub off the attractively priced drugstore lipstick caking on her teeth. "I don't guess your predecessor bothered to introduce herself at the time, but the next time they marched her into Wonderful HR to give her the what for she pulled your name out of a hat and packed her bags."

LATER THAT EVENING ON THE phone from my suite at the Intercontinental, Meredith couldn't imagine why I cared about what some half-pint air bandit drunk up on kiddy liquor might have heard about me through the grapevine. "The important thing is *you* didn't drink."

"God no. It was like an in-flight relapse prevention course," I said. "She clearly implied that I'm one of a string of perfectly qualified instant rejects hired only because the parent company held a gun to their head."

"Is this the Pineapple Upside Down woman? Her version of events would appear to be the result of some very wishful thinking."

"Maybe. I can't figure why the new team didn't cut her loose on day one."

I gazed out the window of my King Classic Oceanview Suite beyond the moonlit channel of the Intracoastal Waterway onto Biscayne Bay. Come morning, billionaires' yachts would zigzag an outlying cluster of barrier islands adjacent to dozens of megaton ocean liners berthing out of the Port of Miami.

"It really bothered her I scored a room upgrade," I told Meredith. "I gave the lady in charge a wad of Wonderful swag."

"Seriously? Did this little individual just fall off the turnip truck?"

"Hopefully she fell into it. Her room overlooks the place where they park them."

"See? Not even on the ground for half an hour and already karma is a bitch," Meredith said.

I picked up an event program the size of a small metropolitan phone book I got at the check-in desk, whose front cover had been purchased by ZZZZZoom! and featured a riot of graphics from its debuting slate of video games.

"Their new creative chief is in from San Francisco to give the keynote address on the 'Future of Storytelling for the Global Family,'" I said. "I should try to introduce myself. Our acquisition wasn't much of a story until he came aboard and now everybody's champing at the bit to find out what he has up his sleeve for us."

"Excellent," said Meredith. "You do what you went there to do and let Half-Pint worry about the return flight sky marshals zeroing in on the load in her underpants."


JONATHAN P. PARK HAD COME up as a troubled Koreatown youth who served his fresh and edgy scripts around town disguised as a pizza delivery boy. Generally credited as a forerunner of prime-time animation, he'd picked up multiple Emmys by the age of twenty-five for his groundbreaking work on *Universal Loser*. A ninth-grade geek has the power to destroy the world by way of a nuclear cartwheel and the help of his faithful sidekick, a homeless kickboxer whose super-amped double jab was built on the bones of a dozen dead guys.

"*Own. Your. Story.*"

Now in his late thirties, Jonathan preached to a packed house in the thirteen-thousand-square-foot grand ballroom at the Intercontinental Miami. Cutting a fit and chiseled figure in a hand-tailored Brioni suit, he wore a wireless body mic tucked seamlessly into his hairline, like a Broadway performer determined to bring the illusion worthy of a thousand-dollar ticket by integrating every spare orifice.

"You *are* your story. The difference between you and it must be imperceptible to today's audience, technology-trained by the age of two to sniff out your inner fraud."

A chuckle emitted from the crowd.

ZZZZZoom!'s newly appointed wunderkind danced around a clear acrylic presidential teleprompter, set center stage, angled at forty-five degrees and barely perceptible to the audience, immersing himself within living, breathing sketches of his astonishing work splashed across the stage.

I had picked up his bestselling book, *Own It*, at the check-in desk, but had only a moment to leaf through it the previous evening.

"Perception is a more lethal weapon than even deception in the storyteller's arsenal," he said from the stage.

Our fingers flew across old-school laptops and savvier electronic tablets retrofitted with late-generation touchscreens made to feel like ordinary paper meeting the tips of a thousand inspired styluses.

"I knew a girl, teenage runaway, probably on the pipe. Passed from foster to foster, beyond help and hope. She took off from an aunt's house with three homeless men and murdered the first woman she met up with. The first kill might have been spun as accidental—had she not tasted blood and shortly murdered again."

A gasp from the crowd.

"What has happened to this country?" asked Belinda through bits of hotel-sized chocolate chip muffin stuck to her teeth.

I would have shushed her, but I was already pretending I'd never seen her before in my life.

"Once again, our little juvey gets off scot-free," said Jonathan from the stage. "She claims self-defense, can't remember a thing. Does anybody know her name?"

Surely one of the thought leaders in children's entertainment hailing from every corner of the globe could solve this riddle with or without the aid of a flying monkey, but you could have heard a pin drop in the cavernous Bayfront Ballroom.

I hoped to speak loudly enough to be heard from the second to last row without coming across as a show-off, since the standing-room-only crowd already resented me for having grabbed one of the last seats.

"Dorothy," I said, weakly raising a forefinger. "Dorothy Gayle."

Shielding his eyes, Jonathan pointed in my general direction, squinting through the dark. "That's right, somewhere from the back. Dorothy Gayle. And who was the heroine of my tale?"

"Dorothy Gayle!" repeated the enthused crowd en masse.

"Err!" said Jonathan, making the sound of a "wrong" buzzer.

"Elphaba," I said, more confidently this time.

I stood up, prodded by a small group of Shanghai engineers who dispersed the aisle as though I'd landed my house in some new world order Munchkinland. "Otherwise known as the Wicked Witch of the West," I added, bringing it up another notch. "You told the story from her side and made Dorothy your villain."

I left out the part where this is the plot of a long-running Broadway musical, for God's sake, and slipped out the back door to a big round of applause.

A spotlight found my empty seat and Belinda Rockland leaning into it, redirecting any and all credit to herself, if only for the greater glory of Wonderful Girls, she would later claim.

I made my way out of the ballroom and back in again through a door in front—just as Jonathan P. Park finished up to a thundering applause.

I fought the throng rushing him off stage for a private moment. Like rock star roadies, his handlers formed a circle to escort him out a back door, but I raised a Wonderful Lavender card above my head. "She's from Wonderful Girls!" someone said. "Let her through."

All in one balletic move, Jonathan P. Park snatched the card from my hand and stowed it in his shirt pocket. "I'll call you, Wonderful Girl," he said over a shoulder and disappeared into the crowd.

MAKING MY WAY THROUGH THE lunch buffet, I thought about a nurse at Betty Ford who generously overapplied her sparkly green eye shadow, earning the nickname "Elphaba" among my snarky Orange County housewives crew. I couldn't help wondering if I'd put the wrong spin on my entire life story. Nurse Elphaba had done nothing wrong, other than woefully misjudge her color family, but I'd cast her as an antagonist during a painful chapter when it seemed easiest to do that with just about everyone I met. If I was truly the architect of my own story, perfectly able to spin it however I liked, why hadn't I ever done it?

Though I wasn't quite sold on either the theory or its author, pending further investigation I carried my copy of *Own It* out to the bustling marina on a buffet tray.

I reached the last available umbrella table at the same time as another refugee from the indoor swarm.

"You take it, hon," said a familiar voice absently beneath the brim of a rhinestone baseball cap.

She had a cell phone to her ear, and I hadn't gotten a clear look at her face, watching her scoot off to jockey for position near the contingent from the Communist Party of China State TV on the slim chance they didn't turn out to be lingerers.

The best I could do was keep a hand on my own table and hope I even had the right person while waving my free arm in her general direction.

"Diarra? Diarra! Over here!"

Orphaned as a tot one starless night when Ethiopian warlords wiped out her entire clan, Diarra Demissie narrowly escaped death herself by wandering through the Sub-Saharan Desert for days in search of the Red Cross.

You could see where she wouldn't be a fan of awkward public confrontations even now, especially given our proximity to all that nastiness with Castro at the Bay of Pigs. Equal parts optimist and pragmatist, she credited the long odds she'd already beaten in life to a sixth sense for ballistics of any kind pointed in her general direction.

She found herself slightly disoriented within a rabid swarm of liquid lunchers overcrowding the bayfront tiki bar and twirled around once or twice before landing exactly where she started, smack dab in front of me.

"Diarra Demissie," I said, grinning from ear to ear. "Of all the gin joints in all the world."

"Jaycee Grayson? Oh, my my."

Offering up a wide and pearly smile, she twisted me into a familiar hug with arms like a pair of elongated cinnamon sticks. "How wonderful to see a friendly face," she said, unfurling herself to take a step back.

A gorgeous mass of beaded dreads capping her thin and willowy frame partially obscured the words "*Black Woman Speaking: Listen and Learn*" in rainbow lettering. Her runway-ready black T-shirt probably came courtesy of Balenciaga—or maybe the guy on the corner washing car windows for change. Things could go either way with Diarra. She towered like a queen over this subsection of showbiz hacks, who mostly set our sights on the kid space only after embracing its inevitable world dominance.

"What brings you to this freak show?" I asked, wholly perplexed.

Diarra had come up as an indie vocalist on the LA music scene in her early career and missed nineties-rock-legend status by an inch. Though we both viewed our graduate studies at UCLA as a last-ditch effort to grab on to something solid, we did plenty of age-inappropriate drinking with the undergrads we taught filmmaking basics right up until graduation day. Diarra shortly got popped for a DUI winding her way through the canyon and reprioritized some things, such as staying alive.

As I lurched forward in the studio system no matter the personal cost, Diarra sacrificed any notable success to become a leading member of Hollywood's Sober Mafia, or so I heard. People like us tended to lose touch over time.

"The Mango Sangria is the free daily special—five bucks each to add the frozen vodka shots," a harried cocktail waitress reported, landing a tray full of sweating glasses in front of us.

"We'll just have the water," I said a little uncomfortably, helping myself to a pair of glasses and sliding one over to Diarra.

"I've been nominated for the big Kidgie award," she said, changing the subject. "Have you seen the Nike 'Don't Tell the Kids' campaign?"

*Oh no, not that! Had she really ended up schilling shoes?*

Where my work in school wowed the judges on technique, Diarra was the artist, raising a voice so fresh and confident her thesis film was rumored to have taken both the US and UK Student Academy Awards before it even locked.

In a coming-of-age musical comedy, an aspiring Ethiopian dancer receives US citizenship at the exact moment she gets her first period. She comes out to her American family as a young Black lesbian fresh for the fight—although nobody hears a note in the big, show-stopping *Ekista* folk number above a riotous party pulsing with the pain of the motherland.

"I haven't had a chance to look at *every* TV commercial up for the Grand Kidgie," I fibbed. "But yeah, I heard Nike is the one to watch."

"The client killed it on sight," she said, heading that one off at the pass. "We brought in teen athletes and asked them to run like a girl, throw like a girl, that sort of thing. They stood there like idiots, fumbling the ball, playing with their hair."

"That's disappointing."

"The younger athletes played fiercely," she said. "It turns out that girls must be taught that we're ridiculous. By then, the boys are loving it and we've given up. Not the kind of message that sells a lot of sneakers."

"Did I do something at your wedding?" I blurted out. "I know I had a lot to drink, but so did everybody else who went into the creek, and isn't losing your head the whole point of a Topanga Canyon ceremony?"

"Maybe not the *whole* point," Diarra said. "We would have done the commitment poems we wrote, the ancestor prayers at sunset. But let it go, boo. We're astonished to this day your sister managed to make it all so beautiful."

Meredith might have staged a moonlit canyon wedding for Diarra and her wife, Liz, without ever previously meeting either one of them, but I knew how to inspire her to action. "They're completely broke getting their little production company together," I said. "They can only afford to serve hot dogs and tofu pups at an outdoor recreation area."

"For Chrissake, a wedding is supposed to be a memory. Who wants to remember a tofu pup coming back up on the way down the canyon?"

Sure enough, Meredith made magic for sixty guests on a budget of three hundred bucks—a lesbian mountain luau with skewered veggie "not-kabobs" in individual boxes bound with white tulle. Guests heated our own dinners over a communal bonfire, followed by a vegan marshmallow sundae bar set a little too close to that creek for my taste.

"I told her not to put it there, but you know how stubborn she is," I told Diarra. "Anyway, she finally threw me in the drunk tank. For a girl who did *not* need to get sober, it's kind of growing on me."

"Oh, honey, I always knew you'd figure out just how fabulous you are," she said, visibly relieved by my news.

She tapped my *Own It* book on the table between us. "I missed him speak just now, but I did read the book, and he works a very interesting program."

"Wait, what? Are you saying Jonathan P. Park is one of us?"

"Jonathan P.P. often visits the rooms," she replied, preserving his anonymity for formality's sake. "I don't know him personally, but he doesn't strike me as the sort he pretends to be in public. If he leaves his true self behind to get a reaction, the two of you might have some things in common, my love."

Jonathan P.P. flamed out early and hard, not only doing drugs in honey wagons across the backlots, but also selling them to vulnerable extras, assistants, and hangers-on.

"Lord knows he didn't need the cash," Diarra said. "It seemed like he wanted to get caught, and when he had a cocaine heart attack during a live audience taping, Human Resources rode along in the ambulance and severed his multimillion-dollar overall deal by the time they got to the gate."

"Human Resources. Neither human nor resourceful," I tsked.

"Nobody heard from him for years. I guess he went to Seoul and ran the anime scene before resurfacing in Palo Alto and getting in with the dot-com crowd."

"This is so wild, Diarra," I said. "I was thinking what a poor judge of character I can be, and boom, you walk back into my life."

"You know I don't believe in accidents."

She showed me a dog-eared in-flight magazine article from her plane ride down about an eleven-year-old aspiring to become the first girl on the International Space Station. "I wasn't certain why she called out to me until I ran into you."

Anastasia D'Alessandro was a pint-size fifth grader with an IQ of a hundred and sixty who was fluent in seven languages by the age of four.

In training under her parents, Boeing engineers working with the Italian space agency, she hoped to defeat space radiation, particularly hazardous for youngsters, with new technology in development. "They're not sure when they'll have everything in place, but they are getting close."

"Wow. I like it a lot, but it wouldn't work for Wonderful Girls."

"Wonderful Girls? That's where you've landed?"

"We're desperate for something fresh, but they have zero interest in developing backward from the reality space," I said. "They have a formula, and parts of it still work. This kid would need some serious obstacles holding her back to even open a conversation."

"After she was diagnosed with autism spectrum disorder, she not only refused to give up but also integrated exploratory therapies into her space training."

"Give me the magazine."

"For real?"

"The only thing I know for sure is we've paid enough dues, you and me. I'll get back to you."

MY CELL AWAKENED ME AFTER midnight, and I squinted in the dark to read a number I didn't recognize.

I thought hard about whether to pick it up, having run into my last Hollywood boss at a one-minute pitching round-robin that forced us both to talk incredibly rapidly.

She'd turned twenty-seven and already forgotten the whole nasty bowling alley mess she was never involved with, anyway, promising to call me for mocktails and dancing at Gloria Estefan's hidden salsa club above her cloistered Lincoln Road restaurant before we left Miami.

We did some air kissing and traded empty well wishes before moving on to another vacuous exchange of nonessential ruminations. I picked up my cell, thinking about a good out on the whole event and settled on Legionnaires' disease, coughing up a lung into the receiver.

"It's J.P.P.," said a covert voice on the line. "Meet me in the Bayfront Ballroom."


JONATHAN P. PARK LOOKED AT me the way men do when women give them too much information about the things that go on among us in their absence and make the mistake of expecting them to understand a single word we're saying. After a while they're just watching our lips move, because that is never a bad thing to watch. Provided no televised sporting event is within earshot, they may even let us finish before offering up a declarative response.

"Homie don't play that," Jonathan said simply after I wrapped it up with a long, frustrated sigh.

We'd been sitting together covertly for an hour or so in a dim corner of the empty ballroom. Wearing my London Fog thrown hastily over the Juicy Couture track suit I planned to wear to the airport in the morning, I felt as though our encounter had every hallmark of a Deep Throat reporter session at the Watergate Hotel.

On the other hand, Jonathan P.P. bore little resemblance to the slick snake oil salesman who'd appeared earlier on stage, sporting a backward baseball cap embroidered with the word "Seoul" and K-pop idol parachute cargo pants paired with an overflowing white hoodie. At times I had to make sure he was still slouched down inside of it somewhere.

"Are you ready to own it?" he asked, emerging from his impressive headwear to suck boba tea from a fluorescent pink straw.

"No! I'm trying to tell you I haven't been empowered to own anything. I often feel duped and double-crossed, which is why I need your support in getting my project produced with a very exciting up-and-coming filmmaker." I splayed the in-flight magazine article on the table.

"What are you looking at me for?" he asked. "This is *your* story. You can't be waiting on somebody else to tell it, or you'll be waiting one long-ass while."

"It's just been really tough," I said with a long sigh.

"It's been really tough?" He could barely stifle a laugh. "When they kicked my butt off the lot, they stuck me with the tab for a two-million-dollar heart transplant." He opened his hoodie and showed me a deep scar bisecting the center of his chest. "You think I sat up in Betty Ford eating bonbons and wetting my baby diapers? Try ninety meetings in ninety days on an old-lady walker and an oxygen tank. I wasn't even thirty. Not a word of that this boy didn't manifest for himself, and I never stopped believing I'd write myself one sweet-ass happy ending."

Personal responsibility held the key not only to Jonathan's recovery, but also to life itself.

"I met my wife online when I was fifteen and she was thirty-two. Real fancy chick, dental hygienist by trade, goes to church and stays there to serve cookies to the poor. After I hop five buses to meet her at Denny's, she takes one look at my sorry ass and hightails it right out the door."

"She probably didn't want to get arrested," I said. "You could have been a decoy from that news show where they track down internet pedophiles."

"It wasn't like that," he said with a chuckle. "I tried her again three years later when I signed my first deal. Said she could give in now, or I'd be back again in another three. Her choice. She's upstairs now sound asleep so she can wake up early for her Salt Glow Spa Facial."

I thought about Abel Dreaux and how easy it had been for me to shut him out before we even started. If I didn't like the sound of his story, I could tell him one I liked better.

"Why would anybody put your spin on their life? Put your dreams in the middle and plot your own plot to get there, it only takes six daily steps. Let me hear them."

"Manifest, Do Your Best, Speak Your Truth, Don't Assume, Just Resume, and Never Take It Personal." I ticked off his simple six-step credo, though I couldn't help but correct that last one. "Never take it *personally*. We're looking for an adverb there."

He'd probably had enough by that point and glanced at his ten-thousand-dollar Breitling watch, reaching for the daily event sheet sandwiched in a menu holder.

"Are you interested in the Friends of Bill W. Sunrise Scuba Service?" He initialed a twelve-step meeting in burnt-orange ink with a spendy custom Copic Sketch Marker favored by commercial artists and tucked the flyer in my hand. "That'll get you the back half of a sober kayak."

"Thank you, Jonathan, but I have a plane to catch first thing," I said, evoking a solid out on underwater sharing and prayer. "When are you planning on being in Littleburgh?"

"Not sure," he said. "I've got a five-B portfolio to catch up on, can you beat that?" He hoped to fly in for our fiscal year planning meeting after the holiday break, weather depending. "Meantime, try a little less talkie and a lot more walkie. If you need me, reach out anytime."

I wasn't clear how to do that, exactly. He hadn't exchanged his card for mine earlier, and his handler claimed he didn't do that. *Germaphobe*, she mouthed. I considered informing her that germs are delivered from carrier to receiver rather than vice versa, but she'd already squired me off to an empty hallway.

Jonathan had set out two cell phones on our meeting table, checking each separately from time to time. Did he have a bookie? Cross-addiction commonly afflicted substance abusers in recovery who fell prey to equally unhealthy habits, such as blood sucker slots or live infinite blackjack. Maybe he got addicted to online auctions and drained his wife's dental hygiene savings bidding on diecast miniature figurines from the Franklin Mint.

Flashing me some type of gang sign from the Kogi BBQ movement for all I knew, he slipped out through a darkened back kitchen. I had to wonder why he hadn't gone with the freshly vacuumed receiving area opening wide onto multiple vacant elevator banks.

Under his clearly worded advice, I would have to suck it up and manifest my own destiny, which by all rights would put me in the driver's seat without a care in the world.

I would return to Littleburgh ready and willing to spin it to win it while speaking my truth and refusing to take things personally. Beyond that, not everything had to make sense, which was good, because as with everything Wonderful Girls, so very little would.

CHAPTER NINE

# Kayla Flynn, the Most Wonderful Girl with a Fake Résumé and a Real Future as Mrs. Weissfluggen Buick

I ARRIVED BACK AT WORK carrying a crushed Key Lime Pie box like a battered battle prize. Baked the previous Friday morning at Fireman Derek's Bake Shop & Café in downtown Miami, the coveted confection accompanied their Famous Guava Cheesecake, but I ate most of that as I sat shivering at the shuttered arrivals-level coffee shop of the Dane County Airport later that night.

I had trouble manifesting myself transport of any kind into the village. Icy streets crippled the whole region after the first big storm of the season Abel Dreaux forecast with alarming precision. A layer of rock salt melted golf ball–sized hail into a muddy road paste crisscrossed with tire skids. I refused to call nine-one-one to track him down, theorizing the towing of stranded motorists from roadside ditches took precedence over a sticky conversation about why I'd left behind my personal two-way radio.

I regretted sending away Belinda Rockland earlier when she offered me a ride into Littleburgh in her gigantic husband's enormous Chevy Silverado. "Course, you'll have to take the box."

She referred to the vinyl-covered back section and the trove of stolen treasures crowding the cab for the final leg of its trek to her home coffers. "You'll only have to lie down flat between the bigger bags for a half hour or so. That is if they've got the backroads cleared."

"Thanks, but I think I'll take my chances with a cab."

I waved her off on the steady elbow of her quiet giant, watching a mammoth ice block tainted with motor oil frozen to its back bumper approximating the one that took down the *Titanic*.

By the time I met up with her again in the office parking lot on Monday morning, she looked me up and down suspiciously. "What is that, the meeting pie?"

"I carried it in my lap on the plane. Seated next to you. For three hours."

"I guess you didn't make it yourself," she huffed.

"How about we start with a taste of the tropics?" I shortly proposed upstairs at the executive conference table.

"I'll give it a try," volunteered Kayla Flynn, who introduced herself, oddly, as the new diversity hire.

I'd never seen a more translucent individual, the general color of the membrane inside of a hard-boiled egg, who always appeared to me as though she had not quite hatched. She bobby-pinned a sheath of thin, pale blond locks to either side of a middle part that could be drawn like a pair of drapes around her entire head and face.

No mere intern, Kayla brought almost seventeen months' experience as a former assistant video editor for a chain of optometry clinics, earning some notoriety for her creative work in and around the tristate area.

When I inquired precisely which states these numbered, Kayla needed a moment, savoring that last tart bite of pie.

"All three of them, I believe. Also, I'm engaged!" She flashed a heart-shaped diamond on her ring finger. "His name is Ronald, but you all know him as the junior Mr. Weissfluggen Buick. Am I bragging now?"

The only entry on Kayla's résumé I could ever independently confirm, other than those she would later lift directly from *my* résumé, was a credit she had earned in homemade soft-core internet porn and presented under the heading "Student Film."

"The employee has a right to express herself artistically," noted Wonderful Recruiting in a memo I would shortly receive in response to my concerns.

"I'm not all that familiar with the demands of homemade internet porn," I acquiesced in a return email. "I have seen my share of student films, however, and I must agree this is some groundbreaking work. Carry on."

Somehow, I suspected that in my short absence, Casey Klinkhoffer had sold this bunch on the ridiculous notion that the best diversity hire is the least qualified one.

"Oh yes, Casey worked very hard to bring us just the right pick for your new program," Trudi confirmed brightly in our afternoon sit-down.

"Nearly forty percent of the UW–Madison student body is nonwhite," I said, gritting my teeth. "They're known for their friendliness to LBGTQ+, and they have a top-rated film school. Is there a reason we skipped over all that and landed on the future Mrs. Weissfluggen Buick Jr.?"

"And I'm going to stop you right now," Trudi said. "I think you need some training in nondiscriminatory hiring."

"I certainly do not. I bring a long track record in cultivating diverse talent."

"Not by our standards," Trudi said. "You've implied that Kayla makes an inferior candidate for a position she already has due to the color of her skin—or possibly her sexual orientation." She lowered her voice sharply to choke out that second thing.

"I haven't implied anything," I shot back. "I'm stating unequivocally that the whole point of implementing inclusive hiring is elevating otherwise unheard voices. We're hearing plenty already from the Kayla Flynns of the world."

"Oh no, that kind of thinking will not be tolerated here at Wonderful Girls." She reached behind her desk and handed me the dreaded HR brochure, "Manager Training and Redirection."

*Don't ever mistake HR for a friend,* Meredith had so often forewarned me. *Think of them as the company prosecutor, and you're the defendant of some regrettable set of charges that you've already copped to in the form of a weekly paycheck.*

"I very much look forward to working with Kayla," I said, hitting the gas in reverse.

I would have to find another time to mention the six-foot-tall Ethiopian lesbian I intended to hire to direct our first-ever feature film, blasting an only slightly radiated, neuro-atypical child into outer space.

"I'll put you in touch with my sister," Trudi said. "She's the expert on helping management navigate company culture."

"Pardon me, did you say your sister?"

"Trina Oldham, in HR," she said. "She and I are twins. Haven't you been introduced?"

"I think I'd remember that."

Utterly terrified, I imagined Trudi and Trina roaming the office hallways on plastic trikes searching for human resources violations, stopping only to fingerpaint suspicious doors with the word "Redrum" stamped with identical bloody handprints.

"Right," Trudi remembered. "Trina has only recently returned from maternity leave."

Trudi had mentioned something about her clan's preferred delivery method, and I had to wonder how much Wonderful leave time her twin sister had clocked splaying herself on the family table to give the world another blubbering Oldham.

"Do you want me to run your studios, Trudi?" I asked. "That's what you brought me here to do, but I can't help you if I'm unable to prioritize my own projects or even hire my own staff. On top of that, you've put the keys to the physical plant in the hands of someone having a difficult time moving forward in any tangible way."

"And all that has shifted a bit in the last few days," Trudi said. "Let's take a walk over to the Photo Studios once we've finished up here and I'll ask Casey to go over your new job description."

"Casey Klinkhoffer? What would she know about executive job descriptions?"

"All part of the reorg," she said. "I guess we've all had a busy five days. Belinda tells me you made quite the splash at Kidgitalscreenfest."

So that's where we were going with all this. I should have expected a punishment of some sort for over-connecting with certain individuals Belinda reported as potential threats to the glorious reign of the Big Five.

"Did I mention what a splash Belinda made at the awards ceremony?"

Her Kidgie Award–nominated Super Bowl ad featured a girl and her Wonderful doll reuniting with a Clydesdale foal after they got separated in a forest fire. It all seemed a bit Budweiser derivative to me, but this drivel easily bested Diarra's buried Nike campaign.

When Belinda's name was called as the Grand Kidgie winner, she required a covert shove to the podium. She'd ordered a third round of Moscow Mules for an otherwise sober table and disappeared all six copper mugs beneath the skirts of her ballgown.

She had to have worn heavily elasticized support panties made for the big girl, I theorized, watching her clink up to the microphone like a Wonderful Celtic bar wench lopped in half.

"She was quite effusive in her thanks to the entire team," I said. A souvenir copy of *Own It* on Trudi's desk served as her signal that she would be reading every word, if she hadn't already. "If Jonathan wears an open collar, you can see the top of the scar where they had to install the new heart after all the cocaine," I blurted out.

"And isn't that just the inspiration we need around here," replied Trudi, delivering it straight down the middle.

Aided by those big eyes and creamy skin—touched only by regular, ordinary bar soap—could she indeed communicate disingenuity combined with abject disgust, both equally undetectable to the naked eye? "You assured me these folks were all about tech," she added. "And here they've brought on this huge entertainment presence to shake things up."

"I'm confident he'll stay in his own lane," I said.

*Don't Assume, Just Resume, and Never Take It Personally.* I'd already forgotten the other three *Own It* credos I would need to move forward with my preferred story, but with Jonathan's blessing safely in my pocket, this entire line of conversation had been of little import to me.

"I'll let you save any key takeaways you wish to share for the whole team," Trudi said. "We'll kick off our annual planning session when we regroup after the holiday break."

"What a great opportunity for me to loop in Jonathan." *Manifest, Do Your Best, Speak Your Truth*, I remembered, and with that I was six for six.

It would probably take Trudi Oldham some time to decide how much she resented that last zinger, but her story was hers to own, and she could do so however she pleased.

"I've started to see you as a real team player, Jaycee," she said.

"And I've started to feel like one, Trudi," I replied, beating her to her own conjunction for the sheer sport of it.

LATER THAT AFTERNOON, I SAT at the desk of the newly minted Senior Director of Studio Operations. Casey Klinkhoffer walked me through her whiteboard reorg chart with renewed confidence, elevating herself a good five years beyond her expected career trajectory with the simple geometry of an equilateral triangle drawn in dry-erase marker.

"Story, Production, Marketing," she said. "You, me, Belinda. From my understanding, that setup would comprise your typical mini-major Hollywood studio."

She hardly needed my help to anoint herself a department head alongside a pair of vice presidents. "Have you run all this by your boss?" I asked.

"Belinda isn't technically my boss anymore," she said brightly. "The three of us are laterals. I left you some freelance budget, so we won't have to keep fighting over support staff, but we'll have to share Kay for now."

"Kay?"

"That's her preferred name." She circled Kayla Flynn's name inside the triangle she'd drawn and gave the whole package a dry-erase exclamation point. "She also likes Kay-Kay."

"This is some impressive work, Casey," I said, employing my best Trudi Oldham doublespeak. "I do not know where you find the time."

"Neither do I," she replied without a hint of irony. "I do get that Kay-Kay might not be our ideal dream producer, but she is hungry, and I'm confident she'll work her butt off around here."

Kayla had already pulled me aside to request a transfer to San Francisco at the earliest possible opportunity to pursue her showbiz aspirations. "That's a nine-hour commute from LA," I said. "They do have some good restaurants. Fisherman's Wharf. Sausalito."

"Good enough." She beamed.

"So, are Louise and Prudence okay with reporting to me?" I asked Casey.

She tapped a series of "Arrows of Inspiration" targeting our trove of Wonderful publications for potential development as entertainment properties. "I thought you might want to meet with them personally and explain how all that would work," Casey said. "I didn't want to step on anybody's toes."

"You didn't?"

"Of course not, why would I?"

"Well, I'm pretty sure I head up Global Entertainment," I said. "That would encompass both Marketing and Production, where this little Story department of yours appears to bow out just when the fun part starts."

"Don't be such a Negative Nancy," she said. "You know very well it makes sense to cut the Wonderful Swirl. You're the one who came up with that phrase."

*And you're the one who parroted it directly from my lips front and center on your title page!* Leafing through Casey's written proposal to senior management, I had to hand it to her for harnessing all my ideas in a single count of grand larceny. *My* virtual film festival, *my* summer filmmakers lab—all neatly laid out and fraudulently crediting her as owner and originator.

*Casey* would bolster our full-time ranks to save on freelancer costs. *Casey* would leverage social media to scale back on production costs while creating all-new revenue centers. *Casey* would implement color-blind policies that treat all people fairly, regardless of race, creed, or gender—as we are all endowed by the creator with certain unalienable rights. By the end she plagiarized Thomas Jefferson and the Committee of Five.

"I'm not plagiarizing anyone," she said, as though wholly affronted by such a thought. "You and I had a casual conversation one day, back and forth, sharing ideas."

"That's not how it went, Casey. You know it, I know it, at least three Wonderful Mrs. Happys who ear-witnessed your white-collar bunco crime know it."

"Those women were models. How many times do I have to tell you that?"

"You don't have to tell me anything," I said. "I got your number, babe."

I leapt to my feet, glancing at a framed black-and-white glossy on her desk. A fresh-faced, younger Casey sat in a director's chair on the set of a New York–based talk show, alongside a legendary television icon. "Barbara Walters!" I exclaimed, smacking myself in the forehead. "She's the great feminist mentor who taught you to comport yourself like a workplace kleptomaniac?"

"I have no idea why you're being so nasty, but I think I've done some bang-up work here," Casey said. "To feel valued, to know, even if only once in a while, that you can do a job well is an absolutely marvelous feeling."

"Are you even speaking in your own words right now?"

"I'm borrowing from Barbara. It's a very famous quote."

"Which requires full attribution, every time!"

A pair of freelance makeup artists detecting high-level drama hovered outside the open office door, perking up their ears for the juicy details. Pulling myself together, I drew a calming breath before heading for the open studio. "Congratulations, Casey. I look forward to your input on getting the studio up and running," I said with a big fake smile.

"Yup, same here," she returned perkily. "Say hi to the chief."

"Will do."

I continued across the studio floor, threw open a side exit door, and kicked it shut behind me, hugging my light sweater against the damp chill of a drizzly November afternoon over the preserve. I hammered on my cell to call Diarra Demissie. "You can start writing the outline," I whispered.

Underscoring *my* new mentor's ever-important theme of *less talkie, more walkie*, I had declined to triangulate internally news of major inroads I'd made the minute the San Francisco office opened earlier that day. Initiating efforts to secure eleven-year-old Anastasia D'Alessandro's life rights for a forthcoming space station feature film, doll, and accessory line, I'd also asked for story rights to the magazine article Diarra had given me in Miami.

"Will Jonathan Park sign off on all this?" a woman with the ZZZZ-Zoom! legal department responded to my demands.

"Of course, but you'll have to take care of all that yourself while preserving extreme confidentiality," I said firmly. "Is that going to be an issue?"

"We do own you, so I suppose we can represent you on the legal work," she theorized. "In that case, all of our communications would be privileged."

"Excellent. Jonathan is on the road, but you'll need everything in order by the time he arrives here for our annual planning summit—or I assure you he won't be pleased."

"Yes, ma'am, I'll get right on that," she said. "What was your name again?"

Diarra Demissie received the life-changing news of her hire as a first-time feature film director with typical understated grace. "I guess I can clear my calendar," she said. "Is this an official Jonathan P.P. production, or are we going rogue?"

She knew me all too well. "Let's start by getting you paid for the script," I said. "I'm still feeling my way around how they do things here, and I'm pretty sure it's everything I ran away from."

"Ah. Funny how that works."

"Men can be horrible, of course—the casual threats, the backhanded violence and microaggressions," I said. "How is it that horrible women came as such a surprise when we're so much better at all of those things?"

JOCKEYING FOR SNOWY ROADWAY POSITION while tightly gripping the wheel of my winterized Porsche Cayenne with both hands, I made my way home from the office well after hours, pummeled by intermittent showers of freezing rain melted with a spray of thirty-below-safe windshield wiper fluid. I held my own against crazed soccer moms at the wheels of kid-packed SUVs, amped-up college students buzzing about in dented economy cars, and bullying pickup truck drivers with ominous bespoke snowplows.

Even while putting on a brave public face, I had definite plans to burst into tears upon my safe arrival home to my in-progress fixer-upper, where the projected repairs had grown exponentially in scope during my Miami trip. The roof had been partially removed to accommodate the rebuilt attic, now leaking into multiple buckets throughout the kitchen.

Tightly wrapped tarps duct-taped to cardboard protected my newly installed butcher-block countertops, half-finished cabinet woodwork, and reconditioned oak flooring.

Though Elijah and his wife had gone home for the night, I discovered the dining table set for a party of one, with some type of animal haunch dangling from a string in the fireplace. It sizzled on lingering embers, releasing a gorgeous aroma of foraged meadow garlic, sweet fennel, and wild leeks seasoned with rosettes of basil and wild licorice.

Unclear whether I was looking at an expertly butchered raccoon, a wetland waterfowl, or some other beast of dubious origin, I was too hungry to demand particulars and concluded, like so many culinary adventurers before me, that whatever I devoured tasted just like chicken.

I'd found a miniature sailboat crafted from shaved pine tree bark floating in an icy mud puddle at the foot of my front steps. It appeared to be an expression of gratitude from my Hmong family for the winter coats and school supplies I'd left for them in the same general spot.

Its open hull burst with sappy, fragrant pinecones, studded with tufts of edible chickweed, wild violet, and elderberry foraged from my property for medicinal tea during the coming cold and flu season. Toothy orange hedgehog mushrooms, along with a fluffy hen of the woods, topped a trove of stacked oyster mushrooms and wavey chanterelles for creamy fall soups and hearty winter stews, alongside prized morels—elongated toadstools with ridged caps uniquely shaped to sequester browned butter in a sauté pan.

Detecting no signs of life from the two-way police radio I'd brought home from the office, I had a passing thought that a glass of Sauvignon Blanc might serve as a welcome end to my uneven day. Like an unpracticed bandleader, I had no faith in my ability to tease any such delicious high note from an evening alone without fear of loosening a deafening trumpet or screeching clarinet.

Though I might never learn to tame the voices in my head, the loudest of these belonged to my inner Betty Ford counselor. "I want you to put down the craving and pick up a pencil and paper," Mr. Y. barked, jolting me to attention. "Write it out, then light it up." These letters were to be burned as therapy, he reminded me, circumventing the intended recipient and offered up to the skies.

Adhering to imaginary orders like my own relapse prevention robot, I opened my laptop and scribbled out an email without bothering to research an address.

*Dear Barbara Walters:*

*I have always admired the barriers you broke as the first female network news anchor. Likewise, I have come a very long way, to a very weird place, to rank among only a handful of female studio heads.*

*I do not hold you in any way accountable for the disappointing actions of your former mentee Casey Klinkhoffer in attempting to steal my thunder. Mistaking her for the dear friend and close confidante I hoped she would become cut far deeper than her betrayal of me as a colleague.*

*In the end, the student became the teacher, and my lesson is rejecting disloyalty and disrespect of any kind in favor of enlightenment. For that I am forever grateful.*

*Standing tall in the sisterhood,*

*Jaycee Grayson, VP Global Entertainment, Wonderful Girls*

I held off on hunting down a sprig of lavender and patchouli from Naomi's jelly jar of fresh herbs on the kitchen counter, declining to perform the suggested witchy granola dance while printing and sacrificing my missive to the firelight. I never quite understood how a hit of aromatherapeutic carbon monoxide would substitute for a nice glass of port on the nightstand.

I let it all lie in my unsent digital outbox and headed upstairs for bed, pausing to look across the thick black fog choking the lake. I could barely make out the flashing beam from Abel's lighthouse—until I jumped at the electrifying sound of an incoming radio transmission.

"Two-Two-Two, Two-Oh-One. Ten-eight, in service, over," his voice crackled from the radio, forcing my giddy schoolgirl smile as I clicked on.

"Two-Oh-One, Two-Two-Two. Ten-two, receiving, over."

"You've been ten-seven, Snow White," he said. "Nice to hear your voice."

"I've been under the gun, Copper," I said. "Not like you, with this severe ten-thirteen still in the area. I'm scared to drive back to work in the morning, or ever again."

"I've been up for the last seventy-two hours straight helping to clear the roads," he said. "I may or may not be awake right now."

I laughed. "Wait, are you being serious?"

"As a heart attack," he said. His voice sounded a bit lower and perhaps somewhat more theatrical than I remembered in person over the encrypted airwaves, as though he were hosting an old-time radio show, and I was his late-night guest star. "I took an Ambien and sometimes I can't tell whether I am asleep or I'm not asleep," he added.

I'd heard Ambien horror stories back home, of course. Guys I worked with would wake up from time to time with unexplained prostitutes in their beds demanding jewelry and cash—but I wasn't sure if I believed Abel Dreaux could be out cold across the lake while also speaking to me so lucidly.

"Hopefully you won't be summoned in the early-morning hours to the scene of a violent raccoon crime," I said.

"That would get ugly for me quickly," he volunteered. "The Crime Scene Unit would draw my blood and racoon defense attorneys would come out of the woodwork. I've prearranged with my night dispatcher certain questions I must answer correctly, or she'll go ahead and pass the call through to the sheriffs."

"Repeat the word 'bananas' if you feel awake right now," I suggested.

I listened to him breathe, unclear if he'd fallen even more deeply asleep while pressed against the radio switch. "Come back, Two-Oh-One. Were you planning on asking me out for a date, over?"

He perked up. "What did you have in mind, over?"

"I'm looking for a police escort to the council of alders meeting next week. I'm trying to look important so I can get my house plans permitted without incurring a substantial fine from the federal government."

"Roger that," he said. "Would you let me cook you some supper first? I make a mean goulash."

"Hungarian goulash?"

"Sally's goulash. I'm a picky eater as a rule, so I learned a couple of her recipes."

"Do we really have to eat Sally's food? You're not planning on inviting her, I hope."

"Aw, shucks, did I mess up already? I don't know much about dating; I only ever went on the one date."

"You probably won't even remember asking me out in the morning. Are you *bananas* right now, Two-Oh-One?"

"Negative, cannot confirm," he said.

I was upstairs now in my panties, pulling on a white flannel nightgown. Unconvinced he would remember any details of this conversation, I sucked in a breath and changed tack.

"In that case, I want you to tell me about Robyn Apuna and please skip the shame. I'm from LA, we don't have that."

I heard the flick of a Zippo lighter as he drew in a long breath.

"Do you smoke?"

"Only when I'm asleep." He took another long draw. "I met her in a depression support group after the divorce. She asked for a lift home on my motorcycle. The right answer was no, but those were some dark times."

"I'm not judging," I said, sinking into my bed and pulling up the covers. "I've had my own dark times, Copper."

"You? Come on, Snow White."

"You know what I'm finding? Sometimes you take warmth and kindness on its own terms. It doesn't always look like it's supposed to."

I pictured my Hmong family throwing themselves on the mercy of the seas in a handcrafted pine bark sailboat on the slimmest of chances they could escape war-torn Vietnam during their blackest hour.

"I'm an old fool," Abel said on a long, guilty exhale. "I don't know what you'd want with me, anyway."

"I don't know about Robyn's standards, but you can't smoke if you want to date me," I chided. "Bad for your health."

"I know you're out of my league, don't think I don't."

"I'll be the judge of that. We'll only have a problem with her if you're not over it."

"I couldn't see my way around putting her out in the street, even after she started trying to kill me in my sleep. After that I locked her out of my bedroom, and it was just me helping the kid. I know that sounds weird."

I drew in a sigh. "You can take me out, but I can't make any promises beyond the goulash. I mean, dueling a pistol-packing psycho for a sleep-talker's affections is beyond *bananas*."

Another long pause.

"We're just another failure," he mumbled. "I don't know how to make you happy."

I wasn't a hundred percent sure who he meant to talk to, but I'd certainly been excluded from the mix.

"Ten-one, unable to copy, over," I radioed back off another protracted silence.

Perhaps we'd passed some marker beyond light flirting, an elastic sadness connecting us more profoundly, that we might or might not dare bridge in the clear light of day. I felt confident we were the only two people in Abel Dreaux's life engaged in a promising dating relationship, for whatever that was worth, and I would have to spin another small win tomorrow.

"Two-Two-Two, ten-seven, out of service. Sleep tight, Copper. Over and out."

I SAW ELIJAH THE NEXT morning on my way to work and asked him what I'd eaten for dinner the previous evening.

"Canada goose, miss," he said, slinging a shotgun over his shoulder.

The dreaded Canada goose! Of all the nerve, fleeing Betty Ford only after I engineered my escape and sniffing me out here.

"Can you teach me to shoot one down?" I asked, tackling the frost on my car windows with the metal blade of an ice scraper.

"No, miss," he said firmly. "I hunt all the geese we need." Killing a wild bird is known as a blood sport for a reason, he further informed me, and there would be plenty of plucking, cleaning, gutting, and butchering not fit for a woman like me.

"A woman like me needs to settle a score," I insisted. "You and Naomi can do the rest."

Why stop at writing unsent letters when I could stare down my demons on the other end of a rifle barrel? My sobriety would take a turning point when I borrowed a whole new brand of survival skills from my new friends living off the fat of the land.

Perhaps that telegraphed a warning shot to anybody standing in my way that they might want to move out of it.

CHAPTER TEN

# Yameena Abbasi, the Most Wonderful Girl with an Animatronic Pirate and Pending B-2 Visa

WISCONSIN HAS ONLY TWO SEASONS, the saying goes, winter and construction. I would need to leverage the turning of all four seasons I'd never known in my California life, an endless amalgam of exacting brightness, to wrestle the whole of my adventure into submission.

Having arrived in the late bloom of summer, I had barely gotten my bearings before the rampage of fall color turned a slippery brown. Stiff winds denuded trees and branches, persevering awkwardly against the elements in a jumble of rotting vegetation. The chilly reception I'd received amid a chorus of workplace spite accompanied at-home hammering and squealing chainsaws like a musical score gone awry, marking races to intermittent finish lines before winter promised to freeze us all where we stood in some human snow globe scene.

As Meredith and I planned her upcoming Thanksgiving visit, she took issue with the nature of my budding romance with Abel Dreaux occurring over the muddy nighttime airwaves. "I'm cautiously optimistic about all these deep and meaningful conversations," she said during our afternoon phone call. "I just don't understand how you expect to enjoy a solid relationship with someone who may or may not be out cold."

"Ask your husband," I replied.

Shopping the Wonderful Girls employee store with the cell phone cradled against my ear, I looked at discount baby things, a guilty pleasure I often indulged after the lunchtime rush.

"I told you not to do that yet," Meredith said. "It's way too soon, and it's very bad luck."

"Sorry. I never heard that." I briefly considered returning the pink gingham playsuit in my hand and un-shopping my mostly full cart, but I couldn't help diving into a bin of assorted pastel onesies in search of newborn sizes.

I didn't exactly know how far she was into her pregnancy, since it went against her nature to delve into the nitty-gritty details so many women like to share—such as her navel had popped out that morning or her labia had fallen below her hemline—and I felt grateful for that.

"Listen to me, Jaycee. Your guy is taking a federally controlled substance. It's probably highly addictive."

"It's a hypnotic, not a narcotic," I said. "I look at it like a truth serum, listening to what spills out of him in the dark. Sometimes he sounds almost mythological regaling the events of his day—like a warrior fresh from the hunt, or an emperor from another time. The other night he said something about laying down his sword at my quivering feet. Maybe you should slip a nice zombie pill to old Butch sometime."

"Butch doesn't need any extra sleep," she said flatly.

"Abel doesn't take it *every* night," I clarified. "Cops get slammed with the weather this time of year and sometimes they see such hideous things they couldn't possibly get to sleep on their own."

"Did you know his ex-wife is a phlebotomist? A literal bloodsucker.

Unless that's a different Sally Dreaux." I could hear Meredith clicking around her computer over the phone line.

"Are you internet stalking these people? Please don't do that," I said. "Seriously, talk about premature."

"I wanted to make sure he's really divorced."

"Is he?" I had to ask, wincing.

"Three years. She got the cash on hand and half his future pension. He got a nice piece of property, judging from the county surveyor's drone shot. Too bad you can't run over and look around."

"Once again, I do not care to do so," I said. "Butch is still coming for Thanksgiving, right? I need to make sure I have enough of everything. Sheets, towels."

"He wants to. I thought we were headed to Chicago, though."

"That's Wednesday and Thursday; I made room reservations at the Chicago Athletic Association, and we can have Thanksgiving dinner there. I thought we'd drive back here on Friday for Eugenie's leftovers party."

"Eugenie? The maladjusted not-daughter, Eugenie? Come on."

"I mean, she didn't directly invite us yet, but Abel promised he'd put something together once we have a head count."

ABEL AND I MADE THE half-hour drive to the nearby Village of Mt. Horeb a week or so earlier, after Eugenie phoned to ask for his help plumbing a clawfoot club she'd picked up at a thrift store. We stopped in the central hub of the original Norwegian settlement to look at the legendary wood-carved troll statuettes that line its charming main drag. Abel phoned Eugenie to ask if she wanted anything special from Sjölinds Chocolate House and mentioned that I'd come along for the ride.

We arrived at Eugenie's a few short moments later, discovering the house locked, lights out for the night well before eight. "Maybe she knows I've annoyed Casey Klinkhoffer at work," I told Abel by way of one possible explanation.

"This isn't about Casey Klinkhoffer, by golly."

"Eugenie needs to behave like a grown woman," I said, gently touching his arm. "She's involved her husband and daughter in this childish stunt."

"I guess I'll drive you home." He hung his head in embarrassment.

"Or we could find a place to make out," I volunteered naughtily. "Do you know any good lovers' lanes where the cops won't find us?"

He drove straight to my house, where we ran inside through a torrential downpour. Rolling around on the couch in my open great room, we kissed madly like a pair of teenagers for a few stolen moments—until one of the Mennonite boys happened upon us. We bolted upright, in a jumble of zipping jeans and untucked shirts.

"Sorry, I thought you'd gone for the night," I mumbled.

"As you were, young man," added Abel over a shoulder as we ran back out to his truck, laughing.

"I don't hear any delightful Dreaux family holiday invitation," Meredith said on the phone, unimpressed. "I hear a pair of horned-up pariahs wandering Littleburgh looking for a broken streetlamp."

"It is kind of hot, to be honest," I said. "Obviously, I can keep a better eye on the pacing since I gave up drinking, but not having any real privacy also helps. I should thank Sally personally for blocking me from Abel's bed."

"I wouldn't call Little Miss Sally an expert on pacing," Meredith quipped.

"Her goulash recipe didn't turn out half bad," I said. "It's basically elbow macaroni in canned tomato sauce with ground beef."

"I think that's called Hamburger Helper."

"Not after Naomi Petersheim gets her hands on it," I said. "I'll shoot you her take on it if you want but remember to add bacon drippings if you swap in any kind of game meat for the ground chuck."

"Game meat? Do I need to go find my trusty Girl Scout bow and arrow?"

"Either that or your favorite shotgun. Just work around the buckshot."

NAOMI DID NOT SEEM THE least bit bothered by my ongoing kitchen renovations, availing herself of a newly installed stove and old farm sink in need of a decent faucet to make bone broth from stores of assorted game her husband stalked and killed for the family table. She froze the mystery elixir in glass Ball jars and butchered the meat to leave behind in twine-tied brown paper packages. Handwriting her instructions for sautéing thick venison chops, wild turkey cutlets, or delicate rabbit loins alongside Hmong-foraged wild mushrooms, she tucked a roll of hand-churned butter and a jar of skillful demiglace in the fridge.

"Grass-fed demiglace costs like seventy-five bucks for an eight-ounce jar at Williams-Sonoma," Meredith said on the phone. "And here I thought these people gave you the heebie-jeebies creeping around the place."

Indeed, she and Elijah rarely spoke as they toiled together, often long into the night, ferrying lumber or passing an odd assortment of hand tools among an even odder assortment of nameless friends they often brought along. I could only conclude they made crop circles by the light of the harvest moon.

It appeared my Hmong had removed all detectible evidence of their handiwork by the next morning as I puzzled on the eerily silent scene from my overlook.

"Coffee, miss?" Naomi asked, materializing from somewhere in the marshy mist.

"Oh, you scared me." Nearly startled out of my bedroom slippers, I became even more distracted by whatever she offered on her breakfast tray. "Is that your rocking Friendship Bread?"

"With baby sweet potato and black walnut."

"Really? Did you grow all that?"

"No, miss. You did."

She sent me off to work with a smile on my face and a savory pocket pie in my lunch bag. I wouldn't give it another thought until I heard music throbbing from some hidden corner of the house I could never track down. I decided a radio had been left turned on somewhere and it would lose power randomly with the shoddy knob and tube electrical wiring Elijah uncovered, shaking his head gravely. "Just add it to the bill," I said, covering my ears.

One dark, rainy evening I heard a pulsing, frantic rhythm that I traced as it grew louder with every footstep I took into the darkened great room. I tried to flip on a light switch but discovered it disabled—just as I saw the silhouettes of Elijah and Naomi levitating two feet off the ground!

At my startled scream, they screamed back, stumbling off either side of a shared stepladder obscured by the legs of the pub table. This created an optical illusion of suspension above ground as they rewired an overhead chandelier lowered onto the tabletop.

"Oh my God, I thought you were hovering!"

"We don't hover, miss," Elijah said curtly. "We get up and walk like regular folk." He not only delivered a compound sentence, but also more words than the sum he'd uttered in my presence.

"Yes, fine, I get it," I said, throwing up my hands in surrender. "Why do you never talk? And where is that music coming from?"

They exchanged a look.

Reluctant to divulge any long-held secret to the "English," they'd come to view me as the rare outsider they could trust in our short time together developing Hmong-foraged delicacies for the home kitchen. That was the way I saw it, anyway.

I crossed my arms to signal I was waiting. Naomi begrudgingly removed a pair of ear buds stashed in her bonnet. Elijah pulled his from somewhere inside his mass of curly hair.

"Does this have something to do with the crop circles?" I asked.

"We like metal," said Elijah.

"Heavy metal," added Naomi.

"We're headbangers, miss. We also like to sing."

"And dance."

"Jigging. Clogging. Polka."

"We're very good."

"Now you know."

"They belong to an Old Order that doesn't necessarily view technology or outside entertainment as evil on its face," I explained to Meredith over the phone. "They can enjoy music and even dancing if it doesn't involve a lot of unnecessary touching. I guess at my house they can let loose and rock out without worrying about breaking down the spiritual life of the whole church."

"That's a lot of words for two people who don't talk," Meredith replied.

"They didn't tell me all this," I said. "I heard most of it from Freddie Weissfluggen."

"The mailman?"

"How many times do I have to tell you that's Harlan Meidlemeister? Freddie Weissfluggen is the president of the alders. I think we might be dating."

"You're dating another guy now? Does Abel know about this?"

"Why would I tell him? Freddie is Abel's boss, so that's a little complicated."

"You think?"

"Abel introduced Freddie and me when Abel and I were technically on our first date, so again, awkward."


PRIOR TO HIS ELECTION AS head of the council of alders overseeing village police services, Freddie Weissfluggen had earned local legend status as a military hero. He suffered a severe spinal cord injury after his copilot ejected from a F-16B Fighting Falcon during an aborted Air Force Reserves training exercise out of Madison's Truax Field.

The plane malfunctioned and burst into flames, but Freddie managed to land it alone in an open softball field, avoiding dozens of schoolchildren at recess, and eventually returned the thirty-three-million-dollar aircraft to service. He received both the Airman's Medal and the Service Cross Medal of Valor without seeing a day of overseas combat.

I hadn't noticed Freddie's confinement to a wheelchair at the city council meeting. He sat at the head of a table, exhibiting enormous patience while arbitrating a contentious argument between two Main Street shopkeepers in progress for many years over a proposed streetlight initiative on the otherwise wide-open three-block stretch.

He had not shown any special interest in me, beyond a passing intrigue with the request for easements I had put in around improvements already well underway to my purportedly storied house and its protected surrounding wetlands.

When Freddie drove out to my house to look around one afternoon, Elijah's Mennonite workers improvised a ramp from some spare lumber. He wheeled himself up the front steps with a pair of well-muscled arms. "You're out of ADA compliance," he informed me at the door.

"Can we work with that if it helps push things along?" I asked. Fighting the foul weather clock, we had a partially complete boardwalk and a fully rebuilt second-floor lookout.

"I don't know. How many disabled friends do you have?"

"Right now, there's only you," I said with a coy smile. "Does every permit applicant get a house call from the guy in charge?"

"Well, sure," he said, a bit perplexed by any suggestion otherwise.

We sat at my pub table drinking Hmong-foraged herbal tea and discussing the pros and cons of formally establishing whether the rumors of my property's historical significance had actual merit.

"I can do some research," he said. "I should warn you that getting locked in to the Prairie School history could mean coming before the full committee to fix a cracked window."

He wore his shortly clipped, sandy hair so ruffled you had to wonder if he cut it himself in the bathroom mirror and left the barber chair for folks with time to waste. Partially obscuring a hard-won eye injury from the accident, his thick black glasses sat a bit too low across the bridge of his perky, turned-up nose, and he exhibited an unvarnished earnestness that made me uneasy for reasons I couldn't put my finger on.

I opened my bag to grab a pen and paper—and a coveted pair of tickets to the big UW–Madison Badgers–Minnesota Gophers game landed on the table.

"Uff-da! Where'd you score those?"

"I'm not going to lie," I said. "I got them for our visit today from my mailman."

"Harlan Meidlemeister? That guy's quite the operator."

"You know him?"

"I know everybody. I bet you paid a pretty penny to attempt the bribe of a public official."

"I didn't mean it like that," I said. "I want us to be friends."

"Hot dog, I knew you liked me!" His cheeks flushed a bright red. "I just knew it. Yes, I will go out on a date with you, Miss Jaycee Grayson."

My plan had been to offer him the pair to use on his own, but whatever it took.

"You have balls of steel, Jaycee," my sister said on the phone.

At thirty-four, Freddie seemed both a bit too young for me and a little too nice.

"On the other hand, I am a sucker for a uniform," I told her. "The guts it took to land that fighter jet. Meanwhile, I haven't heard from Abel in days, and the weather will only get worse from here."

"Okay. Now I get it. You're putting the squeeze on Officer Snooze Alarm to pay more attention to what he might miss if he doesn't snap to."

"You can call it whatever you want, Meredith, but I am manifesting every part of my own story, and I am spinning it to win it. You're just annoyed you can't run me anymore."

"I never wanted to run you," she replied. "I've had to run you from time to time to keep you from hitting a wall, and I'd like to see you avoid hitting another one."

I happened upon a separate back room of the employee discount store, where a display of discontinued items approximated a *Peter Pan* stage revival.

Dolls, clothing, and accessories strung from fishing wire appeared to fly in and out a back window of a Victorian nursery and off into the twinkling night. I made an audible gasp. "This is the cutest thing I have ever seen," I said. "Wait, I'll send you a pic."

"No baby gifts!" Meredith barked. "I'm hanging up, I have a meeting." *Click.*

"Can I help you?" asked a lovely Pakistani woman in her late thirties. "I'm Yameena Abbasi, the new Assistant Floor Manager."

"Did you do all this yourself?" I asked.

"I'm starting another on the boys' side," she said with a nod.

In an adjacent side room, she'd fashioned an impromptu Neverland, alive with the sound of chirping birds and fluttering fairy wings over an island trove themed around pirate games, plush animal toys, and glittering treasures of virtually every variety she'd grabbed from the store shelves and buried beneath a mound of playground sand.

"Did you want a beach bucket and shovel?" she asked. "Twenty dollars for whatever you can scoop up and fit in."

Yameena said she wanted to challenge herself creatively while taking a break from advanced studies in visual anthropology back home in Lahore at the University of the Punjab, while her husband, Yusuf, sought his doctorate in biomechanical engineering in Madison.

She pointed overhead to a trio of startlingly lifelike animatronic Lost Boys hanging upside down from the ceiling, where they swashbuckled for control of an adapted ZZZZZoom! arcade game blinking and clanging its digital golden doubloons.

"Yusuf enjoys playing around with our boys in his spare time," Yameena tossed off, handing me an oversize gumball to place in the beak of a giant parrot perched on the shoulder of a steampunk Captain Hook. This set off a Rube Goldberg flood of gumballs rushing over a cleverly configured Hot Wheels–type track, through which Hook lifted his sword for long enough to allow mine to pass through and return to me in a tiny gumball treasure chest.

"Argh, there's the booty," squawked the parrot.

"Thank you," I said.

"You're welcome, nice lady," the parrot returned.

"These are only little nuggets of ideas," Yameena said humbly. "We haven't much of a budget for display, and I only work part-time."

"Are you available full-time?" I asked. "Is Yusuf available? Are the boys? We could get everybody temporary work permits and B-2 visas, whatever you need."

I TRACKED DOWN BRAND MANAGER Rebecca Lavery in the deserted employee cafeteria, framed by a picture window and a heavy downpour of freezing rain.

She sat in a hidden corner nook before a stack of parenting magazines, diligently highlighting each in a color-coded system she'd devised.

"My daughter can't stop wetting the bed, and the doctors have completely failed us," she looked up at me and explained, tying her always freshly shampooed hair into a knot at the back of her head. "I am determined to find a solution that actually works."

"Oopsie Heroes," I told her, getting out my cell phone to search for the popular bedwetting app. "It's supposed to be ninety-eight percent effective within six weeks and it works with a sensor in the bedding, so it doesn't upset the child. I emailed you the link to the app store."

Casting aside the cumbersome magazine stack, Rebecca threw back her head and laughed, as if I told her a joke last week she just now got. "You probably wonder why you ran away from home to join up with a bunch of hardheads in the middle of freaking nowhere."

"That's not why I'm here, though," I said, lowering my voice. "I want to be in business with you, Rebecca Lavery."

"With me? What kind of business?" Intrigued, she gestured for me to sit down.

"Packaging rolls up under you, right? Point of purchase display, immersive retail, that kind of thing?"

"What we do there holds up with our messaging across traditional lines," she said. "We haven't seen the need for any major updating over the years."

"Only because you don't know what's happening out there," I said. "ZZZZZoom! has unveiled some pricey new technology our competitors have to pay for, but it's ours for the asking."

I plopped my Fran MacNeill doll in front of her, signaling the grainy marching band tune from its embedded speaker chip, whose batteries were running low.

"Girls today want high quality, reliable sound they can listen to on their own devices. The new tech synchs your phone at point of purchase and boom, you get a downloadable song delivered to your inbox."

"That's very cool. And there's no cost to us?"

"Not for the tech. The problem is we haven't got the content. Ideally, we'd get our own music label up and running, with a celebrity attached to record an anthem unique to every character."

"No doubt the margins are there to produce original music," she said. "I don't know about the appetite for that internally, though. Have you talked to Trudi, or Belinda?"

"Have you heard the expression when a door closes, find a window? You're my window. Please don't make me jump out of it because I'm all out of options."

She had reached this wall before; I could see it on her face. "How much are we talking to get this going?" she asked. "It's nearly the end of the fiscal year and my budgets are drying up."

"This is only the tip of the iceberg." I opened a photo gallery on my phone, flipping through images of vendor booths I'd visited on the floor of Kidgitalscreenfest.

"Once you've synched up your phone, whether online or in-store, a doll pops up in a hologram for a chat about any related item you might pick up," I explained. "Tagged merchandise is selling at up to two hundred times above forecast in focus groups."

I showed her another image of a life-sized talking doll. "Facial recognition software matches the girl with her doll of choice, and from that point only the two of them can converse back and forth together."

"A real-life imaginary friend," declared Rebecca.

"We wouldn't need much time to train the artificial intelligence, which is less complicated than it sounds."

"Holy cow. This is a lot more than packaging. You're talking about reconceiving the entire brand for a new generation."

"We'd launch a space-age character and traditional movie concept to support the whole assortment. Right now, I'm looking to create a few quality prototypes to show Jonathan Park what we can do creatively with their tech," I said. "Your strategy has been stalling and hoping they'll go away. They're not going away. At some point, they'll have no choice but to take the business away from us."

"You know who I would love to talk to about this?" she mused. "Happy Lindstrom, the mother of the brand, wouldn't that be something? I don't know that she'd be available, but I wonder if she'll be in town this weekend for the holiday parade. The Wonderful Mrs. Happy float is a big deal."

"Hold up now," I said, savoring this juicy tidbit. "You're telling me Happy Lindstrom herself rides the float? Or is it a Wonderful Mrs. Happy actress they put up there to fool everyone?"

"Either or, I guess. They like to have a few of them on hand working the crowds, but she still comes around from time to time. Trudi often visits the family on holidays and comes back with some great story from the old days."

I finally got the picture, even if Rebecca Lavery had been sold a different one altogether. "Do you know Happy personally, Rebecca?"

"We've never met face-to-face," she said. "She conferences into meetings now and then, or she did until the acquisition. She was already pursuing other interests by the time I came on board five years ago."

"Wait. Happy didn't hire you as a college sophomore?"

"What? No. Who told you that?"

"I don't know. Press release, something like that," I waffled. I wasn't prepared to reveal my various sources, reliable or otherwise.

"Trudi drummed up all that PR fluff. I guess it still works as a brand story," she said. "I worked on completing my master's thesis here, which took me forever, what with the kids underfoot—but Trudi hired me. I know what you're getting at."

"You do?"

"Of course. Trudi isn't an easy person, but you can't let her chase you off when you've got these great ideas cooking," she said. "You want my advice? Never make microwave popcorn with Trudi around. Even the smell of it makes her crazy.

"Nobody expected everything to blow up like it has, and some of us have done better with it than others," Rebecca said. "Don't give up on us just yet."

I gestured to a photo of Rebecca's family on her cell phone wallpaper, where a rowdy clan of towheads mugged in front of a firetruck with their fire captain dad. "Lucky you," I said with a wink. "In LA, the dating theory is firemen are to women what porn stars are to men. Maybe it's different when you're married awhile."

"No, he's still a porn star," she said with a smile.

"I think we'll be good partners." I extended a hand to shake on that.

"It doesn't work that way around here," she said. "I'll authorize the budget to get this going but we aren't going to be friends."

We'd been obscured by the central fireplace during the entirety of our discussion, but suddenly discretion seemed of utmost importance. "Start telling people you're offended by the way I hold my car keys, and if need be, I'll pick a few cat fights with you in the executive conference room."

"They'll all be onto us at some point," she said. "By then the day will be saved, God willing, and the creek don't rise."

THE LITTLEBURGH TURKEY TROT MOVED at a head-spinning clip through all three blocks of Main Street, due to the ongoing failure of the controversial stoplight legislation.

Even the Littleburgh High marching band seemed to be playing at double-time as Abel Dreaux kicked off the parade in his village police chief cruiser. He acknowledged me with a somewhat formal nod, speeding past with his overhead lights twirling.

"I don't care to socialize where I work," he said one evening while proposing we drive all the way into Madison to grab a Butter Burger at Culver's.

"I work here, too. Everyone works here, why else would anyone be in Littleburgh on a weeknight?" I asked. "I suppose there's the meat auction at the Elks Lodge. Did you want to check that out?"

"Not a chance," he said. "See that woman walking into the corner convenience store? I put her kid in cuffs last week for riding around town on the hood of his buddy's car. Did she thank me for bringing him home safe? Nope. I'm the bad guy in her eyes."

"What a nasty person and a terrible mother," I said. "I would think most Littleburghers would want to see their police chief out and about the village. Why not buy you the occasional doughnut?"

"You don't know the rural underbelly like I do." He pointed to a nondescript residence set back from the street. "That's the neighborhood whorehouse," he said. "Yep, I know all the dirty secrets in this town, and they aren't pretty."

It looked like an ordinary home to me, with a basketball net over the garage door, surrounded by a white picket fence in need of a paint job. I had to wonder whether it was the whore or the house whose secrets Abel Dreaux policed like the Village Chief of Hyperbole.

Captain Freddie Weissfluggen led the 115th Fighter Wing of the Wisconsin Air National Guard, pointing directly at me and waving with the singular enthusiasm of a good politician. He sat on the back ledge of a premium red Cascada convertible sponsored by Weissfluggen Buick, the local dealership his father owned. I pondered what my see-through assistant, Kayla Flynn, was doing in Freddie's passenger seat before identifying Ronald Weissfluggen, Freddie's younger brother, as the fiancé Kayla had boasted about.

Weaving the implications of that spindle into our tangled web, I nearly missed the half-dozen Wonderful Mrs. Happys marching alongside the Wonderful Girls float. They tossed candy, toys, trinkets, and mini dolls into the throng of what I imagined to be all twenty-one thousand six hundred and twenty-four Littleburgh citizens reported on the last census.

As the float whizzed past, I managed to exchange a curt look with the ever-officious Casey Klinkhoffer, directing traffic through a headset and mouthpiece, having appointed herself producer of the entire event.

More significantly, I nearly missed my chance to get a look at company founder Happy Lindstrom, according to the sign on the side of the float.

I raised my cell phone to try snapping her picture, but an overly zealous child intercepting a strand of play pearl beads tossed from the float knocked it to the ground.

I hardly got a glimpse of the woman riding the float, though I recognized her face without question as that of a dear friend I'd met in passing months earlier in Frank Lloyd Wright's kitchen.

## CHAPTER ELEVEN

# Robyn Apuna, the Most Wonderful Girl with Poor Rifle Skills and an Ear Clip Blasted into the Ceiling

MEREDITH EXHIBITED FLAGRANT DEFIANCE OF our number-one road trip rule prohibiting her from singing aloud with the car stereo. The more experienced winter driver, she wailed her way through a heavy snowfall with the specific intent of annoying me while we headed back to Littleburgh from our Thanksgiving side trip to Chicago.

"You are in violation." I flipped off Shania Twain just as Meredith opened her mouth to join in for another round of country whining with off-key crossover appeal.

"Hey! I'm harmonizing here." She flipped the switch back on.

"Sorry, no." I kicked it off with my foot. "Most people admit they can't sing and don't do it."

I can't remember a time when Meredith and I weren't arguing about something, or when she wasn't slightly ahead. Once she became certified by the State Bar of California as a licensed professional, I could pretty much expect to remain seated at the defense table for life.

She had arrived in Madison two days earlier pregnant and moody, cutting an alarmingly bloated appearance even without her husband, Butch, in tow.

"His sister Joanne planned to take her brood to the in-laws, but they got sick, terrible flu going around back east. Now they're doing their big O'Cochlain thing in Worcester, what could he do?" she said. "He really wants to see your house, though, maybe next summer."

"Don't apologize to me," I said, grabbing her bags from the luggage carousel. "It just bugs me it always puts you in a bad mood."

Butch's last-minute power move to be somewhere else doing *something* else would ensure he controlled our trip remotely.

"Narcissistic abuse," Mr. Y. labeled this cycle back at Betty Ford. "Your bro-in-law is what we in the business call an emotional vampire. He's got his woman good and addicted, and he'll never take his knee off her neck. Dude's a parasite, a tick, a leech, a sponger, any of that sound familiar?"

"Every word. Finally, we're speaking the same language, Mr. Y."

"*Her* drug of choice is *her* problem, *comprende*? Next time you want to drink over it, sit your ass down and write Mr. Wonderful a letter, a poem, a haiku, whatever it takes."

"I'm not writing Butch a haiku," I said. "That would be a complete waste of nonrhyming meter. I've never even seen him read a regular book."

"It's not for him, princess, it's for you."

My sister was utterly appalled to learn I had shared details of her marriage with a "retired" drug addict named Mr. Y. "This is how you spent your time in therapy, complaining about me to some poor bastard who can't afford a whole name?"

"Mostly we watched murder shows," I said. "He was only allowed to talk during the commercials, or if he recognized one of the cadavers."

Her hands clamped around the steering wheel as the wipers fought the heavy snowfall. "You need to shut up now. Hand me my tub of Garrett's Caramel Cheese Corn."

We had eaten less than an hour earlier, a six-course Thanksgiving Day meal seated by the massive Christmas tree at the center of the famous Macy's-Marshall Field's Walnut Room.

Admittedly, I didn't know much about gestational weight gain, but I did have the internet. Only halfway through Meredith's pregnancy, she should barely be showing, but she'd already puffed up well beyond the girth of the average expectant mother over the entire nine months.

Never a subject fit for open discussion, her weight would remain a literal elephant in the room as we mostly argued over various interesting dishes I would and wouldn't try. "What's the problem with lobster bisque?"

"Lobsters are basically cockroaches. You never noticed the resemblance?"

"You like shrimp."

"I hate shrimp," I said. "You're looking at a plate full of peel-and-eat poop veins."

Respectable families milled about dressed in their holiday best, set for an upstairs visit with Santa Claus. Two grown women squabbling over their soup like a pair of fishwives needn't derail any child's Christmas dreams. "Please stop telling me what I do and don't like," I said, gritting my teeth. "You've been doing it for forty years and it still hasn't worked."

"I'm only saying you may be missing out on some things."

"I'm missing out? You wouldn't even get off the museum bench to check out *American Gothic*!"

I'd worn my hair in a low bun with a lace collar and pearls so she and I could stand in front of the famous Grant Wood painting and imitate the humorless rural farm couple. "That's how you thank me for the cute little pitchfork from the gift shop."

"That was just tacky," she sniffed. "And what you did to the North Lion."

Edward Kemey's eight-foot-high bronze sculpture deters tourists from climbing up to take photos when its motion sensor signals an ear-splitting roar.

I mounted the big cat's elevated pedestal, crawling underneath to scratch its oxidated green patina belly. "Take my picture!"

Flatly refusing, Meredith crossed her arms, declining to acknowledge me at all after a recorded voice threatened to call the police. I took my sweet time dismounting and snapped my own suggestive selfie under his raised tail and hindquarters.

"Please stop embarrassing me," she said, her lower lip quivering as she fought back a flood of tears. The thing about Meredith is she hardly ever let loose and cried, but even watching her try not to would get me right in the gut.

"Are you seriously crying because I embarrassed you? God, I'm sorry."

"I can't stand how you're always so goddamn fearless."

"Fearless? Why would I fear a sculpture?"

"Because I'm afraid of everything. I'm a total hypocrite. Always have been."

"Did we even go to the same Girl Scout camp?" I scoffed. "I don't think they put too many scared people in charge, although I couldn't have cared less about any of it."

"Not caring about anything *is* a kind of fearlessness. Throw another set of dice in the air and see where it all lands. Free as a bird."

"Where's all this coming from? Did Butch leave you?" I asked hopefully.

"Butch will never leave me, don't be an idiot."

"Then what? Is it because you're so preggers?" I figured "so preggers" was a safe enough euphemism for "extremely fat."

She forced herself to push forward. "I tricked you into moving here."

"What? No, you didn't. Obviously, you wanted me to get a life."

"Will you shut up, please?" She was having trouble finding a place to start, but I could tell she'd gone over this more than once in her head. "Do you remember when I came to Betty Ford waving around all those papers? I wanted you to think you were out of options."

"I *was* out of options," I said. "What are you saying?"

"All those weeks you were down there, I felt like you were finally safe, and I could breathe. It was the strangest feeling, like I had been set free into the wild. I didn't know what to do with myself. I really think that's how I got pregnant out of the blue."

"Whoa, that wasn't my fault. How old are you, fourteen? Get a condom, for God's sake."

"Butch is very large. They're often out of stock."

"Oh no. Just no." I covered my ears, thinking back to our escape from Betty Ford. "You lied to me?"

"Not exactly."

"What does that mean? You either lied or you didn't lie."

"Of course, you had a case," she said. "You were clearly wronged, legally, provably wronged, and I had an obligation to walk you through all that. I was just so tired of watching you slam your head against the wall, year after year, fighting a fight you weren't going to win."

"You do not know that! Now you're telling me what dream to dream?"

"Those people weren't fit to lick your boots!" she said. "I thought if I could sell you on the same dream, in a different place, you'd grab on to it and run. We could back it up later if it didn't work out, but in that moment, yes, I lied—because it's what *I* wanted."

"You gave up on me because it made you feel good?"

"Jaycee, I will never give up on you. Never, ever. I found some women willing to make a legally binding obligation to be nice to my baby sister. You earned a break and I made damn sure you got one. How is that wrong?"

"Because I'm not a baby, and I don't need a caretaker. God, take care of yourself."

She looked small to me sitting there, as large as she'd become, the buttons of a navy peacoat she'd worn throughout her school years stretched taut over her swollen breasts and enormous belly. I saw her as a nine-year-old girl, shortly after our mother left, sitting under that weeping willow tree assuring me what a happy event that had been while she quietly died inside.

"Are you going to forgive me or what?" she asked.

I felt the falling snow on my hair amid a whirl of traffic as the decorative holiday lights twinkled along Michigan Avenue somewhere in the middle of the country. "Maybe something bigger than us both called me here—a frontier spirit, I don't know. You don't have to blame yourself for everything that ever happened on the planet."

She covertly wiped her nose on my sleeve, letting an elongated sigh onto the frosty air as if to confirm her own existence. "I searched myself on the internet the other day and there was nothing there."

"That's not possible. Unless you got ahold of that new spyware they give to actual spies."

"My name appears in a couple of Chinese drywall cases among a long string of other names. It isn't very interesting at the end of the day."

"It isn't very interesting now." She shot me a look.

"What? I thought we were truth telling." I laid my head on her shoulder and offered up an idea to dispense with this existential midlife crisis of hers within the day. "Let's take a side trip on the way back and hunt down the real Happy Lindstrom."

"What in God's name for?" She pushed away my head. "Get off me."

"Wait. Hear me out."

Though Freddie Weissfluggen insisted no library had ever existed in or around Littleburgh, he did know of one near the Village of Black Earth, where Abel Dreaux supplied me with an address for the home of a Mr. and Mrs. Henry Lindstrom.

"What's all this about, Snow White?" Abel replied to my request for information one night over the radio.

"I'll thank you for the intel when I get back, Two-Oh-One. It'll be a big, wet, juicy kind of thank-you, tied up with a pretty holiday bow, over."

"Jeezaloo, Two-Two-Two. Was there anything else you needed? Hit me up with a list, I'll come over and fill it, over."

"I think we'll save all that for another night, Copper. Nighty-night, over and out."

Meredith warmed her feet and hands on a sidewalk grate in front of the museum, blowing on the thin generic gloves she'd picked up at the airport. "Can we skip the badge bunny banter?"

"If it turns out to be Happy and Hank's house, we pop in, introduce ourselves around the family table, and leave behind a nice box of Frango Mints." She and I had already stocked up on the famous Chicago confection. "The worst that could happen is I get another piece of proof that there is no Happy Lindstrom and Trudi Oldham is a fraud."

"Happy obviously exists," Meredith said, dismissing the whole idea and putting an arm up to hail a cab to take us back to the hotel where we'd garaged my car. "You saw her at the Thanksgiving parade."

"I saw a woman I recognized on a Mrs. Happy float they trot out every year," I corrected her.

I asked Freddie Weissfluggen if he'd interacted with Happy Lindstrom that day. Adding his name to the growing list of those who denied knowing her personally, Freddie only confirmed a hefty donation to his alder campaign made in her and Hank's names.

"You don't need a side trip," Meredith said, opening the door of a cab stopped at the curb. "You need to call your friend Mr. Y. for a nice long phone session."

"Alrighty then. Catch you later."

"Aren't you coming back to the hotel?"

"I'm going to walk over to the ice rink at Maggie Daley Park to work on my forward takeoff waltz jump. I've been having some trouble landing on my back outside edge, but my half flip and double Lutz are improving, so hopefully I'll escape any serious injury."

I'd never laced up a pair of skates in my life and intended to jump on Foursquare to track down the nearest hot latte but figured I'd stick it to her on the fearless front.

By the time I got back to our room, she had acquiesced to a short look around Black Earth, known not only for its historic train depot and former local meat market converted into an antiques mall, but also a small children's library.

"I'm not giving Happy Lindstrom my Frango Mints," she said, gathering up her things. "The woman is a billionaire, she can buy her own."

HAD THE WEATHER COOPERATED, THE whole plan might not have devolved into a death-defying arctic thrill ride with strong career-killing implications for extra measure.

The storm had subsided by the time we located the turnoff for Black Earth, and only a light snow fell as we traced a winding creek north to the edge of town.

We pulled up to a fashionable stone pillar mailbox matching the address Abel had given me at the foot of a cloistered backroads drive. It sloped sharply upward through dense red and white oak, carpeted in fresh snow and obscuring from full view a magnificent A-frame perched on a twenty-acre hilltop.

"You'd need a good set of snow tires to get up a hill that steep," Meredith said.

Near a sign warning away trespassers, an old man with a snow shovel over his shoulder in the company of three young boys toted a pair of improvised cardboard box sleds.

I lowered my window and flagged him down. "Excuse me, sir, would you happen to know if this is Happy Lindstrom's house?"

"Who's that?" he asked, cupping an ear.

"Happy Lindstrom," I repeated. "She started the big doll company over in Littleburgh?"

"Wonderful Girls," he said with a friendly smile. He tapped the youngest boy on the back. "Run on up to the house and tell Trudi or Trina some folks are looking for Mrs. Happy."

"No, wait. Don't do that!"

Too late. The boy took off in a sprint up the steep drive. The whole lot of them wore fluffy wool trapper hats with built-in earmuffs, and the old man seemed hard of hearing to begin with.

"Trudi and Trina?" Meredith questioned in my ear.

"My boss and her twin sister who runs HR!"

"Oh, hell no." Meredith gunned it forward a few inches, getting hung up a snowbank. She threw it in reverse and dug in even harder, spinning her wheels deep into the icy ridge—and lodging us firmly at the foot of the drive.

The old man approached the car with the two remaining boys. "You want to try rocking it? You're blocking the drive there pretty good, and I expect some folks trying to head out in a minute or two."

"He expects some folks trying to head out in a minute or two," Meredith repeated to me under her breath.

She nodded at the old man and gave it some gas while swinging in and out of forward and reverse.

"Hold up now, you don't want to overload your transmission," he said. "Awful fancy car you got here. What is it, Swedish?"

"Stockholm's finest!" I readily agreed.

Porsches are German, of course, but I wasn't about to leave behind an accurate vehicle description on the slim chance we managed to slip out of this pickle before Trudi and Trina arrived from on high pedaling their plastic Redrum trikes.

"It won't budge," Meredith said flatly. She leaned her head out the window. "Sir, do you think your boys might sacrifice a pair of those cardboard sleds?"

"Isn't that a good idea," the old man said, tapping another boy on the bottom. "Run up to the house and get your dad so we can give these ladies a good hard push."

"No, wait, don't do that!"

Too late. The second boy took off in a sprint up the drive, as the first boy trotted back down with a card he handed off to the old man.

"I guess they get a little tired of lookie-loos coming around," the old man apologized, handing me the card. "You understand."

The standard-sized calling card was white with Wonderful Lavender typeface offering a Murphy, Arizona, post office box for the Wonderful Mrs. Happy.

"She always writes back," the boy told me with a full-on lisp. He was about six years old and couldn't have had more than a handful of working teeth in his entire head. "Be specific if you send her a Christmas list."

I jumped out and helped put the cardboard under the back wheels for traction, and then joined the boys and the old man in front as Meredith hit the gas in reverse to give that Porsche Cayenne the Olympic ice curling push of my life.

THE NEXT MORNING, MEREDITH AND I crunched back and forth through the snow in front of my house, unloading the shopping bags we hadn't bothered with the night before. Though never confirmed to begin with, our invitation to Eugenie Dreaux's leftovers party later that evening had been affirmatively withdrawn, Abel told me over my cell phone. He had been disinvited himself after a big family blowup the previous day over Abel's absence at the holidays buffet Sally put on in her tiny house. "What could I do?" he said. "Robyn shot herself in the head."

"She killed herself?"

"No, she's alright. She clipped herself in the ear, though, blasted her favorite cuff clear into the ceiling. Took me a good half hour to dig it out of there and work out the dent with a ball peen hammer."

"I don't understand how any of this would have been your problem. Doesn't she have her own family?"

Robyn's mother and stepfather had called and asked Abel to meet them at the hospital but then never showed up themselves.

"They only just got married themselves," he told me. "I'm the only real stability she ever had, so they figured they could lean on me in a crisis."

"Unless you had a previous commitment," I said. "You can tell me to mind my own business, but Eugenie had every right to be mad. So did the rest of the girls."

145

"They've made a rule now where Sally and I attend these events solo so as not to confuse the children. You understand."

"Not really. I didn't shoot myself in the ear." I put the phone on speaker so Meredith could get a load of this nonsense and I wouldn't have to repeat it later. "Where is Robyn now, Abel?"

"Seventy-two-hour psych hold at St. Mary's," he said. "I guess she shacked up with some enlisted guy near the army base at Fort McCoy, but I don't know that he's got a personal vehicle at his disposal. If he doesn't come fetch her, I'll drive over and deliver her to his doorstep, by golly."

"Oh, that'll be good," I said, making no attempt to mask my sarcasm. "The three of you can talk holiday gun safety, appropriate ear jewelry and such."

Harlan Meidlemeister came by with the mail just then, and I hung up with Abel.

"Harlan, would you do me a favor and bring the chief his spare radio this afternoon?" I ducked into the car and handed it to him. "Let him know I won't be needing it for the foreseeable future."

Meredith looked at me awestruck. "You are a fearless warrior."

"I have some strong feelings for Abel Dreaux, I can't lie. But that would only be my problem right now if I'd already given in and slept with him."

"Oh, so that's your secret."

A far less experienced dater, Meredith had certainly slept with Butch O'Cochlain quickly, back in the day. They met when he showed up at one of her frequent gatherings as a plus-one of another guest among a dozen or so casual gourmets.

Her diminishing fan base had started canceling last minute with flimsy excuses, having settled into promising relationships and age-appropriate leisurely pursuits requiring matching golf togs and Fitbits with color-coordinated jogging suits.

They obsessively checked their cholesterol, sharing newfound drug interactions and food restrictions Meredith found offensive enough to ignore and take her chances with the occasional bout of anaphylactic shock over dessert and coffee.

That night she produced a hearty pot of *boeuf bourguignonne* to lop up with crusty homemade baguettes, followed by a towering croquembouche comprised of miniature profiteroles and wisps of caramelized sugar.

By the time Butch commandeered karaoke hour with back-to-back Neil Diamond he'd fallen in love with her food, she fallen in love with feeding it to him, and they'd both fallen in love with the sound of his voice.

She pulled me aside to ask if I could disappear for a while.

"What did you have in mind, Chateau Marmont? The Hollywood Roosevelt? Not the Peninsula Beverly Hills!"

I had been couch diving in her upstairs loft for the previous few months while hammering out a very promising new screenplay and banked on the loan of a fine metallic credit card, something in a rose gold or platinum alloy that would catch the flashing light of a successful transaction.

She went out the next day and rented me a practical WeHo duplex with off-street parking and a nearby coin laundry.

Her buyout of Butch's share of a Marina del Rey condo he'd leased with some unscripted producer buddies living on unemployment became a point of contention between them for many subsequent years. In Butch's eyes, she had not only cut short his bachelorhood but also diminished his ever-dubious career aspirations as an unemployed producer.

"That's how they keep their prey on the hook after the up-front love bombing," Mr. Y. told me. "She's only in charge until he pulls away, and then she gets herself all turned around looking for the next fix."

With all Meredith's talk about being weak and hypocritical to the point of irrelevance, the fact is she had fewer and fewer choices to make over time.

"I'm still not quite sold on the point of him," I had equivocated early on, when the subject was still up for discussion.

"He says the same thing about you."

"Tell him I'm your sister, Meredith, not some bad life choice you made in a panic because that's what all your Smith friends did that year."

She and I watched Harlan Meidlemeister disappear down my service road in his mail Jeep with Abel's radio in tow. "I've been dating since I was fifteen and I've always been good at it," I said, slapping my hands together dismissively. "With liquor out of the picture I could go pro."

I knew I couldn't teach my sister to protect her own heart, certainly not against this baby predicament she would soon face with a husband so clearly not up to the task.

This would be our last trip as just the two of us, and while I'd wanted it to be special, so far, we'd mostly bickered. On top of that, she didn't look well.

"What do you want to do this afternoon? We talked about checking out the National Mustard Museum, but you're probably tired. Did you want to lie down?" I asked.

"You amaze me," she said, mystified. "You just risked your entire career and blew up a promising relationship in the span of twelve hours, and your plan is to move on and delve into mustard."

I was hardly ready to move on. This unhinged Robyn individual plagued my every thought—what did she look like, what did she smell like, why her in the first place, given the high price of admission she'd exacted from day one?

I'd never even seen the motorcycle that had connected her and Abel, a pair of star-crossed depressives destined to share nightly prescription sleep aids and biweekly true confessions at their community center support group.

I couldn't mute the image of this magnificent specimen crisscrossing Wisconsin on his bike, pistol locked and loaded in a thigh holster, youthful arms clenched tight around his waist, a wild heap of hair flying high on the wind.

He told me there hadn't been much between them after they pulled up their pants, but the potency of their sexual pull to the exclusion of all he held dear hardly cheapened her in my eyes. As long as our bond went unconsummated, theirs would remain a powerful wedge between us.

I forced myself to return to more pressing issues in the present.

"So what if Trudi did spot us from way up in that house through some superpowered butterfly telescope?" I theorized. "I could say I met Happy a few times and tracked her down to say hi."

"Then she'd just think you were entirely inappropriate instead of completely off your gourd," she said. "Do you think that old guy could have been Hank?"

"Take it from me, a drinker like Hank would have been way too loaded for snow play by that hour on a holiday. Who knows, maybe Trudi's family went up there to pay Happy a holiday visit."

"I don't hang out with my old boss on Thanksgiving," Meredith said. "I used to send him a rum cake before he retired, and then what was the point?"

"It's still entirely in the realm of the possible Happy never existed, and that whole place is an elaborate front for the big scheme she and her twin sister cooked up."

Meredith tried a spoonful of the hot soup. "Holy God, what am I eating?"

"New Glarus Black Currant Beer Cheese Soup," I read from the handwritten label on Naomi's glass jar. "It's alcohol-free."

Naomi wasn't above using appropriately crafted beers in her recipes and took her personal cheesemaking to the next level with a striking variety of tangy farmhouse wheels at various stages of ripeness aging on my pantry shelf.

"She said to add venison sausage crumbles on top, but I don't know where she left them. We have smokers, freezers, extruders. She just ordered a huge dehydrator."

"The Tribest Digital?"

"I don't know what that is. Ask her yourself when she comes home."

"Home? She lives here?"

"Not really," I said, puzzling over that a minute. "She'll sleep in the back room if it gets late working on something more complicated, a sous vide or what have you."

"What about Lurch?"

"Funny you should ask." I tossed her some pine nuts Naomi toasted and stored in a peanut butter jar.

She twisted open the top and inhaled the contents with deep appreciation, like something she intended to lay out in neat lines on the coffee table and snort.

"I'm sensing some serious tension between the two of them," I said. "They hardly talk at all when we sit down to eat and only seem happy when they sing with their friends across the marsh."

"What kind of singing?"

"I don't know, Gregorian? It's more like chanting than singing, but something about it feels familiar," I said. "Whatever they have going on, I get the feeling she wants something more and he's not in it."

"You need to stay out of that," Meredith said. "Way out. Look at the life you've built for yourself. Your professional test kitchen, your carpenter elves. It's like you're hosting a North Woods cable access station. And do you really have to antagonize every woman you work with?"

"No. Just the ones who insist on getting in my way."

"I wouldn't overplay my hand with that guy on the coast, either," she said. "I know his type."

She lay down on my great room couch in the glare of the afternoon sun over the lake, perfectly capable of managing my new life just as handily as the old one, even with her eyes closed.

Something felt off-kilter about what should have been a moment of quiet satisfaction that I'd been able to shelter her from the coming storm she would soon face, if only for a couple of days.

Still under renovation, my home had kitchen cupboards for salvage and used appliances set out on the porch to be hauled away, with piles of uninstalled bathroom tiles stacked up in the hallway.

Still, I had hunkered down and made inroads toward creating a comfortable hideaway without leaning on Meredith for anything, and this marked an inner thanksgiving the two of us celebrated in relative detente.

I looked across the water to the lighthouse at the locks, feeling a pang of regret over the crackle from a spurned radio I would not hear after dark.

A disturbed young woman I'd never met lay smiling in a mental ward perfumed with germicides and gunshot residue, toying with a slightly dented ear cuff like a badge of honor she'd be hard-pressed to top, short of getting the job done.

All would have been well enough in my world, if only I hadn't later picked up the bright white hand-stitched Amish wedding quilt Meredith wrapped herself in while napping and stained with a river of blood.

CHAPTER TWELVE

# Lila May Grayson-O'Cochlain, the Most Wonderful Girl Who Never Was

BEFORE DAWN ON A GRAY, early December morning, I lay with a rifle poised at the edge of a bog alongside scattered shagbark hickory and bitternut trees that had dropped a rich bounty of avian bait onto a snow-dusted savannah.

Abandoned at the first sign of frost, an Asian pear orchard flanked the field, its delicate apple-shaped fruit once destined for upscale markets but now unfit for human consumption and scattered over newly sprouted barley and winter wheat.

Elijah Petersheim discovered a flock of Canada geese gorging themselves on this rotting buffet, bulking up for their migration south while fattening their livers to three times the normal size. Seasoned and boiled in glass jars, fattened Canada goose liver would become the centerpiece of a humane foie gras recipe Naomi played with and stacked in neatly labeled tins in my pantry. Its taste would be especially smooth and rich, flavored with hints of hardy wild herbs, acorns, and juniper berries the obese gaggle fed on since late fall, kissed by a frosty mist rolling over the snow-sprinkled landscape.

Elijah loaded my rifle with large guillotine-styled broadheads and told me to aim for the head and neck.

"You'll only kill or miss with these," he said, in case I worried about maiming the birds.

The feathers would be brought home to Viroqua and plucked for goose down, the meat cured, and the prized fatty livers seasoned and boiled in glass jars.

"I won't miss," I promised him.

I'd never had a real rifle in my hands, but I'd spent my youth with a Metro Liner bus pass and a pocketful of tokens at the ready, shooting up digital aliens, predators, and mortal enemies among a small crew of legendary gamers swarming arcades in and around the San Fernando Valley.

"You'll get a shoulder bruise from the kick," he warned.

"And I'll wear it proudly," I said.

Elijah hadn't necessarily wanted me to join the hunting party of somewhat uncomfortable Mennonite men and boys, who spoke among one another in a soft pidgin German, despite being fully bilingual.

I told them I had a score to settle with this tenacious beast who'd made a big mistake tracking me to the hard-won safety of *my* Midwest roost.

"They are good eating," Elijah said, scratching his head over my uncharacteristic display of machismo.

I wore a blaze orange vest and cap to match my camouflage jumpsuit in a look I'd borrowed directly off the cover of this month's Cabela's catalogue.

"Sometimes it's good to call a *lot* of extra attention to yourself," I said.

The men and boys wore somewhat less flashy garments over their practical dark pants and suspenders under homemade winter coats accented here and there with brightly colored scarves and vests. They'd swapped out their straw hats for elongated stocking caps they called "woolies" and wore collarless plaid flannel shirts. The goal was to avoid shooting each other by accident while complying with both the will of God and the State of Wisconsin Hunting Safety Ordinance.

The boys trotted downwind from our hide to place a few dozen decoys in silhouette that I couldn't help but covet for decorative reuse on my fireplace mantel.

Elijah accessed a goose call he wore in a collection strung around his neck, growling into it in a deep voice that mimicked the short, quiet grunts that the birds on the ground made to their friends in the air.

He choked the end with his hand, sliding it up and down to make loud, prolonged snoring sounds they exchanged as a special greeting at feeding time. He may not have much use for plain English, but Elijah Petersheim spoke fluent Canada goose.

"Are they really this gullible?" I whispered.

"Yes, miss." He gestured to the skein gathering over the open field. "All yours."

I aimed my rifle with the searing focus of a trained sniper and picked off the first five flying fatties appearing in my viewfinder—reaching my daily bag limit in under a minute.

At forty yards away, I could clearly see my handiwork motionless on the fertile feeding grounds in a jumble of broken necks, fractured beaks, and dead eyes—and promptly burst into tears.

I HAD NOT BEEN MYSELF since Meredith left town after an overnight stay in the hospital for observation.

"It's normal to have spotting for some time after a miscarriage," she insisted after I took her in. "I don't know why you won't believe me. They say it can last for several months or more, depending on what kind of procedure you have afterward."

"That wasn't spotting. That was hemorrhaging," I said.

"Thank you, Doctor Vadge, the Vagina Team will look into that crack assessment and get back to you," she snapped back.

She seemed perfectly clinical about all of it while I stood by her hospital bed giving in to hysteria. "I'm still not following you," I managed through a flood of tears. "When did you lose the baby?"

"At sixteen weeks. I've told you that twice now, did you want to synch Outlooks?"

"But that was over a month ago," I said to this cruel woman I'd obviously never met before. "I talk to you practically every day, sometimes three or four times a day. When were you planning on telling me?"

"I needed some time to sit with it before this multiple-award-winning dramatic performance, can you blame me?"

When I couldn't find a tissue and honked my nose on Meredith's bedsheet, a scowling nurse came by to shut the door, presumably so I wouldn't upset the legitimately sick people on the ward. She ducked in for a moment to pull a fresh sheet from the closet and remove the one I'd soiled with my snot.

"Please don't use or touch anything," she said curtly on her way out, pausing to refer to a second bed that remained vacant. "We might get a patient with urgent medical issues, and we like to keep things in order."

"Pull yourself together, please," Meredith said to me. "I'm not in the mood."

"Does Butch know?"

"He was there. We went in for the ultrasound and they couldn't find a heartbeat. They thought there might still be some hope, but it turned out there wasn't. You should know this has been very hard on him," she added.

"It would be good if we don't make this all about Butch," I said.

"He lost a baby, Jesus Christ. What have you lost, a cute idea? Something to play with when you're in the mood and spoil from time to time?"

"I bought a shit-ton of baby stuff, and I had to hide it all over the house!" I wailed. "I was scared to death you would find it, and we'd have another stupid fight about how wrong and bad I am all the time."

"Come here, you weirdo."

I got in the bed beside her and almost pulled out a tube they had dripping something or other into her after issuing a diagnosis of slight dehydration and mild anemia.

She also had a slight temperature, which could be a sign of infection somewhere in the body they wanted to get under control.

"Ow!" she said. "You're on my arm, move."

"You move, you're the one who gained seven hundred pounds." I waited for the other shoe to drop. "I guess we can't call this a pregnant pause," I quipped.

"Listen to me, Jaycee. Everything I'm going to be in life I am right now, today." With her back to me as we spooned, sister to sister, maybe some of this felt easier for her to spell out. "Try to accept it, I have. You, though, all your doors are open. None of us can see what's on the other side, but you know very well how to get up and walk through them."

"I'm dying to break into the psych ward," I confessed. "I'm pretty sure Abel's ex is locked up down there."

"Don't, they'll keep you. Look at you, you're a wreck."

The dour-faced nurse delivered Meredith's dinner tray—dry slices of turkey they'd probably served the day before with watery instant mashed potatoes and some kind of whipped pumpkin in a plastic dessert cup neither one of us would touch with a ten-foot pole.

I tried to make myself smaller in Meredith's bed so she wouldn't chase me off, annoyed at having to serve a bed tray like some low-rent part hostess. She was a highly trained medical professional who'd done three tours in Afghanistan, where all the men wanted her for all the right reasons.

"Stop making up stories about the nurse," Meredith interjected after she'd left, having no trouble whatsoever reading my mind. "She's probably feeling overworked because women with families wanted the day off."

"That's a story, too. It's just a boring one." I looked out the window toward a serenity garden where a statue of the Virgin Mary surrendered to a soft snowfall with wide open hands. "Did the baby have a name?" I asked.

"We were thinking Lila May."

"Lila? After Mom?"

"We just liked the sound of it," she fibbed. "May is Butch's grandma on his dad's side. Lila May Grayson-O'Cochlain."

"I'm sad, my sister."

"I'm sad, too, my Jaycee. Now you're my only baby."

"Well, I guess there's that."

I GATHERED ALL THE FORBIDDEN pink and lacy things I'd bought for the new arrival that wasn't to be in overstuffed shopping bags to bring along when Freddie Weissfluggen took me to find my Hmong family.

He seemed certain they had scattered from the edges of my property to winter among a raft of itinerant workers sharing utilities and other services courtesy of a state grant at an indoor farmer's market on the grounds of the converted drive-in movie theater on the village outskirts.

The families tended orchards of late-harvest apple varieties—Fuji, Jonathan, and Golden Delicious—that could escape injury after freezing more than once on properly covered trees.

Manning several dozen covered stalls, adults and children backed up their RVs outside to sell hardy crops like turnips, beets, and celery root, along with onions, leeks, garlic bulbs, and a miscellany of gnarled winter squashes kept fresh in cold storage for months.

"Would you recognize the family?" Freddie asked. He and I wheeled down a central corridor of what used to be the drive-in's refreshment and recreation center.

"Not a chance," I said with a shrug. "I've only seen them a few times from a distance."

With Christmas in the air, a crafts fair bustled with shoppers looking for holiday decorations, floral arrangements, and gifts.

I heard some carolers singing a familiar, unaccompanied, Medieval-sounding Christmas hymn in glorious four-part harmony from a busy stall at the end of the corridor, where a long line snaked around the corner and nearly out the door.

An overhead sign painted on a live edge walnut plank welcomed gourmet shoppers. "Homey Naomi's Farmed and Foraged Foods," I read. "Oh wow. I think that's my Mennonite."

"Naomi Petersheim," he said. "She put together the most popular stall in the market this year, hands down. It's not just a shop, it's an experience."

"I had no idea," I said as we elbowed our way to the front of the line for a closer look. "I thought everything she made got sold at their family store in Viroqua."

"Tourist traffic slows down out there this time of year," Freddie said.

Naomi displayed the fruits of her labor from my kitchen construction site on hand-hewn wood shelves and neatly stacked blocks of bailed hay.

A pyramid of Homey Naomi's Crabapple Maple Jelly crowned a large wooden barrel, beside smaller jars of pricey venison, baby boar, and wild hare demiglace.

Wedges of homemade farm cheese had been cut from large wheels, with cubes for sampling set out in small wooden bowls according to age and sharpness, along with a selection of jerkies, sausages, and Homey Naomi's Venison Slim Jims. Packets of dried Hmong-Foraged Herbal Cold & Flu Tea and bags of dried Hmong-Foraged Field Mushrooms fanned out beside a selection of soups, stews, and bone broths bursting forth from a freezer case.

I never imagined Naomi to be an entrepreneur, but it all came together for me in an aha moment. Though momentarily she would be expected to produce a large brood of children whose raising would surely occupy nearly all her time and energy until the moment of death, she seized upon this fleeting window in early marriage to capitalize on other talents.

Elijah and their friends bustled about singing a lovely a cappella rendition of "O Holy Night" in pidgin German while serving samples on wooden trays.

Canada Goose Fois Gras drove demand for the entire line of locally sourced items, though stocks of the highly seasonal delicacy were running unfortunately low. Elijah gave us the last few coveted samples on fresh-baked sprouted wheat crackers topped with a spoonful of Quick Pickled Root Vegetable Relish. "There's more of everything at home," he said.

"Where's Naomi?" I asked.

"In the back. She worries the attention isn't modest."

"See you at the barn dance, buddy," Freddie said with a friendly tap on Elijah's tray.

"You guys go to a barn dance together?" I asked.

"Everybody heads over there after the market," he said. "That's where I got to be All Square US Wheelchair Champ."

"I don't know a thing about square dancing, but I've always wanted one of those skirts."

"It's the spirit of community and resilience you're after," Freddie said. "I'm thinking about building my congressional campaign on it."

"You've got my vote, Freddie Weissfluggen."

"Good, because I'll be looking for someone by my side once I start campaigning."

"By your side? What do you mean by that, exactly?" I asked.

"Door knocking solo for village alderman was way too much," he said. "You're looking at an undertaking ten times that size for a congressional run."

I wasn't a hundred percent sure if that was a marriage proposal, but I hadn't taken Freddie all that seriously up until then. Abel Dreaux owned a piece of my heart I'd never exposed to anyone in our late-night radio calls, despite his disinterest in providing much more in the cold light of day. Here stood a real live square-dance champ determined to go the distance.

"Everything works," Freddie assured me cheerfully during one of our early dates at the Hubbard Avenue Diner, smack in the heart of Littleburgh. He showed me off to passersby in the front window like a prize he'd won. "I do need some pharmaceutical assistance, but I'm confident you'll be pleased with the results. Not that I'm trying to rush you."

"I'm having brain freeze." I pushed away the large chocolate malt I sucked through a straw. "I'm not necessarily thinking clearly right now, but you are cute."

"I'm determined as heck," he assured me. "Nobody says I won't walk again and I'm taking that as two thumbs up, green light go."

He'd signed up for a promising spinal cord injury trial at the university combining electrical stimulation with stem cell therapy to help the body reorganize itself through adaptive changes.

"It's not a matter of if, but when. Wouldn't it be something to make a walk to the podium for my big acceptance speech?"

"You should wait until you earn the speaker's gavel. That would make the history books."

"Hot dog, you're good."

"I'm learning to own the story of my life," I said. "It's this method one of my bosses came up with for being in charge of your own destiny."

"I never needed any special method for that," he told me. "You stay alive. You never flinch."

I felt another galvanizing charge between us as we left Naomi's winter market booth, burdened only by the heavy shopping bags I'd brought for the Hmong hanging from the back of his chair.

"Hey, Freddie! Hey, Jaycee! Whoo-hoo, over here!" yelled Kayla Flynn, waving her arms to get our attention without losing her place in line.

"Does she follow you and whoo-hoo wherever you go?" I had yet to meet the elusive Ronnie Weissfluggen, but here was Kayla out and about on her own again, giving us little choice but to offer a quick hello.

"How crazy is this?" she said, leaning down to give Freddie her signature extra-long hug. "What are you guys doing here?"

"It's a winter market. We came for some winter market things," I said flatly.

"What about you?" Freddie chimed in off the awkward pause.

"I can't live without Homey Naomi's Cream of Wild Mushroom Soup," she gushed. "I'm stocking up before she sells out again." Freddie smiled weakly. Kayla smiled back. I wasn't feeling one bit smiley; something was very wrong here, though I couldn't quite put my finger on it.

Shortly after I'd first spotted Kayla and Ronnie on Freddie's Littleburgh Thanksgiving parade float, Freddie and I ran into her while on our date at the big Badgers–Gophers game that gripped the entire town.

"A brat is not a hot dog," Freddie explained to me firmly while we waited in line at halftime to order ours with caramelized onions and sauerkraut. "Brats are sausages cooked raw in pilsner or lager, preferably New Glarus, before they're grilled off."

"I don't drink alcohol," I said.

"Why not?"

"Let's say I finished up early."

"Got it," he said. "The beer mostly cooks out, which is why Sconnies like to wash our brats down with more beer."

"Hey, Freddie Spaghetti," Kayla interrupted, eavesdropping on our conversation while standing behind us in line. "Wait, how do you two know each other?" she puzzled once she had our attention.

"He's my alderman," I said. I didn't know how much she had overheard, but I was not pleased to find her within earshot given the sensitive subject.

"Such a small world," Kayla said, leaning down to give Freddie a big hug. *Did she hug all men a beat or so too long or only her fiancé's brother?*

Now she'd appeared again by happenstance, wearing a flaming red Santa's hat and flashing Christmas bulb earrings, in case you were thinking of making any other person in the general vicinity your center of attention.

Freddie and I said our goodbyes and left her waiting in line at Naomi's stall to go browse some craft booths around the corner. "So, when were you planning on telling me what the deal is there?" I asked casually.

He looked back to make sure she was out of sight. "She and I had a thing. It was a long time before she ever got with Ronnie, but we kept it under wraps for a lot of reasons," he said.

"Such as?"

"She worried my story might overshadow her career."

"Her career in editing optometry videos?"

"She wanted a lot more at the time," he said.

"She still does. I'm pretty sure she's not going to find it."

"I hadn't heard from her in forever until I started dating you," he said. "She must be stalking my social media. I check in a lot—people want to know what their head alderman is up to, catch up with him if they can."

"I don't know, Freddie," I said, shaking my head. "Sometimes we think something's over because that's what we want to believe."

"She called it off with me, could not have made things clearer. I'm not proud of hooking up with her from time to time after that, but I swear it's been years."

Having seen Kayla's "student film," I understood how persuasive she could be with her clothes off.

"Nowadays, I do not see or talk to her at all, unless Ronnie puts something together," he said. "Even then, I keep it short and sweet."

"Then why did she start stalking you all of a sudden?"

"It might be something about you." He shrugged, taking his phone from his pocket to show me a text he'd received. "Yep, she just hit me up for sex. She's done it every time she's seen us together."

After all he'd been through, I did not feel it was my place to let Freddie Weissfluggen know he had been victimized by an emotional vampire unlikely to ever take her knee off his neck, borrowing a phrase from Mr. Y. He would have to figure out his own story and whom he wanted at the center.

"You do you, Freddie, but I can't have these theatrics at work," I said. "I'm dealing with a lot there already, and I don't need her running around telling people I stole her boyfriend."

Freddie was younger than me, Kayla was younger than he, and none of it was a good look. I'd told Freddie up front I had been dating Abel Dreaux until recently and I didn't know how that might play out in the end. Either way, things could get awkward with Abel's department falling under Freddie's supervision.

"I like being with you," I said. "I can't commit to anything more."

"Yet. I'll just have to keep working on wearing you down," he said with a confident grin.

We happened upon a Hmong booth selling winter foliage, berries, and pinecones. Every variety of foraged evergreen branch and stem—dogwood, birch, willow, and hazel—exploded over the brims of five-gallon white plastic buckets.

A Hmong woman in her late thirties braided variegated ivy around bendy red berried-holly branches to make wreaths studded with fragrant sprigs of eucalyptus, rosemary, and bay.

She displayed them on a table alongside handcrafted bark sailboats I clearly recognized as the kind my Hmong had gifted me, each filled with a selection of nature's décor by custom order at the booth.

Two preteen girls tending the table intermittently returned to their schoolwork, pulling pens and notebooks from a pair of Wonderful Lavender book bags I was happy to see put to good use.

"This looks like my family," I whispered to Freddie.

"Awesome job with the school supplies," he said. "We've got a new program underway to try to get all the kids registered in school, but we get a lot of resistance when they don't have anything they need."

"I hadn't realized it was that bad," I said. "Maybe I should have saved some of the baby stuff for Naomi and Elijah to pass around Viroqua."

"Nah, it's a little bright for their crew," Freddie said. "Anyway, they like to get things done among themselves."

After quietly stashing the bags under the table, Freddie and I had nearly reached the exit at the far end of the central corridor when one of the Hmong girls tapped my shoulder and produced a pair of fragrant holly wreaths in either hand.

Her little sister handed me a bundle of mistletoe, rosehips, chestnuts, and hawthorn in white paper tied with knotted vines. It looked like dried potpourri and smelled like the season.

"My mother says thank you for everything," the older girl said shyly before covering her mouth from the heady embarrassment of it all. The two of them giggled and scurried off.

"Looks like you've got some fans there," said Freddie.

"I don't know how they've been looking out for me all this time when I never see them at all."

"You're only ever alone here if you really insist on it," Freddie said.

I did not want to view Freddie as a backup plan, but with winter closing in like an ice tomb it seemed apropos in the moment to crown each other king and queen of the night market and get on with it. With a pair of matching holly wreaths on our heads, we prepared to face the music.

THE ANNUAL HOLIDAY DANCE AT the village barn rollicked with jigging, clogging, and country waltzing set to upbeat Christmas tunes.

My first try at a wheelchair square dance, I had trouble adhering to the partner instructions to either hold on to the back of Freddie's chair or stand and push it. I struggled mightily to keep up with a manic caller directing "Rockin' Around the Christmas Tree" and nearly flew off the back in either case. I would have been mowed down by another chair on an allemande left had Freddie not swung me around on a crossover circulate and put me in his lap against regulations for a final round of do-si-dos.

"If he calls a Patrick Swayze, get ready for a Jennifer Grey," he said, raising his arms to demonstrate an above-head lift.

*This was a guy with some serious upper-body strength.*

"Our official state dance is the polka," Freddie informed me. "Some people aren't sure it merits that honor over the Chicken Dance or the Hokie Pokie, but we can't let you go home without trying your hand at it, no siree Bob."

Miners, lumberjacks, and factory workers immigrating from Europe in the nineteenth century brought along their rollicking couples' folk dance at two-four time, flaunting the staid minuets and quadrilles of the abandoned aristocracy in humble village taverns across the Midwest.

Exhausted from her earlier triumph at the market, Naomi was about to relinquish her closing polka with the seven-foot-tall Elijah, but I spotted Kayla in line at the bar giving me the stink eye and declined.

She'd brought along the fabulous Mr. Weissfluggen Buick, Junior, who seemed a bit bored with the goings-on, compared to, let's say, an important potluck at the dealership.

"You two headed to a toga party?" Ronnie asked.

"Just playing around." Freddie reflexively removed the wreath from his head, and with that released the both of us from the brief, magical bond of our Hmong winter forest spell.

He must have felt a buzz in his pants just then, pulling his cell from his pocket and checking a text for yet another salacious offer he couldn't refuse—or maybe I imagined that entirely. I took off my wreath, too, and hung it from the side of Freddie's chair.

IT TAKES A SPECIAL KIND of girl to hit up her fiancé's brother for sex while he's out on a date with her boss and show up later to give it another shot using the would-be cuckold as a beard.

I shared that precise sentiment with Barbara Walters later that night when I drafted another email to quell a craving for a nice rum toddy or two to close out a day that left me both privately vexed and determined to fight back hard.

*Dear Barbara Walters:*

*I once heard you quoted as saying, "Deep breaths are very helpful at shallow parties." I recently went looking for some of your more famous expressions to catch Casey Klinkhoffer in the act next time she has the unmitigated gall to claim another woman's ideas as her own.*

*She and Kayla Flynn are quite the pair, each with a unique reason to diminish my prospects in love and in life for the simple reason that so far, I've allowed it.*

*I promise you here and now neither will succeed going forward because I am a fearless warrior.*

*Standing tall in the sisterhood,*

*Jaycee Grayson, VP Global Entertainment, Wonderful Girls*

Flagrantly defying Meredith's advice, I pulled the card with Mrs. Happy's Arizona post office box from a coat pocket.

I had been thinking about her earlier, listening to that glorious music in Naomi's market stall, and couldn't help but envision Happy Lindstrom calling attention to her wares with clever sketches performed in that drive-in decades earlier. A local working gal, she, too, had wanted something more for her own family.

Had she been keeping a tighter grip on Hank's drinking by enlisting his partnership with her business venture? Had he lost both his church choir gig and day job, threatening the family's reputation and finances before Happy saved the day?

Women are survivors as a rule, and whether Happy Lindstrom was a real person or the byproduct of a recent college graduate's desperation to hit on something bigger, her story began to make perfect sense to me either way.

"*Dear Mrs. Happy,*"

I wrote on a piece of Crane's stationery trimmed in cranberry and gold for the season.

*"I don't know if you remember me, but I believe our fates crossed recently in Frank Lloyd Wright's kitchen. I wanted to send holiday greetings from Littleburgh and let you know I have been treating Marion Mahony Griffin's secret architectural gem well. If I have the wrong person, my apologies. Until we meet again, Jaycee Grayson, VP Global Entertainment, Wonderful Girls."*

I licked the envelope and affixed a Santa stamp, leaving it in the mailbox for Harlan Meidlemeister to pick up in the morning.

I went out back to the lake with my little bark sailboat, filled with the contents of the fragrant twig and berry packet the little Hmong sisters had given me.

Lighting a candle for my only niece, Lila May Grayson-O'Cochlain, I slid a paper cup over top to shield the flame from the wind and secured it into the hull with a few drips of candle wax before setting the vessel free on the rolling waves of the chilly black lake, hardening to ice beneath the surface.

The flame appeared to power the sails for some time as the boat did not capsize, nor did the light die, as the tiny craft sailed off into the fog.

CHAPTER THIRTEEN

# Louise Atwood, the Most Wonderful Girl at the Symphony with Oboe Dreams and Pot de Crème Wishes

KAYLA FLYNN LACKED THE NATIVE imagination to see her future in a former doll hospital where hopeful children sent injured Wonderful Girls for refurbishing. The service had all but disappeared over the years in favor of a loyalty program offering a revolving assortment of brand-new, healthy dolls for a very attractive price.

Holdovers from a lost era, hollow body cavities and fleshy limbs dangled from peg boards in various stages of disrepair, with overfilled boxes of severed heads organized by hair length and wig color scattered around the musty warehouse as if by a serial killer with a severe case of OCD.

"Brr. It's chilly over here," Kayla announced on arrival.

"I'll order you a Wonderful Lavender space heater," I said.

She was probably parroting Casey, who came to resent her

own proposal to go halfsies on Kayla's time shortly after the swindled studio expansion project reverted to me.

As promised, Rebecca had casually offered to underwrite the tech-forward Brand projects I'd proposed as a means of inspiring confidence with the big boss during his upcoming visit, leaving Trudi little choice but to acquiesce.

"Trudi wants us to use this space to work more efficiently on the Brand Management project," I told Kayla. "It's all very high priority, and it has to be in the can by the time we break for the holiday."

"Casey says shooting the catalogue is high priority," she countered.

Among her lowly move-in and clean-up tasks, she organized garbage bags filled with assorted doll underpants by size and style, all well beneath her pay grade judging by the occasional audible harumph. "This place feels like a really long walk back and forth to the Photo Studios, especially in foul weather conditions."

"We'll look into digging you a tunnel and put another Wonderful Lavender space heater down there. Remind me to talk to Facilities."

"I don't think you understand what's coming," she said. "They say we can expect another polar vortex from the North Pole. Or was it the South Pole? One of the poles. There's going to be a lot of snow."

"I'm not looking forward to that, either, Kayla, but the primary job description at your level isn't 'Whiny Weather Girl.' It's 'Creative Problem Solver.'"

"What? Casey said I'm Associate Producer."

"I'd have started you as an assistant something or other, to be honest, made you earn the bump to associate. Filmmaking is a craft. The only way to learn it is through a long-held system of faithful apprenticeship."

"Apprenticeship?" she sniffed. "I have plenty of skills and experience already."

"Great! Let's focus on your most important contribution, that upbeat positive attitude of yours. You've shared your larger goals, and I'm going to help you reach them, even if I do have to kick your sweet little butt."

Another audible harumph, followed by an ever-so-slight eye roll.

"I might be careful with that one," Louise Atwood later advised me. "She and Prudence have gotten chummy lately, and apparently Kayla has been complaining about suffering some anxiety working under you. She says her hair is falling out."

"That is unfortunate," I said, genuinely alarmed. "It's a little stringy already."

"Stop me if this is none of my business, but are you dating her fiancé's brother?" Louise whispered, although we were alone in my office with the door closed.

"We're friends," I said.

"Kayla told Prudence she's stressed enough with the wedding plans, and now with the boss involved in her personal life she feels like she has to be 'on' all the time."

"Wow. That is quite a unique spin on things," I said.

"I had a feeling. Honestly, I don't know why Prudence would want to entertain that kind of gossip."

Prudence resented reporting to me perhaps even more than Kayla within the new structure and said so in a lengthy email to Trudi and me.

"I have devoted my entire life to the literature, and it hurts me deeply to see these beloved heroines pulled from our pages only to be publicly debased via garish, money-grubbing technologies," she repeated over and over, employing any number of similar words and phrases.

Prudence's proficiency with a thesaurus outmatched only her flagrant disregard for economy of language. *How had she fit so many big ideas in those tiny storybooks?*

Louise, on the other hand, shaped up not only as an unexpected lieutenant, but also the only colleague among five hundred or so to offer me a social invitation.

Kayla had left early for her class in making the origami flowers she planned to use at her wedding to cut down on the cost of real ones. She often multitasked while in meetings and on conference calls, absently folding pieces of pastel-colored paper into springtime buds in lieu of taking the team notes I'd asked her to keep.

As for Prudence, she always knocked off at the stroke of five to mind her strongly held work-life balance.

"Did you have any interest in the symphony?" Louise asked.

"Me?" I looked around, certain we had a visiting ghost. Maybe one of the dismembered Wonderful Girls self-healed and sprung to life in some low-budget horror movie I lived in.

"The Doctor is off at a chronic kidney disease conference in Akron," Louise said. "They have a sandwich counter in the theater lobby with the most divine chocolate pots de crème. The guest conductor is a woman, which is far too rare. They're doing an Elgar cello concerto and Tchaikovsky's Symphony No. 5."

"You had me at chocolate pot de crème," I said.

AT NEARLY A CENTURY OLD, the ninety-one-member Madison Symphony was a highly respected regional orchestra in residence at the Overture Center, an elaborate performing arts complex situated on the Isthmus, with seven theater spaces and five galleries including the Madison Museum of Modern Art.

"Happy Lindstrom made sure employees would always have access to discounted tickets," Louise told me as we entered the twenty-two-hundred-seat Overture Hall among Madison's glitterati, hugging our coats against a damp, cold drizzle over a muddy layer of snow on the ground.

A massive lobby curtain constructed of two-thousand-pound annealed glass panels gave way to a soaring view of the capitol, spotlit in splashes of red and green for the holiday season. "She and Hank were apparently big patrons of the arts," she added.

"Apparently? Didn't you work with her at one time?"

"Oh, I never met her in person," she said. "We only started putting the storybooks in the doll boxes ten years ago, and Trudi needed an editor."

"I heard you and she were high school friends."

"We were, but I went away to Stanford, and I'd been teaching at Berkeley for several years when she reached out."

"A fellow Californian? Get out."

"The Doctor hails from the Santa Barbara area," she said with a chuckle. "We are fond of the coast but made our way back here to set up an old-fashioned country practice after Prudence was born. Other than two horses and a smelly old Lab, she's our only."

"Wow. That is not at all the picture I had in place for you."

"It's terrible how we put each other in tiny little boxes," she agreed. "Maybe we're so busy doing that with the dolls we forget to be fully fleshed women in the workplace."

Once again, I had to conclude that Casey either had the story all mixed up herself or purposely laid out a convoluted version of things as a trap. Maybe she wanted to discourage me from even trying to penetrate a perceived wall of resistance among these supposed lifelong pals to create some false alliance between the two of us.

I wonder if Trudi knew I'd been asking around about the company's origins and the physical whereabouts of its founder.

Lately the door to Happy's grand corner office had been closed, except when schoolchildren came around in tour groups. Shown around the Wonderful Mrs. Happy's legendary workspace, they sampled candy kisses foil-wrapped in shades of Wonderful Lavender. I suspected the whole suite had been constructed not as a working office, but an elaborate stage set.

"I'm so grateful you and I got a chance to work together!" Louise said.

She felt underused in her previous role, especially after Prudence came aboard, but welcomed the opportunity to work alongside her loquacious daughter and kept her own dissatisfaction under wraps. "Obviously, I'm a music lover, so I'd love to get involved with that. I did want to share that I'm proficient on the oboe."

"Woodwind instruments are always intriguing," I said dubiously. "Right now, we just need a few lines of dialogue written for the ZZZZ-Zoom! prototypes."

"Screenwriting, how exciting!" she said. "I'd also love to give some notes on this top-secret feature script of yours."

"Oh sure," I said, wondering how she'd gotten wind of that. "I mean, if you think you can keep your lips zipped about the details."

"Mum's the word," she said as the lights dimmed, muting the hum of the crowd. "I know Prudence can be snippy, but that's the generation. She'll come around when she sees the opportunities you're bringing."

I FIGURED THAT MIGHT BE a while once Prudence joined Kayla to report me to HR for compromising their long-term health. Three different types of lethal spores had been affirmatively identified in the warehouse with a mold test kit Kayla purchased online.

She demanded reimbursement of forty-nine ninety-nine, plus shipping and tax, and another six hundred for follow-up stain-testing at a mail-order lab, pending future medical damages totaling an unknown sum. Potentially leading to liver cancer, should she somehow ingest a large quantity of moldy food, the moldy air had aggravated her seasonal allergies well ahead of schedule.

I advised her to spritz her desk with Clorox and double up on the Claritin. "She said you recommended a lethal drug overdose," Trina Oldham told me when I sat down in her office for our overdue meet and greet.

Trina wanted to "visit intriguing opportunities" for "strengthening supervisory performance" of "promising newer talent." This was HR doublespeak for she'd shortly be issuing a formal reprimand she'd already written, and it was important she first pretend to hear my side.

Kayla had neither prioritized an upbeat positive attitude nor faithful apprenticeship of senior teammates, according to her dated and time-stamped documentation of *my* assorted infringements serving as a cover sheet for *her* deluded manifesto of self-entitlement.

"We'd like you to offer Kayla a more meaningful workplace experience," Trina said.

"I'd like to offer her the Presidency of the United States," I replied. "Should we go through the usual process or march her up to Washington and demand they print out the nuclear codes for her origami wedding flowers?"

She and Casey both had to be in business with Trudi for anybody to receive this cockamamy diatribe as anything other than the ludicrous ranting of an oversexed madwoman with a chronic runny nose.

"You're her manager," Trina insisted. "You need to manage her learning experience so that she can be more effective in the performance of her job."

"She doesn't want learning, experience, or her job. She wants my job, without performing anything, except the occasional sneezing and coughing fit."

Where Trudi wore a fixed look of pleasant surprise, Trina's expressions ran the gamut between somewhat perplexed and deeply concerned. Beyond that, the only way to tell them apart was an active cold sore on Trina's upper lip, though you couldn't count on that with the good antiviral medications available over the counter.

"Did you tell Kayla you wanted to 'kick her sweet little butt'?" Trina read verbatim from her own neatly hand-scribbled notes on a white legal pad.

"That's a bit out of context."

"Threatening language is never appropriate." She talked so softly I wondered if she had extra-thin office walls and an office mole on either side listening in with a glass cup.

I once sat next to her table in the noisy lunchroom, though, and had to read her lips to get that she wanted to borrow my ketchup.

"Kayla says she wants a future in showbiz," I said firmly. "Candy-coating things would do her a great disservice. Getting back to Prudence, I'd like to focus her lifetime devotion to the literature somewhere beyond endless love letters to herself."

"I see." Trina laid down her pencil, signaling the importance of taking things off the record. "Are you aware that your employment contract has a moral turpitude clause?"

"Moral turpitude? Have I done something criminal, vile, or socially deviant I should know about?"

She shrugged. "I just wanted to toss that out as a reminder that we hold Wonderful management to an unusually high ethical standard."

"I'M NOT GOING TO DIGNIFY any of this with a response," Meredith said on the phone later that night. "Your boss may be on the warpath, but she can't up and sever a perfectly valid employment contract without cause. Hang on a sec."

Exasperated, she picked up a ringing landline. "Hello? Yes, but I already told someone they'll need to let themselves in with a pass key. Room nine sixteen."

She came back to her cell phone. "Sorry, I'm in Atlanta on business. Where were we?"

"My perfectly valid employment contract."

"Iron-clad, with a pay-or-play option to renew," she said. "They can only get away with firing you with cause."

"What kind of cause?"

"You have the company manual, read it," she said, unusually wound up, even for her. "You can't steal their trade secrets and sell them to the competition, that kind of thing."

"What about my drinking history? Kayla might have heard me talking to Freddie and went and yakked about it."

"So what?" she asked, incredulous. "Workers have medical issues outside the office. Have you shown up naked at work high on meth and operated the heavy machinery?"

"Don't give me any ideas," I said with a sigh. "At least now we know they've been jerking me around from day one. My boss perceives anybody at her level who isn't a trusted old pal to be a clear and present danger."

"Hang on a sec," said Meredith again. She called out to someone at her hotel room door. "Hello, I'm in the bedroom, please come in."

She came back to the cell phone, extremely harried. "Jaycee, I have to go. Hotel security is here."

"What? Why?"

"I'll call you back."

Ten minutes later, she returned the call, sounding much more relaxed. "Sorry about that. Have you noticed how high off the ground the beds are nowadays at the better hotels?"

"Not really."

"Well, they are. Try sitting on the edge of one at a Ritz-Carlton or Mandarin Oriental, your feet won't come near the floor. Anyway, I reached out earlier to grab my glasses off the nightstand, and I fell off."

"Oh my God, Meredith."

"I tried to get up, but I was completely stuck between the bed and the nightstand with literally no way to wedge myself out."

People told this kind of anecdote at Betty Ford, with a punchline about realizing it was time to get sober. I wondered if she'd lost any of the baby weight, or if she still felt so torn up about the loss she had to stuff down her feelings with more and more food. How many hotel security guys had it taken to get her off the floor?

"I hope you didn't hurt yourself," I managed. "How did we spend that whole time talking about my stupid job problems with you lying there trapped?"

"How we do things, you and me. I guess I'm feeling like my old self again."

"Did you get a decent dinner at least?"

"I haven't had any dinner," she said. "I only got out of client meetings an hour ago. Not all of us have a professional chef in residence."

"We could have had you," I reminded her. After spending her junior year at the Sorbonne, Meredith lined up a job in a Paris patisserie while taking cooking classes at the Cordon Bleu. "I never knew why you chickened out of that. Something about you couldn't keep staying with your French family?"

"I lied about that," she said. "I had everything all worked out but got scared of what would happen if I didn't keep walking that straight line, dead ahead."

"I would have helped you. That was our plan."

I worked as Meredith's sous chef when I was coming up in the business and wanted to compensate for the cash she'd cheerfully fork over when I couldn't make the rent.

Playing the charming maîtresse d'hôtel at her extravagant dinner parties, I would not only fetch and serve, but also clean her house the next day.

We joked about opening a fabulous teahouse together when we got old, the kind where you couldn't get a table unless you knew someone—until Butch came along and derailed all that with the squeal of a hot karaoke mic.

"Let's both try living healthier, though," I proposed on the phone.

"Just a freak accident," Meredith said, fully entrenched in her story. "It could have happened to anyone."

MY PERSONAL COMMITMENT TO A healthier lifestyle lasted until the following evening, when Freddie took me to The Hilltop in the nearby Village of Cross Plains. "You've never done supper club?" he asked, incredulous. "Put on your hungry pants, girlie."

Sharing plentiful taxidermy, wood paneling, and year-round Christmas lights, Wisconsin's kitschy supper clubs exuded a cool sixties vibe, holdovers of a bygone era when family-owned taverns and dancehalls served a weekly ritual of Friday fish fry, Saturday prime rib, and Sunday broasted chicken.

"We'll start with the cheese ball and a relish tray, both givens," Freddie said, giddy as a schoolboy. "I'll have a hand-muddled brandy old-fashioned, also a given."

"I'll have a Shirley Temple," I said weakly. "Extra cherries, please." Crowded into a corner of the bar, we waited for a table with sufficient aisle space to accommodate his chair.

"Oof, I'm sorry," he said. "Does visiting a bar freak you out?"

"Nothing I can't handle. Wisconsin has a lot of bars."

"Second only to Montana and North Dakota per capita," he said.

"All of them combined couldn't serve me enough booze once I get started. When do you think we'll get a table?"

"We can seat you now if you can share the long one in the back with another party," the hostess interjected. Unfortunately, Casey Klinkhoffer with her husband and another couple comprised the other party, stowing their coats near the front door.

"That's Eugenie Dreaux and her husband, George," Freddie said.

Ever the politician, Freddie steered me from that awkward table arrangement without missing a beat, while also exhibiting a definite interest in appeasing the interlopers joining us for a chat.

"Hey, we thought we'd skip out on the crowd here, maybe check out the Tornado Room downtown," he fibbed. "You go ahead and take our table, have fun."

"You're the man, Freddie Spaghetti," said Casey as Marshall and Pendleton buzzed about underfoot. "I've got to get some food in these two or else shoot myself in the head." She gave me a forced smile and shepherded her brood to the back table, while Eugenie and I paused to exchange glances.

"Do you know Jaycee Grayson?" Freddie asked, cutting through the discomfort like a human butter knife. "She's a good friend of your dad's."

I searched for a hint of her father in her sweet, heart-shaped face, but quickly remembered the two of them shared no more blood than she and I did. "Nice to meet you, Eugenie," I said. "Your dad and I dropped by to see you a while back, but we didn't find you at home."

"I remember," she said. "My daughter had the sniffles, so we put her down early. I guess our wires got crossed." For some reason, I believed her. She had no trouble whatsoever looking me unapologetically in the eye.

She and Casey had been childhood friends at Sunday school in the village church, where Eugenie played piano, and Casey ran the stage productions.

I wondered if Casey knew the circumstances of Eugenie's birth, something the eldest Dreaux daughter hadn't learned herself until she was fifteen. She found some old diaries in which her young mother had selfishly preserved details better stowed in the vault and never spoken of again. Eugenie took the news hard, of course.

"I sat her down and told her she's my daughter and I'm her dad and that's that," Abel told me, visibly guilt-ridden. "I made her promise never to tell anyone anything different. I know that was wrong, but I was trying to protect her."

Eugenie never forgave either parent for deceiving her and hadn't invited them to a wedding reception her sisters threw after she ran off to the Bahamas to elope with George Gissinglund, a boy she'd met in college.

"He likes to talk a lot," Abel said. "He's a banker by trade, though, so she'll never go hungry."

With the birth of her six-year-old daughter, Zoey, the ice began to melt among the three of them—but it froze back over harder than ever with the ugly divorce between Sally and her dad, especially after gun-toting Robyn rode into the picture on the back of Abel's bike.

"Can I meet the movie lady?" Eugenie's husband, George, stepped up to the bar and extended me a hand. He appeared to be a big hand extender as a rule, a heftier sort with preternaturally bushy eyebrows and a forceful grin. "You know, my wife and daughter do a little modeling here and there."

"We've posed for your catalogue a couple of times, thanks to Casey," Eugenie said, brushing him off. "It's an awful lot of fun."

"Eugenie auditioned for *Star Search* as a kid," George added. "You people didn't want her."

"I didn't work on *Star Search*," I said, not about to take the heat for dashing Eugenie Dreaux's dreams of becoming a child star at a time when I myself was only in the twelfth grade. Though Abel had mentioned she'd majored in musical theater in college, I was surprised to learn he had spoken much about me.

"Eugenie sings like a bird, so does Zoey, if you ever needed anything like that," George said.

I never expected to meet an aggressive stage parent while perched on a barstool next to a stuffed elk's head protruding from the wall, but I should probably steel myself for that kind of thing now that we are headed into production.

"Shoot me a voice demo, I'll take a listen." I handed Eugenie my Wonderful business card. "We're not in full swing yet, but I guess you never know. And say hi to your dad for me."

I wished I hadn't thrown that last thing in the minute it came out of my mouth.

"Oh sure. He and my mom have Zoey tonight, so we'll see them later at the house."

He *and* her mom were babysitting. Why did they both need to do that; was the child some tapdancing whirling dervish? I get that Eugenie and her husband wanted a date night, such as it was, but it occurred to me that Abel and Sally might also be having one.

"I MISS YOU, SNOW WHITE," Abel said when he called very late that night, supposedly by coincidence.

"Are you serious?" I said groggily, annoyed he felt free to wake me up out of the blue. I hadn't heard from him in weeks, and I'd never once spoken to him on my cell phone. "Where did you even get my number?"

"I'm a cop," he said.

"In that case, what took you so long to call?"

"Word is you've been dating my boss," he replied.

"Word is you've been dating your wife."

"Sally? Why would I date her?"

"You don't seem to have a problem living with her."

I heard the flick of a Zippo lighter, and he took a long draw off a cigarette.

"You're not even awake right now, are you?" I said, already knowing the answer. "This is *bananas*, Copper."

No response. Another pensive draw of the cigarette. "If you want to talk to me, next time try it in the daylight."

I hung up. He called back!

"It's very late," I hissed.

"Too bad. I want to make a deal with you."

"You don't have any cards to play," I shot back.

"How about you come out to my place and I'll show you my lighthouse?"

"That's not a deal, it's a vaguely intriguing opening offer," I said.

"Why keep fighting it? You know you want to."

"I want a lot of things that aren't good for me," I said. "Fighting them is second nature. Why don't you ask me again when you're not on drugs?"

No response. "Please put out the cigarette before you conk out. I hate you but I need you alive. Abel!"

"Yes."

"Put out the cigarette!"

"Roger that, Two-Two-Two."

"Nighty-night, Two-Oh-One, over and out."

If this meant Abel and I were dating again, it also meant it was time to make a choice between him and Freddie.

I wondered if Abel had been more involved than he cared to admit with both his ex-wife and his ex-girlfriend all along. Nor could I escape the sinking feeling that Freddie was obsessed with his brother's fiancée, whether he even liked her, and would eventually cave to the relentless sexual pressure she showed no outward interest in ever withdrawing.

Would Casey tell Kayla she spotted me out with Freddie—or should I be more concerned she'd report back to work that I'd been out drinking at a bar? If so, was all of this put together the textbook HR definition of "moral turpitude"?

The only thing I knew for sure is I didn't care.

One rarely falls asleep laughing out loud, outside of a mental health facility. Maybe I'd taken up residence in one of Wisconsin's old-school supper club sanitariums and didn't know it yet.

CHAPTER FOURTEEN

# Summer Jessup, the Most Wonderful Girl with a Threatening Tomato Pincushion on Her Wrist

SHORT-HANDED IN A MINIMALLY FUNCTIONING warehouse studio, I toiled alone deep into the night on my Island of Misfit Toys preparing for Jonathan P. Park's upcoming visit.

"Reducing your staff constitutes a demotion, and they haven't established sufficient grounds for that," Meredith advised me over the phone. "I can put them on notice we consider any such shenanigans to fall under the equitable doctrine of prevention."

"The who what?"

"It excuses a contracting party from performing as agreed when the other party prevents them from doing so. It's a way of crying breach of contract, but I don't know we want to fire the first shot just yet."

She was probably rushing around the house gathering clothes that would stretch to fit within reason to take on holiday in the California wine country.

"Butch has a long list of vintages he wants for the new cellar he has underway in the spare bedroom," she told me. Earmarked as the baby's room, it had evolved into another playroom for Butch. "He's designed quite the sophisticated setup, with floor-to-ceiling wine racks and its own cooling system. It's nice to see him excited about something again."

Butch rewarding their loss with his personal home bacchanalia felt like too much to bear, but at least he was unlikely to cancel on her at the last minute.

"I'm sorry you and I won't be together," I said. "I can't remember the last Christmas we spent apart."

"Just keep your head down and forge ahead," she said. "Your boss can play all the games she wants, but if she intends to force you out, she'll have to do better than scaring you."

"Scaring me? That's a laugh," I said. "I never thought running my own show would be so entertaining."

At a brown bag lunch meeting, Prudence worked herself into a frenzy over how her tenuous association with me might impact her future career prospects.

"Somebody should tell Jonathan that nobody volunteered for this team," she said, hovering over a pile of walnuts like a covetous squirrel. "How did you intend to address any misperception he may have around that?"

"I hadn't thought about it."

"Don't you think you should?"

"Why don't you put together a deck walking him through some of the changes we've made across the company?" I suggested. "Show me a draft when you're done."

"I think I'll show it to Trudi first, and then give it to you," she said, not the most artful of backstabbers. "Then I'll show it to Trudi again."

"And what is your ideal contribution to the project?" I asked Kayla. She still had issues with the insufficient heating and would often wrap herself in a crocheted throw, exuding all the fashion sense of a living-room couch. "Anything you like," I urged her. "Use your imagination."

"Wow, okay. In that case, I'm confident in my ability to executive produce."

"That's certainly imaginative," I said. "What did you have in mind?"

"I could start with the music video."

"What music video is that, Kayla?"

"Aren't we doing one?"

"For what purpose?"

Kayla had requested a private sit-down with Jonathan to share her work, which was followed by the cold realization that that would be difficult to do in her case. He might respond to an experimental eyewear commercial she'd shot out of focus as a clever visual metaphor, but she wasn't taking any chances.

"We're doing a theme song for the new movie. Shouldn't we have a video to go with it?"

"What an excellent idea, Kayla." *I said that part out loud and kept "knock me over with a feather" to myself.*

Diarra and Louise not only tweaked the hush-hush movie script based on the real-life adventures of Anastasia D'Alessandro, but also collaborated on "Anastasia's Theme," to include with the purchase of the proposed character doll and debut with Kayla's visuals across our social channels.

They recorded a rough scratch track over the phone, accompanied by Diarra's ukulele with Louise on oboe and took turns singing the rhyming verses:

> *She once felt out of place,*
> *And rocketed to outer space,*
> *Orbiting the moon and the stars.*
> *Minimizing irradiation,*
> *The International Space Station*
> *Looked a lot closer than Mars.*
> *There's nowhere she'd rather be,*

*Than hanging out in gravity,*

*Dodging all the flying debris.*

*She's a footnote in history,*

*Eliminating every mystery*

*As to spacesuits made in Size She.*

*She's a wonderful girl, fully interplanetary,*

*Defying her atypical neurodiversity.*

*She's a wonderful girl, conquering astronomy,*

*An extraordinary girl hero like me.*

ALREADY MIFFED THAT REBECCA LAVERY had done an end run around her in supporting my concept for Jonathan's welcome event, Trudi had barely given me the time of day ever since.

Far too passive aggressive to come out and say she disliked me at first sight and planned to replace me with my own underlings the moment that became feasible, she'd pop by from time to time to say hi.

"And someone's burned a bag of microwave popcorn," she announced, making a casual tour around the studio as if to sniff out the culprit. She peered beyond the glass window of the small recording booth, ducked into an editing bay, and checked over shoulders in the electrical and engineering shops to make a vague show of interest in the goings-on.

"I'm not asking the individual to come forward," she said. "Let this be a friendly reminder that we all need to exhibit restraint around behaviors others may find offensive."

"I don't think anybody microwaved popcorn," I said when Trudi reached my office. "Yusuf might have burned his burrito."

I had the freelance Pakistani family poached from the employee store hard at work assembling the basic elements of the retail experience. Yameena and her husband, Yusuf, had mocked up the "Imaginary

Friend" doll we named "Iffy" as a conflation of the project's initials, able to chat exclusively with the girl whose face she recognized as her match. They had already installed ZZZZZoom!'s voice command software that functioned like an Alexa device, and we all trained Iffy's generative responses in casual conversation among ourselves.

"I'm ordering ramen for lunch," Yameena would say. "Iffy, do you like ramen?"

"I don't know Roman," Iffy responded. She could not only talk, but also sing, skat, beat box, and rap, and her cheerful voice was engineered to sound like a hipper Shirley Temple.

"Ramen is a bowl of hot, delicious noodles," Yusuf told her.

"Iffy, do you want ramen for lunch?" Yameena repeated.

"I want a bowl of hot, delicious noodles, yo," Iffy responded.

"I want a bowl of hot, delicious noodles, yo, *please*," Yameena corrected her, reminding Iffy of her manners.

Their boys, Hassan and Hamsa—ages fifteen and sixteen and available to work only a few hours after school—already had the interactive character hologram nicknamed "Holly" in alpha testing.

Preparing to demo her merchandise-related chat feature, they worked to feed in Louise's pricing and sales copy as updatable voice data.

True to form, Trudi pulled me aside in my office to emphasize total disinterest in the improbable milestones met in a few short weeks. "How much time in total does this Pakistani family have invested in the tamale making?" She couldn't get her racist tropes straight, so I had trouble finding them offensive.

"They're pretty good about recording their time," I assured her. "Yusuf often brings his students along to intern for us, and that's a zero-cost product enhancement."

"No, I don't feel comfortable with that, and I doubt Trina will, either."

"Tell her to check the Fair Labor Act," I replied. "It's on the up-and-up for them to work in exchange for college credit, provided we offer a bona fide educational opportunity."

"We have a brand halo to consider," she sniffed. "We'll have to pay them something. I wish you'd tell me these things before you go and implement them on your own."

"I highlighted the internship in my original proposal for the studio," I reminded her. I could either shoot her a copy for re-review or ask Casey Klinkhoffer to come over and refresh Trudi's memory by pitching my idea as her own.

If anybody could construe free PhD engineering candidate labor as a bad thing, I had to give that to Trudi. The project would be quietly killed shortly after my overproduced sideshow stopped gumming up the works internally if she had anything to say about it.

"Jonathan has shared his excitement about what we're doing, of course, but I can always tell him we need to pare back," I said.

"And that won't be necessary," Trudi replied. "However, you have squeezed all the company funds out of this you're going to squeeze. Consider that fair warning." At last, a direct threat. In some sense I appreciated it.

In truth, my only independent confirmation that Jonathan even received news of our progress came through random approvals he initialed and routed back to me through his legal team.

As his visit neared, though, he phoned my cell to share random snippets of feedback. I'd get a call from Kuala Lumpur, Quito, or Calgary, from what I could make out over a delayed international cell phone connection, in the wee hours of the night.

"Does she float?" he asked in a non sequitur even wide awake I'd be hard-pressed to decipher.

"Who is this?"

"J.P.P., who's this?"

"Hi, Jonathan, it's Jaycee Grayson."

"Who?"

"Jaycee Grayson, head of studio at Wonderful Girls." I sat upright in bed and reached for my iPad on the nightstand to take his notes. "Are we talking about Space Station Girl?"

"I'm loving the concept, but I need to know more about the execution."

"For the movie?"

"No, I get all that," he said.

*J.P.P. loves the script!* I recorded in my notes.

"I'm thinking about the doll," he said. "She needs a float function at zero g."

"I suppose we could explore some options for that in the packaging," I said.

"Own it, J.G."

*Click.*

"WE'VE HAD A LOT OF fun with gravity in the movie script, but I have no funds on hand to make that happen in the real world," I complained to Louise Atwood the next day at the studio.

"We could always do something old-school," Louise said. "Maybe she could come out of the box inside a big helium balloon."

"That wouldn't get it. Cute idea for a birthday party, though."

"Research and Design falls under Summer Jessup," Louise said. "I say throw it on her desk and walk away."

"I'm afraid of her tomato pincushion. Something about it gives me a voodoo doll vibe, like she stabs it while thinking about me."

"Now you're fictionalizing," Louise said. "I wouldn't describe her as warm, but she might pull through for you. Only Summer predates Trudi around here."

Hold up now, how could that be? It was high time I paid Summer Jessup a visit.

THE RESEARCH AND DESIGN CENTER made perhaps an eerier workspace than mine, with sewing mannequins scattered about half-dressed in mismatched bits of clothing like headless corpses of women and girls ages two and up.

Rolls of fabric crowded every corner and splayed open on long project tables running the length of the workshop alongside half-baked toy and accessory designs.

Color swatches pinned randomly alongside drawings, photographs, and magazine clippings on inspiration boards for proposed character dolls represented a mashup of regional cultures and histories. No fewer than forty machines stretched across an industrial sewing room, though it had already been shuttered for the season behind darkened glass windows.

Summer had a personal sewing machine on her desk, a vintage Singer she pumped with her foot, in lieu of a computer or phone. Notoriously bad about returning calls and emails, she nonetheless seemed miffed with me about being left out of the loop on details around the Space Girl prototype she'd been asked to put together.

"I have no idea how to work this way," she said when I popped by her office. She focused on constructing an adult-sized ballgown out of stiff scarlet-red taffeta and what appeared to be several miles of tulle, as if to emphasize an endless list of other priorities. "We can mock up a rough assortment, but typically we spend months researching these characters under a uniquely curated board of fashion historians with specific expertise in the subject."

"This is a real girl," I said. "Call her mom and ask what she wore to school this week."

Summer referred me to a mishmash of sample clothing and accessory items she had already put together and pinned on a pegboard. "Her 'meet look' would be the Spandex skinsuit she trains in, and we'd offer the Boeing space suit, helmet, and gloves worn for spacewalks as an option. Okay?"

"Can you think of any way to indicate her weightlessness in space?" I asked hopefully.

She gestured toward a drawstring cocoon on a pegboard behind the door and spoke through a mouth full of long pearl-topped pins I worried about her swallowing. "They sleep sitting up in a bag that attaches to the wall, so they don't float away. We can offer that in lieu of pajamas in both girl and doll sizes."

"I like it, but it doesn't convey a powerful enough image."

She played with the fearsome tomato pincushion on her wrist like a ticking clock and picked up a sketchpad and pencil, apparently willing to give this about twenty more seconds. "We can reverse-engineer the doll stand included in the box."

She made a quick drawing of a doll attached to coiled fishing wires from a control bar, like a bouncing marionette. "She'd hang overhead from an optional glow-in-the-dark cosmos above the girl's bed, while moving her arms and legs and twirling in space."

"Wow. You're pretty good at this," I said. "I guess you've been at it awhile."

"Only since tenth grade. That's more years than I care to count."

"So, you knew Happy Lindstrom?" I tossed out casually.

"I lived with her. And Hank, and the kids, when they were all still around."

"We're talking about the real Happy Lindstrom?" I asked, trying hard to mask my incredulity.

"That's the one," she said. "We worked out of her garage, and she took me in after things got rough with my stepmom."

I let this sink in a moment as she went back to the ballgown.

"Anything else I can do for you?" she asked.

"I appreciate your help, Summer, you have no idea," I said earnestly. "I've been left to my own devices on pretty much everything and the guesswork is killing me while I try to meet everyone's expectations in a vacuum."

"I guess there's no excuse for that, even at this time of year." It seemed to occur to her just then that she bore some responsibility for the treatment I'd received from the team. "I often think Happy must be terribly disappointed in all of the backbiting that goes on around here."

"I imagine so, but how would that kind of news get back to her?"

"Oh, she pops in to check up on us now and then, although she doesn't always announce herself. Once I caught her in a warehouse uniform driving by on a forklift."

"Fascinating. I always had an inkling she might disguise herself among the Wonderful Mrs. Happys."

"That I'm sure of," Summer said. "She does have a tell, though, even when she's trying to fly under the wire."

"What kind of tell?"

"Probably I've said too much already."

Though Summer wasn't half as standoffish as I'd imagined her to be, she thought better of revealing company secrets to a relative newcomer with one foot out the door, from what she'd been given to understand.

Taking a step back, she compared the dressmaker's dummy to a desk photo of a young woman in a pageant sash and gown.

"Is that your daughter? She's beautiful."

"She's competing for Miss Wisconsin next month. She's pretty much managed to put herself through college with the scholarship money. The big dream is Miss America."

"I know the folks who produce the televised event," I volunteered. "Very nice guys, I'd be happy to make a few introductions." In truth, they were a couple of jackasses I once met at a three-camera workshop in Vegas and hadn't talked to in years, but they would probably be happy to jump on a call with the kid and tell her how awesome they are. "I'm sure they'd be helpful in introducing her to life behind the scenes, especially if she has any interest in television."

"Does she ever," Summer said. She put down the pins and even slipped the tomato pincushion from her wrist, revealing a permanent indentation from its elastic band. "Look, I know Trudi can be prickly. She and I have had our own disagreements, but can you imagine the stress she's under to appease every mom and girl in the world in every way humanly possible? It all got so big, so fast."

"Classy problem to have," I said.

"Unless it messes up *your* family and *your* marriage."

I couldn't tell if she was directly referencing Trudi or sharing a personal detail, but I had to admire her kinder, murkier gossiping style.

"In my case, I never talk about my situation," she said. "You'd be hard-pressed to find anybody in the building who even knows I'm single again."

That wasn't exactly so, as she was alternately known as Thrice-Divorced Summer Jessup, but I didn't want to burst her bubble.

"Your secret's safe with me," I promised. "You probably escape some of the village scandalmongering living all the way over in Black Earth."

"Black Earth?"

"Isn't that where Happy's from? I figured you still lived out that way."

"Oh, they didn't build the place up there until a few years ago. All the talk about Hank's drinking, and what that meant for her image, chased her further into obscurity. They started front and center in Main Street Spring Green. Near Taliesin."

With that, I'd assembled all but one outstanding puzzle piece. "What's the tell?" I asked bluntly.

"She loves popcorn, snacks on it all day when she's working. If she's in the office, you'll smell the real Happy Lindstrom coming long before any confirmed sighting."

I TOLD MEREDITH ON THE phone that night more than one mystery had been solved. "Trudi doesn't hate the smell of popcorn; she just doesn't want anyone else making it so she can detect Happy's presence in the midst and be on her best behavior."

"What's the other mystery?" Meredith asked, though I could tell she wasn't in the mood for intrigue.

"That our company founder is a real live person who hasn't got it in for me and still has a seat on the board."

"I guess it's safe to say she owes you a favor, considering the literal shit you've been through together," Meredith said.

I wouldn't expect such a thing to be repaid, nor even spoken of, but I hoped we would get a chance to reconnect.

Though her given name was Helen, Summer Jessup had shared, she earned the nickname "Happy" in childhood after her decidedly good-natured demeanor and only began to use the moniker again in connection with her Wonderful Mrs. Happy character.

"It turns out I had her number all along because Happy's second home in Arizona is a setup," I told Meredith. "She built a whole town that only looks like a town, but it's actually a living art gallery."

"Please tell me what that means quickly so I can go take a nap. I'm tired."

"You can visit the gas station, but the pump doesn't work because it's a piece of artwork. There's nothing behind the façade when you try to go inside. You can look in the shop windows, but you can't buy anything—expensive luggage, brand-name clothing, designer shoes."

"I don't even like shoe shopping when you *can* buy the shoes," said Meredith wearily.

I figured Butch was pushing her too hard to grow his spendy wine collection on their Napa trip, considering all she'd undergone physically in the previous months. "You do sound exhausted. Where are you?" I asked.

"Home in bed. Butch went wine tasting without me after I got an infection."

"Oh wow. What kind of infection?"

"A highly contagious staph infection called MRSA. I can't have contact with a lot of people."

"Your husband is not a lot of people, he's one person. I can't believe he left you alone when you're sick with some flesh-eating virus."

"Please don't blow this all out of proportion," she said. "I guess I've had it for a while, but they've been giving me the wrong antibiotics and they don't want it to spread to other areas of the body."

"What other areas?"

"Anywhere, I guess. Brain, lungs. I probably picked it up during one of my procedures."

"Procedures?"

"After I lost the baby," she said, annoyed by my probing. "I've undergone the routine series of follow-up care; do we have to get into this again?"

"I feel bad that you're alone at Christmas."

"I feel worse that you are," she replied in a bid to one-up me. Her eyes were probably closed, but she did have her priorities.

"Diarra's coming next week," I said. "She has to stay with me for her meetings with us because there's no money for travel expenses."

"That is just wrong," Meredith said. "You've been there almost six months, and they haven't given you a single thing to do you didn't have to beg, borrow, or steal. Even if they do force you to resign, we could easily make a case for constructive termination."

"Meaning what exactly?"

"Meaning it'll cost them several million dollars to force you out—and that's if we don't file a suit for punitive damages. Juries don't look favorably on companies upending workers' lives under false pretenses."

No routine infection would hamper Meredith's bent for sisterly litigiousness given her guilt over foregoing my previous case.

"Nobody's forcing me out just yet," I promised. "I have a few aces to play over the next few days. I'm starting in Spring Green."

THE SPRING GREEN DOLLAR GENERAL store had been one of the few successful businesses on a once-charming village main street that fell upon hard times after a Walmart Superstore moved in up the road.

Then a stay-at-home mom, known more commonly during that era as a local housewife, Happy Lindstrom volunteered at the Frank Lloyd Wright house, which subsequently hired her part-time as an especially popular tour guide among visiting school groups. Bothered by the lacking literature centered on the historic women of the region, she built the Spring Green Village Library with a Youth Literacy Grant from the Dollar General Corporation.

Happy expanded her platform to include fictional girls, scripting harrowing adventures to act out during a Saturday morning musical story hour. When she took her show on the road, the community inherited care of the library, and the event remained popular to this day—especially during the winter months when snowbound children had nothing much to do.

Though not at all sold on a children's library as the sexiest location, Kayla envisioned the construct of her proposed music video only in the loosest of terms as "totally rad."

My concept, conversely, involved the Wonderful Mrs. Happy hosting a group sing-along of "Anastasia's Theme." Schoolchildren colored rocket ships and solar systems while dreaming of space travel, intermixed with black-and-white clips of an astronaut-in-training we come to realize is an eleven-year-old girl. "The only words we hear are the child's," I said with a dramatic flourish. "'Coming soon from somewhere in outer space.'"

"Yeah, I guess that could work," replied Kayla, absently folding her growing garden of origami wedding flowers.

"You'll have to make it work because Freddie already made the arrangements. Your only required input is 'thank you.'"

I'd asked Freddie to secure the location with specific intent to telegraph fair warning to Trudi that I'd deciphered the truth behind the legend of Happy Lindstrom despite her machinations and would use it for my own purposes if need be. It also sent a message to Kayla, who seemed to view Freddie as her property belying any outward reality between the two of them.

"I thought you were dating the chief again," she said. "That's the rumor, anyway."

"It's just as unprofessional to comment on rumors as it is to pass them around," I said. "You might want to write that one down."

She didn't.

Kayla probably suspected that Freddie and I failed to gel as a couple, although I didn't formalize this with him until a few nights later.

"We can't keep stringing each other along," I said during an evening walk down snowy Main Street that should have felt uniquely romantic. "The fact is we're both under somebody else's spell, whether or not that person turns out to be good for us."

"I've told you again and again Kayla called it off with me," Freddie said. "She can't handle the chair, or my political ambitions, or anything else about what I want or need. Heck, she went and got herself engaged to my little brother, how many ways can she say we're finished?"

"I believe you," I said. "Sadly, every time we've talked about this, you've told me what *she* wants. That puts her in charge, and I can't possibly strike you as someone who'd let another woman run any part of my life."

"I'm not a total rube," he said. "This stuff comes up in my program; it's all tied together, the physical obstacles, the cycle of mental abuse—but I can't view myself as anybody's victim or I don't know a single thing about who I am."

"It happened to my sister, and she is no victim," I said, putting a hand on his arm. "She's brilliant and caring to a fault, the strongest person I've ever known. You'll work your way out of it when you decide you want that more than something you only wish you wanted."

We paused under a streetlight in a light snowfall, in full view of holiday shoppers buzzing about both on foot and in a blur of speeding cars.

"Meantime, you work on your stoplight to help slow down all our lives to a reasonable pace. Maybe you and I can revisit things down the road if we're ever free at the same time."

I leaned down to give him a hug, and he abruptly pulled me into his lap, kissing me long and hard. I hadn't expected explosive chemistry between us, but I had trouble breathing after I stood up—and did not dare look back after briskly walking away.

"So, I'll text you then," he called after me. "Every day. A woman needs to hear from her alderman."

"Wait until after the thaw."

"Merry Christmas, Jaycee Grayson."

"Merry Christmas, my friend."

I'm sure that one sliced right through the heart, but somebody had to do it.


"I DON'T THINK YOU AND Freddie qualify as idle gossip when you were spotted last night making out in the middle of the street," Kayla promptly informed me the next morning at the office, emboldened by whatever side deal she had going with Trudi and Trina to be as lippy as she liked. "Anyway, I don't think the video is going to work out. We'll all be out for the break by then, so I'd have to be paid at least double time."

"This remains your project, Kayla. You proposed it, you're going to make it happen," I said firmly. "You'll need to figure out the camera and lighting equipment you need and write up a production plan."

"Well, I guess I could borrow Casey's V-RAPTOR." She couldn't help but be titillated by the opportunity to get her hands on a forty-nine-thousand-dollar high-speed camera system over the holiday. "The supervisor has to arrange for anything we want to borrow, though."

"That's a hard no," Casey told me when I popped over to the Photo Studios to put in a request. "I'd like to help Kay—"

"Kay?"

"That's what she likes, Kay or Kay-Kay, I've told you this before. Try listening to other people occasionally. You can't take anything out of here without express written permission from Trudi, and even then, I'd have to push back. Honestly, Jaycee, do you have any idea how much pressure the rest of us are under with real work this time of year?"

"Just because you couldn't steal it out from under me doesn't mean it isn't real," I replied.

"Is that supposed to inspire me to do you a favor?"

"Probably not," I said with a sigh. "Truthfully, I don't even have budget for talent."

"Don't look at me. I've contracted all my Mrs. Happys for advance work on the spring catalogue; I doubt you'll get any volunteers for anything extra."

"Louise wants to play Mrs. Happy," I said. "I also have the featured mom and girl singer lined up. If you care about your bestie, Eugenie, and her talented young daughter, I'm confident you'll support them in every way possible."

CHAPTER FIFTEEN

# Diarra Demissie, the Most Wonderful Girl with S-O-B-E-R and D-Y-K-E-! Tattooed across All Ten Fingers

I KNEW DIARRA DEMISSIE FAR too well to buy any appearance of familiarity she tried to project with traveling second class. Having spent much of her early career on the road to fame, she knew what it looked like to live high off the hog with a big record label footing the bill.

"You're such a good sport," I said, meeting her at the Dane County Airport. There was no limo, no entourage, and only one crazed fan trying very hard to keep things under wraps.

"I'm just glad everybody likes the movie script."

"Not everybody's seen it, though."

"Has *anybody* seen it?"

"Everybody who matters," I said.

"Not a problem." She drew in a calming breath, continuing down the breezeway toward baggage claim. "I imagine folks will have more notes for the script once we get into my storyboards."

"Oh wow. You didn't have to do all that work for this little meet and greet," I said. "I meant that literally."

"All good. I get all the details we need to work out internally. Let's call recording the single an added extra between friends—unless it goes platinum, of course." She had lined up some musician friends from Milwaukee to play on the track we planned to produce in-house during the visit, when one of Yusuf's students, a popular campus DJ, volunteered to do the sound engineering.

I pulled into a convenience store along the airport service road for a quick lunch of sipping canned chicken noodle soup to condition Diarra's vocal cords.

We picked up a side of Cheez-Its and a Cherry Pie Larabar to split for dessert. "Stock up for the studio, whatever you want," I urged her. "A skeleton crew will have to work these next few days, but we'll have meals brought in and I have my corporate card for anything else we need."

"So, we really have gone rogue," she said, doing the math. "Part of me hoped you were exaggerating about the perceived lack of support."

"It's more than a perception, to be honest, but I promise I've got everything under control. If there's anything special you want, though, tell me and only me."

"That doesn't exactly sound under control, babe."

"We have a few allies in the building, but trust no one as a rule of thumb. Whatever happens, do not expect to rely on my assistant for anything."

Along with her ukulele, Diarra brought along an acoustic guitar and a small amplifier Kayla would shortly break.

"Oh, honey, I don't understand why that nasty little person hasn't been fired."

"You've never been at the mercy of the corporate machine," I said. "It's the nail sticking out that gets hammered down."

Long determined to stick out as boldly as possible in life, Diarra shuddered at the thought of toeing the company line and gave me an empathetic hug as we returned to my car, slogging through a muddy snowdrift.

I didn't know what the year-end holiday party had on the menu, but with employees invited to bring their families, I pictured it overrun with sticky children, chicken fingers, cocktail weenies, and a full complement of Wonderful Mrs. Happys I no longer felt pressured to sniff around after in search of fresh popcorn.

Bolstered by the presence of a qualified partner in crime, though, I did want to get Diarra into the office for some last-minute introductions before the closure. "Do you think you can handle it? We don't have to stay long."

"I don't know. Do I have time to change first?"

She looked like she'd just gotten out of the world's hippest salon chair, with waist-length braids beaded in gradating shades of red and her gorgeous set of lips painted a slick blood orange. Wearing a floor-length faux fur vest in a zebra print over a long-sleeved velour bodysuit and thigh-high vinyl boots, she looked every inch the sought-after industry multihyphenate.

"Please don't," I said. "You're everything I ever dreamed of and more."

DIARRA AND I BARELY STEPPED foot into the festive goings-on inside the glass atrium of the Happy Wonderful Place when Trudi pulled me aside and said we needed to talk in her office.

"And it's nice to meet you, Diarra," she said with a perfunctory nod once she had the two of us seated uncomfortably at her desk. "Jaycee, I'm afraid we have a few problems with this whole arrangement. For starters I have some issues with this screenplay you've taken it upon yourself to commission without proper authorization."

"I'm sorry, I thought Jonathan took care of all that," I said. "We can work on streamlining procedure going forward, but I thought it important we give him the reins on this one."

"I can integrate any notes you may have," Diarra volunteered.

I could tell she found Trudi's curtness confusing in the way it belied her permanently delighted facial expression—but Diarra could be delighted with the best of them.

"This was only a first draft," Diarra added. "We'll keep writing until we get it right and won't shoot a frame until it's locked."

Diarra didn't know she herself hadn't been locked in the director's chair, and I had no idea who'd slipped the script to Trudi. I was going with Kayla, by way of Prudence, who lifted it from Louise without her knowledge. Maybe the Doctor had been an unwitting accomplice somewhere between glandular disease conferences, but either way the timing was not good.

"Please give us a little rope to put our vision forward before the opinions start mucking up the whole thing beyond all recognition," I implored Trudi. "That's how movies end up with ten writers and no box office."

"And you're the expert?"

"That's exactly what I am, which is why you hired me," I said. "And how very fortunate for us that someone with Diarra's credentials had availability to fly in and share her thoughts this time of year."

"My wife and I have never spent Kwanzaa apart," Diarra said with a sigh. "It hardly feels like Karamu without a pot of jerked goat on the stove."

"We can jerk some goat for the crew," I said.

"Nobody's jerking anything in this office!" said Trudi. She had no idea what goat jerking might entail or why it presented a problem.

Diarra and her wife, Liz, observed the seven principles of the seven-day Pan-African winter holiday during dinner each night, lighting seven candles—three red, three green, and one black, representing the diaspora.

"Please don't take any of this as complaining," Diarra said apologetically. "I'm humbled and flattered by the opportunity, and I intend to deliver beyond your wildest imagination."

Trudi's wildest imagination probably told her that this cinnamon-smelling, candle-burning Karamu observer belonged to the Symbionese Liberation Army and had some explaining to do about all that business with Patti Hearst. On the other hand, it's unlikely

Trudi would wish to appear discourteous to a person of color sporting curled blue eyelashes and leopard-print nail polish, with the characters "S-O-B-E-R" and "D-Y-K-E-!" tattooed in rainbow colors across all ten fingers. "Jaycee, please enlighten me on the disco party you're planning with these men from Milwaukee."

"Are you referring to the musicians coming in to record?" I asked, unable to stifle a laugh.

"*These Men from Milwaukee* could be their band name," Diarra said, misreading this ridiculous rebuke of me as a jocular creative brainstorm.

"The campus is closed to give *everyone* a break," Trudi said. "Security, Facilities, Sanitation. As intriguing as all this sounds, you'll have to go with the version you've already recorded or find somewhere else to host your friends."

"All we have is a click track, meant to establish tempo and structure," Diarra clarified. "Louise and I made it on FaceTime."

"We'll need to overdub that with the fully mastered song I promised Rebecca," I added. "That's only fair when she already put up the funds."

"Could you excuse us, Diarra?" Trudi asked. She either felt it impolite to discuss money in front of a sober dyke or had a hitman lurking in the hall prepared to knock her off.

"Go hang out in my office," I called after Diarra. "Help yourself to my giant box of Wonderful Peppermint Patties and grab a few Wonderful pens and pencils while you're at it."

Trudi trained her clear blue eyes on me in oversize ocular judgment. "Rebecca Lavery didn't understand the level of disruption this fanciful overstepping would cause, or she would never have entertained your proposal."

"She said that?"

"I'm saying it. I also regret to inform you that Kay-Kay is unavailable for this music video extravaganza you're planning."

"It's Kay-Kay's extravaganza and she's the one planning it," I said. "That's what a 'producer' does."

"She's had a change of plans. She's expecting a friend in town during the break to help with her wedding."

"Her June wedding half a year from now? Why didn't she just say so?"

"Because she's afraid of you," Trudi said.

"I'm afraid of *her*. You have no idea the things she's capable of."

"She's a vulnerable young girl," Trudi said, aghast. "Where is your empathy?"

"Where's yours? Maybe I haven't been the greatest mentor to her, but how have you mentored me? And to contend now that I've violated internal procedures *you* never told me about?"

"We expected you to bring more refined management skills and hit the ground running. Both Kay and Prudence describe you as a very poor communicator," she added.

"Only because I rarely communicate what they want to hear. I'm determined to pass on my hard-won survival skills because in our business that's the only real protection a 'vulnerable young girl' has."

"Perhaps you may see it that way, but I've received too many confirmations of Kay-Kay's allegations to ignore them."

Signaling surrender, I got up and headed for the door, stopping to line my pockets with candy canes from a jar on her desk. "Like I said, you learn to survive in this business. Just bear with me until next week, okay? If Jonathan doesn't like what he sees, I will voluntarily resign, and your free candy will be safe from my clutches forevermore."

"Do I have your word on that?"

"You can have more than my word." Would something scribbled on a Santa Claus cocktail napkin stained with jerk sauce and black candle wax be legally binding? "I'll have something on your desk first thing," I promised.

Once we were safely in the car, I told Diarra by way of apology that Trudi fancies herself a liberal. "She once mentioned to me that she's pro-choice."

"What choice is that?" Diarra asked. "Premium or unleaded?"

WHILE I HOPED TO ENLIST Naomi's help on studio catering, I found her crying in my home kitchen and learned she had pressing commitments elsewhere. "My father wants to see me betrothed by the spring thaw," she said.

"Betrothed? Aren't you already married to Elijah?"

"No, miss," she said with a wince. "Elijah is my brother."

"That is such a relief! I thought the two of you seemed a little off, but I couldn't quite put my finger on it. Can't you say no to this betrothal, or at least make them wait?"

"Wait? I'm nearly twenty."

Since their mid-teens, Naomi and Elijah had been on *rumspringa*, a customary period of "running around" with little formal obligation to the church—but would soon commit to baptism and marriage to formalize a permanent commitment to their way of life.

"We appreciate your kindness in allowing us to extend our freedom time with you," Naomi said.

"Naomi, you are welcome here anytime for as long as you need to stay. I don't like the idea of you being forced to do anything on some imaginary schedule in the name of God."

"Anabaptists always have a choice," Naomi insisted.

"What if you walk away? Will they shun you?"

"We don't do that, miss," she said with a patient half smile. "It's why we split from the Amish."

Who was I to tell Naomi Petersheim that personal independence was the one true path to a happy life? She would never know loneliness, struggle to make the rent, or confront some pervert in a bowling alley determined to bring her down a peg.

On the other hand, her future lay at the mercy of men so stubborn they wore the same set of clothes for the last six hundred years. "When does this whole betrothal deal go down?" I asked.

"The elders will make an announcement within the month, once I've accepted an offer." While Naomi's mercantile success had caught the eye of quite a few boys, she theorized, none seemed especially supportive of a wife succeeding in an aggressively commercial lifestyle.

"Isn't that shocking," I said. "I won't pressure you then, but we do have a lot of food around here. If you want to use it up to do some catering in the studio, you could make a few extra bucks."

"What happens in the studio?"

"Music, dancing, technology. Head banging is optional. Whoever told you money was the root of all evil was probably a man, and he definitely lied. Money is power, and if a woman gets enough of it together, money is freedom."

IF IT'S TRUE THAT AN army marches on its stomach, Naomi rallied the troops to victory like a five-star general executing firm orders for congressional budget cuts. Round-the-clock, she manned a crafts table piled high with healthy snacks like salted root vegetable chips and spiced game jerkies, along with iced herbal teas and sparkling apple cider garnished with orange slices and cinnamon bark served from five-gallon Red Wing jugs.

Three times daily, she set out a selection of home-baked breads and fresh-tossed salads and ladled up hot bowls of her famous soups, stews, or braises. Warm slices of molasses-rich shoofly pie or fruit cobbler with hand-scooped ice cream and hot coffee rounded out mealtime for under a buck twenty-five per person, all in.

Diarra planned to feature Eugenie and Zoey Dreaux as our main mom and space girl vocalists and have Zoey solo on the last line, if she could deliver it.

"'Conquering astronomy' feels like a tongue twister when you're missing your two front teeth," I told Eugenie when I phoned to make the offer.

"She knows the whole thing," she announced, arriving at the otherwise shuttered campus with Zoey in tow. "I homeschool her, so we've made space travel a big subject these past few days."

Diarra took Zoey into the recording booth while I gave Eugenie some costume options for the library shoot. "Typically, we'd want an eight- or nine-year-old for this, but you've probably heard I have a thing for your dad," I said. "He tells me the two of you are his whole world."

"I think you have me confused with my sister Jacqueline—she's the tomboy. My other two sisters have boys, which Dad always wanted himself."

On the contrary, Abel told me raising daughters had been the highlight of his life. They'd painted his nails and rolled his hair in pink foam curlers, playing dress-up with him for hours while Sally was off at work.

"I'm not confused," I assured Eugenie. "You're the only daughter your dad has spoken about in any detail."

Just then, we heard a loud yelp and turned around to watch Hassan and Hamsa hoisting Kayla in the air in front of a sweeping green screen.

Strapped into a motion capture suit to animate the astronaut training clips, she appeared over stock footage of the swirling galaxy. "I still don't understand why I have to stand in for the astronaut girl when I'm an almost married adult," she whined.

"You fit the suit," I said, flashing her a big smile and two enthusiastic thumbs up. Let her label me a scary boss after I not only gave her the rare opportunity to produce her own piece, but also the starring role in a seven-hour thrill ride through the universe.

I turned back to Eugenie. "I don't know if your dad mentioned I invited him to the shoot tomorrow."

"Is that necessary?" she asked, mulling over her costume choices on a clothing rack. "He and I haven't talked much since Thanksgiving."

"It isn't my intention to meddle," I fibbed. "I need him on hand for crowd control in case word gets out and the whole town shows up clamoring for a part. You're welcome to bring some guests of your own. Your sisters, maybe, or your mother?"

"Respectfully, Miss Grayson, I'm going to give you a piece of advice."

"Jaycee. Please."

"Don't ever voluntarily get between my parents. They never made their own relationship look the least bit fun, but anybody who dares point that out only ends up getting hurt."

"Obviously, I don't know your mom," I said. "What I do know is your dad probably deserves a little forgiveness for being a man. I wish

I could forgive my dad for that, but he's been gone awhile now, so I missed my chance."

"My sisters hate me for sucking up to you," she blurted out. "They're rooting for Mom and Dad to get back together, like that wouldn't be a total disaster."

"I remember wanting that, too, for some reason—long after my mom ran away to join the circus," I said. "Anyway, I hope you girls can see your way around this rule you've made about neither parent bringing around dates."

"*She* did that!" Eugenie said, rolling her eyes. "She doesn't even want to date. She just wants to punish him for doing it because she's a control freak."

"Aren't they all? Mothers, I mean." I'd neither had one nor been one, of course.

"When us girls got to be teenagers, she told Dad we'd need more closet space," Eugenie said, making her case. "He built us a walk-in down in the basement, but by the time we came home from school she'd packed it to the gills with *her* stuff."

"Maybe with a younger mom everybody grows up together and everything gets to be a big competition."

"Why do you keep taking her side?" she asked icily.

"I don't know," I said, wondering about this myself. "Maybe it's because I was raised by someone way too young for the job, and I often wanted to kill her for doing it all wrong. Still do."

I handed Eugenie two shopping bags full of merchandise in lieu of payment for the work. "One of the dolls works in a beauty salon, and the other in a clinic for small animals. Hair and hamsters were the two subjects my sister and I settled on when our dad brought home ladies who were chasing him."

Something in her expression said she found me a kindred spirit in some small way. That didn't necessarily make us friends, but I might be welcome at her table sometime. Regardless of whether her mother and sisters ever came around, Eugenie wouldn't be hiding the knife while serving the meat loaf and forcing a smile while stabbing me to death. Good enough.

The two of us watched Diarra working with Zoey beyond the glass partition of the recording booth, where she struggled to keep her grown-up-sized headphones from falling forward as she sang her heart out into the mic.

"We're having a little party at JavaVino tomorrow night after we wrap," I told Eugenie. "Diarra and the band plan to play a set. I hope you and George can make it."

"Am I invited?" Kayla interrupted, eavesdropping like a champ on solid ground. Hassan and Hamsa had given her a short break, and what do you know, she chose a spot directly behind me with her listening ears on.

"I thought you couldn't make it tomorrow," I said.

"I can't go to the library thing, boring. I don't mind helping the band later, though."

Though she had indefatigable stars in her eyes over some passably noted musicians in the house, I couldn't afford to advise her to wipe them away and make a run for it.

"We have a lot to do and no one to do it," I said with a resigned sigh. "Ask Diarra if she needs an extra set of hands at the gig. For the record, your credit on this one is 'roadie.'"

I'D NEVER BEEN NAKED IN a lighthouse before, but after sleeping with Abel for the first time in his watch room below the flashing dome of the cupola, I felt far less inclined to give it up to any man at ground level.

"You can't imagine the drama," I gushed to Diarra the next morning. "The spotlight over the shoal, the snowfall on the icy water rushing in and out of the locks."

"How was the sex?" she asked, cutting to the chase.

"That man has a *lot* to offer," I said. "So much so that he's developed some highly advanced foreplay techniques to keep from killing the woman on the way in."

"Impressive," she said. "From my general understanding most guys would head on in, anyway, but what do I know?" She sat on my bed cross-legged, playing around with a tune on her guitar.

207

"Can you think of a more apt metaphor for physical passion than the Littleburgh locks?" I asked.

"That one would take some convincing for this beautiful lesbian."

"The whole point is maintaining a difference in levels between two opposing bodies of water dying to get at one another," I said.

Constructed more than a century earlier to accommodate a canal system between Lake Mendota and the Yahara River, the original lock gave way to the harsh elements time and again. "The last time it broke, the village flooded, and they had to evacuate. Abel and a couple of the sheriffs went house to house. He was swept away more than once but fought his way back against the current and marshaled every Littleburgher to higher ground."

"I thought the ex-wife barred you from the property even with your clothes on," Diarra said, bringing *me* back to higher ground.

"Have you been talking to my sister?"

"She has some reservations."

"She needs to take a look in the mirror," I retorted. "Have you seen her lately? She claims it's baby weight, but she gained most of it after the miscarriage."

"We were talking about you, lovely."

"I'm telling you I've never had a more romantic Christmas in my life! Sally Dreaux went back to her family in Anowaka, but don't you see that's all part of the excitement? What if she came home early and surprised us *in flagrante delicto*?"

"So what if she did? She has no claim on him."

"The idea of it is still a turn-on, I don't know why. Then you have the gun-happy ex-girlfriend running around; they can only keep her locked up for so many days at a clip."

Diarra had been absently strumming her guitar, but she stopped and put it aside. "You know, boo, sometimes after we get sober life starts to taste a little too plain vanilla," she said. "We indulge ourselves in inventions of the mind because we crave living in the thick of the cray-cray."

"Abel isn't the least bit cray," I said. "That man is a rock."

He had suited up in his dress blues the day before for the library shoot, hoping this would be his moment to reconnect with Eugenie.

She and Zoey wore coordinating sailor-style dresses, accepting Abel's outstretched hands on either side, just as Diarra directed, twirling his daughter and granddaughter like toy soldiers.

"He put in a decent performance in the role of himself, but frankly I find him a bit dusty," Diarra said. "You didn't mention he smokes."

She only knew this because she'd bummed a cigarette off him outside during a break. "You didn't mention *you* smoke," I said. "Aren't you supposed to be watching your voice for the gig tonight?"

"What have you got there?" she said, conveniently changing the subject.

"I wrote Abel a poem for Christmas." I'd discovered poetry at the behest of Mr. Y. to express myself to myself, along with writing my unsent grievance letters to Barbara Walters. "It's about the 'L' word being too dirty to say out loud."

"You're seriously in love with this guy?"

"I'm seriously *in like* with him."

Diarra picked up her guitar and cobbled together a tune, singing the words I'd written.

> *Heart-shaped tests to take,*
> *Some stranger's nest to make,*
> *It's no why wonder we escape,*
> *Shake it off, run, and cut bait.*
> *Unless, unless, just wait.*
> *Hey, how'd it strike you*
> *If the "L" just means I like you? I like you...*

"I wrote a song?" I asked.

She took a pause to work out a few chords. "You're writing one now, girlfriend." She sung another verse.

*Not an end, a new beginning*

*Where like must mean we're winning.*

*We'll share some all-night sinning,*

*Save the crazy underpinnings.*

*Yeah, like's a sexy word,*

*Come on, let's buck the herd and play…*

She reached over to her amp to give it some boom, and her voice soared in a husky mezzo soprano as she deftly switched chords with her right hand and picked out the melody with her left.

*Oh, the "L" just means I like you,*

*I've got a little crush.*

*My knees go weak, my head goes mush.*

*Still Abel, what's the rush?*

*I like you…I like you…I like you.*

"I guess we've got the title," I said, feeling high off the rush of creation. "Is this not exhilarating? You can call him dusty if you want, but I've never felt more creative than when I'm with him."

"Oh, honey, he's not here," she said. "This is you and me creating."

A frightening thought seized me. "Am I making him up? What if none of this exists in the real world because I'm constitutionally incapable of being honest?" I paraphrased a basic tenet of our sobriety program.

"Truth can be pliable, depending on who tells it and for what purpose," she said.

"Ah. Like you and being a smoker."

"The student becomes the teacher," she said. "In our case, we don't drink or use no matter what. Beyond that, put me down for whatever gets you through the night."

KAYLA SHOWED UP TO THE coffee bar to shoot the rock documentary certain to be her ticket to the top. "You go get that thing, Kay-Kay," I said, tossing around some meaningless platitudes to appease her.

"I appreciate your support, Jaycee."

"Yup, own your story and whatnot," I urged her weakly, in no mood for an authentic détente. I resented sharing my victory lap with her after she left me in the lurch to shoot *her* music video myself.

Abel didn't know quite what to make of "I Like You." *Diarra and These Men from Milwaukee*, who apparently liked Trudi's band name enough to claim it on future recordings, dedicated their first track to Abel in its world debut.

"Nobody ever wrote me a song before," he whispered in the dim candlelight of our table for two, looking around uncomfortably. "It has my name in it."

"Have you arrested any of these folks recently? Or are you nervous because Eugenie is hearing the unvarnished truth about how it is between you and me?"

She, too, looked uneasy, seated at the bar listening to the band with George. *Sally could babysit alone tonight, I thought.* "Here's your eldest daughter, meeting you halfway at her own peril among the other girls," I told Abel. "To my mind, this means she loves you very much."

"I still think of all my kids as about ten years old," he admitted.

"You don't have any kids. You haven't had any for a good twenty years. What you do have is a hot Hollywood girlfriend you strip naked in lighthouses and ravish deep into the night."

Liberated by that reality after many years of false imprisonment, he didn't even need to be indoors to make love to me that night.

He took me (at his insistent phrasing) in the steamy back seat of his squad in a dark corner of the vacant coffee house parking lot long after hours. In a naughtier version of rock, paper, scissors, like beats love, hands down—and danger covers all the bases.

I'd traveled this road enough times to know the dynamic of who owned which part of whom would soon switch gears with the messy squeal of an overloaded auto transmission. Throwing caution to the wind, for the moment I saw Abel as my calm before the storm, however much of my fertile imagination that took. Replacing my drug of choice, my invention of a personal police chief as preserved in poetics would have to offset the high highs and low lows up next as we danced into the New Year on a blizzard of uncertainty.

CHAPTER SIXTEEN

# Rebecca Lavery, the Most Wonderful Girl with a Newly Shampooed Head on the Executive Chopping Block

ONE RARELY SEES A MAN dressed from head to toe in white, but Jonathan P. Park arrived on the Wonderful Girls campus in the back seat of a chauffeured Cadillac Escalade wearing a single-breasted Dolce & Gabbana suit in shades of cream and ivory with a vanilla-toned striped silk tie.

He hugged a hooded, floor-length Tibetan lambswool coat trimmed in arctic fox fur, entering the building under a heavy snowfall approximating a walking polar vortex.

After three straight days of white-out conditions, a layer cake of snow blocked doorways and windows at least halfway up, and icicles the size of medieval jousting lances clung to the building ledges, occasionally collapsing under their own weight and impaling to death innocent passersby.

I already knew the general tenor of the news he would deliver to the rest of group.

The previous day, I'd been bustling about the executive conference room ensuring everything would be set up just so well in advance of his scheduled arrival to meet with the senior team.

"Let's put Diarra at the head of the table," I told Kayla. "We'll need a dozen of the screenplays in binders so everyone will have their own if Jonathan wants to do a table read."

"Yikes. Who's going to make all those copies?"

"That would be you, Kayla."

"Me? Oh wow. I'd have to find one of those big machines that do the collating and the three-hole punching, or I'll get totally confused. I wouldn't know where to start if you wanted to go with something crazy like two- or three-sided."

Though confusion and Kayla Flynn went hand in hand, I might have expected *some* interest in paperwork, what with her crack origami skills. "I have every confidence you'll figure it out," I said, nudging her out the door.

A couple of minutes after she stomped off in a huff, the conference room phone rang, and I picked it up. "Jaycee Grayson."

"Kayla tells me you need a large number of copies," Trina said. "That would not meet the standard of an appropriate assignment at her level."

"Actually, it's quite a challenge moving a project through multiple rounds of color-coded rewrites," I explained. "The assistants typically undertake the copying and pagination to familiarize themselves with the material."

"As an associate, Kayla only assists herself. Did you need more training on this?"

"That would be an excellent use of my time, of course, but I still wouldn't have the copies for our guest," I said. "You're not suggesting I copy twelve hundred script pages and put them in giant binders?"

"They have an industrial-sized machine in Shipping. I understand it's very user-friendly."

"Never mind, Trina. I'll have Kayla run the draft to an outside vendor." I hung up.

The phone rang again. I picked it up, hissing into the receiver. "What now? Does Kayla require the services of an Alaskan dog-sledding team to mush her over to Kinko's?"

"It's J.P.P.," said Jonathan's voice. "Let's meet at my chalet."

I couldn't comprehend how Jonathan would have pinpointed my location in the building to get a call through to me from Reception.

I wondered if his advance security detail had staked out the office these last few days. Maybe they surveilled us covertly, crouched behind a potted Ficus plant here or traveling mail cart there, communicating furtively into their wristbands. Reflexively, I shut the mini blinds.

"Welcome to Wisconsin, J.P.P.," I said. "Did you want me to bring Diarra Demissie along?"

"Who?"

"The woman who brought us the project. We could ask her to go over the storyboards," I said. "I'm excited to see them myself."

"Let's save that for another time. I'll send my car."


SHAPED LIKE A SPOOL OF thread perched atop a spindle, his slope-side chalet comprised a perfect circle hewn of North Woods cedar wood and white pine anchored to a cylindrical core with a spiral staircase providing interior access.

Sky-high picture windows gave way to a three-hundred-and-sixty-degree view of the Tyrol Basin's twenty-two downhill runs and three-hundred-foot vertical drop I never knew existed.

I hadn't eaten an authentic California Cobb Salad in some time and figured Jonathan traveled with produce boxes from the San Joaquin Valley filled with hydroponic lettuces, strawberries, and Hass avocados ripening to perfection in the cargo hold of a private jet.

"Are we spinning?" I asked as we sat down to lunch.

"Don't go getting queasy on me, J.G."

He picked up a remote control and slowed the twirling chalet to a barely perceptible speed.

"When did you get in town?" His initials were embroidered in gold on the black linen napkins, scrawled across matching plates, and etched into the crystal stemware in a bold geometric sans-serif font.

"A couple days ago. I'm planning on staying awhile."

"Awhile? You're not seriously going to move into our offices?" I asked with a nervous chuckle.

"I'm still feeling my way through things. I do like that crazy flower petal setup in the corner."

"That's the Wonderful Lavender Space," I said. "Happy Lindstrom's office."

"Don't know her," he said, drawing a blank. "So, about your Space Station Girl script, we're going to tear that one up and adapt the live action movie into an animated TV series."

"That would definitely involve some tearing up." I nearly choked on an aero-gardened grape tomato. "Wouldn't you want Diarra Demissie in this conversation?"

"Who's that?"

"The writer," I said, trying to hide my exasperation. "I've sent through multiple documents indicating I also planned to bring her on to direct."

"Sure, she could direct an episode or two, why not?" he said congenially. "Have her send over an animation reel."

"She's not an animator, Jonathan," I said. "She did bring us this property, and we should at least throw her a bone if we're completely changing directions."

"We bought it from her outright," he countered, waving away an Asian woman in her early fifties twisting a tall wooden pepper grinder over his salad. I certainly hoped she wasn't his much older wife but suspected otherwise and smiled at her weakly.

"We bought the kid's life rights, we picked up the magazine piece," he said. "I've signed quite a few checks because you asked me to."

"I don't want to appear ungrateful," I said, eager to appease him. "Diarra feels comfortable with her salary to date, but her input has merit going forward, regardless of the legalities."

"Like I say, I'll take a look at her work, but I don't think we'll need another staffer on the writing team." He replaced some wayward chunks of iceberg lettuce set alongside neatly arranged rows of smoked turkey, candied maple bacon, and trendy jammy eggs. "I'm bringing my guys into town for a couple of weeks to hunker down and knock out the first season."

"Your guys?"

"From *Universal Loser*. Been manifesting that one awhile now waiting for the right project."

I knew the type. Harvard Tasty Pudding jerks looking for steady gigs to pay the rent while infiltrating the stand-up circuit; late-night talk show writers who decided they needed more emotional depth once they turned twenty-five.

"May I ask how a girl on the spectrum redefining one small step for mankind is the right project for these gentlemen?"

I pushed away my plate. The twirling chalet indeed nauseated me, and I hoped his former dental hygienist wife had not prepared a sugar-free dessert.

"I don't get the pushback, J.G.," he said. "All these months you've sent me your ideas to approve, and we are all systems go. Don't even get me started on how amped the ZZZZZoom! team is to get cracking on Iffy and Holly."

"I don't understand. How would they 'get cracking' on fully functioning prototypes?"

"The software can do more than your people came up with, lots more. They did an awesome job, don't get me wrong. Our tech team can build on that to show the sub brands all kinds of crazy functionality. You own it, J.G. Give yourself a big pat on the back."

"Did you like the song?" I made a last-ditch effort to maintain control of anything at all I'd put forth. "Maybe you could use 'Anastasia's Theme' over your show's opening titles."

"I like that old-school sound personally, but I've got a Māori guy in New Zealand doing electronica the kids go nuts for," he said. "We want you ladies hyperfocused on the dolls. I had a chat with your boss about this late last night."

"Late last night?" I never thought of Trudi as existing after dark, figuring she powered down around sunset and dissolved back in on the morning elevator like Mr. Spock.

"That one spooks me out with that kooky twin of hers," he said with a shudder. "The whole lot of them give me the heebie-jeebies. The pincushion lady, that little half chick gabbing about the moving image and her grandmother's jelly roll. I've got to pick my battles, J.G., you understand."

"Of course I understand! I've never encountered a narrower minded bunch of scheming, plotting naysayers," I said. "I've come a long way in countering all that with some solid work you've rewarded by taking it off my desk."

"We've got all kinds of stuff for you to do," he insisted. "These gals are down for bringing a broader base of characters to life so we can grow the international markets."

"There's no appetite for that here, Jonathan. These women are xenophobes, and that's a very kind word for it," I said conspiratorially, lowering my voice to a whisper against xenophobic eavesdroppers. "Our diversity hiring program has one person in it and she's literally transparent."

"You keep right on manifesting that feature film of yours," he said, offering me a minted toothpick from a once-priceless Chinese cloisonné box devalued entirely with another frilly monogram. "Anything you get past the senior team gets my green light, sight unseen."

"What about the new TV show?" I asked. "I'm contracted as Executive Producer across all entertainment platforms."

"Yeah, we'll be looking for global distribution, and my name brings a little sumpin-sumpin to that party, am I right?"

"You're taking my credit, too?"

"Only in theory," he said, smiling congenially. "I'm all the way down for checking out some writing samples, though."

THE SCRAPPY TEAM MEMBERS WHO'D hunkered down to beat the clock on Jonathan's arrival had cleared the studio just as speedily with bad news in the offing and little motivation to come back for their garbage. Louise picked up plastic cups and plates abandoned on random filing cabinets in a scene resembling a frat house the morning after the chapter lost its charter.

"Jonathan wants me to audition for my own job," I said, trailing after her. "It would be quite a demotion, actually, on the off chance I land it."

"Thank heavens they haven't fired all of us. The Doctor and I just took out a home equity loan on our outdoor dream kitchen so we can enjoy picturesque holiday meals in the barn."

"With the barn animals?"

"Martha Stewart does it beautifully." She discarded a half-eaten egg salad sandwich on stale harvest bread left on top of a powered-down 3D printer. "How did I get stuck with this? I think I'll go home early and finish the rest of my workday there."

"No, don't. I want to get together with Prudence and Kayla for a team huddle."

"They went over to the Photo Studios to work with Casey. Something about producing stop-motion animations for the new play portal. Casey says nine-year-old girls with iPhones use our product to get fifteen million YouTube hits."

"I said that, actually, but let's not split hairs." I cracked a fresh box of dry-erase markers and handed one to Louise, assuming my rightful position at the whiteboard. "We're still a team, right? We'll just have to keep throwing everything we have against the wall at a great feature film concept until something sticks."

"I'd like to help, you know I would," Louise said. "I don't know that I'll have the time, though, with the rest of the storybooks to map out for the year. That takes a lot of bandwidth."

"A dozen storybooks? That's six hundred words in total."

"It's a complicated process," she said.

"Et tu, Louise?"

"What do you mean by that?"

"Welcome to workplace bullying," I said. "It's highly contagious. Grown-ups are much more efficient at it than kids, and women make men look like bush leaguers."

"I agree you've been beaten up on, but I'm exhausted," she insisted. "I wanted this just as much as you did, but there comes a time to call it quits." She gathered her coat and scarf, heading for the door. "I'm going home to pet my dog and feed my husband."

"Or you could feed your dog and pet your husband," I said, getting the door and letting in an arctic blast of air. "Why don't you milk a horse and ride a cow while you're at it? Martha Stewart does it 'beautifully.'"

"I won't accept a cheap shot from you," she said, wearing a brave smile deep into the persistent snowfall. "Call if you need me, Jaycee."

Was it any wonder my team deserted me when the chips were down? They hadn't exactly been supportive when the chips were up. Who needed them, anyway? It was time I paid a visit to my high-ranking secret ally, Rebecca Lavery, openly and without fear of repercussion!

I found her alone and dejected, however, packing an empty copy paper box on her desk with personal items.

"Oh no!" I rushed in and shut the door behind me. "Please tell me you didn't get fired."

"It turns out that quietly acquiescing to the word 'downsized' increases the amount of the severance package exponentially," she said stoically. "Also, they let you pack your own stuff without dispatching some goon from Security."

I sunk into a chair, head in hands. "I did this."

"I don't believe that for a minute," she said.

"What else did you do wrong other than support me?"

"ZZZZZoom! felt it beneficial to integrate a holistic experience across all their sub-brands," she said. "That's why they invested in the tech to make it work. It makes sense to roll up everything under their umbrella."

"Did Jonathan decide to off you? Or did Trudi and Trina throw you to the wolves to save themselves?"

"Does it matter?" she asked. "Like it or not, the three of them run the show now and the remaining team serves at their collective mercy. At least they didn't come for you."

"Only because they haven't figured out how to break me yet."

"It won't be pretty, I won't lie to you," she said. "They used to make Veronica pee in a cup every afternoon after lunch."

"Who?"

"Your predecessor. I can't remember her last name."

"Nobody ever can," I said. "How sad is that?"

"I would much rather walk away with my head held high than be subject to death by a thousand cuts."

"I have a two-year contract with an option to renew. I'm not going anywhere until I'm good and ready."

"They'll continue to insult you, though never openly," she said. "You will become frustrated, who wouldn't? Eventually, confusion turns to paranoia. Can you trust yourself to deliver anything of consequence?"

"They didn't count on the steely nerve of a pro gamer," I said. "I volunteered to resign if Jonathan didn't judge my work up to snuff. I'd say putting his own name on it and enlisting his buddies to lap up my greasy leftovers wins me that round, game, set, and match."

"Whatever happens next, at least you won't have regrets," she said with a long sigh, getting up to shut her blinds for the last time. "I put my head down and looked the other way more often than I care to admit, but my future holds countless opportunities to brag about ever having known you, Jaycee Grayson."

I would reward Rebecca Lavery for putting that freshly shampooed head on the chopping block for me with a small but pivotal role in the fantasy movie of my life. "I'd like Emma Stone and Julianne Moore alternating in the part of you at pivotal life stages," I said.

"I've always admired Jodi Foster. Yes, I know she's aged out of my all-important ingenue chapter and has always been quite gay. Call me a rebel spirit."

How neatly family photos fit inside the preferred office exit box alongside inconsequential items that defied abandonment—a personal-sized hand lotion, a tiny bottle of Tabasco. A ball of collected rubber bands from the morning newspaper to keep on hand in the kitchen drawer. What a thin tissue held everything together, I thought. How easily any of us could disappear unnoticed in an instant.

Rebecca left behind a half-drunk mug of coffee with a kiss of cherry Chapstick on the rim that would sit there for weeks, its cream curdling to a solid, affronting even the hardy night cleaners, who eventually tossed it in the trash.

Before she'd even vacated her prime Wonderful parking space, coworkers converged in her newly available office on the hunt for good discards—a Wonderful Lavender pencil holder and automatic sharpener, a giant jarful of gummy worms, her holiday candy of choice.

I comforted myself with the image of Rebecca arriving early for the first time anyone in the Lavery family could remember. She surprised the kids stuck home with her porn star fireman husband on a long, lovely snow day they would all remember fondly and well.

ALTHOUGH DIARRA DIDN'T SEEM QUITE as delighted by the news of her demise, resentment came at far too high a price to even consider indulging it free of charge.

"We had a good run, boo," she said affirmatively. "I can't help wishing you'd been more up front with yourself about what you were really dealing with here."

"I'm sorry. I believed through and through I could make this happen."

"Maybe you've learned a lesson in acceptance."

"Why would I need that?" I asked. "I'll always put up a fight for what I want, even when I know it's easier to stay down for the count."

"I guess you can afford to get up and take another hit when nobody holds you accountable for much of anything."

"Was that a dig? You don't do digs."

"I know," she said, a little perplexed. "I'm sorry, boo. Maybe I'm annoyed with myself right now for seriously overreaching on all this.

Liz and I are trying to adopt a daughter from Colombia, and I'll have to come up with a good excuse for my abrupt lack of employment."

"A daughter? Why didn't you tell me?"

"Tell you what? I don't know if it's going to happen yet," she said. "I try very hard to live in this moment and trust the universe to bring the rest of them. I want that so much for you, lovely. Just let go. Drop the rock."

"What rock?"

"The one convincing you time and again that you run everything when we are all powerless. Things we never thought possible happen once we surrender and not one minute before."

"Well, isn't this a pickle."

Here she was preaching the exact opposite of Jonathan's *Own It* and yet we all three stayed sober under the general tenets of the same program.

"My sister seems to think I've been dreaming the wrong dream all my life, but now that I've figured out the right one, I'm just supposed to sit around and wait? For what exactly? A sign of some kind?"

"I wish I knew." She packed up the last of her things and zipped her bag.

"Please let me take you to the airport," I said, trailing her downstairs.

"No. You go back to work and devise a crafty new plan for making an end run around the next thing that gets in your way. I know you want to," she said with that big, easy grin of hers.

"I do. I want that so bad. Please stop reading my mind. I get enough of that from my sister."

"And call your sister. Mark my words, honey, the rest of this nonsense means nothing."


MEREDITH SOUNDED AWFUL WHEN I talked to her at home that afternoon on the phone. She'd come down with a bad case of bronchitis and Butch had taken her to urgent care earlier in the day.

"The brain trusts treating me overdosed me on antibiotics these last few months and now everybody wonders why they've stopped working," she said.

"You sound like you're hacking up a lung."

"I think I just did," she said after a series of wet, wheezing coughs. "They gave me some syrup with morphine, and I'd have to call it my new favorite thing. Whoo-hoo."

"I like hearing you buzzed for a change," I said. "I always thought your big problem was you didn't drink enough."

"I'll drink more when I get over this. At first, I thought I had Parkinson's disease."

"Parkinson's disease? Where'd you come up with that?"

"My Google self-diagnosis," she said with a worn-out, rasping titter. "Writing a brief at an arbitration in Seattle last week, the pen flew right out of my hand."

"That's weird."

"I don't have enough oxygen in my bloodstream with the lung infection, according to the world-famous pulmonologist," she said. "Frankly, I didn't find him all that sharp."

"I don't like the sound of any of this. What happened to Butch?"

"He went to find an oxygen tank. They've sent me home, but the insurance covers a nurse to pop in and hook me up."

"Hook you up to oxygen? Jesus, Meredith. Maybe I should fly home."

"Fly home because I have bronchitis? You're hilarious," she said with a cute giggle she seemed to discover for the first time.

I thought about what Diarra said. Maybe I did need to drop the rock and stop trying to control everything with a world-famous pulmonologist in charge.

"I am going to send you some flowers at least. Why can't I ever remember your favorite?" I reached for my iPad and found an online florist with a get-well bouquet that had a fuzzy monkey hugging the rim of its vase.

"Stargazer lilies," she reminded me. "We got in a huge fight about this planning my wedding. You called them ugly."

"Not ugly, unoriginal. I said fuchsias were ugly, and I forbade you from using big pots of them all over the reception tent," I said. "I've always felt bad about that, actually."

"Don't feel bad. I did this to myself." Her voice broke, and I could tell she was trying not to cry.

"Don't cry, Merry." It got me right in the gut when she cried. "You didn't do anything to yourself."

"I did, though. All my health stuff started with my weight and everything's harder to treat because of it. I decided I'm going to have that surgery."

"Okay. People seem to do really well with that." I chose my words carefully, tiptoeing around this long-forbidden territory. "Obesity is a disease, though, not a moral failure. I'm super proud you're taking the cure."

"This isn't how we do it," she said, still fighting to hold back tears. "I get you out of messes. I feel like I've messed up everything. Like every single thing, since we were born."

"Good. Then we both get a new beginning," I said. "When does the surgery happen? I'll schedule some vacation time."

"A while, I don't know." Annoyed with herself already, she'd gotten into it all prematurely. "I'm supposed to lose some weight on my own first, and in the meantime, you said you have two hundred movies to write."

"Two hundred and fifty-two," I said. "They're just one-sheets, it won't kill me. It might take a few more months working overtime."

"I think everything is going to be okay," she said, suddenly sounding so sleepy she might nod off right there. "I feel so tired."

"Yeah, take a nap. How do we always end up talking about me? I love you, my sister."

"I love you, my Jaycee. You'll always be my baby sister girl."


ABEL WANTED TO GET UP and leave shortly after we had sex later that night, but when he felt around on the floor to find his clothes, I pulled him back under the covers.

"What kind of man turns down the warmth of a naked woman in this weather?" I asked, slithering up against him.

"What are you doing to me right now?"

"If you want to smoke, go out on the terrace. You're not fooling anyone."

"It's twenty below, Snow White. I need to go home and let out Pavlov."

"Have Sally do it. What's the point of having a roommate if she can't let the dog out occasionally?"

"Please stop calling her my roommate," he said. "It takes her quite a while to walk across the property in the snow when she needs to use the toilet."

"Come again? Sally doesn't have her own toilet?"

"We have some plumbing work left to do on the tiny house. You know the deal on getting waylaid by the weather."

"So, she's showering in your bathroom?" I asked, incredulous. "She stands there naked, feet away from you in the steam, and shaves her legs?"

"She uses the girls' bathroom, and I wouldn't know what she does with her legs." He got back up and jumped into his jeans. "She set up a cot in my dining room for nights when the snow makes it too hard to get back and forth."

"The two of you *are* roomies," I said, milking this one for all it was worth. "I bet you have slumber parties and drink hot chocolate together. What have you told her about me?"

"Not her business," he said. "Obviously, she knows who you are. I left my Apple Watch on the kitchen table, and she read a couple of dirty text exchanges between us."

"How charming," I said sarcastically. "I guess she won't be expecting Mary Poppins."

"Sally and I are friends. Have been since we were kids. I'd have to call her my best friend if I'm being honest."

I watched him lace up his boots—my favorite pair, big and sturdy with knives tucked into pockets on either side that he wore to break up bar fights out near the Interstate. "If she's your best friend, I guess that doesn't leave much room for us," I said.

"It leaves plenty of room," he insisted. "She and I only get so far nowadays even talking about the kind of stuff you and I have going. We have to use a code word to pull things back if the girls are within earshot."

"What's the code word?"

"'Bananas.'"

"That's *our* code word, Copper."

"That's right, it is," he said, only vaguely recalling this. "Let's you and I get another one. How about 'crabapples'?"

"I like 'bananas,'" I said. "Give her another one."

Mildly amused, he kissed me indifferently on the forehead. "She doesn't need to be over there worrying about me at this hour. I put her through enough with my job over the years. Don't pout, Snow White."

"I'm not pouting about you. I've had the lousiest day—maybe not ever, but in the top five." I rolled over and turned my back to him. "You're not the only one who sometimes has trouble sleeping."

He pulled a prescription bottle from his jeans pocket and shook it. "There's only three left, try breaking them in half."

"What is this, an opioid? I'm not supposed to take painkillers. Too addictive."

"It's a mild antianxiety medication," he said. "It takes the edge off so you can get some rest when you don't want anything harsher in your system." He took my face gently in his hands and gave me a suitable kiss goodbye, leaving the bottle on the nightstand.

"Don't forget to call me," I said. "I worry, too."


ABEL COULDN'T HAVE BEEN GONE twenty minutes when the phone rang. I looked at the incoming number and sat up in bed. "Meredith? What's up?"

"It's Butch."

He and she had been married for twelve years and together for fifteen, but I couldn't remember the last time he called me. He didn't even have my number on his own phone. "Butch? Is everything alright?"

"Nothing's alright, Jaycee," he said. "Meredith's gone."

CHAPTER SEVENTEEN

# Yancy O'Cochlain, the Most Wonderful Girl at the Nonpracticing Catholic Girl Scout Funeral Mass

I DIDN'T CRY AT MY sister's funeral because I had nothing to cry about. People don't just up and die out of the blue, and though I was willing to show up and play along, I refused to accept any of this nonsense as my new reality.

I stood in the vestibule of Our Lady of Malibu, not far from the cliffside villa showcasing J. Paul Getty's collection of Greek and Roman antiquities plundered unlawfully from protected Italian ruins, wondering how I got here.

My sister, meanwhile, had supposedly been reduced to ashes in a five-hundred-dollar Ricco Deruta soup tureen from Sur La Table.

"It's her favorite pattern," Butch told me the previous week when he phoned from the funeral home. "She wouldn't have the garbage they want you to buy with the funeral package in the house."

He meant to say *he* wouldn't have it in the house, where he wanted me to believe Meredith no longer lived, as ridiculous as that sounded to anyone who knew her.

While the matching porcelain ladle went missing en route to the church, I should accept as fact her alleged widower's contention that my sister had elected to spend eternity in there where the clam chowder belonged.

Butch had a business relationship with a roving Irish priest named Father Fitz, with whom he traded promising estate planning prospects where funds had been reserved for elaborate final wishes. Now on a fixed budget for the rest of his life and undergoing a deep psychic change in his spending habits, Butch had arranged a discounted mass for Meredith, a nonpracticing Catholic, who would have gotten quite a kick out of Father Fitz's bold and enthusiastic pay-per-view Irish brogue.

Despite cutting a few corners here and there, the newly frugal Butch couldn't help but boast about certain touches that made his wife's big send-off more of a testimony to his social influence and impeccable taste than to her well-lived life.

The swanky California redwood–gabled chapel, where Meredith's theoretical ashes rested in the warm glow of Tahitian vanilla–scented candlelight, ranked among Southern California's toniest devotional venues, Butch wanted me to know.

When I saw the supposed remains of my larger-than-life sister tucked into a tidy mosaic bye-altar, he anticipated a fit of hysteria and grabbed me by the shoulders to help me shake it off in advance. "You can't put in your big performance here," he said. "We'll have to do all that another time."

I didn't want to put in my performance there and appreciated any preferred scheduling information he might want to share, given his expertise with all things death and dying. Hospitals had been his favored stomping grounds since childhood; he knew how they worked and how to work them.

Exhibiting an Irishman's native affinity for life-threatening illnesses, he often talked about shepherding his favorite elderly O'Cochlains to a considerable family plot in South Boston, where their people had immigrated to escape the Potato Blight in the mid-nineteenth century.

Fully in his element, he had remained stoic from the moment he called to report Meredith's loss. "Get her back!" I demanded. "There was a pulmonologist, where is he? Call the pulmonologist, Butch! What's wrong with you?"

"She's dead, Jaycee. Why aren't you hearing me?"

"People don't die of bronchitis," I said with a nervous chuckle. "That's ridiculous, what are you even saying?"

"She had methicillin-resistant double pneumonia. I don't know what she's been telling you, but she's been in the ICU for five straight days."

"Nope, not true," I insisted. "She was home this afternoon."

"No, she wasn't," he said. "They *wanted* to discharge her when they couldn't do anything more for her, but she had trouble breathing later so they put her on a ventilator and her heart stopped."

"They can start it back up with the electric paddles," I said frantically. "Tell them!"

"They beat on her for a really long time, kiddo. After a while they were only hurting her."

"No, no, no. Put the doctor on speaker."

I could hear sounds in the background, beeping and scraping, but not the frenetic, crash cart, code blue sound of hope and life. There was some clanging of dirty instruments, a whoosh of water in a sink, the hum of resigned chitchat. I sat there quietly a moment, listening.

"Never mind," I said.

Only then did I sit up and turn on the lights, staring blankly into my phone. I planned to stay right there and never move or speak again.

"I brought her your lilies from the house," Butch said.

His voice broke, and he gave in to huge, inconsolable sobs.

He had grown a little teary-eyed at their wedding, but beyond that I'd only known his emotions to range between mildly frustrated and comic book angry, with an imaginary smokestack blowing its top above his shiny bald noggin.

"She has the little stuffed monkey with her in the bed right now," he managed to get out. "I can't talk long; I'm donating her eyes to a blind kid they have waiting."

"Boy or girl?" I asked, though I don't know why that mattered. "How old? What grade?"

"I don't know, Jaycee. Nobody tells you much."

I would have to spend the rest of my days searching for my sister's eyes on every child I saw.

Had we stayed on the line together, I might have broken down and cried with Butch O'Cochlain of all people, but a hospital chaplain arrived to administer the last rites and he handed me off to the head honcho, his older sister, Yancy.

The picture of funereal efficiency, *his* sister made it out from the East Coast while *my* sister lay dying—which I found suspicious on its face, especially when Yancy set about acquiring the exact pharmaceuticals sufficient to sedate a large man with a known propensity for self-immolation.

She would further stabilize his condition wherever necessary over the next days with silky shots of Jameson administered covertly from a flask she kept filled inside his jacket.

"What would you like to offer at the welcome table?" she asked me over the phone. "Maybe a nice mass card with the Irish Prayer?"

She knew very well I held her brother in exceedingly low esteem and had no intention of letting that impact the noble tone she intended to set for his event.

"Is that the one about the road rising up to meet me?" I asked. "Why would I want the road to do that?"

"It's always a hit with mourners, dear."

She was the type who could call you dear without coming off the least bit condescending.

An agreeable redhead who spoke to most everyone with the ease of a preschool teacher, she had teased-out red hair like a cone of cotton candy spun on top of her head, with a petite lower body and broad shoulders that added up to chronic back pain she endured like a champ.

I often fantasized about burying my face in her ample bosom, intoxicated into submission by the overpowering fragrance of Jean Nate Bath and Body Splash.

"Let's think about things Meredith would like," she said. "How about a commemorative bookmark?"

"She did like books," I said. I spoke about Meredith in the past tense for the first time and automatically corrected myself. "She loves books, always has."

"All of this is going to take some time," Yancy said with the kind of sympathy that turns you into a useless puddle of goo. "After a while life goes back to normal, but we do have to go through the motions."

A fifty-ton shrimp trawler plowed into her husband of eighteen years one morning as he chugged his motorboat into the local marina to pick up a tank of lawn mower gas. Living in a vegetative state for some time propped up at the family table, he finally went to Jesus as the O'Cochlains gathered to argue one magical Christmas Eve.

"I joined Butch for the visitation yesterday and Meredith looked lovely," Yancy told me. "The pale pink blush on her cheeks worked beautifully with a hint of lipstick and they had her hair pulled back in the sweetest chignon."

"That seems like a lot of work for the crematorium," I said. "Butch told me it took some doing to find a place to accommodate her size."

"We've handled all of that, dear, you don't need to worry yourself about a thing," she said firmly. "Now, I have a number of catalogues if you wanted to pick out that bookmark."

"Memories of Literary France" had a gold tassel and a George Sand quote in French and English on either side. *Il n'y a qu'un seul bonheur dans cette vie, aimer et être aimé.* ("There is only one happiness in this life, to love and be loved.")

"Perfect," Yancy said, declining to note any irony around that sad sentiment regarding the husband who loved her not a whit in either language. "We'll use a lovely photo I found in the nightstand drawer. Meredith was so svelte during her time in Paris."

"She lost a lot of weight eating like French women eat and getting around the city on foot," I said. "She was a different girl before she met Butch."

Yancy glossed over the implication that Meredith's life would have been better had she never met him at all.

"Butch isn't doing well," she said with a long sigh. "One minute he's on the floor crying his eyes out and the next he's cursing at the skies."

*Guilty conscience,* I thought. Maybe he smothered her to death on a lark with his overstuffed La-Z-Boy seat cushion or poured a cup of antifreeze into her hospital water pitcher, if only to instantly regret offing the cash cow. "It's always on the husband," I said.

"Of course, dear, but it's also important we involve the sister."

I didn't know whether she'd chosen to let another dig slide by, or she honestly didn't get it. Either way, she would enjoy assuming the role of Butch's minister of propaganda, previously played so blithely by poor Meredith.

Yancy would soon be carrying around the Kate Spade Dakota Leather Crossbody I bought Meredith in Chicago to apologize for the unfortunate North Lion incident. Who wouldn't suck up to a newly flush little brother who never earned a dime in his life and suddenly had Meredith's huge retirement portfolio all to himself?

"What are your thoughts on the guest book?" Yancy asked. "You're going to need addresses for the thank-you notes. I'm happy to help you with our side of the family."

"What are we thanking them for? All their tearful Irish whiskey drinking?"

"You know what, dear, I think this is too much for you right now," she said. "You do what you need to do to get yourself in shape for next week and I'll handle the rest."

BY THE TIME I ARRIVED in the church, Yancy had a regal white leather-bound book with gold-trimmed pages splayed open for business beside a pile of the froufrou memorial bookmarks.

That long-faded Girl Scout sash, with its frayed merit badges dangling from broken green threads Meredith had hand-sewn with a young overachiever's confident whip stitch, became the star attraction at the reception table. People whose names I didn't recognize—Meredith's neighbors and friends from work, Butch's distant relations—killed time waiting in the receiving line making out cryptic icons for First Aid, Archery, Campfire Cooking, and the coveted Outdoor Recreation Challenge.

Anyone wondering about her physical limitations later in life would learn that she could just as easily choose between ministering to their poison oak rashes or hunting them down like rats to skewer for lunch on a flame-roasted stick. What a beautiful send-off.

Photo collages dated from our childhood were taped to white posterboards and propped on wooden easels beside fragrant floral wreaths Yancy deemed elaborate enough to decorate the front row. The most perfunctory of these, a tidy pyramid of lavender tea roses in a white ceramic urn, had arrived with a computer-generated teleflorist card, *"From the joyful, thoughtful women of Wonderful Girls."*

"Did you want that one up at the altar?" Yancy asked.

"Not really. Did anyone send fuchsias? I should have sent some myself, so what if they always look like they're falling over dead? I'm the worst sister ever born."

"Don't you dare say that. Remember the fun you and I had at the wedding?"

The Shelter Island deer made a meal of Meredith's wedding tent centerpieces set out the night before, sending Yancy and me scurrying to the mainland to improvise towering baskets of all-night superstore fruit into the wee hours.

Despite their being held on opposite coasts, the two ceremonies mirrored one another nearly identically—the same pair of plaid bagpipers greeting the same dressed-up guests on what could have been the same church steps. They played a hopeful "Amazing Grace" at the nuptials and a sorrowful one at the funeral, with Butch's extended brood heading for the right side of the aisle and Meredith's smartly dressed Smithie friends to the left.

Women of tremendous substance—a federal appeals court judge, a nuclear physicist, head mistress of a lauded Connecticut prep school—the

Smithies hadn't managed to upend the controversial marriage ceremony in Shelter Island, New York, where one of them begrudgingly lent out her family's beach house.

By the time the happy couple made a memorable entrance at the reception by seaplane, even the most strident member of their feisty flank was drunk enough on Negronis or Campari and sodas to let down her hair and go with it.

Come to think of it, the same Patrician faces, give or take an intervening brow lift or two, had peopled Meredith's college graduation, the third major event measuring her short life with the ominous toll of church bells.

Then a ninth-grade LA punk, I skateboarded in and out of the academic procession from the residence at Albright House to the Quadrangle, where young women dressed in white bent on building a better world formed concentric circles to reject the patriarchy out of hand and award one another's diplomas.

Covertly chewing watermelon bubble gum, I coordinated the very same untied black Chuckies and white denim jacket with my reluctant formal wear at all three occasions. Clearly I had not necessarily evolved into the serious sort one entrusts with a dear friend's death bed confessions even these many years later.

I could only listen in on their updated chapel chatter for any hint of mutual concerns around the true nature of Meredith's demise.

*"Good Lord, I'm not saying he literally killed her, but he may as well have."*

*"Let's not go there, ladies, it's disrespectful to her memory."*

*"Nobody knows what goes on between two people behind closed doors."*

*"Maybe they did love each other, just not the kind of love we'd want for dear Merry."*

*"What are the odds they'll serve buckwheat at the repast? I'm back on Sirtfood and killing it."*

On the Boston side, the folks ran unapologetically large-boned and the opinions loud and proud, with long, growling "ah's" where the "r's" should rightfully be to punctuate *their* take on things—where Butch somehow ended up on the short end of the matrimony stick.

*"He thought he married up, but then she gained all that weight, the poor bastahd."*

*"He stuck with her for years when plenty a fellahs woulda run off fast and fah."*

*"He had to support that sad little sistah financially. No mothah. No fathah."*

*"He wanted kids of his own, but no, she had to have the big job and the sporty cah."*

*"And what a beautiful home he provided his bride. Will they have more than one open bah?"*

For her part, Yancy freely acknowledged the marital strain, something she saw no shame in between a husband and wife over time. Butch viewed himself as fully bicoastal and frequently spent summers and holidays back home with the extended O'Cochlain clan, where Meredith hadn't been spotted for years.

"They became close again during her illness, though, so sweet to watch," she said. "Playing Yahtzee by her bed for hours, shaking the dice and cooing like newlyweds over who had the better roll."

"He took off her toenail polish when she went in for the hysterectomy," added a self-styled first cousin, twice removed. "Painted it right back on her when she came out of the anesthesia."

*Hysterectomy? Toenail polish? Yahtzee?*

None of these randos offered a lick of reliable information since they clearly had the wrong Meredith. My Meredith may have withheld a few secrets from me here and there, but surely, she'd have mentioned her intention to check out early in life just as soon as she and Butch finished up one last round of ER peek-a-boo.

I spotted Diarra in a front pew embedded among the Smithies, but I couldn't catch her eye and had no choice but shoot her a text from the back. *What if I'm only here as a show pony? Butch is probably using me to justify every lousy thing he ever did to Meredith.*

*She wouldn't want you making a scene*, she texted back. *Stand tall and channel Jackie Kennedy.*

She became distracted by some kind of kerfuffle with the church organist, who objected to her singing a Linda Ronstadt piece during the service and insisted she swap in something nonsecular.

Naturally, this offended the Smithies, who theorized that Linda Ronstadt herself was a deity meriting thanks and prayer at a proper Seven Sisters send-off.

As the last of the mourners filed into the hand-hewn redwood pews, Diarra bolted onto the altar with her guitar and delivered a soulful cover of "Goodbye, My Friend" in an overt act of rock goddess defiance.

Though no Michael Crawford, a marginally capable vocalist cued the official procession with his rendition of "On Eagle's Wings," set to the staccato moans of the organ accompanied by the strains of a whiny violin.

With that, Father Fitz processed up the aisle showing some serious theater chops of his own in white and gold embroidered liturgical vestments amid an equally elaborately costumed entourage—clearly expecting some big bucks when they passed the basket among the well-heeled grievers.

No other place of worship in the county offered validated parking with an ocean view, Butch had informed me, and the parish paid a pretty penny to keep unwanted children off the beach.

He fought back a blinding flood of tears under the weight of Meredith's soup tureen held out front like a sacrificial first course for the gods. Even his most ardent supporters waited heart in mouth for him to drop what was left of his wife and spread her all over the floor.

A one-man show if ever there was one, Butch initially had every intention of delivering the eulogy, but Yancy seemed to have convinced him that the bereaved husband needed to sit back and bask in the condolences. Her loyalty would always lie with her brother, but Yancy understood loss, and she knew in her heart mine had been the far more profound.

I marched up to that lectern holding a single white rose plucked from a random wreath and would use it to stab through the heart of anyone who got in my way. You could hear a pin drop for miles along the coast and deep into the Pacific—where the whales sang a quiet mourning song to their newborn calves and even the killer sharks knew enough to stand down and listen up.

"Children are meant to grow up and leave our parents, and if we're lucky enough to find a spouse of our own, someday one of us will leave the other behind."

I looked Mr. Butch O'Cochlain directly in the eye. He had done nothing wrong, other than fail my sister in every way a man can fail a woman.

"A sister is a sister for life, there from start to finish. She refuses to ever leave, even when you politely ask her to."

Though I still felt thoroughly numb, Diarra would come up and sweep up the pieces if I suddenly cracked open and stood there oozing out of my own body like a giant egg.

"If you have a sister with you today, I recommend you apologize to her for whatever fight you last had about something stupid, probably within the last half hour or so. Maybe she sings in the car or embarrasses you in public art spaces. Whatever it is, it won't kill you to reach out and forgive whatever she did so wrong, so you don't have to be me, standing here, wishing you had. I'll wait."

A smattering of women and girls shuffled around in the pews, hugging one another amid a round of apologetic snorting into traded hankies.

"When I was born, someone advised our mother to stash me away when we got home from the hospital so Meredith wouldn't feel jealous of me. Mom asked her if she had fun those last few days. What did she eat? Did she play a new game or read a story? My sister looked at her like she'd completely lost her mind. 'Mommy, where's the baby?'

"Meredith made me her baby from that day on. I'm only here now because she saved me from drowning in a lake when I was four years old and nobody else noticed I'd fallen in. She picked me up off the floor a thousand times since, and she never once gave up on me, not even when I really wanted her to. Goodbye, my sister, my only sister, thank God for you. You rest now. The party's over. I'll clean up."

CHAPTER EIGHTEEN

# Liz Demissie, the Most Wonderful Girl Who Sounds like Javier Bardem in the Afterlife

I LAY WITH MY HEAD in Diarra's lap over the next few days, although sometimes Liz would come in and take a turn getting me to eat a spoonful of Cream of Wheat with manuka honey and warm goat milk.

Unfailingly energetic, Liz had a long, blond-streaked ponytail she tossed around like an exclamation point to emphasize whatever she said. She and Diarra lived in a clapboard Venice cottage not far from the beach, where the three of us walked barefoot in the sand in the mornings side by side. Feeling the sheer power of three women moving through space united, we inspired fellow beachgoers to duck instinctively out of our way.

"Why wouldn't Meredith get help?" I asked. "She wouldn't even talk about it until the end."

"Maybe she was scared about losing control of things." Liz bounced a paddle from an elastic string Diarra bought her earlier when we popped into 7-Eleven for some coffee. "She always struck me as super in charge of it all, even when she definitely wasn't, all of which I mean as a major compliment."

"She was a tiny soul living in such joyful hiding under herself." Diarra thought this through while assembling a perplexing convenience store paper kite. "When this big, huge thing came along and attached itself, she refused to give it one more bit of energy than it already took."

"I think the rest of us would call that addiction," Liz said.

"Little Meredith refused to call it anything," replied Diarra.

"She could call it Charlie for all I care!" I said. "What I'll never get over is how she could leave me alone like this without so much as a word."

"Oh, honey. You don't know what she knew or when," Diarra said. "Nobody does."

"She knew. Even Butch knew. He let it slip that when he joined her on her last business trip for a few days in Seattle she was riding around the hotel on a mobility scooter," I said. "He left her out in the car while he went and checked out the Space Needle."

"Butch can go suck a bag of dicks," Liz interjected, boinging her paddle ball. Some women can say the most vulgar thing and make it sound adorable.

"As much as I'd like to lay the whole thing on him, it isn't really fair," I said. "Even her partners made it a point to tell me how great she had seemed right up until the end. She won some ten-million-dollar court case and took everybody out on the town, kicked up her heels half the night. The next thing they heard she was gone."

"Why try to make sense of a thing so senseless, my darling? Death isn't any more perfect than life."

Diarra had lost most of her family to famine, civil war, and ethnic cleansing, atrocities so devastating she rarely spoke of them, though she remembered well the wails of the survivors. They beat themselves about the head and chest, throwing themselves to the ground and tearing out clumps of their hair in grief. You could see why she would throw in her fortunes with a woman who placed so much faith in that fresh egg of Silly Putty stowed in her pocket.

Diarra's toy kite caught the edge of a stiff breeze. It dipped up and into flight over the ocean with a theatrical salute as the three of us ran after it, leaving a trail of disappearing footprints in the advancing surf.

While I had never known life without my sister, Butch O'Cochlain had stumbled upon her recently in the grand scheme of things on the best day of his life. As I left the funeral, he had promised to send me a few boxes of family heirlooms Meredith had set aside in the garage.

He would never again have to go off to work at a make-believe job, and within a few months he found new love with a widowed pediatric nurse he met on a golfing range over a bucket of balls.

He and I would never speak again.

DIARRA, LIZ, AND I SOAKED in a wooden hot tub on their Venice terrace, watching the sun drop like an orange balloon over the Pacific. I lifted a wand from an assortment of bottles and blew a cartoonishly large bubble off into the night.

"Maybe I'll call the Realtor and see about putting my house on the market. I can't afford it anyway if they're going to fire me."

"Maybe it's time to cut the hot cop loose, too, since he couldn't be bothered to show," Liz said, echoed by a computerized Spaniard. "*Tal vez es hora de soltar al policía atractivo ya que no se molesta en mostrar.*" She used a translator app on her phone to practice Spanish while awaiting approval of their daughter's adoption.

"Who said I wanted him here?" I asked. "His ex-wife decided she'd like to date him again and he told her he'd have to get back to her on that after running it by the girls."

"The grown-up married girls?" Diarra asked. "That's just weird."

"I don't even think Sally wants him back," I said. "She just got triggered after heading down to Cancun for her birthday and Abel told her to get laid by a Mexican pool boy."

"Ouch," said Liz with a full three-sixty-degree flip of her emphatic ponytail. "Why so mean?"

"I can think of meaner," I said. "I don't know, maybe Meredith was right thinking those two had unfinished business."

"Meredith was pretty much always right," said Liz. "*Meredith siempre tiene razon*," repeated her translator.

"Please turn that thing off," I said. "It's like Meredith is still with us but she's turned into Javier Bardem in the afterlife."

"Just come back to LA," Diarra said. "You can stay in the back house."

"No charge," Liz tossed in, sweetening the deal.

They were talking about their garage, where I would sleep in the car. In LA, this is known as a furnished rental near the beach I might have jumped at if I could only bear to keep a secret from the two of them. "Okay, but what if Meredith can't find me again?" I blurted out.

"Again?" asked Diarra. "She paid you a visit?"

"Only once. She was sitting on my couch, plain as day. She told me she had to go because she hadn't been able to get things right in life, but I still had time. I promised her I'd try, but when I asked if I could hug her, she said no, and the first thing I had to get right is accepting that."

"You and I had a chat about acceptance," Diarra said. "You weren't very interested."

"Everything sounds like a bigger deal when dead people say it."

I climbed out of the hot tub, standing buck naked under a blanket of stars. "I have no idea where home is without her." It occurred to me that as much as I no longer belonged here, I had no business returning to Wisconsin expecting to make wrong things right. "I knew it wouldn't end well when Meredith came to my rescue that last time," I said. "Not in a million years would I have guessed she'd be the one who ended up dead because of it."

"What's she talking about?" asked Liz, elbowing Diarra.

"She can't live with us," Diarra said. "She can't even live with herself until she goes back to the desert and finishes what she started."

SHORTLY AFTER MR. Y. REFUSED TO see a former patient whose name he only vaguely recalled, I had to break back into the Betty Ford Center the same way Meredith and I had escaped. Jumping a barrier from the parking lot that turned out to be a row of boxwoods reinforced with chain-link, I bloodied my hands and knees on protruding metal shards while narrowly escaping severe injury to my vagina.

The system of trails snaking across the grounds had been scrubbed clean after the Canada geese moved on in the final piece of a head-scratching migration pattern.

I sneaked into the psych building toward the back of the campus, appearing in Mr. Y.'s remote office at the end of a long hall, where I risked a tasing at the very least. He'd be a fool to lose that last can of deer spray to defend himself against a disgruntled patient with a shiv or a rabid Canada goose who'd missed the last flight out.

"I'm surrendering," I announced. "Do you have a Band-Aid?"

Wholly nonplussed, he reached into his desk for some wet wipes and handed me a roll of medical tape with gauze. "You been drinking?"

"No, but I took a couple of pills a while back," I said. "I did leave one in the bottle."

"What are you saving it for?"

"I don't know, that's why I'm here," I said. "My boyfriend gave them to me, and I don't like him very much right now, but I do trust him for reasons I can't explain. Also, my sister died and decided not to tell me first, although I suspect she knew she was going to, which really pisses me off."

"Those are all good excuses, as if we needed any excuse to use." He scooted back in his office chair to get a better look at me. "Have the cravings kicked in?"

"I never had any cravings for Klonopin, though I could use a nice martini. To be clear, that's more of a passing fancy I occasionally indulge than a full-on craving."

"Klonopin is an anticonvulsant used to treat seizures and prevent panic attacks," he said. "I wouldn't be shaking it up with that martini idea, unless you're after a tasty recipe for death."

"In case you haven't noticed, I've got a little too much on my plate for that." I tended to my severe lacerations for dramatic effect. "I should stop in and see Elphaba about some antibiotics before I check into detox."

His long hair had been shortened to chin length. He wore it down now rather than in that familiar braid sitting on his shoulder. Maybe he'd reached over with a pair of scissors and lopped it off. "Your office looks about twenty percent smaller than I remember and not nearly as interesting."

"I haven't changed a thing," he said, looking around. "That probably means you're the one who's done some changing."

I told him I hadn't been getting to meetings and didn't have a sponsor, except informally through my conversations with Diarra. "And I got into this book called *Own It*," I said. "Doing my best to keep my word. Trying not to assume stuff I'll probably get wrong, anyway. Refusing to take things personally."

"That's Toltec wisdom," he said, a little confused. "It dates to the ancient Mayans."

"Are you sure? I thought my boss invented it."

He threw back his head and belly laughed, showing off an unusually nice set of teeth he apparently took the time to self-whiten. "I guess your boss could be an ancient Teotihuacan priest." He pulled a well-worn leatherbound book from his briefcase. "Toltec means 'artist'—artist of word, music, form, color, and life itself."

"Did they manifest their own stories and spin it to win it?"

"Sort of. They belonged to a secret society of spiritual practitioners who believed we're all just hallucinating our lives. I think you may be one of them."

"Oh no, that's too much." I got out my phone to check my Outlook. "Just find me a bed so I can come off this relapse."

"Not going to happen, Princess. For one thing, you're not in relapse."

"Are you not hearing anything I've said? Did you need me to go back and start again?"

"Please don't. I've got some real tragic cases coming out of detox. That Broadway legend who embarrassed herself again, a couple of former White House aides."

"For real?"

"Nothing is real," he said. "Didn't we just go over this?"

I was in no mood for deciphering sober riddles.

"Look, I'm in some big trouble at work I can't just hallucinate my way around. Meanwhile, my sister died thinking her life didn't amount to anything, and she's probably right, since she devoted pretty much all of it to my dream. Now I'm the only one with a sliver of hope for making either of our lives matter in the grand scheme of things, so I can't just sit around pretending I'm a Toucan priestess."

"Teotihuacan," he said. "A toucan is a parrot. What's the problem at work?"

"They've been testing my urine. I don't really know how all that works, but at some point, they're going to want to see a prescription I obviously don't have."

Trudi and Trina had been relentless in the days before I left for Meredith's funeral, sending Louise to my desk with a plastic cup at random intervals.

"Apparently Kayla indicated she has personal knowledge of an alleged drinking problem," Louise whispered through the door of the ladies' room stall, waiting for me to pee into a cup. "They'll deny hearing that and claim this is all routine."

There were other intrusions—a forensic examination of budget I'd invested into the studio improvements, confiscation of my corporate credit card while confirming its proper use. Meredith would have hit the roof if she hadn't already keeled over and died on me.

"I'm so sorry," Louise said after the news of her loss hit the Wonderful watercooler, triggering a brief truce shortly before my departure for the funeral. "I should have supported you better. I don't know what came over me."

"They're trying to make me appear incompetent."

"I know different." Louise took my hand as if to bind an unspoken promise, quickly realizing I hadn't washed it after making my latest deposit. "You do that. I'll take your sample."

I looked at Mr. Y. dubiously across his desk. "Most people are good with sticking their necks out until it's either you or them," I said. "Who's going to pick you, especially when you're in relapse?"

245

"Again, I'm not hearing a relapse," he said. "It wasn't your drug of choice, and you didn't go looking for a high. All good?"

"All good? I just told you my sister died because she refused to give up on me, which basically means I killed her!"

"Sorry, no. Your sister isn't in this one."

"There is no me without her, don't you get it? She used to think I had no fears, which is mostly true, because it was her job to do all that for me," I said, choking out the words. "Now I'm afraid of everything that happens next because nobody's ever going to love me like that again. I wouldn't even want them to."

Finally, I surrendered to a river of tears, welcoming the salt burning the edges of my tongue as happy news that I remembered how to feel.

Mr. Y. waited only a moment or two, then got up and showed me the door.

"What is wrong with you?" I wailed. "Can't you see I'm crying?"

"I do see that, yes. How long did you plan to keep at it?" He checked his watch.

"What are you, an animal? Should I get on my knees and beg to come back, is that what you want? I admit it, okay? I made the mistake of my life leaving recovery!"

"You never left recovery. Do you know what some people wouldn't give for that?" He looked a little wistful, hanging my bag on my shoulder and pointing me toward the door. "Take it and go."

"You're seriously sending me back out there to taste some more of my own dumb?"

"Only until you stop liking it. I feel like you're this close." He pinched together a thumb and forefinger, his breath cinnamon hot in my ear. A Dentyne man. I pictured him making the drive across the desert to refresh his stash from some back-alley candy man selling in bulk.

"Can I at least have some gum for the road?" I asked, stifling a final sniffle. "I'm fresh out."

He tossed me a pack warm from his shirt pocket and added a fresh box of Kleenex to my scant pile of necessities. "Use them all. Don't buy another box anytime soon."

"Is that some Toltec grief ritual?"

"No, I just worry about the environment."

Sensing I wouldn't be back this way any time soon, I snapped a mental picture of Mr. Y.'s nondescript office. Just as quickly, I dismissed my Betty Ford chapter like a smeared Polaroid at the bottom of an old shoebox in the attic, lost to time with the fornicating raccoons of summer.

"We're probably not supposed to, but can I give you a hug goodbye?" I asked.

"Bring it in."

I stood on my tippy toes and wrapped my arms around his well-muscled neck, burying my face in that terrifying snake tattoo. Leaving my Kleenex box intact, I wiped my residual snot on his collar. "I, too, share your concern for the environment," I said.

"*Via con dios*, Princess."

## CHAPTER NINETEEN

# Trina Oldham, the Most Wonderful Girl with a Wearable Self-Milking Playtex Creamery

**K**AYLA HAD A CHANGE OF heart about her copy-making duties after the *Universal Loser* crowd moved in and converted Happy Lindstrom's hallowed corner office into a writers' room for *Spacy Stacy*.

Reconceived as a kicky war between the sexes about three junior high science geeks and their wannabe astronaut gal pal, the groundbreaking feature film would become forty-four irrelevant episodes overdubbed in nine languages and broadcast all over the world.

I had never seen the generous girth of the binders Kayla procured and set around the writers' table, stuffed to the gills with Jonathan's hand-drawn character rotation studies, model sheets, and animatics.

The underlying screenplay received precious little attention, since most of the guys hadn't bothered to read it.

Watching my Hollywood nightmare resurrect itself and march into my hard-won Midwest territory on thousand-dollar Vans Chukka boots, I had an urge to pick up a rifle and reduce them to a batch of smug overpaid comedy writer foie gras.

Desperate to stave off any outward appearance of approaching middle age by dressing like Eminem in his youth, they wore backward baseball caps, unbuttoned plaid flannel shirts over black crewneck tees, and baggy cargo shorts exposing their well-toned, shaven calves to the cruel Wisconsin elements.

"Did I look that cold when I got here?" I asked Louise from our Wonderful hideout down the hall.

"Look at you now, though," she replied with an equivocating shrug. "You're a study in appropriate layering and functional footwear."

I shifted uncomfortably from side to side.

"Are you okay?"

"I have to pee again."

"Didn't you just go?"

"I overhydrate when I'm nervous," I said, heading back toward the ladies' room. "Do not take your eyes off the milkmaid until the wolves have dispersed."

Kayla leaned down like a geisha to exchange flimsy footwear for cozy mukluks with disposal toe warmer packs she planned to slip under the table and change out every four hours.

Reaching around her as if she didn't exist at all, they mulled over an assortment of mini bagels with cream cheese on a catered platter.

Kayla had never brought Louise and me so much as a coffee stirrer, and here these guys got hot mocha cappuccinos with fresh-grated chocolate she would refresh throughout the day like a traveling barista.

"That Kay-Kay is one talented kid," Jonathan reported after his sit-down with her earlier. "How about that sweet music video she put together?"

"I'm sorry to tell you this, Jonathan, but Kay-Kay had nothing whatsoever to do with that project. She wasn't even present for the shoot."

"Don't be like that, J.G." He put a finger to his lips as if to keep me from embarrassing myself with disinformation. "Very cool effect she came up with for the motion capture work. She walked me through her shot list frame by frame."

"Was it written in Punjabi by any chance?"

He wasn't quite as impressed with the *actual* footage Kayla did deliver from the JavaVino gig, an arthouse jumble of jump cuts zooming in and out of Diarra's mouth and onto her wobbly uvula in extreme close-up. "Maybe she comes off a little extra," Jonathan said. "She reminds me of me at that age."

"In what way?" *Maybe he had a severe mold allergy? Could he not get enough afternoon origami flower folding?*

"She's an outsider in her own life stuck up here in cow country, but that kid knows what she wants and she will have it. Some of us are born to spin the story to glory."

*And others have to rip off unsuspecting Mayan priests.*

I SAT BESIDE TRUDI IN Trina's office for my latest double come-uppance, where my authorization of company equipment for Kayla's supposed project raised all four identical eyebrows.

"Is there a reason we have to keep talking about Kayla?" I asked. "I just went over all this with Jonathan."

"We see the team as *victims* of your negligence and abuse," Trudi said. "Let's focus on all the ways in which *you've* cast aside the greater good to service *your* whims."

"Unethical hiring practices."

"Irresponsible expenditures."

"We've prepared quite a regrettable list."

Trina's low talking forced me to the edge of my chair, splaying my upper body over her desk to decipher the freshly stocked drivel falling out of her mouth like trout over a waterfall.

"Look at yourself," Trudi said. "You exhibit an arrogance multiple staff members find off-putting."

"Which multiple staff members? Don't I have a right to address their concerns directly?"

"Actually no." Trudi slammed shut her folder. "We have an obligation to shield the employees against retaliation."

"Why would I retaliate when I've done nothing wrong? We've gone over and over this."

Trudi took this as some sort of cue to initiate a bizarre round of fast-paced double-talk. "Certain medications are known to alter various perceptions," she informed me.

"Your medical information is private, of course," said Trina.

"Unless you were to request employee assistance," added Trudi. "Which we could make available as soon as this afternoon."

"Unless you opted out, at which point things would get complicated."

*Good twin, bad twin. What a couple of amateurs.*

"Ladies, this is a fishing expedition!"

I evoked the precise words of a stoner kid from Boulder I met waiting for an airport taxi outside Betty Ford. "They'll think you've consulted some hardcore hippie from the cannabis industry," he said. "Nobody wants those dudes coming around stinking up the place, even if they did get a clean screen on you, which is rare. My stepmom hasn't got zilch on me, how do you think I got sprung?"

He lit up a spliff in the direct shade of Betty's famous garden bust to prove his point.

I summoned his moxie to stare down Trudi and Trina both.

"So, what was it, a faulty tester? An unidentified adulterant? I'm willing to go with improper storage or labeling and call it an honest error, but unless I see some legally certified lab results for counter-testing, I am concluding this pathetic line of questioning now."

"There's no need to get nasty over a routine wellness check," Trina said. "Workplace safety is always top of mind here at Wonderful Girls."

"No harm done," I said, reversing positions. "Can the three of us agree we are very different kinds of women?"

"Hundred percent," said Trina.

"Hundred and fifty."

"That isn't a thing, Trudi, but what the heck. Maybe the sum of our parts does add up to substantially more than what today's girls need. I know I'm ready to make a fresh start."

"I find that very hard to believe," Trudi scoffed. "You've flatly refused to work on Jonathan's new show."

"Those guys don't want me up there. I'll hardly open my mouth before I get shut down by some lame joke about women talking too much."

"How would you explain the support Jonathan has offered Kayla?" Trina asked.

"There's always a Kayla. A harmless vagina in the room is there to perk up the big pecker in lockstep with the lesser peckers."

"I see what you've been dealing with, Tri. She's a shock jock, stuck on the wrong station."

"She was your hire, Tru. I was on leave." Trina pulled a pair of suckers from a jar and gave one to Trudi.

"Excuse me, how is it okay to reduce me to some third-person trope while going to your special place with nicknames and lollipops?"

Finally coming out of some weird candy time revery, they both looked at me as though surprised I was still there. "I have no idea what took me so long," I announced, "but I would like to lodge a formal workplace harassment and discrimination complaint."

"Against Wonderful Girls?" Trina asked, aghast.

"Against my direct supervisor, Trudi Oldham!"

"That is patently ridiculous," Trudi sniffed.

"Who led the charge to undermine, ostracize, and degrade me since the day I walked in the door? Wrong origin, wrong culture, wrong birthplace, wrong marital and maternal status. I'm quoting the Fair Labor Act now, posted in *your* employee break room, where I've routinely been made to feel different for eating two lunches with one fork!"

"Trudi, please leave."

"I will not." She crossed her arms.

"Get out. Let me do my job."

With that, Trudi squeezed her ample rear past me and exited in a huff, slamming the door behind her.

"Before you go on, Jaycee, I need to inform you there have been significant shifts in our needs since your hire," Trina said. "We've had trouble finding you suitable work."

"Oh please. There's plenty of work that isn't ever going to get done, because you can't find a soul to do it within a thousand miles of this ungodly outpost of gender dysfunction."

"Is it possible *you* weren't the right fit?"

"I don't have to fit!" I shot back. "I'm supposed to be a square peg in a round hole. I can be any hole I want to be. It's called creative disruption, and it's why you pay me the big bucks."

Though Trina didn't appear to follow me, any talk of hole size and large payments meant calling in the fleet. "An allegation against the organization is bigger than San Francisco. I'll have to involve Tokyo."

"What is this, the Battle of Midway? We don't even have a wall in this pathetic operation to line up that crew for a piss."

"The warehouse facilities are within a short well-lit walk with priority plowing," she insisted, wincing at the image I'd drawn. "That said, it is going to be quite a lengthy process involving a sizable contingent, what with the incoming legal, translation, risk management, and global security teams. That's not even counting your assigned caseworker from Wisconsin Victim Services on hand to watch for any coercion or intimidation tactics from those sneaky Pacific types."

"You're bluffing."

"Am I?"

"Oh, you are good," I said. "But I'm better. I know what you've been up to, Trina Oldham. *J'accuse!*"

"I haven't the slightest idea what you're talking about."

*Neither did I, but I was on a roll.*

"This whole place is just one thin line on some ginormous spreadsheet in the sky that only makes sense until it doesn't, and then boom. Acquisition."

"Yes, we did that already. It's been nearly two years now."

"In that case, maybe we're due for something more hostile in a takeover," I theorized. "Only the next time we get gobbled up by some monstrous conglomerate, the leftovers might land somewhere in the vicinity of *your* hot little hands."

"Really? And how would I make that happen?"

"People get old and die, fade away, dole out their share of the spoils to sycophantic pets who spend turkey time with them in cozy wintry hideaways."

I scanned the photos on her bookshelf, an alarming display of yearlings, birthed in the bathtub, fattened for the fight at *Mommy and Me* and booted off to preschool. I lost count at round eleven, when I became distracted by the frightening elasticity of this woman's cervix.

"Risk, by definition, carries too much risk," I continued. "There's nothing as risky as innovation and originality. Why rock the boat? Why do anything when you can sit quietly in the basement until the next big bonanza falls out of the sky?"

"What a colorful story," she said. "While I don't appreciate the vaguely drawn character assault, I can't fault you for showing the skills to deliver *something*."

"I'm not here to deliver. I'm just another shiny foreign import who turned out to be so unreliable I got marked for a quick return to some godless port of origin."

"Yes, very entertaining, lots of hyperbole. Excellent work."

"I don't do any work! Nobody does! We all twirl around in circles all day with our thumbs on our foreheads. Oh, we might go out and pick up another annual award recognizing our failure to innovate in any meaningful way. The people need something uncontroverted to celebrate in these troubled times."

"Even if there were a shred of truth behind this fiction you're weaving, why wouldn't you point the finger at the primary beneficiary of any such profiteering scheme?"

"Happy Lindstrom? She's barely in the picture and you know it," I said. "She earned a right to go off and build some fake desert strip mall in the name of high art. If only she hadn't entrusted her original vision to a pair of empresses with no clothes. Ironically, you might just get away with this wacky Orwellian notion that inertia works, the longer you're willing to kick back and watch it all burn to the ground."

"Are you finished?"

"I don't know, am I?"

"Stop asking questions! I'm the HR Generalist."

"Is that your title?"

"That's a question!"

"Sorry. After you."

"Firstly, I hardly know Happy," she huffed. Masking her anxiety, she gathered some papers to file, but they flew to the floor, and she scrambled after them on hand and knee. "I spent my early career in Namibia managing my husband's church in service of our Lord Jesus Christ."

"You call yourself a Namibian Christian?"

I crawled after her under the desk.

"You dragged me here under false pretenses while my sister was dying. You might as well have killed her yourself. She was a big, beautiful, fairy forest queen and you're a petty little criminal selling your soul on the flimsy hope of earning a few extra nickels."

Trina Oldham had supposedly taken live shooter training at a monthly Women in Soft Goods meeting in Wauwatosa and couldn't be easily intimidated by the senseless rantings of a disgruntled underling. Louise warned me during one of our ladies' room urine-testing chats that Trina would run, hide, placate, disarm, or fight back in whatever order necessary.

"I recognize this is a difficult time, but I would ask you to control yourself," Trina low-talked across her desk.

"What is uncontrolled about the truth, other than nobody's allowed to speak it around here?" I low-talked even lower. "If you wanted to get something off your chest, I'm listening."

She eyeballed a heavy industrial stapler and a good, strong umbrella with a wood-carved duck bill handle. "You haven't got a shred of evidence as to this Marxist theory of yours."

"Maybe I do, maybe I don't," I said. "You'll always have a conscience, though, unless you left it back in Africa. Those must have been some crazy times, just you and the hubs, him Tarzan, you Jane, no screaming brats or bitchy twin yakking about overcrowding your share of the womb."

Trina silenced a beeping alarm from beneath her button-down blouse, as bright orange lights beamed from either nipple.

"If you'll excuse me, I'm having my afternoon expression."

She crawled over to a mini fridge to grab a sterile BPA bottle and settled back into her chair, emitting a long sigh.

"I'm sorry, are you milking yourself?"

"Even if my office lactation options were any of your concern, I'm perfectly able to multitask," she said, clearly affronted by my curiosity in her fully automated, wearable nursing station.

The gentle churning of a seven-level system grew more intense as it thumped from cup to cup against the desk. She wriggled around a bit, then sat up ramrod straight, locked and loaded. "Where were we?"

As I slinked into my chair deeply humbled by the efficiency of Trina Oldham's Playtex creamery, it occurred to me she had been robbed of unique DNA at conception.

Harlan Meidlemeister had revealed in dribs and drabs that the Oldham twins could barely reach the cash drawer when they started working the register at their dad's market. When one twin neglected to ring up a four-pound Folger's canister rolling by on the conveyor belt, both twins took the blame for its unexplained disappearance. Witnesses couldn't say which Oldham twin later returned a total of twenty-five Folger's cans at a succession of markets along the highway, netting an eventual four hundred and eighty-four dollars in cash.

Although my loose-lipped mailman must have been a tyke himself at the time, he claimed personal knowledge of a large cash donation Old Man Oldham made that spring to the 4-H Club. A pair of genetically engineered piglets for the twins to raise were gifted in return, dispensing with the entire matter before opening day of the Dane County Fair.

What came to be known as the Oldham Family Folger's Affair had been swept into the dustbin of Littleburgh history years before the Greater Dane County Expired Coupon Scam. A two-for-one special ignited a legendary five-village run on Skippy Peanut Butter, my source went on to report in rain, sleet, and shine. Driftless shelves had been emptied of nut butter of any kind as families stocked up for the hectic back-to-school lunchbox season. The local couponing clearinghouse declining to honor an unusually large invoice from Oldham Grocery signaled a visit from the Wisconsin Department of Justice, but they quickly dismissed the entire matter as a simple accounting error after Mr. Oldham purchased both that coupon clearinghouse and its only major competitor.

By that time, Trina's new groom had whisked her off on a mission deep in the African subcontinent, while Trudi's star rose like a meteor over a glass atrium she aptly christened the Happy Wonderful Place. Had Trina been forced into some regrettable lifelong enterprise under a thumb imprinted with her exact match—or was it the other way around? Either way, the executive half of Trina's mutated ovum uprooted her idyllic life bilking her chosen prince's pulpit, only to banish her to the basement for a twice daily pump and dump. I considered inviting Trina to shed the bonds of bovine servility and walk with us, if only I had the slightest idea who we were or where we were going.

"Listen to me, Trina," I low-talked, nice and easy. "Weren't you the one who brokered my employment contract even as your water broke?" I took a shot here, figuring on the odds.

"And?"

*Bingo.* "It was *your* grit and determination that led me to the edge of the wilderness, where Clara, Tara, and Sara were born."

"Dolls aren't born. They're not even real." An electric jolt marked a sharp transition between her stimulation and suction cycles.

"Movies make everything real."

"A movie? That's what you're after here?"

"Yes, a movie! Stay with me now!" *These women had really lost the plot.*

An alarming screech signaled a code red from Trina's phone.

"Now you've shorted my self-cooling function," she said curtly, dialing down the temperature and jerking her wayward Frankenbra back into place.

"We're no longer in my wheelhouse," she said. "However, I'd be very surprised to see you get a forty-million-dollar expense approved."

"What if I figure out a way to bring it in for less?"

"You'll have to run all that by the senior team. In the meantime, you may expect to receive a second letter of reprimand around the personnel issues we've discussed."

"What happens if I get a third letter?"

"There is no third letter. Our contract stipulates mutual obligations to one another, and you have failed to sell us anything that works. Your beef isn't with me. It's with yourself."

If Trina Oldham had proved herself adequately human and resourceful to hopscotch around a criminal referral to the Department of Justice while simultaneously cranking out a block of baby swiss, I could darn well become my own Meredith.

"Apparently, you're not familiar with the Equitable Doctrine of Prevention!" I said. Either I'd remembered my sister's verbiage correctly or babbled some meaningless legalese. "You can't make a contract with me and prevent me from doing my part."

"I'll investigate your assorted charges and get back to you with a final determination. Right now, I need to think happy thoughts about my baby." She leaned all the way back in her chair, cuing a terrifying rush of rabid gurgling.

"Not so fast."

I splayed myself across her desk so near her face I smelled a hint of human cottage cheese about to spoil her dual-function barn party. "While you're working on all that, I'm going to need some of those free mochaccinos with the grated chocolate on top. Have Kayla bring that over on a tray with the leftover mini bagels. I like mine scooped and toasted," I said. "Do me a favor and hold the cream cheese."

CHAPTER TWENTY

# Naomi Petersheim, the Most Wonderful Girl on the Lam from the Lord under Orders from the *Ordnung*

AFTER RETURNING TO THE OFFICE from Meredith's funeral, I found a small stash of condolence cards on my desk, but none seemed to be from folks I knew by name.

Predictably, even Louise refrained from offering a written word of support in the event things got as ugly as they were about to. A bouquet of grocery store mini carnations from the security gate sat wilting in a Styrofoam cup of water, and the cafeteria people sent over a half-dozen limp chocolate-covered fruit pops stuck in an upside-down half cantaloupe.

I opened a lovely linen envelope, sealed with a dollop of silver wax and stamped with the letter "C." and read the handwritten note inside.

*Dear Jaycee,*

*Life sometimes brings enormous difficulties and challenges that seem just too hard to bear. But bear them you can, and bear them you will, and your life can have a purpose.*

*With sympathy,*

*Casey Klinkhoffer*

She lifted it word for word from the back jacket of Barbara Walters's triumphant memoir about being iconic for a full half century after her mom let her dad dick her around, to paraphrase the Wikipedia entry I looked up.

I threw on my coat and boots and marched over to the Photo Studios through the deep snow.

Prudence stood outside Casey's office, fussing with some items on a wardrobe rack.

"Whatever it is, I'm not involved," she said tersely. "I have to get these to the illustrator and I'm late for a lunch appointment with my trainer."

"How fascinating. Anyway, I don't recall asking you for anything, Pru."

"'Pru' is not my preferred name. If you're using it to diminish me in some way, I will not hesitate to report you to HR."

I snatched a half-eaten oatmeal cookie from a hallway coffee cart.

"That's disgusting," she said.

"It could use a few raisins."

As she turned on a heel and stomped off, I had to wonder if that was just how she walked. "Hey, nice chatting with you, Prudie!" I watched her disappear down the hall and sneaked into Casey's office.

Her cell phone sat on the desk in sleep mode. Breaking into it would be a challenge far beyond my technical skills, but I grabbed it anyway and made a run for it.

EXASPERATED BY MY FREQUENT TRIPS to the ladies' room, I managed a last-minute doctor's appointment with a top urologist at UW–Madison.

Escorting me to an exam room, the nurse handed me a paper gown and told me to remove my clothing so the doctor could perform a pelvic examination.

"That's a bit excessive," I said. "It feels like a little urinary tract infection. I get them all the time."

"We're a teaching facility," she told me, as if that should explain the enthusiasm. "Do you have any issues with a female student observing?"

"I'm all for offering my body to medical education while I'm still alive."

"The good news is it's nothing serious," an officious little fellow shortly announced after a quick look under the hood.

"What's the bad news?" I asked, sitting up in the stirrups to close my knees for business.

"No woman likes hearing this, but an overactive bladder is often associated with the onset of menopause."

"Menopause? I'm barely forty."

"The estrogen levels start to reduce at this stage, causing structures around the pelvic organs to weaken." Making a big show of scribbling something important in my chart, he mainly struggled with whether to order a nice fat pastrami on rye for lunch while covertly eyeballing a take-out menu displayed on the counter.

"That's it? You're not going to do any tests?"

Returning his attention to me, however begrudgingly, he probably decided to stick to his low-carb diet and avoid another ill-informed cholesterol conversation over dinner with the trophy wife. "We can give you something to reduce episodes of urinary incontinence."

"Incontinence? Like I said, it's just an annoying feeling that I need to go again when I just went."

"If you don't need the medication, don't take it. Whatever makes you more comfortable, ma'am."

"It's miss, actually. Shouldn't my relationship status be central to this type of diagnosis?"

"May I ask if you have a burning sensation with urination?" interjected the young female resident present for an alleged education.

"Only because I go so much," I confided, gal to gal. "We have this super scratchy toilet paper at my job, like they're doing whatever they can to cause mutual discomfort." I made a mental note to add that to my list of workplace grievances.

"Are you having pain during intercourse?" she asked.

"I get where you're going, Doctor," he said, waving a hand in her general direction. "We can comfortably rule out diagnoses in consideration of the demographic."

"Excuse me," I said, waving a dismissive hand in *his* general direction. "I have plenty of intercourse across a *wide* demographic."

"Are you exclusive and monogamous with your current partner?" she asked.

"Of course. I can't speak for him, but what woman can? He lives with his ex-wife."

"Who is also likely a very low-risk, very middle-aged woman," chided Doctor Misogyny, wedging himself between her and me. "Just a guess."

"Would he have any other current or former partners that might give you cause for concern?" she persisted.

"His last girlfriend is twenty and totally bonkers," I said. "She lives on an army base."

"Woot!" she exclaimed, doing a highly inappropriate touchdown dance before pulling herself together. "I'm sorry, but I never get to be right about anything around this place. I should have gone to law school."

ABEL AND I SAT IN his squad in front of my house while he was on duty, distracted by the backdrop of coded prattle crackling from his radio. "You gave me chlamydia, Copper."

"No, that couldn't have been me," he said, rejecting the entire matter out of hand. "I don't even have any symptoms."

"Seventy-five percent of the population is asymptomatic, but thankfully I'm not one of them."

He patted my knee dismissively while grabbing a bite from a ham sandwich sequestered in a brown paper bag tucked between the seats.

I wondered if Sally was packing his lunch now. "I guess you don't plan to apologize, but there's some paperwork to be filed with the Wisconsin Department of Health. They can help notify everyone you've slept with."

"Everyone? Jeezaloo, Snow White! I haven't been with anyone but you in a dog's age."

"That doesn't make a whole lot of sense right now, does it?"

He sighed. "I guess I could have picked up something from Robyn, although I don't know how. I haven't seen her in I don't know how long."

"They'll need to screen me for everything now. Hepatitis. Genital herpes. Syphilis and gonorrhea."

"Please stop naming sex diseases. What do I know about dating, an old guy like me?"

"Why would you have slept with Robyn after you and I met?"

I was disgusted by the thought of her disease in my body, as though I had fallen prey to a regimen of overzealous Ft. McCoy recruits lined up outside the latrine to have at me.

"Maybe you and I hadn't gotten together in that way just yet. I might have been with her around Thanksgiving."

"After she shot herself in the head?"

"It was her ear, and she barely clipped it."

"You blocked anything real from ever happening between us by hooking up with her," I said. "You claimed to be single and available, and I believed you."

"I was! I still am!"

"You're really not." I let this sink in myself. "You don't even want to be free, or you wouldn't have let six different women come between us, time and again."

"Six different women? Where'd you hear that hooey?"

"I'm talking about your six emotionally stunted daughters, one of whom you married on a technicality."

"Here you go, bringing Sally into the middle of things."

"I didn't bring her anywhere," I said. "She moved in and tried to get you back knowing full well we were involved."

"She blew me off, if that makes you happy," he said with a dismissive shrug.

"Isn't that a fascinating turn of events. Would you care to elaborate?"

He hesitated. "Did you say something to Eugenie about Sally being a lousy mother?"

"What? Of course not!"

"Well, that's how it got back to Sally. She's been the family translator since the girls grew up and wanted the different feminine products and such, all kinds of colors and shapes. Can I help it if I don't always speak the best 'girl'?"

"'Girl' is not a language. Who knows what kind of gibberish that woman ferried back and forth in a pathetic attempt to stay relevant." A cold realization washed over me. "I bet Sally and Robyn look alike give or take a few years—big doe eyes. Long tangled hair that can never get enough brushing."

"Eugenie tell you that?"

"Wild guess! You only feel okay when you're looking down and pulling up a woman who's every inch smaller than you. Finding one you saw as an equal made you feel off-kilter."

"Not true. I love how it is with us," he said. "Been looking for you forever."

"Yet you can't stay awake long enough to take me on a proper date. We've never gone to a movie or sat in a coffee bar playing checkers. I don't even know if you like those things."

"You knew winter was coming and this is how it would be."

"Winter is always coming," I said. "And this is always how it's going to be."

He quieted me with a hand, focused on some coded chatter over the radio about a bank robbery days earlier in another part of the state and a possible armed suspect heading in a different direction.

"I've got to go." *No, he didn't.* "I'll call you later." *No, he wouldn't.*

"Skip it," I said. "Next time you get an urge to see me, jump in the lake and swim over."

"It's frozen solid. Even in summer that current is dangerous as heck."

"No frozen lake or dangerous-as-heck current would ever stand between a man and the woman he wants," I said. "If you want some help getting off the pills, I know some folks."

"Why would I need help to stop taking my meds?"

"Because you're an addict."

"I'm a cop." He wrestled with the suggestion that both things could be so with an elongated chuckle.

I jumped out of the squad. "You should know I didn't write 'I Like You' for you. I wrote it for myself."

"It has my name in it."

"I have a Wonderful pencil. Consider yourself erased."

*DEAR BARBARA WALTERS:*

*I read somewhere that you advise women to steer clear of little fights and fight the big one. My problem is I fight the wrong ones with the wrong people, and fighting in general takes too much energy. I guess like a lot of women I waited for some empty suit to swoop in and save me from me, but I've recently had some hard lessons about how short life is, and I'm done waiting for anything.*

At home contemplating all three unsent Barbara Walters missives in my email outbox, I looked at an image of little Marshall and Pendleton on Casey's pinched cell phone and had second thoughts about breaking into it for an email address she may never have had. How could I claim such bitter disappointment among all the women who'd betrayed me to my face if I needed to force Casey into a corner on whether her most obsessive conquest even existed?

I proceeded to give over my unsent outbox to the universe, saying a slightly revised prayer out loud.

*God, grant me the serenity to accept Casey Klinkhoffer's thieving and deception.* Delete.

*The courage to accept the things I cannot change, such as Kayla Flynn's lying and whoring.* Delete.

*And the wisdom to tell the difference between Trudi and Trina Oldham at the end of cold sore season.* Delete delete delete.

I heard a rustle outside my window and got up to flip on the exterior lights. I made out the silhouette of Naomi seated on my back steps with a basket in her lap, shivering in the twilight. She seemed like she might be waiting for someone on the sly, but I ran downstairs to fetch her in from the cold. "What are you doing out there? Come inside before you freeze to death."

"My father says I can have more time," she said.

Though she had dressed modestly in her usual garb, her long thick blond tresses reached her waist, freed from their customary *kapp*.

"You don't have a single split end," I said. "Can we figure out how to bottle that?"

"I mixed liquid castile with summer chamomile and the last of the wild roses from the knoll. I left a bottle on the kitchen sink."

"I thought that was dish soap."

"It is."

I suddenly needed this girl in my daily life to get any reasonable degree of clarity around being a woman. "How much time did your dad give you?"

"As much as I need to make the right decision for God," she said. "That is what the *Ordnung* says, and even the men must accept it as law."

"High five, girl," I said, raising my right hand.

Unsure how to respond to that, especially while tying on an apron, she slipped past me up the stairway and into the main living area. "The winter market has closed for the season," she lamented, buzzing about fluffing pillows and ferrying my dirty plates to the kitchen. "The orchards and fields have been picked and hunted; the cellars stocked. I've no way to earn my keep until the weather breaks."

"You don't need to earn anything around here," I said. "Why don't you have a seat?"

"Miss?"

"Sit down. Take a load off."

She sat uncomfortably beside me on the couch, drumming her hands on her knees.

"Maybe you really want to use this time to figure out how to make a greater impact on your community," I said. "Naomi, you're a leader."

"I'm no leader, miss." Her cheeks flushed a bright pink over her lightly freckled skin. "I'm just a cook."

"People don't line up down the street for just a cook," I said. "There's a farmer's market on every block, with an Amish granny at the candy counter—and who doesn't like a nice, hot Mennonite muffin? Yours became an addiction because you harnessed all your talents to reel us in and keep us there with music and song. Maybe not dancing, but you get where I'm going."

"There's dancing. Twice daily jigging and clogging with make-your-own aebleskivers. Couldn't you get a ticket?" She got up to fetch some wood, stacking it on the fireplace with the precision of a Jenga tower.

"Do you have any idea the kind of money your brother has taken me for on this renovation? Maybe he gives you a cut if he's feeling generous, but why must the woman submit to the man's whims where she's the primary headbanging jigger and clogger?"

"Because the kitchen is my dance, a private dance, for me. When the music stops, I like going back inside myself."

"Stay there," I said. "Homey Naomi could function fine with you behind the scenes. A fictitious Mennonite farm gal out front would open an enticing brand conversation."

"A brand conversation about what?" She had never heard the term but seemed to like the sound of it, turning her back on me to mask her intrigue. Lining up twigs of dried lavender and rosemary for kindling just so, she released a twirling plume of lightly fragranced smoke into the air.

"About how to make life beautiful with what folks have on hand."

I watched the firelight cast a berry-hued glow over her shiny locks. "How to make calming fires and wash our hair and dishes with the same sweet-smelling soap. Organic and sustainable are nothing new, but you're doing something unique in foraging the land for things most of us never saw."

A flickering of torchlight outside against the reflection of the soaring picture windows snapped Naomi out of her own flame-lit revery. "Oh dear, now I'm late."

"For what, the late-night ride of Paul Revere?" I cupped my hands against the glass to peer outside.

"Please don't confuse me."

She scurried over to the basket she'd brought along and pulled out two boiled chickens and a chicken liver, a bag of uncooked rice, a bottle of Chinese wine, and a folded heart made of gold joss paper that smelled of sandalwood. "The people of the market are very sorry for the loss of your sister," she said, delivering a script of some kind.

"What happened to the other chicken liver?" I asked.

"That is odd, isn't it?"

She scratched her head, clearly overwhelmed by the assignment, as dozens of multigenerational Plain People intermixed with wandering Hmong assembled at the edge of the hard-frozen lake, reflecting the starlight overhead like a sheet of glass.

"The Hmong believe we must call the soul to the afterlife with music." Naomi led me out onto the chilly overlook, where a young Hmong boy beat a ceremonial drum against the mournful whine of the qeej—a long, willowy flute on arched bamboo shoots. "The truth is your sister needs no special guidance into the arms of God," she whispered.

"The mailman told me your people don't mix well with their people," I whispered back.

"Harlan Meidlemeister? What does he know?"

When the drummer stopped, the flute carried on its departure song alone, and the mourners released their illuminated paper sky lanterns, a flock of glowing doves sailing bravely into the unknown. "The Hmong say we must light her way as she re-visits her life," Naomi said, adding another dubious aside. "The truth is her soul has already ascended to heaven with God."

As a newly minted Toltec, I had my own beliefs, but I freely accepted the sum of whatever these folks preached. Just when I thought I was meant to walk alone, we became family, a tribe of fellow misfits bonded by the ravages of winter. Together we'd survived its inevitable losses without exchanging a single word, sharing comfort in the silence of the prairie's hidden fringes.

"How would you have known my sister died?" I asked Naomi, tears welling in my eyes. Maybe they had a manual of some kind revealing the key to my own life absent of Meredith's, some complex jumble of undying adoration and mutual resentment I could conjure in place of the persistent ache at my core.

"Freddie Weissfluggen keeps us up on things," Naomi said. "He worries about you, that one."

"Freddie?" I asked. "Is he here?"

"No, miss. I don't know how they work things on the other side, but in these parts, when you tell a boy to go, the kind ones stay gone."

She handed me a dish towel hanging from her apron string and left me to dry my tears and get on with it as she headed into the kitchen. Twisting her hair into a knot, she buzzed about taking an inventory of what we had on hand. After putting on a big pot of water for the rice, she began to slice and portion out the chicken for the crowd.

"They'll come inside now for the feast of small pigs," she said. "Go fetch my hatchet."

"Your hatchet? For what?"

"For the small pigs, of course. We'll have to butcher and roast them." She clapped her hands impatiently. "Go on. Shoo."

Meredith and I would never open our chichi SoCal teahouse, but her legacy just might live on in the most unexpected of ways. Pending a substantial infusion of cash, Homey Naomi's Farmed and Foraged Foods, a limited liability corporation, might even be taken seriously in a highly competitive marketplace as a woman-owned gourmet products empire built one small pig at a time.

CHAPTER TWENTY-ONE

# Fran MacNeill, the Most Wonderful Girl on the Football Field Kicking in the Wrong Direction

WINTER RELEASED ITS HOLD ON Wisconsin only begrudgingly, as the temperatures rose in bursts of false hope, giving way to infant buds on bright green twigs. Spring bulbs peeked above the snow like periscopes—when another blast of brutal cold trampled all signs of sunnier days to come.

Despite my best efforts to chase away every critter in and around my house months earlier, I woke up listening for the ribbits, clucks, and grunts of frogs, toads, hedgehogs, and marmots taking the bait of a fleeting warm spell. I heard only the sound of persistent hammering coming from my back porch.

I threw on my London Fog over a pair of flannel pajamas imprinted with dancing snowmen to run down and tell Elijah to come back with a groundhog.

Freddie Weissfluggen rolled himself around my completed network of walkways, tacking up approved village construction permits.

"You're late," I said.

"I'm early. You told me not to come back until spring," he replied with an easy grin. "Come here, let me show you something."

I trailed after his chair along the zigzagging boardwalk, tracing the fragrant planks of fresh-cut pressure-treated timber designed to have minimal impact on the wetlands.

"Where are we going? Should I get my boots?"

"I don't know. Maybe I should get mine," he said mysteriously.

He stopped short, and I almost plowed into him as he wheeled around to face me.

Using the newly installed wrought iron railings on either side, he hoisted himself up—and for the first time ever, took a few steps toward me.

"Freddie," I gasped. "You're walking!"

"It's an experimental spinal implant that works like a cattle prod. You're seeing it for the first time outside of a medical setting. Who knows what'll happen down the road."

I threw my arms around him and almost knocked him over. "You're a rock star!"

He steadied himself upright, supporting himself on the railing. "Jeepers, does this mean you'll marry me?"

"No, Beaver, it does not. I can't even think about dating right now."

"I'm going to take that as another tentative yes."

I couldn't recall a first yes, tentative or otherwise.

"I admit I'm a little under the gun," he said. "I need a running mate for my congressional run."

"Freddie, I've been to rehab twice now, although this last time I had to break in and I hurt myself *down there*."

"Gerald and Betty Ford made something like that work all the way to the White House. Meantime I've brought news about your house."

He reached for a document-sized manila envelope stowed in the pocket of his chair. "Does the name Marion Mahoney Griffin ring any bells?"

"Wasn't she Frank Lloyd Wright's mistress?"

"No, she was never his mistress. They were more like frenemies, until he kept stealing all her best ideas and taking the credit. Kind of like you and Casey Klinkhoffer."

"Wow. Are you saying this house has some kind of curse?"

"Not at all. It's how she restored her reputation—only it killed them both in the end."

"My house killed Frank Lloyd Wright?"

"Pretty much. How's that for a claim to fame?"

One of the first female architects in the world, Marion got so fed up with Frank she married another architect and skipped the country, Freddie said. "Then Frank went and told the press her work with *that* guy was even more subpar. Making matters worse, just when Marion was about to get famous in places like Australia and New Zealand on commissions Frank couldn't touch, the husband up and died on her."

She returned to Chicago brokenhearted and alone, living out the rest of her days in relative obscurity—until a pair of world explorers who knew of her triumphant work abroad inherited a remote parcel of Wisconsin marshland.

The lush site overlooking a hidden corner of Lake Mendota only became habitable with the damming of the locks at the mouth of the Yahara.

Marion came out of seclusion to design her only known solo commission—a stone's throw from the greatest living work of her archnemesis.

"Wouldn't you know the old buzzard managed to gum up the works one last time?" Freddie said. "*He* put *his* name to *her* drawings and got everything so turned around they were both long gone before the builders broke ground."

He unfurled a time-worn, hand-inked drawing of "Littleburgh Love Cottage" Marion might have imagined late one starlit summer evening in the glow of a lantern by the shore. "You might want to donate this little gem to Bob the Cobbler."

"The shoe guy? What for?"

"He runs the Littleburgh Historical Archives from the back room of his shop. I found your house plans hiding in plain sight next to a partial collection of commemorative stamps from the Wisconsin Pavilion at the 1964 World's Fair."

"Behind the expired shoe polish? What kind of way is that to treat Marion's legacy?"

"Bob didn't know what he had," Freddie said. "He'll have it in the front window now, where the whole world can stop and take notice every two minutes and twenty seconds, once I get a majority vote on my traffic light." I looked at him dubiously. "It could happen."

I glanced back at the home renovations I'd integrated into Marion's stubborn design. Whether she'd ever stopped back in to have a seat on my couch, I always felt her presence, like a polite knock at the door I never got to answering amid the bats in the attic and creaking floors at my feet. "My sister wanted me to belong somewhere without having to put up a fight every day of my life. I really blew it here, Freddie."

"Why are you talking about yourself in the past tense?" Freddie asked, propping himself up behind me with a firm hand on either shoulder. "Like it or not, you have a family out here now, and they'll be looking at you to finish what you started. I can't see where you'd need to put up a fight for anything on your own land, but you do have a rifle, and I hear you know how to use it."

"It's Elijah Petersheim's rifle, but I am the best shot in the county."

"You care to make a wager on that one, missy?" he said with a wink.

Freddie Weissfluggen, the legendary Littleburgh badass, had refused to abandon a thirty-million-dollar fighter plane while literally on fire. That had somehow slipped my mind until the fine morning he posted himself like a lookout over my fledgling boardwalk while I slept alone waiting for the overdue birth of spring.

Hands on hips, he crossed his newly functioning legs at the ankles, dwelling in the endless possibility of the awakening prairie—and toppled backward over the railing!

"Oh my God, Freddie!" I leaned over and looked down. "Are you alright?"

"Oh wow, pain. Pain. Pain. Pain."

He sat up on his elbows in the slushy marsh, wearing a huge celebratory grin. "Pain, Jaycee! I. Feel. Pain!"

"Please don't sue me, Freddie. I couldn't possibly have enough homeowner's insurance in place to afford breaking Littleburgh's finest a second time."

I ran down the ramp, tromping through the stinky swamp cabbage to kneel at his side.

"Maybe I'm not broken anymore!" he exclaimed. "My ankle hurts like holy freaking heck, excuse my French."

"How am I going to get you up? I'm not sure what time Elijah's coming. He's been mad at me since I put Naomi in business college. Now he and I have to get our own supper three nights a week."

"Lie down. We'll play the cloud game."

Had I dared look up at the sky, I might have found Meredith shooting me a lascivious wink as I lay beside Freddie and watched his chest rise in the dewy sawgrass.

Maybe Tara, Sara, and Clara—conjured up by a frustrated housewife in a garage just down the road—would march through a cumulus cornfield in defense of a generational sisterhood still struggling to make sense of it all.

Clasping his hands behind his neck looking skyward, Freddie made out a shape in the clouds. "I see a two-headed baboon riding a boogie board there to the right. You see it?"

"What I see is a woman somewhere in the middle of her life about to lose everything she never knew she wanted."


BANISHED ALONE TO THE STUDIOS among that alarming collection of chubby limbs and headless torsos comprising the remains of my loyal support team, for weeks I'd churned out endless movie synopses—each declared uninteresting, overpriced, or generally unworkable by the senior team members.

My attendance at their meetings had been perfunctory, in the event I received an invitation at all.

Belinda Rockland stopped me flat at the door of a five-year marketing road-mapping session integrating my entire group scheduled in the Wonderful conference room after Louise quietly gave me a heads-up.

"I don't work with you," she said. "I work with Jonathan."

"And Kayla, Louise, and Prudence," I said. "We're the entertainment team."

"All that rolls up under Jonathan now. He likes to phone in from the road."

"This sounds suspiciously like whistleblower retaliation," I said. "A serious federal offense."

"I wouldn't know about any of that. However, you may grab a slice of my famous Strawberry Jell-O Poke Cake on your way out," she added magnanimously. "I'm not a monster."

"How absolutely dreadful," I said. "It's high time somebody told you people don't want to see their food jiggling around on a fork."

Try as she might to get in my face while pushing the plate out of my reach, her eye line only met my bra line. "No Poke Cake for you," she said, slamming the door in my face.

"You're a walking anachronism, with the baking skills of a Jiffy box, Belinda Rockland. Someday my Mennonite is going to clean the floor with you!"

I felt I'd already won that round in some small way, despite standing alone in an empty hallway.

Jonathan deflected any potential exposure in Trina's supposed fair employment investigation by offering Kayla a step up as his right arm in San Francisco. She promptly canceled her wedding, shredded thirty-two hundred origami flowers, sold the ring, purchased its worth in cryptocurrency, and left Ronnie Weissfluggen holding the proverbial translucent bag.

Louise and Prudence, meanwhile, managed promotions to co–Lead Story Producers on *Spacy Stacy*.

Now in script development on its second season by way of a virtual writer's room, the serial yuk fest entered production at an overseas animation house.

"Is your passport up to date?" Louise asked Prudence. "I haven't renewed mine since the Doctor and I went to London for the opening of the Chunnel."

"I have a passport, Mother. Why must I prance halfway around the world Gangnam Style to interface with a bunch of animation geeks who barely speak English?"

"Because it's your job," said Louise stoically. "You are a doctor's daughter."

"And you're a doctor's wife," Prudence replied with a dutiful sigh.

"I DON'T GET THAT," FREDDIE said when I relayed their annoying refrain to him one night at the studio. He'd taken to passing by to share a sandwich after hours.

"Nobody gets it," I assured him.

As a last-ditch measure to accomplish something, anything, as I ran out the clock on the inevitable, I marched over to the employee discount store and asked how many Wonderful Girls they had on clearance.

"Four hundred and twelve," said the high-school-aged stock girl, checking her inventory wand. "We're talking the Wonderful losers, though. The ones nobody wanted."

"How dare you talk that way about little Fran MacNeill!"

"You have to pay more for the popular girls," interjected a gal down the aisle. "We have another two-eighty-one at fifty percent off if you're okay with open box."

"I'll take them all," I said. "Put them on my employee badge."

"I don't think we have that many bags," said Girl One.

"Are we even allowed to clean out the whole place?" asked Girl Two.

"Can either one of you operate that forklift?" I asked. "I'm staging a revolution."

Even I didn't know what that meant, but both One and Two seemed to like the sound of it.

We rolled back to the studio in a lurching parade of heavy equipment and female disenchantment, piled high with unblinking rejects trailed like scattered defectors across the Wonderful lot in our wake.

Now I had six hundred and ninety-three battle-scarred troops lined up around the soundstage as though briefly sidelined from some brutal foreign field.

Ripped and torn limb from limb, none would escape physical mangling, twisting, and ripping, often beyond all recognition, enduring the ravages of animation rigging.

Posed in rest and anticipation, walk and run, exaggerated and extreme, as though preparing for secondary movement, my harshly lit front row of Fran MacNeills approximated a coroner's photo lineup from a comic book slasher film.

I knelt on the floor in front of the green screen wall, clicking frame by laborious frame with an iPhone perched on a tripod.

Freddie walked on crutches clamped to either elbow, strapped in a harness to catch the occasional lift from the dormant motion capture system to hover over me while I worked. "How long will it take to finish the big touchdown sequence?" He puzzled over the composition of my miniature football field, flipping through my hastily written script. "It looks like you've got the main gal kicking in the wrong direction there."

"I'm more interested in her emotional journey," I lied. "What do I know about constructing the first-ever doll-driven sports spectacular? At twelve frames per second, I figure I can string something together within the next ten or twelve years."

"Let me grab a couple of volunteers from the Village Welcome Booth to give you a hand."

"With what? You're looking at the sum of my camera equipment. I don't even have an extra charger, and I'm using all the free outlets to move around the space heaters. They've powered down the furnace on me."

"That's a code violation," he said. "I could have this whole campus shut down."

"That should inspire confidence," I said sarcastically. "My big boss flies in for my 'performance review' week after next and I haven't heard a peep from Admiral Yamamoto."

"Didn't we get that guy at Guadalcanal?"

"The point is *I'm* history, Freddie."

"Evoke ADA protection," he suggested. "Alcohol use disorder is a legitimate disability. They can't fire you if you can prove your medical history was in any way a motivating factor."

I wondered why Meredith never mentioned that strategy. Either she hadn't wanted me to view myself as a victim of corporate ableism, or she couldn't get far enough beyond the shame of her own addiction to raise the guardrails on mine. "How would I prove it?" I asked.

"Comments, remarks, uncomfortable exchanges," he said. "You'll need witnesses, but people will step forward to corroborate disability discrimination if they have something to hang their hats on."

"Can you reach my hanging hat, please?" I asked. "It's freezing in here."

He grabbed a coonskin cap he'd gotten me from the Wisconsin Historical Society from a wall hook and helped me into my trusty London Fog.

"Isn't that big boss of yours in recovery?" he asked.

"He knows how to spin it, though, that's his thing."

I thought back to my first bizarre after-hours encounter with Jonathan in Miami, the secret calls, the clandestine meetings.

"Our stories were too alike for him to risk validating mine, but he did leave something behind." I felt around in my coat pocket and pulled out a burnt-orange *Earthenware E17* Copic Sketch Marker and crumpled Kidgitalscreenfest flyer.

"How's that for corroborating evidence?"

The initials *J.P.P.* scribbled in burnt-orange ink memorialized Jonathan's invitation to that *Friends of Bill W. Sunrise Scuba Service*. "I'd love a big Perry Mason moment revealing the missing marker from his two-thousand-dollar set."

"If you wanted to skip all that and negotiate a nice exit deal, I'm your man," he said. "You're looking at a certified disability discrimination victims advocate, with an actual certificate somewhere."

I looked around the stage, remembering the string of indignities that led me here the previous summer.

Had I really come this far to just walk away?

"I was so desperate to *make* a movie, I forgot what I really wanted was to *fix* the movies."

"What's wrong with the movies?"

"They're not *about* anything. Anyway, they're not about me, or the kind of world I want to live in. I thought these women would get that, but obviously I was wrong. Let's get out of here, Freddie."

"Wait, you just gave me an idea."

Strapped into the harness, he bounced after me as I powered down the stage. "I have some funding to get cell phones into the hands of at-risk girls living off the grid. Maybe we could bring them in here to show them a way to express themselves besides calling nine-one-one."

"I don't know. I guess we could try to sneak in a little something while I still have the keys."

"Why sneak anything?" he asked. "We'll line up the school buses at the gate and call the media. If Trudi wants you gone, let her announce it on the evening news."

"School buses? How many kids are we talking about?"

"We don't actually know, but I'd like to take an opportunity to corral as many as we can accommodate. What if the TV people helped out for a few days?" he asked. "We could use their mobile vans, the satellite systems, all of it."

"My dream was to do a mini film fest."

I grabbed a sketchbook to divvy up the soundstage into a succession of individual mini sets. "Imagine awarding the winner a global distribution deal in the parking lot just when she wondered if anyone was listening."

"I told you we would be good together," he said, scrolling his phone contacts. "There are many benefits to dating a political animal."

"Okay, wait. Stop." I put down the sketchbook. "I'm not dating you, Freddie. The best I can do on a personal level is not totally hate the idea of us knocking boots someday."

"Boy howdy."

I couldn't help but smile. "You don't even know if you'll like me once I'm ready for anything like that again. Right now, I'm just a story you like because I want you to like it. Just be careful with me, Freddie."

"I never knew my own brother's story until yesterday," he readily admitted. "I fessed up to him about Kayla, and it turns out he's been running around with her sister Lola since the ninth grade. Now he's got something else going with the lady who answers the phones at Weissfluggen Buick."

"This town needs a better selection of winter sports," I said. "The thing is, all my friends thought Abel had nothing to offer me but a lot of talk, but that was my doing. I like living inside my own head, and I shut him out for a reason. What if he didn't love what he saw?"

"What if he did?"

Defying gravity on his motion capture strings, Freddie swam around me just above head in tightening circles.

"He'd have to be a far braver man than he turned out to be," I said.

"Maybe you don't care to reveal your truth to anyone just yet. Seems to me you'd need to see an unrivaled exhibition of courage, and that doesn't come along every day."

Looking back years later, one tiny moment in *our* story revealed itself that night, a mosaic that made sense only when you stood and looked at it from a distance.

"I can commit to an exclusive flirting partnership," I said. "I'll toss in door-to-door campaign rights with extra fawning and gushing. People will talk."

"That could get out of control over time."

"How about some moon and stars in the immediate?"

Heading into the engineering booth, I cued a familiar galaxy of swirling lights.

Freddie Weissfluggen and I found each other somewhere in space and shared an electric kiss. He swooped me up in his arms, and we twirled off together to a dangerous place in the continuum, although it was hard to tell in an infinite cosmic vacuum. "How high are we?"

"Not sure," he said. "I tend to lose perspective with you."

"Hot dog, Freddie. I knew you liked me."

OVER THE NEXT DAYS, AN unseen river emerged from the Driftless tundra, as girls gathered in the studio to announce themselves in an aspirational world heretofore off-limits to all but a privileged few.

Given their inconsistent exposure to media of any kind, they imagined an explosion of vivid screen stories revealing hidden pockets, people, and cultures of the plain in a collection so unique it would go on to gather steam internationally.

I exchanged my feature-length sports spectacular for an interactive documentary that would later premiere in Meredith's honor at the triannual World Girl Scout Conference in Luxembourg, capturing our movement of tiny voices rising from the fringes, empowered by advancing technology to belong at the center.

With that, I left behind a digital footprint continuing the conversation among ten million Girl Scouts and Girl Guides around the globe, outlasting even the most defective Chinese drywall dispute.

"Yes, fine, an admirable theme," Trudi noted.

I'd rescued her from the crushing parking lot melee and escorted her through the Wonderful mini stages.

"Promoting the product to those who can't afford to buy it amounts to a cruel and pointless exercise," she noted.

"Actually, things only got more interesting after we ran low on dolls."

I directed her attention to a Ho-Chunk tribal dance modeled in hand-painted Claymation. "The girls found some good, pliable mud out back, mixed in with some chicken manure from the smell of it. Did you see the spoken word oral history the shelter kids are doing with shadow puppets?"

"And see to it that you leave the studio in better condition than last time you upended things to serve your own whims," the conjunction queen offered in another dubious non sequitur.

"What happened to you, Trudi?" I asked, truly mystified.

"You saw. I was nearly crushed by that throng near the giant satellite."

"They're beaming their work to the Australian Outback, even though most of them aren't wearing their own shoes," I said. "What I meant is what happened to you that you can't be happy today?"

I hardly expected her to remove a rubber mask and reveal herself to be the true psychopath at the center of her own story, but I hoped to see some small hint of humanity behind those ethereal blue eyes.

"I get to be Happy every day," she said. "I would say that's a pretty neat hat trick all in all."

As she strode out defiantly through the nearest exit, a disembodied doll head rolled to my feet. I discovered Yameena and the boys obscuring themselves within a pile of them in a dim corner, avoiding echoes of Trudi's ugly tamale-making accusations the previous winter.

The boys scrambled back to the stages, prepared to effect various technological triumphs with nothing but spare parts.

"I'm sorry they had to overhear that exchange."

"Don't be ridiculous," Yameena said. "Yusuf and I haven't had a real chance to express our gratitude to you. The boys had received such an unkind welcome at school, and though I liked the idea of America, I wondered if I'd ever have a go at it before you reminded us who we came here to become."

"I did all that? And here I thought I was just being pushy." Turning my camera lens on her, I hit record.

"Don't ever stop pushing," Yameena said. "In my country few women have such a luxury."

"Did I ever thank you for pushing me to reach out to those TV guys?" Summer Jessup asked, eavesdropping nearby.

I located her through my blinking lens, where her daughter, the newly crowned Miss Wisconsin, posed for photos with the giddy girls.

"That was more like foisting," I said, thinking back. "Honestly, those guys struck me as a bunch of jerks, but I needed a favor."

"Now I owe *you* one," she said. "Once they informed her that the industry's devotion to beauty queens doesn't extend to runners-up, she somehow found the confidence to take that crown. Next stop, Miss America."

"As Dale Carnegie said, 'action breeds confidence and courage,'" Casey Klinkhoffer offered up in possibly her first-ever properly attributed quote, however uninteresting. She had slipped in with the sullen Marshall and Pendleton in tow. "Do these adorable boys really not qualify for the free phones?" She stuck out her lower lip.

"Is there trouble at home? Maybe they feel threatened by a neighbor or clergyman?" I asked, taking a stab at vulnerable child humor.

Narrowing her eyes, she jerked Marshall and Pendleton by either hand so hard they nearly flew out of their Air Jordans. "Time to go. Mommy will take you for ice cream."

"Casey, wait." I pulled her cell phone from my pocket and handed it over. "I swiped this off your desk a while back. I can't explain why in a way that would make any sense."

She glared at me even as Marshall wiped his nose on Pendleton's sleeve, and Casey reflexively clocked them both upside the head. "There's always been something off about you," she said.

"That wasn't a compliment the first time, Casey, but I liked you, anyway. I'm sorry for my part in everything. I think under the pressure to deliver in new jobs we just kept missing each other. More than anything, I hoped to find a friend in you."

I waited for her to apologize for claiming credit for my ideas, colluding with a useless underling to undermine me, raising ongoing questions about my fitness for duty, and paving the way for group rejection before I ever set foot in the place. I expected some insight into the deep, pathological insecurities for which she firmly intended to seek revolutionary new mental health treatment at a remote Alsatian lab.

She offered only a firm handshake, as if willing herself to the rank of someone authorized to fire me on a lark. "Let's definitely stay in touch, wherever you end up."

"Am I going somewhere?"

"Aren't you?"

"I'll let you know, Casey."

"Great! See you around!"

SOME MONTHS LATER, I WOULD encounter Casey's socialite mother speaking to a sober group and learn that Casey's teenage brother committed suicide during a psychotic breakdown resulting from chronic drug use. Casey hadn't wanted return to Wisconsin in adulthood and only arranged the move to save her marriage to a stockbroker who lost all their money day trading. Whether she'd been triggered by rumors of my struggles with addiction, I came to view Casey Klinkhoffer in a different light.

*Never judge a chick until you've walked a mile in her shoes,* Mr. Y. replied to one of my Betty Ford rants about some self-entitled hallmate who'd done me wrong in line for the washing machine. *You don't need to forgive the sad individual living inside your head rent-free,* he said. *Put that bitch out in the street and put your own head to better use.*

Even if I had anything relevant on hand to burn or delete, I couldn't get inside my front door at home that night. Harlan Meidlemeister had stacked a pyramid of cardboard boxes from his friends at UPS on my porch, which I soon discovered to contain the trove of mementos Butch had stored in my sister's Laurel Canyon garage.

Hoarding every unwanted gift Meredith snatched back from me that desperate Hollywood night when I planned to sell off everything I owned, she must have convinced herself that I would someday see the light.

She'd boxed up the Dr. Seuss–looking MacKenzie-Childs candlesticks and the cloying hand-painted daisy plates and matching plate holder I never liked or wanted. She managed to throw in the empty Krispy Kreme box amid the IKEA bag and cardboard padding, smelling of ten-year-old sugar and grease, a Proustian reminder of the dozen doughnuts she'd made off with and the bag of holes she left behind. The Hallmark store "You Can Do It Wish Doll" she'd named Aurelia still wore her rusted "Go Girl" bracelet and star-shaped charms.

Her tenacious pride in me, clinging to hope on my behalf all those years, brought a tear to my eye where it all seemed so sickly sweet at the time. My sister not only refused to release her fierce grip on me in life but also was determined to keep hold of it through all eternity.

"You are beyond stubborn, Meredith Grayson-O'Cochlain," I said tearfully to my couch. "I miss you so much, my sister."

I uncorked the Chinese wine calling my name since Meredith's Hmong funeral and sent it down the drain with the last pill in Abel's bottle.

I knew perfectly well how to script my own ending without a trained victim's advocate in the room. Following a long line of Toltec warriors to my destiny, I relished the idea of an epic showdown none of them saw coming the day they messed with Jaycee Grayson.

All this time I'd waited for some obtuse message from on high. If Meredith's delivery indeed served as my surrender orders from the great beyond, relinquishing my own agency over the grand scheme of things would shortly pay off with that inestimable power I had never quite figured out how to tap.

I strapped myself in for the bumpy ride to a surprise finish line only one woman in the world could guide me across unscathed.

CHAPTER TWENTY-TWO

# Helen "Happy" Floyd Lindstrom, the Most Wonderful Girl of All

ALTHOUGH HAPPY LINDSTROM FOUND NOTHING good about getting old, getting old and ungodly rich at the same time had its upside. Folks sat up and took notice when she walked into a room, but in her view, this served only to tip their hands as to the reception she would have otherwise received. After a while she stopped walking into rooms at all, slipping in and out of them on the sly, a truth-seeking fly on the wall maintaining a stronghold on the self-respect she'd have otherwise surrendered at the door.

Her withdrawal into obscurity even as she gained worldwide acclaim had served her well as a life plan that only became more delicious in its third act. She recently vanquished a nasty case of colon cancer while perched atop her prized Numi 2.0 smart toilet featuring a custom bidet, seat-warmer, personalized drying function, and self-cleaning UV light. What unhappy housewife wouldn't want to grow up and become a healthy Happy Lindstrom?

People mistook her late-life refusal to freeze like a

deer in the headlights for their inspection as an instinctual shyness, when in truth extroversion had come naturally all her life.

She'd grown up Helen Myrtle Floyd, a daughter of the Great Depression, whose family of tenant farmers fled the Oklahoma Dust Bowl, driven west by drought and generational poverty. They got as far as the Yavapai-Coconino County line outside Flagstaff, Arizona, where Happy worked after school in her father's humble roadside gas station off a historic stretch of Route 66.

Happy had a knack for improvising Old West characters—Annie Oakley, Belle Starr, and Calamity Jane—foisting overpriced relics and mementos onto well-heeled tourists en route to nearby ghost towns. She hawked cactus-shaped keychains and ashtrays, spinning souvenir shot glasses and gold mining plates atop carved Hualapai walking sticks, and costumed herself under a stack of cowboy hats adorned with rattlesnake hat bands, a selection of tin sheriff's deputy badges affixed to her denim blouse. She drew and spun diecast metal cap guns, holstered on either hip, replicas of the formidable long-barreled pistols favored by Doc Holliday and Billy the Kidd.

Popular, pretty, and book smart, she loved reading about most any subject, dancing alone in the mirror, and singing as a soloist with her church choir. Just shy of high school graduation—a family first—she had every best intention to go the distance until Hank Lindstrom passed through town.

A handsome and charming Wisconsin college student and volunteer church choir director set to inherit his father's lucrative accounting business when the old man retired, Hank didn't strike Helen as the type she could afford to turn down in exchange for one afternoon in a rented cap and gown.

Although Happy would spend the next fifty some odd years freezing her ass off on the wrong side of the Donner Pass, as she frequently liked to complain, she and Hank felt content with their mutual choices, all in all, until he showed up one night with the Sauk County sheriffs.

He had no explanation as to what became of the family Buick or the three small children overdue home from a church youth gathering.

Thankfully, he'd forgotten to pick them up, and a good Samaritan treated them to grilled cheese sandwiches at the diner counter before spilling the tea all over Spring Green. Wrapped around a neighbor's hundred-foot-tall Montello cottonwood, the Buick had fallen across County Road C and shut down traffic in both directions for three days.

Happy soon accepted the fact that she had not married as well as she'd planned and took on a series of odd jobs that exuded a deceptive sense of dignity—library assistant, museum gift shop cashier, and well-read docent.

Ironically, projecting the image of a respectable homemaker not only quieted the chattering ladies of the village, but also ignited her wild success in the business world. Hank's drinking raised growing suspicions of philandering requiring an ever-shorter leash, sewing a famous brand from a seedling of female unity as the Lindstrom family took its show on the road to flee the gaze of an unforgiving matriarchy.

A HIGH SCHOOL CHUM OF Summer Jessup's, Trudi Oldham not only came with a personal recommendation from Happy's teenage ward but also a family name. Trudi knew who she was and what that name brought in these parts, initially comporting herself as a loyal and enthusiastic collaborator on the top floor of Littleburgh's famous dollhouse.

After Trina left Trudi holding the bag on the coupon scam and slipped off to Africa with Pastor Fabulous, Trudi threw in her fortunes with a local boy not fit to lick her boots. Shortly after the wedding, he passed up a bump to assistant manager at Oldham Grocery to start a home business restoring classic trucks that rarely turn a profit.

When children didn't come, Trudi endured a series of painful fertility treatments before giving up and seeking formal adoption of two boys she'd fostered since infancy. With that, an aunt of some kind, or so she said, returned unannounced from some godawful military post in Gitmo or France, Trudi swore to the judge. She laid claim to the older boy, motivated only by a monthly stipend from that bastion of Soviet communism over the border in Michigan.

Trudi spoiled her only like the runt in a litter of mall puppies rescued from an inferior parentage. Those rights later severed naturally at the end of that lethal meth pipe in a hail of generous funeral balloons and memorial silly string Trudi distributed graveside for effect.

Trudi grew a career flame in much the same manner as she'd dodged youthful incarceration—without a scintilla of personal stoking.

While the ZZZZZoom! sale satisfied Happy Lindstrom's interest in technological advancement and international expansion in the wake of her retirement, Trudi perceived the acquisition as her greatest call to inaction. She set in place a counterintuitive plan to signal a bigger, better, and more hostile takeover by devaluing the Littleburgh operation under her iron grip.

As to just how abject failure was meant to fatten Trudi's coffers, she had done quite well for herself already as an observer in a small pond, reaping the rewards of its wave makers not nearly as well-equipped to endure a nice arctic plunge. In it for the long game, Trudi watched the entire Lindstrom clan trot off to greener pastures over the years and took no special joy in denigrating Trina's parade of overreaching executives brought around to keep up appearances until the big bust. Was it her fault they routinely overvalued their stock and had to be divested?

Their cash-for-complacency scheme might have paid big for Trudi and Trina both, had Happy Lindstrom not received my holiday note in the mail. Happy remembered well our brief encounter at Taliesin and often wondered how I fared. Putting two and two together, she recognized Jaycee Grayson as the energetic idea machine she'd seen cut off at the knees time and again as the Wonderful Mrs. Happy snooping around the office incognito.

After a forensic accounting team completed the unmasking of her unworthiest disciples with formulaic simplicity, Happy Lindstrom surrendered the arid warmth of the Arizona desert weeks ahead of schedule and walked into the Littleburgh offices prepared for a full-frontal face-off.

"Get your feet off my desk, young man," she barked at Jonathan P. Park. He hopped up and brushed the crumbs of a breakfast bar from her caned desk chair. "What have you done, you boor! That is an original Marcel Breuer Cesca, the only one of its kind outside the Metropolitan Museum of Art."

"Hey, hey," he said, admiring his own good taste. "Is that other one up for sale?"

"Look at this," she hissed, bending the iconic tubular chrome upright. "A Bauhaus masterpiece mangled beyond all recognition. Will somebody please get the popcorn going!"

The only other person in the room, I noticed a dormant vintage movie theater machine untended for years—and jumped up to give it a whirl.

"For corn's sake, not you. I'll do it myself." She flipped on the interior light and whirling kettle, scooping in an undated harvest of popcorn kernels. "Nice to see you again, Jaycee."

"It's good to see you looking so well," I said, grinning from ear to ear. Happy showed off a desert tan and tennis-toned arms in a sleeveless sheath the color of sunshine. "Jonathan, this is Happy Lindstrom, the company founder."

"Cool-io," he said, a bit confused. "Will you be sitting in on the performance review?"

"That's been canceled, unless this young lady intends to review *your* performance."

"I'm not sure," I said. "Were you provided the complaint I filed with Trina Oldham?"

"She no longer works here," Happy replied. "Neither does her sister."

"Yo-yo, can we dial this back a minute?" Jonathan hammered furiously on both of his clandestine cell phones. "I'm getting that you used to be a big baller around here, but I'm not sure you still have the juice to make this kind of shizz go down."

"You needn't wake the coast; alarms have been sounded in all the right time zones," she said. "Belinda Rockland has also moved on, by the way. If anybody wants to recommend a couple of Change Champions for the recent openings, I'm all ears."

I didn't miss a beat. "A fabulous woman stuck in the toy store could show us the way into the Asia-Africa Growth Corridor with a half-hour PowerPoint."

"That's my growth corridor," Jonathan said. "Hard no."

"And we have a freelance designer from Chicago who'd bring something fresh to a new Integrated Marketing team," I continued. "I don't know that we could coax Rebecca Lavery back in, but she might consider leading that remotely."

"We just cut her loose, though," said Jonathan. "Trimming the fat, cleaning the bean."

"Can I interest you in a promotion, dear?" Happy asked me. "You'd bring the integrity and imagination this one checked at the door with his big boy pants."

"Yo, I'm not some basic bitch over here!" Jonathan pounded a fist on the desk, denting his pinkie ring. "You ladies don't need to pretend I'm not in the room, because I *am* the room should I manifest myself a girlie purple destiny."

"Is that English?"

"Hipster speak," I said. "I can translate if you want."

"I don't have that kind of free time," she said. "Pardon me, sir, but this is the one tiny corner of planet Earth where nobody cares what you have to say. Please don't take that as a challenge to your masculinity because I firmly believe we'd have taken the reins eons ago if only we had your knack for growing a tribe. You become a bigger and better king with every meandering princess you welcome onto the cave couch, but once we park our major prize on a Barcalounger with a TV tray, we're good for life. 'Walk on by, honey, I've got mine.'"

Jonathan needed a moment to react to either a very high compliment indeed or a ding to his flagging manhood somewhere in that parable.

"I'm not in any way qualified to step into your shoes," I told Happy. "San Francisco absorbed every piece of the business I've spent my career earning a right to manage."

"Those morons are allowed to organize their end as stupidly as they want to," she said. "I can't undo any of that without causing the kind of ruckus nobody wins."

"I understand," I said, resigned to the inevitable. "Make me an offer and I'll walk away without a fuss. I've been targeted for pretextual termination based upon a former drinking problem I never once brought into this office."

"Nobody knew she was a drunk," Jonathan flat out lied. "They just didn't like her."

"That isn't true."

"You think they like you?" he scoffed.

"My husband, Hank, used to drink," Happy said. "A scary bout with liver disease dried him out like a dish towel by the stove. Getting old has its upside."

"I might have met Hank last Thanksgiving when my sister and I tried to look you up."

"How is it only the least welcome holiday callers figure that one out?"

Happy had been preoccupied that afternoon with a pair of cloying twins who got spooked by their own incompetence and came around to check the temperature as the Lindstrom family made plans to head west for the early winter. Happy played dumb, letting them tighten their own nooses over the next months, when the numbers would pinpoint the precise location of their dual engine failure to launch.

"Pay the lady," she ordered Jonathan. "Unless you prefer forking over three times her number in legal fees to go on public record with your part in this unholy mess."

"No, I'm good." He scribbled a number on a sticky note and pressed it in front of me on the desk. "What do you say we cash out for something fair and walk away friends?"

"We were never friends." I dropped his twelve-step meeting flyer and burnt-orange marker on the table. "Apologize to Mrs. Happy for lying about me."

Puzzling over the evidence, he took only a moment to do the math. "Okay, maybe I did hear she used to drink, but that is not why I gave her job to a bunch of guys, if that's where this is headed," he said. "I was always going to do that, regardless of what she did or didn't do, because they're *my* guys, and we go back. You feel me?"

"I do feel you, sir," said Mrs. Happy, her voice dripping with sarcasm.

"One of them is nineteen and couldn't write his way out of a pair of pajamas," I said.

"That was me doing a solid for a homie. How is that wrong?" he asked.

Happy leaned back, allowing him plenty of sunlight for self-exposure. "You tell me."

Jonathan P. Park wasn't about to take that bait no matter how buttery delicious the smell of the old broad's popcorn. "I don't make up the rules. No man on this planet takes issue with an available woman of a certain age whose looks are still holding. If anything, *she* has the upper hand with us, provided she's reasonably friendly," he said. "This gal never had a chance with *your* feline freak show across the hall meowing all day about her sus 'left coast leanings.'"

"Wow. Here I thought I only got bullied for being disabled."

"Cry more. I don't play the victim when they come at me with all that."

"Maybe you're okay with racial profiling."

"Damn straight. Wait, what?"

"Or were you referring to my past with the pipe? My ties to gang violence in Little Korea? Not my weird mommy issues."

"Hey. That's my story."

"Yes, it is. Why am I the one losing my job over 'all that'?" I turned to Happy, tapping the sticky note. "We'll need to go higher on that number."

"Get out, you boob," Happy said, showing Jonathan the door.

"Me? What did I do?" He turned to me, exasperated. "Can you find me some cake, no sugar. And get my wife on the phone, I forgot my socks."

"Get away from her," Happy ordered. "Never run your mouth again outside the presence of a civil rights attorney with a bark collar."

"We're on the same team, Mrs. H." He attempted to telegraph something important under his breath while clinging to her doorjamb. "The brass is going to want 'the big shuttie.'"

"The big what? Spit it out, you cretin."

"She has to *ignsay* the *ondisclosurenay*."

"He wants me to sign a nondisclosure agreement," I said flatly.

"Regretfully, you will have to keep what you've endured here under wraps," Happy said.

"I have to give you my story?"

"No. You have to sell us your silence," said Jonathan. "No talkie, all walkie, right out that door."

I COULDN'T HAVE KNOWN THEN that the story of my great adventure in Littleburgh, Wisconsin, would hold much value for anyone but the wonderful girl who lived it. Sequestered cozily away within another woman's architectural self-vindication over a legendary rival perched on the edge of a wintery marsh, I'd written a bittersweet chapter with my sister, Meredith, at the center.

Having learned that life is just a dream, and we are all doing our best to make it up as we go along, I summoned the native fearlessness to walk away from the table that morning without a penny. Suffice it to say, dear reader, I am humbled by *your* investment in all the juicy details.

Jonathan and Happy traded a few choice words before she banned him from the premises forevermore and reminded me a woman need never smile while saying the word "no." I slipped out to make some copies while she took a call from home and later had trouble locating her in the building.

Above the zigzag of conveyor belts zipping their payloads to parts unknown, I caught her on the warehouse catwalk and called out, "Wait! Weren't you going to say goodbye?"

"I'm sorry, dear, I'm late for my granddaughter's birthday party and some bozo went and cleaned out the entire employee store."

"Of all the nerve."

"Give me a hand over here, would you?"

As a stacked lift passed us below, we risked plunging to our deaths. Bending over the railing, we extended our arms to reach out and remove a pair of boxes. The skewed tower teetered off its fork, splaying a trove of Wonderful Girls across the floor, smiling up at us relentlessly from their clear jewel boxes.

Happy and I came up with a Sara and a Tara safely in hand. "Good enough," she said. "The kid can meet Clara next year."

Escaping detection, we crept down a cloistered stairway and opened a corner door onto Happy's beloved nature preserve, a lush carpet of springtime buds.

"It can't have been easy entrusting all of this to anybody," I said. "Why Trudi?"

"Because she was there. Pretty much the same reason I married Hank."

Not at all interested in indulging herself in the blame for somebody else's larcenous heart, Happy power walked across the parking lot as I struggled to keep pace at forty odd years her junior. "Somewhere you learn to stop looking at life like your own private drugstore," she said. "Kind of takes the sting out of things when the dolts at the counter foul up your dad-blasted order."

"I couldn't even figure out which twin was in charge," I said, pumping my arms to keep up.

"Maybe they take turns. That's how me and Hank work it." She stopped abruptly to click open a shiny red Toyota RAV4 hybrid still wearing its clunky winter tires.

"Do you have an extra minute?" I asked, catching my breath.

"Not for another crisis, I don't. What now?"

"You don't have to think about it right now, but I'd like you to consider an exciting investment opportunity." I pressed a Homey Naomi business prospectus on her. "Naomi is much more than an intriguing brand icon. She's a real Mennonite girl who lives in my kitchen cooking up whatever her brother foraged that day in the forest."

"Could you make the brother a sister?"

"I don't know if Elijah would go for that."

She needed only a moment to ruminate on that. "I'm seeing Homey Naomi as an exclusive women's line that picks up in the marketplace where Wonderful Girls leaves off. Picture a gorgeous, grown-up clubhouse, somewhere on the prairie."

"I always knew the girls could grow up!" I declared, feeling fully vindicated.

"Well, certainly. Laura Ingalls grew up, as did Mary, so bravely. The call of the great frontier, emboldened by female fortitude, feels overdue for a contemporary lifestyle reboot."

"I think you might have a knack for this, Mrs. Happy."

"I'm just Helen right now," she said, as though surprised to hear this herself. "Another seat at the table might do me some good. I'll be in touch."

WHATEVER THE FUTURE MAY BRING, hawking my things at a drive-in flea market to keep the lights on seems as sensible an option as ever. I already let go of my prize possession, the "You Can Do It Wish Doll" my sister dubbed Aurelia that long ago night in Hollywood.

Diarra and Liz brought their adopted daughter, Idrina, for a visit to mark my one-year anniversary in Wisconsin, and the four of us took a picnic basket downtown to watch the Fourth of July fireworks decorate the lakefront in bursts, tossed like handfuls of glitter on a child's painting. Pulling fresh root beers from an iced growler—hopping with the flavors of birch bark, sassafras, and summer dandelion—we raised hands against the crackling nightfall.

"To Meredith, forever among the stars," I said, clinking together our foamy mugs.

Little Idrina whispered something in Aurelia's ear, cradling the wish doll I'd passed on when we first met at the airport that morning. *"Mi hermanita, te amo por siempre."*

"What is that she's saying?" I asked Liz.

"I'm loving you, my forever sister?" Liz translated, with a quizzical shrug. *"Habla inglés, mija,"* she prodded, turning to me to apologize. "She's still learning her words."

"We don't know why she babbles like that," Diarra said. "She might be an empath, but they say it'll pass. We keep her away from antiques stores and old hotels or it gets intense."

"My Jaycee, I love you, forever and ever," Idrina said with sudden proficiency. "You'll always be my baby sister doll." She smiled up at me, her eyes sparkling with the mischief of a secret we had kept between the two of us our entire lives.

Meredith was wrong about the things I would have to accept in the wake of her loss. She refused to ever give up on me, and I would never truly let her go. Convinced to my core that life does go on, I outstretched my arms to hug her once again.

## GET THE RECIPES

*Homey Naomi Farmed and Foraged*, our character-curated online catalogue of Midwest-sourced goods and sundries, invites you back to Littleburgh for the next chapter in the Jaycee Grayson Series. Join the mailing list to get *Naomi's Recipe Box*, an exclusive cookbook free to subscribers, featuring 12 print-and-fold recipe cards pulled from the novel. Inside the beautifully illustrated volume, you'll discover hard-to-find organic ingredients, plus ideas, tips, and anecdotes on prairie life from all your favorite characters. With limited edition freebies and discounted subscriber extras, there's lots more to uncover in Jaycee Grayson's horrible, wonderful world, so stay in touch across social media for news, events, and future publication dates. Get more details at WonderfulGirlsNovel.com. Scan for links.

## ABOUT THE AUTHOR

A screenwriter, producer, and former doll and toy company executive, Julie Ann Sipos is known as the familiar "mom voice" behind iconic stories and characters for Disney, Mattel, and American Girl. She studied dramatic storytelling in the MFA screenwriting program at UCLA and now splits her time between Central Florida and Southern California, where she teaches cinema and television writing at Cal State Northridge. *Horrible Women, Wonderful Girls: A Jaycee Grayson Novel*, marks her literary debut. Learn more at JulieAnnSipos.net.